James Hinton

The Questions of Aural Surgery

James Hinton

The Questions of Aural Surgery

Reprint of the original, first published in 1874.

1st Edition 2024 | ISBN: 978-3-36884-716-6

Verlag (Publisher): Outlook Verlag GmbH, Zeilweg 44, 60439 Frankfurt, Deutschland
Vertretungsberechtigt (Authorized to represent): E. Roepke, Zeilweg 44, 60439 Frankfurt, Deutschland
Druck (Print): Books on Demand GmbH, In de Tarpen 42, 22848 Norderstedt, Deutschland

THE QUESTIONS

OF AURAL SURGERY

THE QUESTIONS

OF

AURAL SURGERY.

BY

JAMES HINTON,

AURAL SURGEON TO GUY'S HOSPITAL.

HENRY S. KING & CO.,
65, CORNHILL, AND 12, PATERNOSTER ROW, LONDON.
1874.

PREFACE.

In the following book I have endeavoured to give a brief outline of the subject of ear disease. I have preferred to make it brief, partly because in the present state of professional feeling in England it seems that such an outline of the subject may be more useful than a fuller treatment. But other reasons also influence me; one of them is my feeling that our knowledge is hitherto so limited, that if a full explication were attempted, more of that which is yet doubtful must be affirmed than I am willing to include. The workers in Aural Surgery have been, until the last few years, so few, that in spite of, or rather owing to, their zeal, and the excellence of very much that they have done, a large part alike of the Physiology, the Diagnosis and the Treatment, still remains in the domain of question; and nothing, it seems to me, can be more undesirable on such a subject than to speak with a confidence that outruns its grounds. I have chosen my title accordingly. My

desire is to lay before the reader, if I can, the
general aspect of disease when it affects the ear; to
mention the best established results of examination
and methods of treatment, but, above all, to suggest
the many problems, some of them of the highest
interest, which they open out. By this means, I
may at least avoid the temptation to make a little
knowledge, or a partial experience, spread itself
over a large space, which ought rather to be recog-
nized as still empty; and I shall have failed
indeed, if it does not plainly appear that, so far
from disease of the ear being a barren or un-
attractive field, it is one full of promise.

For to this conclusion, more than all, my own
little study in this domain has led me; that if
there have been in the minds of medical men anything of indifference in respect to diseases of the
ear, or doubt of their power to relieve more than
a few of its simpler forms, that idea is destined
soon to give place to the feeling that very few
fields of practice afford subjects of greater interest
to study, or give a larger reward to the exercise of
skill. Alike for the success which attends simple
and easy modes of treatment, and for the pathological and physiological interest of those cases for
which no yet known treatment avails, it cannot but

be that aural medicine will ere long cease to be a
neglected, and become a favourite branch of practice;
not in the hands of specialists merely, but in those
of the profession at large.

Scarcely anything is needed to make it so beyond
the little trouble that would suffice to render the
surgeon conversant with the appearances of the
membrane; an end to which I trust the illustrations
I have endeavoured to give of the morbid conditions of that organ, in the recently published
" Atlas of the Membrana Tympani," may in some
degree contribute. I have felt it the less necessary
to go into every detail of the subject, because of
the recent publication of other works, of which
such details must be a repetition; as for example
the translation I have had the pleasure of making
of Dr. Von Tröltsch "On the Surgical Affections
of the Ear," and of Prof. Helmholz's "Treatise
on the Mechanism of the Ossicula," for the Sydenham Society; and Mr. Dalby's "Lectures on Diseases
of the Ear," which give an excellent outline of the
subject. I may refer also to a very complete work,
easily accessible in this country, Dr. St. John Roosa's
" Treatise on Diseases of the Ear." *

Also not to repeat what is better told elsewhere,

* New York. Wood and Co., 1873.

I have, with few exceptions, omitted the anatomy of the organ. Nor do I profess to give accurately the credit of their discoveries to each author, nor even to mention the source of every statement made. *Nothing* is claimed as original. The chief part of our recent knowledge comes from Germany, with liberal contributions from America. But unhappily in the former country personal disputation runs so high, especially on the point of priority, that a foreigner may beg to be excused an inevitably unsuccessful endeavour to do justice. The names, among living men, of Bonnafont, Gruber Jacobi, Löwenberg, Lucae, Magnus, Moos, Politzer, Rüdinger, Schwartze, Triquet, Voltolini, Von Tröltsch, Weber, Wendt, Wreden, are held in honour by all whom the study of the ear has attracted, and a multitude of other names compete for our regard and thanks.

In the "Atlas" drawings are given of the membrane in many of the cases mentioned in this volume: a reference is made to them in each instance. The two books are, however, quite distinct.

JAMES HINTON.

London, 1st *March*, 1874.

THE QUESTIONS OF AURAL SURGERY.

CHAPTER I.

GENERAL OBSERVATIONS.

The chief peculiarities of aural disease are determined by simple facts of structure : as, that sound is conveyed to the nerve of hearing by means of a cavity containing air, supplied from the throat by a somewhat long and narrow channel; that this cavity is deeply seated, is bounded both externally and internally by a thin vascular membrane, and is crossed by a delicately-jointed chain of bones. There are also some negative circumstances which are important; namely, that the nervous apparatus is inaccessible to direct observation, and is divided into structures of some of which the functions are at present a matter of doubt. Finally the nerve of hearing is, in its origin, intimately connected with the nuclei of the great nerves of the digestive and respiratory apparatus, and appears to have peculiarly close relations with the parts of the brain concerned in the emotions.

But it is to the part played by air contained within the

tympanum, in the conduction of sound, that the most
practically important characters of aural disease are due.
Generally speaking, the main object of the surgeon will
be to see that this air-containing cavity with the passages
leading to it are subject to no obstruction, either occluding their calibre, or impairing the delicacy of oscillation
of the structures pertaining to them. As the conducting
portion of the eye is a camera with lenses, so that of the
ear is a pneumatic apparatus, and the surgical methods
appropriate are corresponding in their character. Our
business here is with the air—that the channels it should
permeate be free ; that the organs it bathes, and essentially supports by its pressure, encounter no hindrance
in their reception and transmission of impulses.

Bearing these things in mind, aural surgery is simply
surgical common sense, and needs comparatively little
insistence on special points, beyond that which a trained
surgical instinct would suggest. Owing to the structure
of the ear, however — that the tympanum lies so
deeply, and is itself so irregular a cavity with its
only outlet placed not at its most dependent portion,
while, when diseased, its lining membrane pours out
viscid secretion in extreme abundance—one duty lies on
the surgeon, in treating the ear, with somewhat peculiar
exigence : that of ensuring a perfect cleansing. In every
case connected with discharge his sheet anchor is cleanliness.

Another requisite is patience. In so far as the feeling,

so widely spread, that in disease of the ear the resources of medicine are of little avail is justified, its grounds are chiefly two; first the ignorance which until lately invested the whole subject, and secondly, the fact that even the diseases which are remediable are, when they have advanced beyond a certain stage, apt to be tedious in their progress, and especially to be discouraging on account of their liability to temporary relapses. This liability is in great part to be accounted for by the connection between the tympanum and the throat, which is so especially subject to atmospheric influences. But even in cases that on this ground seem to baffle hope, if the affection do not involve the nerve-structure, perseverance will almost always effect a satisfactory result; and such a result is the more often attained because, on the one hand, the hearing may be very considerably below the average with no appreciable inconvenience, and on the other an even extreme amount of permanent damage to the membrane, and to some of the parts contained within the tympanum, may co-exist with a very slightly diminished function. The membrane may be not only almost wholly wanting, but may be so altered as to form irregular fleshy or fibroid masses presenting no visible resemblance to its original structure, both malleus and incus may apparently have been lost, and yet the patient scarcely desire to hear better. Thus, indeed, there arises one of the most interesting problems that the study of diseases of the ear presents— the real relation of the membrana tympani to the function of the organ, which is by no means so simple as would at first appear.

Among points of interest in respect to the structure of the ear may be mentioned its markedly spiral form. It is true that, on an observant scrutiny, clear traces of a spiral form are visible in almost every organ of the body,* but perhaps in none, except the heart, is this fundamental mode of structure so plainly marked as in the ear. It is visible not only in the cochlea, but throughout; the meatus winds with a slight spiral turn—backwards, upwards, forwards, and downwards; the tympanic bone in which the membrane is inserted is a distinct spiral ring, as can be well seen before osseous union occurs; a line traversing the ossicula takes a spiral course; and in the canals, perhaps, this relation is most intensely marked. For not only is each canal in itself a segment of a spiral curve, but the relations of the three canals to each other, lying at right angles as they do, reveal the very secret of the spiral form, which represents indeed simply a continuous motion passing successively into these three directions. In this respect the ear is eminently typical of the whole body, displaying visibly a plan or law of structure which is none the less paramount elsewhere because it is more concealed.

It can, perhaps, hardly be doubted that this markedly

* For the illustration of this fact I may refer to a paper on "Physical Morphology," in the "Brit. and For. Med. Chir. Rev.," 1858. The paper is reprinted in "Life in Nature."

spiral structure is of a functional value : for all motions tend to propagate themselves (at least thro' media in any degree resisting) in a spiral direction. The spiral lines formed on glass rods thrown into sonorous vibrations are well known, and Sir John Herschel remarks* that the waves of sound may be traced in expanding spirals in the air. In the meatus, this form becomes of practical importance, in respect to the removal of foreign bodies, the introduction of the cotton wool or other form of artificial membrane, syringing, &c.—The meatus acts as a resonator to certain tones of the fourth octave (c‴—c⁗), especially to g⁗.†

In respect to the functions of the different parts of the ear the most minute investigations have as yet failed to gain any finally satisfactory results. By means of threads of glass, starch granules, or the plumules of a feather, attached to the ossicles, it has been demonstrated ‡ that vibrations impinging on the membrane are transmitted through the chain of bones, which moves as a whole, and imparts corresponding motions to the fluid of the labyrinth.

Dr. Buck gives the following as the results of his

---

* Treatise on Sound, reprinted from the "Encyclopædia Britannica."
† Helmholz : "Lehre von den Tonempfindungen," p. 175.
‡ By Politzer, Lucae, and others : see the various volumes of the "Archiv fur Ohrenheilkunde," 1864 and subsequently ; and more recently by Dr. A. H. Buck (who used grains of starch) ; "Archives of Ophthalmology and Otology," 1870, No. 2. For the completest details on all these points see Helmholz, "On the Mechanism of the Ossicles of the Ear." (Sydenham Society.)

experiments:—On the dead subject, with a glass tube
attached to an organ pipe inserted into the meatus, the
malleus may be made to make an excursion inwards of
0·43 mm. without injury; but this exceeds, probably very
greatly, its motion during life. The axis of rotation of
the malleus lies nearly midway between its two extremities, so that the head moves outwards as the end of the
handle moves inwards. The rotation takes place upon a
ligamentous structure passing from the malleus to the
anterior and posterior walls of the membrane, and which
is termed by Helmholz the axis-ligament. The upper
part of the head of the malleus moves horizontally outwards, while the part below the articulation with the
incus moves upwards as much as outwards; and the
incus is so articulated with the malleus as to share this
motion; so that it is carried upwards and outwards when
the membrane is carried inwards by a wave of sound.
But in addition to this motion the body of the incus is
thrown slightly backwards, and the end of its long process slightly forwards. The stapes moves correspond-
ingly; namely upwards, slightly inwards, and forwards.
As a result of this, the upper and anterior border of the
base of the stapes is driven farther into the vestibule than
the lower and posterior border. Hence a displacement
of the entire mass of the labyrinth-fluid ensues. An im-
pulse given to the centre of the membrane is communi-
cated from ossicle to ossicle, with a loss in the following ratio :—

Malleus = 4

Incus   = 2

Stapes = 1

But this refers to the utmost excursions; when they are feeble, scarcely any loss occurs in the transmission, so that probably during life the proportion between the motions of the various bones is much more equal than that given above. Section of the tendons of the tensor tympani and stapedius had no effect on the motions. Helmholz * found that the greatest natural motion of the stapes was $\frac{1}{13}$ mm. If the ossicula lie firmly together, each excursion of the long process of the incus will equal only $\frac{2}{3}$ of that of the malleus handle; but the force it transmits to the stapes will be one and a half times as great as that which acts on the extremity of the malleus.

By an arrangement of the heads of the malleus and incus, after the fashion of a cog, both malleus and incus move together on pressure inwards; but the malleus may move very considerably *outwards* without carrying the incus with it, thus guarding in part against the effects of too powerful inflation of the drum.

According to Rüdinger, the malleus and incus and the incus and stapes are articulated by means of a true joint, containing a freely movable meniscus of cartilage, like that of the clavicle. The articulation of the stapes with the fenestra ovalis belongs to the group of the

* "Mechanism of the Ossicles of the Ear."

symphyses, and is similar to that of the bodies of the vertebræ.

Dr. Burnett, of Philadelphia,* has also examined the motions of the membrane of the fenestra rotunda by means of starch granules, observed with a microscope, and found that they corresponded accurately with those of the stapes. A great increase of fluid pressure in the canals stopped the vibrations of the membrana rotunda, and rendered the membrana tympani and ossicula also immobile ; this repressive effect of increased pressure in the labyrinth was greater with the higher than with the lower notes. Mach and Kessel† also found, by the use of a sirene, that the basilar membrane of the cochlea moves from the scala vestibuli towards the scala tympani when the stapes presses inwards.

The same observers ‡ experimented on the effect of traction on the tensor tympani and stapedius muscles, with a view to ascertain whether an accommodation of the ear to sounds of different pitch was effected by them. Traction on the stapedius gave no effect; but traction on the tensor tympani reduced the motions of the membrane under both grave and acute sounds, but more in proportion for the grave ones. The membrane was observed under a microscope, and its vibrations measured by a micrometer ; one millimetre equalling 50 lines. A pipe

---

* "Monthly Jl. of Aural Surg.," July, 1871.
† "Versam. D. Natur forsch." 1871.
‡ "Arch. f. Ohr.," 1873, p. 121.

of 256 vibrations gave a motion of the membrane equal to five lines of the micrometer ; a weight of 3 grammes was then attached to the tensor tympani and the motion was reduced to three lines. On using a pipe of 1024 vibrations, the excursion of the membrane was only $1\frac{1}{2}$ lines of the micrometer, but the same traction on the tensor reduced it less : only in the proportion of 5 to 4.

Carrying their experiments farther, Drs. Mach and Kessel obtained vibration-figures from the head of the malleus, alike for lower and higher tones ; and on uniting the two they found that the two figures were presented together ; traction on the tensor tympani altered the form of the low, but not of the high note.

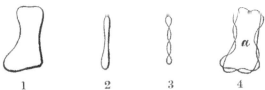

1 2 3 4

DESCRIPTION OF FIGURE :—Fig. 1 shows the vibration-line given by a pipe of 256 vibrations in the second ; this was changed by traction on the tensor tympani into Fig. 2. A pipe of 1,024 vibrations gave the line shown in Fig. 3 ; and on combining them Fig. 4 was formed. Traction on the tensor did not affect the form given by the higher note, and scarcely affected even that of the lower when both were sounded together. The higher note produced more vivid and ample motions when the lower was also sounded.

On the living subject parallel experiments were carried out to test the action of the tensor tympani, but no change could be traced as arising from the act of *listening* to the higher tônes, either in the extent of the movements of the membrane, or in the figures produced. This, however, does not contradict the assertion of Schapringer (who can at will contract the tensor tympani with visible indrawing of the membrane), that such contraction diminishes the intensity of all sounds, since these experiments go to show that the vibrations are in all cases diminished, only for the higher tones less than for the lower. All other attempts to discover an alteration of tension in the membrane during life have also failed. But Dr. O. Wolf holds that the occurrence of such increased tension as a protection against very loud sounds, is proved by the fact that the sounds of an organ-pipe are heard as much as half a tone higher when close than at a distance.* Helmholz has pointed out that contraction of the tensor tympani puts on the stretch at once all the ligaments of the ossicula, except the superior ligament of the malleus.

In respect to the function of the stapedius muscle there is little ground for affirmation. It has been suggested † that it is specially employed in listening, or adapting the ear to rapid changes in sound, an idea to which its supply by the portio dura perhaps lends countenance. Mr. Tóynbee endeavoured to use this function as an aid in the diagnosis of deafness arising from loss of the due

* "Sprache und Ohr." Braunschweig, 1871. I have not been able to find confirmation of this statement.

† As *c.g.*, by the late Mr. Toynbee, "Diseases of the Ear," p. 281; and more recently again by Dr. Allen.

mobility [anchylosis] of the stapes. Professor Helmholz, however, whose opinion must carry the utmost weight, has been good enough to inform me that his researches have led him to consider it simply as a damper of sound. Kessel* assigns to it a strictly counteracting effect to that of the tensor tympani. He observes that the membrane consists of three distinct portions, an anterior, posterior, and superior portion. The superior is the thin part known as Rivini's segment, and most easily yields to impulses, being supposed to be adapted to slight and irregular sounds (answering to the supposed function of the vestibule) : of the lower segments the posterior is the most yielding, and on air pressure in the meatus the malleus rotates inwards and backwards, the hort sprocess moves also slightly downwards, the anterior segment is rendered more tense than the posterior ; and the superior segment is rendered convex while the inferior becomes concave. The effect of traction on the stapedius is, in all respects, the opposite to these movements.

On producing vibrations (in a preparation) with an organ-pipe, the membrane vibrates with a direction inwards and backwards, the anterior portion much less than the posterior. By section of the tendon of the tensor tympani, the excursions of the head of the malleus are increased a fourth, and its rotation also much increased.

By traction on the tensor, on the other hand, the

* *Loc. cit.*, p. 80.

movement of all the parts is diminished, and that
of the anterior portion may be entirely stopped, while
the sound continues undiminished. If now the tendon
of the stapedius be drawn upon the suspended movements of the anterior segment may be renewed, even
while the traction on the tensor is continued. When
a note is sounded with its octave, and the vibrations
of the membrane observed, traction on the tensor is
seen to diminish, first, those of the octave in all the
lower segments; but they continue undiminished in the
thin upper portion of the membrane, and to this is due
the preponderance given by traction on the tensor to the
higher notes, and not to its effect on the membrane as a
whole.*

Dr. Wolf † has investigated the reception of the various
elements of speech by the ear. Among the consonants
sch is heard loudest, and *h* least loud; the force of any
letter depending very much upon the harmonics which
accompany its ground-tone. The vowels range as
follows :—*a, o, ei, e, i, eu, au, u,* pronounced as in
German. In cases of partial destruction of the membrane the vowels were heard disproportionately better
than the consonants, which were worse heard in proportion to the size of the defect, and the better in

---

* These investigations are carried out by means of the *Stroboscopic*
method, which consists in observing a motion at interrupted points, on
a principle analogous to that of the familiar "Wheel of Life." An
account of it is given in the Appendix.

† *Loc. cit.*

proportion to the pitch of their ground-tone, and the
number of their harmonics; a rhythmical utterance
diminished the difficulty. On experimenting with an
artificial meatus and membrane it was found that the
resonance was much greater for the voice than for a
violoncello, and that partial destruction weakened, and
raised the pitch of, the resonance. This was more diminished by hindrances to the propagation of the vibration than by losses of substance. Politzer also found
that weights attached to the ossicula impeded the transmission of vibrations much more than when attached
to the membrane. It must be held, Wolf thinks, that
sounds are conveyed both by movement of the stapes
in the fenestra and by the molecular movements of the
ossicula also. In cases of defect of the membrane, the
last syllable of a word was often heard as if prolonged,
especially with an *l* added. This he ascribes to an
unchecked motion of the stapes in the fenestra, and
therefore infers that the ossicula limit as well as convey
vibrations; a function in which the Eustachian tube participates by permitting their escape.

But it still remains inconceivable how all the innumerable varieties of sound can be conveyed simultaneously
to the labyrinth. Whatever our supposition, every
attempt to imagine the passage, together, of such com-
plexities and delicate shades and varieties of sound as we
are capable of appreciating, thro' such an apparatus as the
chain of ossicula, serves but to make the wonder greater.

Our knowledge of the structure of the membrana tympani has been chiefly advanced of late years by Professor Josef Gruber, of Vienna. He has pointed out (and it is confirmed by Professor Helmholz) that the malleus is attached to the membrane by a small layer of cartilage which is thickest around the short process, and that at that part, though no true joint exists, it is slightly movable upon the membrane. He describes also a layer of " strengthening fibres," situated mostly at the lower and posterior part of the membrane, immediately beneath the epithelium, and running in irregular directions, to which he assigns the function of restoring the membrane to its normal position after tension has been exerted on it. Kessel found that this structure furnished a series of channels, lined with epithelium, thro' which the vessels, nerves and lymphatics, and the membrane pass on their way to the more external layers.

Dr. Von Troeltsch's two "pockets" of the membrane are well known; they consist of two small folds of the mucous membrane of the tympanum, one behind, the other in front of, the short process of the malleus. The chorda tympani nerve runs along the inferior edge of the posterior fold, which also contains some of the proper fibres of the membrane. These "pockets" are of importance, because they seem often to retain secretion. The same may perhaps be said of the folds of membrane which exist above the neck of the malleus and form there a series of minute cavities ;* in these, morbid secretion probably is entangled during catarrhs and so gives rise to the discharges which sometimes take place thro' small ulcerations of the thinner membrane, above the short process of the malleus, and which are often extremely tedious in their recovery.†

Helmholz ‡ has pointed out an advantage, in respect to the reception of vibrations, arising from the form given to the membrane by the arching of the radial fibres. A very small air-pressure upon them is thus rendered equivalent to a great force acting on the malleus, the extent of its movements being proportionately less : they also guard against excessive pressure on the stapes, because, beyond the point at which they are made straight, force applied to them would bend them inwards, and so draw the malleus outwards. The membrane thus, by its curvature, acts first the part of a lever on the malleus, and secondly that of a regulator of the force conveyed. [The corresponding function of the cogs of the malleo-incudal joint in guarding against outward pressure has been mentioned before.] The fibres of the membrane are inextensile, like tendon.§ Politzer, by means of an appa-

* Described at large by Politzer : "Wiener Med. Wochenschrift," 1870.

† See "Atlas of Diseases of the Membrana Tympani," plate xxiii., fig. 1.

‡ *Loc. cit.*

§ Mr. R. Moon ("Philos. Mag.," 1869-70) has argued from the inelastic structure of the membrane that only the waves of rarefaction in the air are transmitted to the labyrinth, and not those of condensation ; and

ratus representing a greatly magnified tympanum, found
that a membrane which, while flat, scarcely responded at
all to either high or low tuning forks, was thrown into
strong vibrations as soon as it was drawn inwards at the
centre, and this equally, whether the sound fell on the concave or the convex side ; * and he considers the different
tension of the individual parts of the membrane between
the malleus and the periphery produced by its curvature
to be an important factor for the simultaneous reception
of different notes. Lucae † has shown that vibrations that
fall perpendicularly on the membrane produce much the
most strong vibrations ; and hence a tuning-fork placed on
the *side* of the head, each meatus being closed, is heard
chiefly on the opposite ear.

Dr. Blake‡ examined the limit of hearing for high notes,
and the effect upon it of perforation of the membrane.
He found that in health it diminished with age from 40,960
(single) vibrations in a second, at twelve years, to 32,768
at fifty ; the sound used being the vibrations of a suspended steel rod, and the distance thirty-four feet ; any
thickening of the membrane lowered the limit ; perforations, as a rule, raised it, especially when situated in the

he ascribes to the muscles of the ossicula the function of restoring the
membrane to the former plane after the rarefied waves have drawn it
outwards. The perception of sound would thus be caused by the flow
of the liquid in the cochlea from the fenestra rotunda to the fenestra
ovalis, and *vice versâ*.

* "Arch. f. O.," B. iv. H. 1.
† "Berlin. Kl. Woch.," 1871. No. 10.
‡ "Trans. Amer. Otol. Soc.," July, 1872.

posterior superior segment. Size did not make so much difference as situation and the degree of retraction of the tensor tympani. An experiment was happily afforded by a case of disease of the membrane, in which an incision, followed by the introduction of a ring to maintain the opening, as suggested by Politzer, greatly improved the hearing, and especially raised the limit of sound from 35,000 to 80,000 vibrations in the second.

Of the labyrinth I abstain from speaking. Very many minute investigations have lately added to the knowledge of its structure ; but the details of its functions may be said to remain as undecided as ever ; especially since the report of a case by Dr. Cassels of Glasgow, in which "the whole cochlea was removed," by caries, " without loss of hearing or impairing the perception of the transmitted tones of the diapason."* This case, for the accuracy of which Dr. Cassels' statement is ample authority, would seem to set aside for the present all the suggestions which have been made, with so exquisite an appearance of reason, by Helmholz, respecting the special functions of various fibres of the laminæ of the cochlea in responding to particular musical tones, upon which doubt has also been thrown from other quarters. Perhaps the other portions of the organ are capable of partially compensating for the functions usually performed by the cochlea, tho' it is hardly possible to understand how the functions of any of the other portions of the labyrinth

* The case is given at length in Chap. xiv.

can have been preserved during exfoliation of that organ.

But clinical experience decidedly indicates that different parts of the labyrinthine structures are appropriated to the reception of different pitches of sound, since the power of hearing certain notes only may be lost, while the rest are unaffected. Such a case is reported by Magnus, and the power was restored during the use of resonators corresponding to the notes involved. In a patient of my own also, a lady aged 40, with whom conversation could be carried on quite easily, the notes of the upper octaves were entirely inaudible. She had never heard a railway whistle. The *pitches* of certain notes also may be altered, as if by mistuning of particular strings within the ear. Sometimes there is a difference, as of half a tone, between the two ears. But the true significance of these symptoms is doubtless yet to be found, and it were a pity to preoccupy the ground with conjectures. Variations of *fluid* pressure of course can hardly account for affections limited to one part of a continuous cavity.

In reference to the effect of section of the semi-circular canals upon the equilibrium of the body, the last experiments appear to show that the effects differ in different animals. Böttcher* found that no movements of turning ensued on careful section of the canals in frogs, and Mr. E. Hart obtained similar results, but Löwenberg* found

* Report in "Journ. Anat. and Phys.," Nov., 1873.

the case different with pigeons. By a modification in
the method of operating, he sought to determine whether
the movements were caused by pain, as supposed by
Flourens, or whether the presence of consciousness was
necessary for these disturbed movements, and whether
the cause consists in an irritation or paralysis of nerves.
The results of his experiments are, (1) the disturbance of
movement occurring after section of the semi-circular
canals of the ear depends only upon this injury, and not
upon any injury to the brain. (2) The vomiting observed
by Czermak in his experiments depends upon injury of
the cerebellum.   (3) The disturbance of movement is the
consequence of irritation of the membranous canals and
not of paralysis of the same.   (4) The irritation of the
canals produces the spasmodic movements in a reflex
manner without the co-operation of consciousness.
(5) The transference of this reflex irritation of the nerves
of the membranous canals to the motor nerves takes place
in the thalamus opticus.   With regard to the statement
of Brown-Sequard, that section of the N. acusticus produces these movements, Löwenberg, operating upon
rabbits, found that section of this nerve from the tympanum yields the same results, but in this case the semi-
circular canals are at the same time partly pinched and
partly pierced.

It may be hoped that before long Professor Ferrier's
experiments will give us a key to the real significance of
these facts.   The slightest affections of the tympanum,

among others syringing with cold water, or with water
much above blood-heat, or the pressure of a column of
cold water upon the membrane, will produce giddiness,
often extreme; the cerebral centres not only of emotion
but of motion being thus eminently liable to be affected
thro' impressions on the ear. It seems, therefore, the
more remarkable that—in strong contrast to the eye—
Dr. Hughlings Jackson should have found no lesion of the
brain or cerebellum that has deafness for its result, result
except thro' mechanically involving the auditory nerve.*

I may add that in one case, that of an elderly lady,
long deaf with symptoms of nerve-affection, I have known
an attack of hemiplegia distinctly improve the hearing;
and quite recently I examined the ears of a woman aged
45, extremely deaf, and found collapse and thickening of
the membrane, with great impairment of the nervous
power, forbidding all hope of benefit from treatment; her
death took place from disease of the heart shortly afterwards, and for more than a week previously her hearing
was greatly sharpened.

A curious statement is made by J. A. Nussbaumer † to
the effect that both himself and his brother always perceived a sensation of colour, as well as sound, from every
excitement of the auditory nerve whether by music or
noises. The colours, however, were not perceived as

* "Med. Times and G.," March 1, 1873.
† "Wiener Med. Woch.," 1873. 1-3. See J. O. Green's Report on
Otol., "Boston Med. and S. Jl.," Oct., 1873.

external, and they differed for the two brothers with
the same note. The statement bears the stamp, perhaps,
rather of disease than of any modification of normal
function, but may possibly have some significance in the
future.

In respect to the functions of the chorda tympani, in
one case in which I accidentally divided it in making
incision of the membrane, there appeared to be a good
deal more than the usual amount of pain, which lasted
for three or four days, and taste was much diminished
along the whole of the corresponding side of the tongue ;
it was regained in the course of a fortnight. It has been
regarded as acting the part of a regulator of the tension
of the membrane by means of a reflex action thro' the
tensor tympani ; but it seems to me that the observation
of cases of disease does not support this view ; the hearing better in a noise, which is so frequent a symptom
in the less favourable class of cases, seems to have no
relation to abnormal conditions of the membrane.

CHAPTER II.

THE diagnosis of diseases of the ear rests on three bases :—(1) The examination of the various parts of the organ ; (2) Tests applied to the function of the nerve ; and (3) The history and general condition. First in importance among these is the ocular inspection. The best instruments for the purpose are the simple, round or oval specula, and a reflector such as is used for the larynx ; one of more than the usual concavity is very useful ; or, by means of a plane one, direct sunlight may be used, and the image of the membrane may be seen on the reflector by others (Lucae). A lens of about six inches' focal distance may be screwed with a joint on the back of the reflector, so that a magnifying power may be used or not, as desired. Ordinary daylight gives the most distinct illumination, and the patient I think is best placed a little farther from the window than the surgeon, not between him and the light.

A speculum provided with a prism, to bend the light into the meatus, has been constructed by Dr. Blake, of Boston,* and Dr. Eysell has proposed a method which

* "Report of Amer. Otological Society," 1872.

he accounts effective for the construction of a binocular speculum.*

Dr. Blake has also constructed small reflecting glasses, like those used by dentists, to be inserted into the tympanum in cases of perforation of the membrane when the state of the parts admits. And it is conceivable that in some cases of minute growths or caries these might be very valuable.

In introducing the speculum, it must be remembered that (beginning from without) the meatus winds, first, a little forwards, and then backwards and slightly upwards, so that there is a tendency for the eye to fall on the wall of the meatus, instead of reaching the membrane; and the speculum accordingly must be introduced well into the passage, and directed first a little forwards, for the most part with a slight pressure on the outer part of the posterior wall, to straighten the cartilaginous portion of

---

* "Archiv. für Ohrenheilkunde," 1873, p. 239. Since a really efficient instrument of this kind would probably be valuable for estimating the irregularities of form presented by the membrane, I append Dr. Eysell's suggestion, which appears as yet not to have been carried out;—" Two prisms of small refracting angles (3°-5°) are so placed in a setting that they touch one another with their refracting edges, and that the border surface of the one lies in the same plane with the border surface of the other that is turned to the same side, and these are introduced between the reflector and the speculum, and as near as possible to the speculum; their edges must be vertical, and the border surfaces above described must run nearly parallel to the median plane of the patient. The observer now, by means of any of the customary reflectors, throws light upon the membrane through either of the prisms, and receives on the right and left eye respectively an image through each prism. With a little practice these are easily made to coincide."

the canal. This will be much aided by drawing the auricle slightly upwards and backwards with the left hand. The anterior wall of the meatus projects slightly in its central part, and so not only hinders the view of the front part of the membrane, but causes the side of the speculum to project into the canal, so that I have often found a perfect examination facilitated by cutting a

FIG. 2.

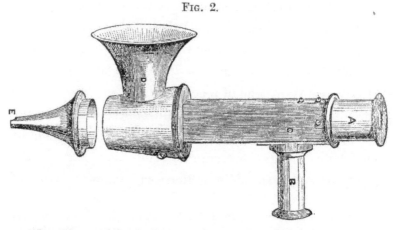

Figure 2 represents the form of speculum I prefer : the notch is seen at E. With it is shown also an instrument, that may be used for demonstrating the membrane ; a prism is introduced at c, and a second observer places his eye at B. Light is admitted at D. It may be used also for other cavities besides the meatus. [Half size.]

shallow notch in the speculum, and turning that side to the front in introducing it. In very young children the passage is extremely short, and the membrane lies almost horizontally.

In the healthy state the membrane presents a surface

of a peculiar glistening transparency, obliquely placed, and of an obvious concavity. Von Troeltsh estimates the angle formed by the membrane with the upper wall of the tympanum at 140° on an average, though it varies much in different individuals. This angle bears a constant relation to certain other characters of the cranial development. In an adult cretin he found it as much as 167°, approximating thus to the almost horizontal position of the membrane in the infant. In an examination, however, which, by the kindness of Dr. Down I was allowed to make of the ears of the inmates of the Earlswood Asylum for Idiots, I did not notice unusual obliquity of the membrane.

The points which specially attract the eye and should be first sought out as the starting point of the examination, are :—(1) The handle of the malleus, and (2) The bright spot. The former commences superiorly with the white and prominent short process, and runs downwards, and generally somewhat backwards, as a broad white line, terminating near—but a little above and in front of—the centre of the membrane at its most concave point (the umbo). The bright spot extends in a triangular form from near the termination of the handle of the malleus downwards and forwards. It is due to the peculiar curve given to the membrane by its oblique position, and concave form, together with the convex curve of its peripheral part.

The extent and form of this bright spot are somewhat

variable. Even in healthy membranes it may or may not reach to the circumference, it may be a single broad streak of light, or may be divided across or lengthwise. If the membrane moves outward, as when the tympanum is inflated, or inward as during the act of swallowing, the motion is generally most delicately marked by the changes in the appearance of the bright spot. In diseased conditions it may be wanting altogether, or from abnormalities of curvature its position may be changed, or several may be present in different parts of the membrane. The colour of the healthy membrane cannot be exactly described, because it varies with several circumstances. By virtue of its transparency its hue is modified by the rays of light reflected from the promontory, and the kind of light employed also affects it; it is more blue by daylight, more yellowish by artificial illumination.

The chief points to note in respect to the membrane are its degree of concavity; the appearance of the reflection of light from its anterior surface; the direction of the handle of the malleus across it; its transparency; its vascularity,* whether there be thinner or thicker portions, or deposits, or parts especially depressed or bulging; and, finally, whether it be wanting wholly or in part, and, if it be, the condition of the exposed tympanic

---

* It should be remembered that prolonged examination will induce a certain vascularity of the membrane; Bonnafont also says that he has known loud sounds produce it.

wall. In addition, we must note the condition of the
meatus, especially whether it be obstructed by exostoses,
which not very unfrequently happens, or contain fluid,
or masses of wax or epidermis, or growths of fungi.
The presence of either a small quantity of opaque fluid
at the bottom, or of flakes of epidermis, may be very
misleading, since they may simulate very closely the appearance of the membrane in some morbid states.
When a layer of fluid covers the membrane a distinct
pulsation is often seen; this generally, but not always,
implies a perforation.

In states of perfect hearing the membrane may present considerable varieties of appearance; differing
greatly in hue, in transparency, and sometimes presenting even dense masses of chalky deposit, occupying a
considerable portion of its surface. In one instance of
not only perfect hearing, but acute musical sensibility,
in a child, there existed apparently a solid rod of bone,
running from the short process of the malleus to the
posterior wall of the tympanum ; apparently a malforma-
tion of the bone.*

The most usual deviation from the healthy state seen
in the membrane is that characteristic of chronic catarrh
of the tympanum, generally accompanied with obstruction of the Eustachian tube. The natural curvature of the
membrane in this case is lost, and it is altogether drawn
in, with a marked concavity. Often in such cases, if

* See Atlas, Plate XI., Fig. 5.

the membrane is transparent and the affection recent, it presents a distinct pink aspect, due to the congested mucous membrane of the tympanum shining through it ; * in more chronic cases the membrane loses its transparency, and becomes white and opaque. When the membrane has this appearance, and there arises the question how far other conditions besides mere closure of the Eustachian tube are present, the form of the surface of the membrane gives us some evidence. When simple closure of the tube exists, the membrane is of a moderately uniform concavity ; if there be present also the results of chronic catarrh of the mucous membrane, the membrane, though it may be very much drawn in, will often have a flat appearance, and in many cases the malleus will be seen not only drawn inwards, but distinctly displaced backwards, and even drawn up into an almost horizontal position, near to the superior border of the membrane. How this displacement of the malleus occurs is not, to my mind, yet sufficiently demonstrated. The formation of bands of adhesion, or shortening of the ligaments of the malleus, or contraction of the tensor tympani muscle, may all be causes, but also it seems probable to me that it is not unfrequently due to a contraction of the substance of the membrane itself, resulting from the continued presence, in the upper part of the tympanum, of collections of viscid mucus, which produce, first, bulgings of the

* See Atlas, Plate III., Figs. 1 and 3.

membrane, and, afterwards, thinning and puckering of
its substance.

In connection with the Eustachian tube another question arises, to which attention was first drawn by Dr.
Jago, of Truro, and subsequently by Dr. Rumbold,*
of St. Louis, namely, the effect both upon the hearing,
and the appearance of the membrane, of undue patency of
the tube. The subjective symptoms are unnatural ringing of the voice in the ear and undue perception of all
sounds occurring in the throat. Dr. Rumbold has also
carefully noted the appearance of the membrane in these
cases, and has come to the conclusion that the functions
of the tube have not hitherto been perfectly apprehended.
He ascribes the concavity of the membrane, in its normal
state, partly to the effect of the continued absorption of
the air within the tympanum, which causes it to be constantly more rare than that in the meatus or the throat,
so drawing the membrane slightly inwards. This difference of density of the air within and that external to the
tympanum, is maintained at a constant pitch by a regu-
lative influence of the tube, which in its normal condition
is not wholly impervious to air, but permits, through its
small superior curved portion, a continuous supply of air;
which, however, has to overcome a moderate resistance
sufficient to maintain the normal concavity of the mem-

* "The Function of the Eustachian Tube in relation to the Renewal
and Density of the Air in the Tympanic Cavity, and to the Concavity of
the Membrana Tympani." St. Louis, 1873.

brane. In other words, the membrane is maintained in its natural concave state, not merely passively, but by a constant balance of opposing forces—its own resiliency, which would carry it outwards, the absorption of the air within the tympanum, which draws it inwards, and the yielding resistance of the tube to the entrance of air, which, in the healthy state, does not suffer the absorption within the tympanum to exceed a certain effect. By the traction of the malleus and of the tensor tympani muscle, Dr. Rumbold thinks the membrane would be drawn merely into a shallow cone; by the continuously balanced rarefaction of the air it is caused to assume a *curved concavity*. Perhaps hardly any arrangement could be more adapted to preserve the membrane in a condition of the utmost sensitiveness to vibration. The proofs adduced by Dr. Rumbold are cases in which, with abnormal hearing of their own voice, the membrane was visibly less concave than normal, and the hearing impaired, all the symptoms being relieved by the injection of fluid into the Eustachian tube. He remarks, also, that the effect of swallowing in relieving pressure of air within the tympanum is not sudden and complete, but only partial, and that, therefore, it cannot be held completely to open the tube, but only to diminish the resistance to the passage of air.

That the normal closure of the Eustachian tube is of a very slight degree is proved by the fact (first noticed by Lucae) that very thin and relaxed portions of the mem-

brane, such as the scars of old perforations, will sometimes visibly move in and out coincidently with inspiration
and expiration. This might be explained by the supposition that the closure of the narrow upper portion of
the tube was effected by the fluid secretion of the lining
membrane, which might move to and fro with the movements of respiration sufficiently to allow a motion in
parts of the membrane which offer no resistance.

Dr. Rüdinger,* of Munich, so well known for his
anatomical investigations of the ear, reports that on
swallowing during a lecture he felt the usual sensation in
the ears, followed on the right side by a peculiar cramp-
like sensation. His own voice sounded louder and of a
different timbre, and even painfully loud, so that, though
interested in watching the condition, he was compelled
at last to perform another act of swallowing, when the
condition ceased. He ascribes it to a cramp of the dilator
of the tube.

Besides their own importance, these observations seem
to me interesting as bearing on a subject that will repay
much more investigation : the part played by spasmodic
conditions of the muscles of the ossicula, and especially
of the stapedius, in producing tinnitus. The cases are
frequent in which no reasonable cause can be assigned
for this symptom but some such affection of the muscles,
due, perhaps, in the first instance, to slight irritative
conditions of the mucous membrane. A clicking sound,

* "Monatsschrift für Ohrenheilkunde," September, 1872.

sometimes audible externally, due to spasm of the tensor tympani, and attended with increase in the concavity of the membrane, as demonstrated by the manometer introduced into the meatus, is complained of now and then.

Another point to be considered in the appearance of the membrane is the prominence with which the bands that run forwards and backwards from the short process of the malleus stand out. This will give important indications of the degree of rigidity that is present. Chronic retraction of the tensor tympani muscle is also held to be a cause of indrawing of the membrane, and in some of these cases the malleus seems to be twisted on its long axis. Lucae has remarked that, in some cases of deafness in children, the membrane may be very concave, as if from obstruction of the tube, when it is not really closed or even much narrowed, but the nostrils are obstructed by swelling of the mucous membrane and excessive secretion, and the tonsillar region swollen, so that respiration is carried on with difficulty, and the air during inspiration is, as it were, sucked out of the tympanum. In such cases treatment addressed to the Eustachian region alone would, of course, fail to give relief. But it may be safely affirmed that in every such case, whether the tube were closed or not (and to me the exceptions to its closure seem very rare), the surgeon's attention would, of course, be given to the condition of the whole naso-pharyngeal region.

In examining the membrana tympani special attention should also be paid to its superior border, to examine the condition of the thin portion above the short process (the membrana flaccida) and of the superior wall of the meatus. Both these parts seem very liable to morbid conditions. The membrane at this part may be densely thickened, or may seem wanting altogether, and the *neck* of the malleus, which lies behind it, seem quite exposed, or at other times a minute perforation may be seen there, or even a red mass of granulations; and very often, especially in conditions connected with long-standing discharge or accumulation of epidermis in the meatus, the upper wall of the meatus at the superior and inner part seems largely excavated, and masses of thickened discharge or epidermic flakes may collect, sometimes to an immense extent, and give rise not only to great local irritation but to general distress. This is quite independent of the formation of the *sebaceous tumours*, consisting of dense layers of epidermic cells, which sometimes form in the meatus, and are also very apt to partially destroy its superior wall.

Thicker and thinner portions of the membrane are easily distinguished, thinner portions being *dark*, as less reflecting; they are also more concave. They are often to be seen as dark spots on a generally thick and white membrane, when they may be assumed to be for the most part scars; but most frequently thinned and sunk-in portions of the membrane are to be seen in the upper and posterior parts, about in the position of the head of the stapes; and they are often in contact with or even adherent to that bone. The cause of the thinning of the membrane in this position is a matter needing to be further explored, but it is almost certain that, in the majority of cases, it is due to the pressure exerted by masses of dense secretion formed during catarrhal affections of the tympanum, and which tend to collect especially in that region; that is, to cling around the ossicula, and very probably to accumulate in the posterior "pocket" of the membrane. I have certainly seen more "bulgings" of the membrane from collections of mucus in this part than in any other, and it seems to me that it is due to its entanglement in that position, owing to the presence of the chain of ossicles; and we cannot but feel how probable it is that mucus that had collected in this position, becoming dense and dry, should give rise to increasing deafness after all appearances connected with increased secretion had passed away. To what extent this is the case is one of the problems on the solution of which the prognosis in a large class of cases depends. For a "rigidity" due to that cause would be evidently much more susceptible of remedy than if it were the result of thickening or hardening of the structure of the mucous membrane itself, or of ligamentous or other immobility of the joints of the ossicula. My experience has led me to believe that the presence of such dried-up mucous secretion investing the chain of bones

is one of the most frequent conditions which determine deafness in the large mass of chronic cases
which occur, with more or less clear history of protracted or recurring attacks of catarrh dating from long
before.

In connection with the presence of abnormal secretions
in the tympanum, other appearances are to be regarded.
The slightest of these is one that may occasionally be
seen in the early stages of catarrh, especially in the
young—the outline of distinct *bubbles* on the inner
surface of the membrane. It is necessary for this that
the membrane should not have lost its transparency,
and that the tube should permit the passage of air; the
appearance will sometimes follow inflation of the tympanum by the india-rubber bag, and the air may be heard
to enter with a slight moist sound. A more advanced
stage of excessive secretion will give rise sometimes to a
mottled or cloudy whiteness of the membrane, varying in
degree at different parts, and which may be seen to be
due, not to opacity of its external surface, but to a
whitish semi-fluid substance in contact with it internally.
Appearances of this kind lend great countenance to
Dr. Jago's opinion that the drying up of mucus into a
thin layer on the internal surface of the membrane
is a cause of deafness, which may sometimes disappear
with a sudden crack, due to the peeling off of the secretion.

Another appearance presented by secretion within the

tympanum is that of a slight yellowish discoloration situated at the most dependent part, and with a curved superior border, *which gradually shifts its position with the movements of the patient's head,* thus showing that it is due to the presence of a fluid. I believe it has not been noticed that the hearing varies in accordance with these changes in the position of the fluid, in cases that have been observed; but the changes in the power of hearing in accordance with the position in which the head is held are frequently very striking, and a shifting of more or less fluid secretion always suggests itself as a possible cause, but not yet with sufficient proof. The secretion in these cases, of course, is perfectly fluid, generally serous; but the existence of even a large amount of merely serous fluid is no evidence that a more viscid secretion is not also present.

Another appearance of excessive secretion is an obscure, yellowish, greenish-yellow, or brownish tint, appearing through the posterior part of the membrane, which is almost always very concave, and the tube more or less obstructed. In these cases the appearance does not change with movement of the head, and the secretion is of dense and viscid character. On inflation of the tympanum a distinct yellow bulging is formed, unless the membrane is firmly held down by adhesions to the inner wall of the tympanum, but even then powerful inflation will often produce a limited protrusion of the discoloured part. In not a few cases, however, according

to my experience, inspissated secretions may be present
in the tympanum, and to a large extent, so as seriously
to interfere with the hearing, without any appearance
characteristic of their presence, the membrane being at
the most white and opaque, and perhaps flattened. In
some of such cases I have found the history—being that
of a distinct catarrh, as, for example, an attack of cold
following a fall into water—a true guide to the presence
of inspissated mucus.

Alike in cases in which excess of secretion is present
and when it is not, the membrane may sometimes be seen
fallen in upon the promontory and more or less adherent
to it, or bound by bands of adhesion to various parts of
the tympanic wall or the ossicula. In the former case
the appearance at once reveals the condition, which was
termed by Wilde *collapse* : the membrane is very much
thinned ; it lies evidently too remote from the eye, and
the outline of the promontory is more or less distinctly
visible ; often the niche in which the fenestra rotunda
lies is clearly marked ; the malleus is seen to run inwards and to rest upon the tympanic wall, or it may be
partly wanting, and most frequently the head of the stapes
may be seen distinctly projecting just beneath the upper
border of the membrane at its posterior part. Generally
the Eustachian tube is obstructed, but if it is pervious,
or can be made so, portions of the membrane may
be blown out into a more or less bladder-like form,
leaving the central part still attached to the projecting

portion of the tympanic wall. The bladdery protrusions
form generally in the lower segment of the membrane.
This condition is sometimes found compatible with hearing so serviceable as almost to be termed good, and it
can almost always be improved if the nerve-power is preserved. One point in respect to these cases is often
difficult to decide, but it is not practically very important,
namely, whether the membrane is really complete and
only fallen in and adherent, or whether a portion has
been destroyed and the edges have become adherent, so
that more or less of the central portion really is the exposed tympanic wall. Some guidance may be given in
determining this point by the appearance of the malleus.
If the lower portion of the handle is wanting there is
little doubt that the adjacent part of the membrane also
is destroyed.

In these cases, and still more in those of more partial
adhesions, and slighter collapse of the membrane, Siegle's
pneumatic speculum is very useful. This is an ordinary
speculum made of vulcanite, the wider end of which is
enlarged into a small box covered in by a glass lens,
through which the membrane is observed, while the small
end is surrounded by india-rubber, so that it can be
fitted air-tight into the meatus. Thus the membrane
can be seen magnified, as if beneath an air-pump; for by
means of an india-rubber tube attached to the box-like
part of the speculum air can be sucked out of the meatus,
and the membrane thus drawn out or forced inwards at the

surgeon's will. Any retracted spots or local impediments to its motion can be thus made apparent. This instrument also (I may here anticipate so far as to say) is very useful in the diagnosis of the seat of tinnitus. There are many cases of most distressing noises in the ear, which are for the moment wholly or very greatly relieved by suction thus exerted on the membrane, and in these cases we may surely feel justified in ascribing the affection to pressure exerted on the labyrinth, through some condition existing within the tympanum, even though no visible indrawing of the membrane is to be seen. Thus, it seems to me, the idea of a primary or even a confirmed nerve affection may be excluded, and we have a means of safely affirming that not only the original but the existing cause of the tinnitus is situated in the tympanum, which is, of course, a most favourable element in the prognosis. I may also add that I have, though in but a few instances, found that permanent relief could be obtained by the patients through the continued careful use of suction on the meatus, by themselves, more or less frequently repeated.

Perforations, when they are large and in an irritable state, so that discharge still exists, are easily recognised after the meatus has been cleansed. The general surface of the membrane is usually whitish and opaque, often covered with more than one layer of half-loosened epidermis ; the exposed surface of the tympanic wall is red and granular, often swollen, so as to appear quite on a

level with the membrane, and the edges of the perforation present a well-contrasted border. But even this
condition, plain as it generally is, may be simulated
sometimes by a granular state of the surface of the membrane (resembling pannus of the eyeball); and which
might be taken for a perforation, exposing a granular
tympanic wall. The granulations on the surface of the
membrane, however, almost always extend also to the wall
of the meatus. Occasionally, such a granular condition
coexists with a small perforation, which it completely
conceals from view. But when the destruction of the
membrane exists but to a small extent, or the whole
membrane has become disorganised, it is often impossible to determine by the eye alone whether a perforation
exists. The only sufficient proof then is the inflation of
the tympanum with air, either of the patient's own blowing, called Valsalva's method, or by the bag introduced
by Politzer, or by the catheter : and the second method
is generally the best. If the air enters the tympanum
freely, and there is a perforation, it will be heard to
escape through the orifice into the meatus with a rushing
or screeching sound, according to the condition of the
parts. The surgeon should listen by an india-rubber tube
passing from the patient's ear to his own. As a rule, it
may even be said that the diagnosis of a perforation should
never be considered final unless air has been heard to
pass through it. Little black patches (of wax, &c.),
adhering to the membrane, are often very suggestive of

small perforations, but, according to my experience, a real perforation very seldom presents such an appearance.

Among the conditions that may accompany perforations must be mentioned polypi growing from within the tympanum, and just appearing at a level with the orifice, or slightly projecting, giving rise sometimes to appearances not easy to interpret. Large polypi occupying the meatus are, of course, easy to distinguish; they generally arise from within the tympanum, and the presence of perforation should be tested by inflation of the Eustachian tube. Often, however, minute growths of this kind are present, and maintain an obstinate discharge, and their existence should be very strongly suspected whenever there is a history of bleeding from the ear. They are sometimes difficult to detect, especially when they are situated deep in the anterior part of the meatus, close to the membrana tympani, where the projecting anterior wall of the passage may almost wholly conceal them. At other times, they may be seated quite at the superior part of the membrane, or close to the floor, or sometimes, in cases of perforation, may be detected half hidden behind the superior, or other, border of the orifice. In whatever position they are, it is impossible to effect a cure till they have been eradicated, and the surface from which they grow brought to a healthy state. Speaking generally, I conceive there can be little doubt that the cause of polypi in the ear is retained secretion ; the fleshy growths which result from diseased bone form a different class.

When inflammation of the meatus or tympanum extends to the adjacent cavities, and involves the mastoid cells (a contingency which should never be overlooked, and which is indicated by pain and tenderness in that region), or when it involves the bony cavities which extend to a greater or less degree above the roof of the meatus, the condition of the meatus is often of great importance, in respect both to diagnosis and treatment. A red and painful bulging of its posterior or superior wall frequently attends such extended inflammation, and in many cases a free incision there will give exit to pus, and avert most serious dangers. It is of importance to distinguish this condition from the much more frequent one of furuncles, which, however, may also occasion a great amount of pain and fever. Sometimes there will be found a distinct orifice in the superior wall of the meatus, from which a very sensitive and irritable fleshy growth may proceed. Whether or not this is always the result of caries of the bone in its ordinary sense I have not been able to ascertain.

The next means of local examination are those by which the conditions of the Eustachian tube and general faucial mucous membrane are tested. Among these, perhaps the priority may be given to the use of the rhinoscope, of which, however, it has not been my habit latterly much to avail myself, finding that, while it was

inconvenient to my patient, it seldom afforded me real
help in diagnosis. Other surgeons, however, speak of it
in high terms.*

The perviousness or obstruction of the Eustachian
tube can, in recent cases, almost always be inferred from
the appearance of the membrane, but not minor degrees

* I subjoin a statement of the conditions which Dr. Pomeroy, of New
York, has discovered and treated by its aid :—
"I. Mucus in the mouths of the tubes, with or without greenish or
greyish mucus clinging or adherent to the post-nasal septum, and
occasionally filling the nares.
"II. Increased redness in and about the mouth of the tube, or
paleness of the mucous lining of the part.
"III. An œdematous condition of the parts near and in the mouth
of the tube, resulting in more or less swelling. The swelling in the
region of the tube, the result of hyperæmia or œdema, may (1) so far
obliterate the mouth of the tube as to cause it to appear as a minute
dimple, or obliterate it entirely, or (2) produce so much swelling of the
collar-like surrounding of this tube as to greatly exaggerate it; (3)
increase the elevation which separates the mouth of the tube from the
fossa of Rosenmüller ; (4) enlarge the posterior extremities of the middle
and inferior turbinated bones, and produce a malposition in the posterior
nares, and give it a rough and uneven outline; (5) cause a ring-like
swelling around the tube, rough, red, and of a macerated appearance.
"IV. Granulations similar to those found in the pharynx in granular
pharyngitis near the mouth of the tube.
"V. An apparent diminution in the mobility of the lips of the tube
during contraction of the muscles.
"VI. Whitish striæ, indicating cicatricial degeneration of the proper
substance of the mucous membrane in the region of the Eustachian
tube."
Dr. Rumbold, among other suggestions for facilitating Rhinoscopy,
has constructed a mirror, the angle of which can be changed after its
introduction ; and draws forward the uvula by receiving it into a tube
closed at the other end by a plate of india-rubber, so that it is retained
by suction. (The Examination of the Cavities of Nose, Throat, and Ear.
St. Louis, 1873.)

of thickening, &c., of the tube, which may considerably
diminish its calibre ; and in long-standing disease, or
when perforations exist, or the membrane is collapsed,
the perviousness of the tube can only be determined by
the passage of air through it.   There are three ways in
which this may be attempted.   1. The simple inflation
of the ears with the mouth and nose closed (Valsalva's
method).   2. Politzer's bag.   3. The catheter.

In either case the result is generally best appreciated
by listening through an india-rubber tube to the sound
of the entering air, but the changes effected in the appearance of the membrane by it are often of the greatest
importance.   Some of these have been already referred
to ; a very frequent one is a great bulging of the
membrane at its upper and posterior portion, where it
may sometimes be blown out by a very slight force
into an almost bladdery form.   In many cases this indicates simply that the patient, having experienced temporary benefit from the inflation, has accustomed himself
to its frequent repetition and carried it too far.   In every
such case, or nearly so, the action has almost or entirely
lost its good effect, and the practice should be carefully
avoided.

The inflation of the drum by means of Politzer's bag
rests upon the fact that the walls of the tube are drawn
apart in the act of swallowing.   The patient takes a little
water in his mouth to be ready to swallow at a signal,
and the surgeon then introduces the pipe of an ordinary

india-rubber bag into one nostril, closes the nostril over it, gives the signal to the patient to swallow, and at the moment of his swallowing sharply compresses the bag. By this means air is forced into the upper part of the

FIG. 3.

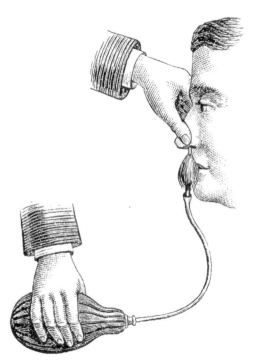

Fig. 3. INFLATION BY POLITZER'S BAG.—It is shown with the box for introducing vapour of chloroform or iodine, described hereafter. The hand should be ready to give the bag a vigorous and sudden pressure. (From Roosa.)

pharynx at the same time that the velum palati is raised and the walls of the tubes are drawn apart, and it rushes accordingly along the tubes with sufficient force to overcome very considerable obstacles. The degree of force used can, of course, be adjusted to the amount of the obstruction. With children great gentleness should be used, and by patience, and accustoming them first to bear the tube in the nostril alone, and then to swallow alone, their timidity can generally be overcome. With very young children the swallowing can be dispensed with, the mouth being kept closed; and with them blowing through an india-rubber tube is often preferable to the bag. The bag should be of a size that can be easily grasped by the patient, if it be entrusted to him to use; and a valve, or an opening in the bag to be closed by the thumb, may be recommended if he is likely not to remember to keep the bag closed until it has been withdrawn from the nostril. The nozzle of the bag should be guarded by a piece of india-rubber tubing.

I think I have observed that the stream of air enters rather more forcibly the tube *opposite* to the nostril into which it is driven. This is, perhaps, easily explained if it be true, as the stream of air would scarcely receive its full *lateral* direction until after its exit from the other nostril had been resisted, so that the opposite Eustachian tube would receive the first and strongest direct action of the pressure. I would not affirm that there is always any perceptible difference, but I think that, even if there be the very slightest difference in the force of the pressure on the two sides, it should be recognised and taken advantage of. For, of course, the chief drawback to the use of Politzer's bag is that the effect cannot be limited to one ear. I therefore by preference apply it to the nostril opposite to the side on which I desire the chief effect, and if the other ear be healthy I desire the patient firmly to close the meatus on the sound side, to guard the membrane from the effect of the pressure. Whether this precaution, however, is really of any use I would not say, because any force which is thus kept from operating on the membrana tympani is, of course, virtually thrown, at least in part, on the structures within the tympanum. I have very seldom observed any evil results upon a sound ear from the use of Politzer's inflation, and then only for a time, but it is, of course, very possible that ill effects might ensue, and the bag should be entrusted to the patient's hands only with precise instructions and careful supervision.

It is sometimes, though I think not often, requisite to use the Eustachian catheter for purposes of diagnosis. This is chiefly the case when, as sometimes happens, both Valsalva's and Politzer's methods give no reliable results—no decided change in appearance or distinct sound. When this is the case, or when the obstruction cannot be overcome by other means, the catheter should be had recourse to. The best form of catheter, in my opinion, is that made of vulcanite, as suggested by Politzer; the utmost care should be used in cleansing it after use (since it is reported that syphilis has been conveyed by means of it); and in every case, at least of its continued employment, each patient should be supplied with a separate one. Several sizes are advisable, and different *curves* are required in different cases, since the dimensions of the pharynx vary greatly. The curve can be adapted to each case at the time; the silver ones being easily bent by the fingers, and the vulcanite ones also after being warmed in boiling water or over a gas flame. Sometimes a very slight curve indeed suffices; and in cases in which the nostril is very narrow I have sometimes found it better to make the curve extremely small, than to use a catheter of narrower bore and larger curve. In respect to its introduction the chief precautions necessary are to keep the beak well applied to the floor of the lower meatus of the nose, avoiding its slipping into the middle meatus as it is passed along; to carry it well to the posterior wall of the pharynx, and then to draw it forward sufficiently before it is turned up into the tube— half an inch, on an average, in women, and slightly more in men. Lately, by Dr. Löwenberg, it has been advised to draw the catheter forward from the posterior wall of the pharynx, with its beak still turned downwards, until it touches the posterior wall of the velum palati, and then to turn it outwards and slightly upwards into the orifice of the tube, which is situated in the same plane. In many cases this certainly renders the process more simple. The peculiar feeling of the catheter slipping into the orifice of the tube is one that cannot easily be mistaken when it has become at all familiar.

It may slip with a somewhat similar sensation into the fossa posterior to it, but the sounds produced on forcing air into it at once reveal the mistake, being harsh screechy sounds, evidently arising in the throat alone. When either nostril, most frequently the left, is impassable for a catheter, it can be introduced through the opposite, and Dr. Noyes, of New York, has adapted the form of the catheter better to this purpose by giving it a slight second curve, carrying its extremity a little more upwards, so as to be more truly in the line of the tube.

The sounds heard during the passing of air into the Eustachian tube are of a value for diagnosis second only to the results of examination of the membrane. They not only decide the question of the perviousness of the tube, and, if the tube be pervious, of the

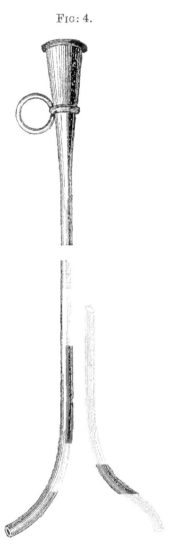

Fɪɢ: 4.

Fig. 4. EUSTACHIAN CATHETER ; a rather small medium size, the size I find most useful. The doubly curved end is Dr. Noyes' adaptation (for the right side).

E

existence of perforation of the membrane, but give evidence, more or less distinctive, of almost every other morbid condition of the middle ear. They have been classified
by various authors with a degree of minuteness which I am
far from saying is either excessive or inexact, for they
present shades of an immense variety, to each one of which
experience justifies us in assigning at least a probable significance. But there are certain characters of the sound
which are perfectly definite alike in their qualities and their
indications. First, there is the sound of the air passing
through a healthy tube into a healthy tympanum, and distending before it a healthy membrane, which each one may
best appreciate by distending his own tympanum. It is a
sound like that produced by blowing gently into a small
bladder, and may be perfectly appreciated by listening with
a tube to any healthy person's ear. When the air is introduced by a catheter into a healthy ear, the sound is a
gentle continued blowing or rustle (*bruit de pluie*) seeming
to come direct into the listener's ear; this is well contrasted with the distant rough sound, evidently not advancing towards the ear, which is heard when the catheter has
missed the tube, and lies merely in contact with the
wall of the throat. If the tube is open for part only of
its length, and there is an obstruction at the narrowest
part, or still closer to the tympanum, but the mucous
membrane is free from excessive secretion, Politzer's or
Valsalva's method gives no distinct sound, or a very
slight one, but the stream of air from the catheter may

be heard with its accustomed rustle, but much more
faint, and evidently stopping short of the tympanum.

With a swollen state of the lining membrane of the
tube, occasioning occlusion, but offering little resistance,
as not unfrequently exists in children, the air passed in
either by Politzer's bag or by the catheter may sometimes be distinctly heard travelling gradually up the
tube, and, as it were, distending its walls, before it
enters the tympanum, as if with a slight stroke. In
other cases, also very frequent in children, when Politzer's bag is used, the entrance of the air occurs with
a slight, but sharp crack, which is always attended with
great improvement of the hearing. In these cases the
membrane has been very concave, and the sharp sound
heard may with every probability be ascribed to its
suddenly resuming a more normal position, the obstruction being situated chiefly at the faucial extremity of the
tube. But the sounds heard on inflation are, perhaps,
most instructive in cases of excessive secretion from the
lining membrane of the tube or tympanum. The degree
of swelling and comparative amount of accumulated secretion will often reveal themselves by variations in sound,
with a great degree of accuracy, on careful examination,
especially if the catheter be used, from the slight squeak
which attends blowing the nose during a cold, to distinct
prolonged gurgling or bubbling, evidently within the
tympanum, and loud creaking or rattling sounds seated
in the course of the tube. Then, finally, there are

modifications of the normal sound of the entering
air indicative not of increased secretion, but suggestive
rather of an unnatural dryness of the mucous lining of
the tympanum, or of abnormal roughnesses and irregularities of its surface. Such are harsh, dry murmurs,
unnaturally loud, on the employment of the catheter, a
hard creaking on Politzer's inflation, or total absence of
audible sound from it, although the membrane on inspection is seen to have yielded to the air. Among these
sounds, one of the most characteristic is a prolonged
"pfiff" on the patient's own inflation, very different
from the slight normal rustle. The signification of this
class of sounds I feel, as yet, to need a better explanation. Perhaps certain atrophic conditions of the mucous
membrane have part in producing some of them, as hypertrophic conditions may be indicated by others; and
the presence of dense and inspissated mucus is, doubtless, the origin of some as yet undefined abnormal
sounds. But these questions need reconsideration in
the light of a new and rapidly increasing experience.

In addition to the sounds produced by the direct
entrance of the air, Dr. Gruber has insisted on the importance of secondary sounds, which may be heard after
the primary sound has ceased, and are due to the reaction of the membrane and other tympanic structures
against the pressure of the stream of air. These are,
however, only sometimes audible, and their precise signification remains to be determined. It must be remem-

bered that inflation may sometimes fail to produce its
natural sound or to affect the appearance of the membrane, not because the tube is really impervious to air,
but on account of valve-like structures existing at or near
its entrance into the tympanum. A case of this kind I
shall hereafter quote; and Mr. Yule,* who is able at
will to open the Eustachian tubes, gives it as his opinion
that such a valve-like condition exists, on the ground of
the greater difficulty he finds in withdrawing air from
the tympanum than in inflating it.

There is another question deserving more investigation than it has received in connection with the act of
inflation of the tympanum, namely, that in some conditions, unconnected either with any acute affection, or
with any previous history of giddiness, the simple inflation, performed without violence, will induce an intense
and distressing attack of giddiness. I have noticed this
effect only in cases in which there was also reason for
believing some affection of the auditory nerve (though
perhaps only secondary to a tympanic affection) was
present; and most probably it is to be ascribed to the
pressure exerted by the act upon the labyrinth. It
might possibly be a sign of a condition otherwise not
easy to diagnose with any certainty: excess of labyrinthine fluid. On one occasion, after introducing the
catheter with no unusual difficulty, and inflating the
tympanum with air in the accustomed way, the patient,

[1] 'Journal of Anatomy and Physiology,' November, 1873.

an apparently healthy man, æt. 28, after complaining of giddiness, fell down in a fit, apparently epileptic (with bilateral convulsions). Recovery soon took place. I ascertained from his medical attendant that he had never been subject to epilepsy, and that no affection of a similar kind existed in his family. He has continued since in perfect health, and under treatment directed chiefly to the throat, and avoiding inflation of the ear, his hearing has considerably improved.

If the tube cannot be opened by either of the above-mentioned means, aided by the use of vapour of chloroform instead of air, a bougie should be had recourse to ; for without its employment the extent of the obstruction cannot be rightly estimated. I find thin laminaria bougies by far the most effective, and absolutely free from objection when used with due precautions: namely (1) never to introduce beyond the isthmus (or narrowest part of the tube) a bougie that should not easily lie in it in a healthy state ; (2) always to withdraw the catheter and bougie *together*, or the catheter first ; this, of course, because the bougie swells, and to attempt to withdraw it *through* the catheter causes it to break ; (3) never to attempt to inflate the tympanum with air on the same day on which the bougie has been used, in order to avoid extravasation of air.

II. The second element in the diagnosis of disease of the ear consists in tests applied to the power of hearing. The voice, the watch, and the tuning fork are the means.

still most relied on, but the notes of musical instruments
are sometimes important aids, especially in certain limited
nerve affections. All the means are yet imperfect, in a
theoretical sense, inasmuch as there is no test of the exact
intensity of either of them. Dr. Lucae has devised an
instrument for measuring the loudness of the voice (a
" maximal phonometer ") in the form of a short kind of
speaking-trumpet covered in at the end with a piece of
elastic sheeting, the movements of which are exhibited
on a dial. By this means the relative hearing power of
different patients might probably be more accurately
tested. But to me it seems that, practically, satisfactory results can be attained by the ordinary methods.
One improvement, however, a suggestion of Dr. J. S.
Prout, of New York, seems desirable to be usually
adopted. It is, in stating the hearing distance by the
watch, to give, not the number of inches it is heard, but
the fraction of the average or normal distance ; using this
normal distance as the denominator. Thus the hearing
distance of the watch I ordinarily use is about forty
inches ; and accordingly I should describe the hearing of
a patient who heard at six inches as W. $\frac{6}{40}$; and of one
who heard on contact as $\frac{0}{40}$. It should be remembered
in respect to the watch that its tick is louder in proportion as it has been recently wound up ; and that it is no
accurate test of the power of hearing the voice. On one
occasion I was consulted by a patient for deafness of a
considerable degree, whose well-hearing brother heard the

watch much worse than himself. Also during treatment the hearing in respect to the watch or the voice may undergo great changes without proportionate change in respect to the other.

In regard to the hearing of the voice, there are differences in the modes in which hearing is impaired, all of which do not as yet seem capable of explanation. But in general it may be remarked that distinctness and moderate slowness of utterance are always of more importance that mere loudness of voice. Some persons hear even a low voice near at hand, but cannot hear at a distance; others the sound of many voices together totally confuses. Not unfrequently the muscles of accommodation seem distinctly at fault, the difficulty not being found in hearing individual slowly articulated sounds, but in following the naturally rapid changes of the voice. Hearing better when listening is very frequent; a person not taking notice even of a loud address, unless his attention is excited, and then hearing fairly a much lower tone. Children are often most unjustly blamed on this account. It is natural to ascribe this effect of attention to the action of the stapedius muscle, as regulated by the portio dura nerve; but I feel that this view is best kept at present in the position of a mere conjecture. When, as is so often the case, and even in conditions of tympanic and not mainly of nerve affection, the hearing is decidedly worse on listening, the assumption generally is that the emotions are at fault.

A very little experience suffices to show that among
people with impaired hearing various articulate sounds
are heard with very different degrees of ease. Twenty,
thirty, and forty and fifty, are badly heard, *e. g.* as compared with the numbers beyond them. Dr. Oscar Wolf
has made some very careful experiments on this point.*
He finds that each true consonant has its own pitch
and accompanying harmonics, and that they are heard at
varying distances ; *sch* is the most audible, *h* the least so.
The vowel-sounds are audible in the following order :—*a*
and *o* the best, then *ei, e, i, eu, au, u* [spoken as in German] .
In perforations of the membrane Wolf found that the
diminished hearing stood in direct relation to the loss of
substance, that the vowels were much better heard rela-
tively than the consonants, and that these were heard
better in proportion to their height in the scale and the
richness of their sound in harmonics. The loss of any of
the ossicula also caused a confusion at the end of words,
as if from lack of proper support to the stapes ; the final
letter, and sometimes others also, seeming to run into a
series of sounds. The difficulty of hearing was diminished by a rhythmical utterance of the words. The
pitch of the *resonance* of the meatus and tympanum,
taken as a whole, is raised by a perforation, so that the
lower-pitched consonants are more interfered with than
the higher. But though perforations diminish the

* 'Sprache und Ohr. Braunschweig.,' 1871. The whole volume is well
worth study.

resonance of the membrane, and so reduce its power of reinforcing sounds, they do not interfere with its vibrating power, and (as experience also proves) impair the hearing much less than hindrances apparently much slighter to the reception or transmission of vibrations by the ossicula. It is hardly necessary to remark that in testing the hearing by the voice the patient should not see the mouth of the speaker, and that in children the watch can be relied on only when the eyes are closed.

Next to the voice, and, indeed, superior to it for some purposes, stands the tuning-fork. We owe the first scientific appreciation of the value of this test to Lucae, who began his investigations by a study of the reason for which a tuning-fork vibrating on the head is heard better if the meatus is closed. The balance of opinion on this point appears to be that the vibrations, which would otherwise escape through the meatus, are thrown back upon the tympanum and labyrinth, and so increase the hearing; but Lucae prefers to ascribe it to a gentle pressure exerted on the labyrinth by the closure of the passage. However this may be, the information practically conveyed by this simple circumstance is of immense value. In one-sided deafness there is at hand a simple, and in the main, most reliable test for the most fundamental of all questions as regards prognosis, namely, whether the affection is confined to the conducting media or involves also the nervous apparatus. In any case in which one ear alone is affected, or one ear markedly more

than the other, it suffices to place a vibrating tuning-fork
on any part of the mesial line of the skull, and ascertain,
with due precautions for accuracy, from the patient
whether it is heard louder on the worse or the better
side, at once to form a rough classification of the disease.
If better on the worse side it depends on obstruction to
the passage of vibrations; if better on the better side the
nerve is probably at fault. Even when there is reason to
believe in the existence of a nerve affection of both sides,
if the tuning-fork be heard louder on the worse side we
may still infer that the difference between the two ears is
(partly at least) due to the lesion of the conducting
apparatus on the more affected side. It is necessary, of
course, thoroughly to guard against the tendency of the
patient to say what he expects to feel instead of what he
really experiences; a tendency intensely strong even in
the most cultivated classes. I much prefer to place the
tuning-fork upon the teeth rather than on the vertex, and
it is best placed on the lower teeth, the mouth being
closed. The sound seems to be conveyed with much
more certainty to the auditory nerve through the teeth
than through the bones of the head in any other way.
Many patients, I find, will hear it well on the teeth, and
yet very imperfectly when placed on the vertex, so that
while its being heard but a short time in the latter situation affords no real evidence that the nerve-power is impaired, I am inclined to believe that its being heard but
a short time when fairly applied to the teeth is very

strong evidence that the nerve has suffered. But the value of the tuning-fork in this respect is less negative than positive. Whatever the other symptoms may be, if the tuning-fork is well heard when placed upon the middle line of the teeth, we seem to be justified in holding that the disease is one that leaves the auditory nerve unimpeded in its function.

It must not, however, be inferred that always when the tuning-fork is heard worst on the most affected side the nerve is implicated. Cases have occurred to me and others in which, even when this symptom existed in the most distinct manner, treatment adapted to remove mucus from clogging the ossicula was thoroughly successful.

FIG. 5.

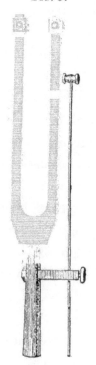

In testing the amount of hearing by the tuning-fork, it seems to me the best plan is to transfer it rapidly from the patient's teeth to one's own, having first ascertained that one's own hearing of it is fairly keen. It has been suggested by Von Conta, however, to strike the fork with a definite degree of force and to note the number of seconds it is heard, having, of course, practised the hand in striking uniformly and discovered the normal duration of the sound. It is good to have various tuning-forks, as

the results are not always exactly the same with different
ones ; and, indeed, I have been, in rare cases, unable
entirely to reconcile them. But the same fork made with
a strong *clamp* will give any note, and one has been constructed by Dr. Blake, of Boston, with a small hammer
attached, the force of the blow of which may be estimated
by a dial. (Fig. 5.)

But it is through observing the effects which closure of
the meatus produces upon its sound that the chief value
of the tuning-fork is gained. The closure may either (1)
increase the sound, or (2) may have no effect upon it, or
(3), in some rare cases, may diminish it. The mode of
testing is to press the tragus lightly, but firmly, back,
occluding the passage, but avoiding pressure upon it,
unless it is expressly intended to note the effects of
pressure. The normal reaction is to increase the sound ;
this denotes, so far, absence of obstruction to the passage
of sound ; if the increase be very great—"doubling the
sound," the patient will sometimes say—we may infer that
the meatus and tympanum are for functional purposes
healthy. If the closure produces no effect upon the
sound, or in so far as the increase is of less than the
normal amount, it indicates that sound does not pass as
it should through the tympanum, and examination will
almost always reveal the fact of some hindrance. It is,
therefore, *a good sign* in any case of deafness that closing
the meatus should have no effect upon the sound of a
tuning-fork placed on the head or teeth, because it

affords presumptive evidence that the lesion lies not deeper than the tympanum. It is held by one eminent authority,* that in purely nervous affections closure of the meatus does not increase the sound of the tuning-fork placed on the head or teeth. This is a point worthy of all examination. My experience had led me to the contrary conclusion ; and in cases that on other grounds I diagnose as nerve-affections, I tend to hold the patient's hearing the tuning-fork better with the meatus closed to be a confirming stroke to my opinion of his unhappy state, as indicating that the source of his affection lies deeper than the tympanum. (3) Rarely, as said, closing the meatus diminishes the hearing of the tuning-fork. On this point clinical experience gives us as yet scanty data. I will, therefore, report a case in which the symptom appears well-marked and unquestionable.

G. W—, æt. 32, a thin, somewhat worn-looking man, consulted me on 22nd November last ; he had been for four years troubled with attacks of giddiness at times, but was otherwise well, and his hearing good. About last Easter, during a cold, he became somewhat deaf on the right side, and a blowing noise came in that ear; he describes it as a little rushing of water, or small windmill. This appears now to be synchronous with the pulse. He was then decidedly more giddy. The deafness continued, on and off, till June ; since then has been better. Had

* Dr. Roosa, of New York. See his ' Diseases of the Ear,' p. 488. I am not aware of any other statement to the same effect.

pain also on the right side of the head. The pain ceased after taking bromide of potassium (from Dr. Leared), and the giddiness seemed better, but has returned. Is worse when worried, or after wine ; digestion weak ; is moderate ; does not smoke. No deafness in family. Had slight syphilis many years ago ; married four months ; not in any respect worse since.

On examination of the ear : watch—right $\frac{20}{40}$, left $\frac{20}{40}$. Tuning-fork not heard fully on the teeth, loudest on the left, the best side. On closing the meatus, tuning-fork heard much *louder* on the left side : much *less loud* on . the right ; the effect being distinctly opposite on the two sides. Sucking air out of the right meatus diminishes the tinnitus for the time. The membranes were fairly healthy on each side ; on the right there was a slight appearance of whiteness at the upper posterior edge, and on inflation, which was free, and with natural sound on each side, the right membrane yielded at that part slightly more than the left. Inflation had no effect on the hearing of the watch. A little wax had been removed from the right meatus by syringing. Throat fairly healthy.

My diagnosis of the local condition was : an increase of fluid pressure on the right labyrinth, with no considerable affection of the tympanum ; this increased pressure causing alike the tinnitus, the impaired hearing, and the giddiness. This opinion was based mainly on the fact of the diminution of the sound of the tuning-fork on closing the right meatus. Increasing the pressure on .

the meatus still more diminished the sound, while insert-
ing an elastic tube into the meatus, and closing it close
to the ear so as to prevent exit of vibrations, but not to
exert pressure, had scarcely any effect. The temporary
relief of the tinnitus on removing the atmospheric
pressure from the meatus, and so drawing the membrane
outward, tends to confirm this view, which is, however,
as yet, matter of theory, and unproved.

Considering next the source of this local condition (in
which I had the advantage of consultation with Dr.
Leared), there appeared to be reason to assign it to the
existence of irregular gout, there being a small deposit,
such as Dr. Garrod has pointed out as consisting of urate
of soda, in the auricle of the left ear. He did not
remember any family history of gout. The iodide of
potassium was ordered; and an ointment of the same,
with Tr. capsici, to rub around the ear.

On the strength of cases analogous to this, I am of
opinion that a diminution of the sound of the tuning-fork
on closing the meatus, indicates comparative free passage
of sound through the middle ear, and some abnormal
condition of the labyrinth, which causes increased
pressure on it, through the tympanum, to operate in-
juriously to its function. I may add that I have not
discovered any really efficient treatment.

There is another condition connected with the reaction
of the ear to sound, of which I do not know the correct
explanation; I have met with it in patients, and ex-

perienced it in a marked manner myself; in my own case it was evidently connected with faucial catarrh, not severe, and affecting one ear only, entirely ceasing after a short time. The condition is a peculiar sensitiveness of the ear to particular sounds, and even to particular notes of the scale : in my own case the sounds were bells, fa″ of the piano or harmonium, and in a less degree fa′ and fa‴. These sounds produced in my ear a distinct clang precisely like the jarring of a loose violin string, lasting for a few seconds : there was slight general deafness also on that side, and the tuning-fork was heard loudest there. It is difficult to me to believe that the seat of the affection was one of Corti's fibres ; I seemed to feel it in the tympanum. But why it was called forth only by special sounds I do not know : the note was much lower than that which corresponds to the natural resonance of the meatus.

Many other anomalies of hearing, especially inability to appreciate certain pitches or groups of sounds, are met with either as idiosyncrasies, or in various abnormal states of the nervous apparatus. Their seat and signifi-cance yet remain to be discovered.*

---

* A "double otoscope" was introduced by Politzer, with the view of testing the escape of sound from the ear. It consists of three India-rubber tubes, about a foot long, connected together in the centre. Of these tubes one is placed in each ear of the patient, and the third in the surgeon's. A tuning-fork is then placed on the vertex of the pa-tient's head, its sound being conveyed to the surgeon's ear, by the two tubes, from both ears of the patient. If now one or other tube be compressed, the surgeon can detect whether sound be transmitted more

F

III. The general condition of the patient. I have left this till the last, because it seems to me, contrary to the advice of some great authorities, best deferred until the local conditions have been examined. Many of the causes of deafness are exclusively local. Even when they are not so, I believe that all of them are aids and guides to a more general investigation, which the study of them much more naturally tends to stimulate than to supersede. But here an infinite task opens upon us. The disease that may not, directly or indirectly, impair the functions of the ear is probably not yet discovered, nor will the zeal of generations exhaust the links that bind even so minute an organ into unity with every other portion of the frame, and tend to make it a sharer in the penalties of every divergence from the state of health. But among the few things we know in this sphere we include such as these:—First and chief, the effect of the exanthemata in children, and of other fevers at all ages, in injuring the tympanum : a source of evil which will be more than half averted, and not a few lives probably be saved, when every medical man shall

freely from one of the patient's ears than the other, a less transmission implying obstruction to the passage of sound thro' the tympanum.

Lucae's "interference otoscope" is a more complex instrument, turning to account the laws of interference of sound by causing the waves reflected from the membrane to interfere with, or reinforce, the impinging vibrations. A brief account of it is given in "Guy's Hospital Reports" for 1867 ; a better one in Dr. Roosa's "Diseases of the Ear," New York, 1872 ; or the reader may consult "Archiv für Ohrenheilkunde," B. iii.

hold it his duty to be prepared to trace the first threatenings of ear-disease in the course of these affections, or rather to anticipate them, so as to note their most unsuspected advance, and give them efficient treatment before their work of destruction is achieved. (2) Gout is one of the chief enemies of the ear, but its effects are rather to be traced, it appears to me, in obstinacy of affections of ordinary kinds than in any specially characteristic symptoms. A peculiar irritation of the meatus, with dull redness and swelling and semi-watery discharge, resisting local remedies, is very characteristic of its presence. Whether the chalky deposits so frequent in the membrane are ever of gouty origin, or whether gouty deposits occur within the tympanum as well as in the auricle, I believe has not yet been ascertained. (3) In phthisis, as is well known, the ear participates, and it has occurred to me not only to strive in vain for, but even temporarily to attain, results in respect to the ear which the progress of phthisical disease soon abolished. In such cases it is our duty, of course, to abstain from painful or even laborious remedies. (4) Syphilis has a certain part in aural disease, but how large a part is not yet decided. Its influence is most marked in its hereditary form, as pointed out by Mr. Hutchinson; every now and then deafness seems a feature of syphilitic sore throat, but if this is a frequent occurrence the specialist does not see much of it. The apparent nerve-defect of hearing, which occurs in the ordinary course of

the disease appears to yield to the ordinary remedies.
What amount of subsequent deafness ensues or remains
after all recognised syphilitic action has ceased, and so
passes undetected as a result of that disease, I cannot offer
an opinion. But I do not think that syphilis is among the
frequent causes of obstinate obstruction of the Eustachian
tube, because the classes among whom I have found this
most frequent have certainly not been those most exposed
to that cause. Of course, the cases of extensive ulceration obliterating the faucial orifices of the tubes by scars
are not here referred to. (5) Albuminuria has been
detected as a cause of tympanic disease in the form of
hæmorrhage, but both this affection and diabetes remain
as yet almost unexplored in this direction. (6) The
convulsive affections of children also stand in a most
important relation to diseases of the tympanum and of
the labyrinth : sometimes a sudden affection of the labyrinth seems to be the starting-point of the symptoms ;
but more often a tympanic inflammation unsuspected is
the source of fever and convulsions, which go on unrelieved for days until a sudden discharge from the ear
reveals at once the source of the evil, and too often the
irreparable nature of its results. (7) Especially the
frequent dependence of inflammatory affections of the
ear upon diseases of the teeth, and mostly of those of
the lower jaw, should not be overlooked ; and no obscure
case of ear-affection can be considered sufficiently explored until the teeth have been thoroughly examined.

(8) The relation also to disease of the ear of abnormalities of the cerebral circulation, of the poison of ague, of the climate of India and the effects of quinine, of exhausting attendance on the sick, of parturition and suckling, of overwork at school, of depressing emotions, of relationship of parents—these and many more are questions which the student of diseases of the ear has to do his best to solve; and not less important—but, indeed, in their practical relations more important—the effects, in their turn, of even lightly regarded affections of the meatus or tympanum upon the general health challenge his watchfulness. For nervous symptoms of the utmost apparent gravity may arise from mere abnormal pressure in the external meatus; and intense depression, amounting even to mania, has been known to cease with the removal from it of foreign bodies or cerumen.

CHAPTER III.

In respect to affections of the auricle I have very little to add to that which is well known. The effusion of blood known as Hæmatoma auris, occurring chiefly in the insane, has received a considerable amount of attention. Drs. Yeats and Needham* have reported cases to show that even when co-existing with pronounced insanity it is not so unfavourable a symptom as had been supposed; and the evidence that violence is generally concerned in producing the affection is becoming more considerable. Dr. Farquharson of Rugby also has observed a very similar condition in boys after football. On the other hand, Dr. Roosa quotes Dr. Hun as holding that the existence of such a tumour, not caused by violence, is sufficient ground for an expectation that insanity may develop itself even in a person perfectly sane; and Dr. Brown Séquard† has found that sections of the restiform bodies in the guinea-pig will produce hæmorrhage beneath the skin of the auricle, generally of the same side, in from eight to twenty-four hours; the

* " Brit. Med. Jour.," July and August, 1873.
† " Tr. Amer. Ot. Soc." 1873, p. 17.

hæmorrhage is soon followed by gangrene : sections of
the sciatic nerve, by reflex action on the medulla, give
rise to the same result, and Dr. Séquard has produced
in his own person flushing of the auricle by pinching the
sciatic nerve. He believes that disease of the base of
the brain, which is however not always attended by
insanity, is the cause of hæmatoma auris. And in this
view it is noticeable that a temporary improvement of
hearing has been reported as coinciding with its occurrence in a deaf patient. In respect to treatment, the
balance of opinion seems to be in favour of evacuating
the clot and using compresses.*— The occasional occurrence of malignant disease will not be overlooked ;
nor the presence of small whitish deposits, rarely painful, of urate of soda, in obscure cases of gout.

The external meatus is liable to occlusion, partial or
complete, and to inflammation.

Occlusion may occur from—

1. Foreign bodies, or the larvæ of insects.
2. Cerumen.
3. Masses of hard epidermis.
4. Sebaceous tumours.
5. Vegetable fungi.
6. Falling together or thickening of the walls.
7. Polypi, and growing together of granulations.
8. Exostoses.

* Dr. Yeats, loc. cit., June 21, 1873.

Inflammation of the meatus is either diffuse, or local, or furunculous ; to which may be added eczema and syphilis.

1. Foreign bodies are almost exclusively met with in children, the chief exception being that pins used to pick the ear by adults will sometimes slip in. This has happened two or three times to my experience, and the point of the pin being generally directed outwards is apt to penetrate the floor. I have not found difficulty in removing them when the meatus and membrane have been well illuminated. A firmly-holding forceps will grasp them, and the point to remember is to keep them well from the membrane. When other bodies enter the ears of children, it should always be borne in mind that there is one, and but one, great danger ; the danger lest the surgeon should suffer himself to be drawn on into hurtful efforts at extraction. No one who remembers how great is the difficulty of abandoning a seemingly simple task in which he finds unexpected difficulties, probably under the eyes of anxious friends before whom an apparent failure will be intolerable, will suffer himself to take up any instrument for the removal of a foreign body from the ear, until after the most patient efforts to avoid it, and the most serious consideration of its absolute necessity. I must be pardoned for speaking earnestly on this point. Even to this day it remains the fact that ears are thus destroyed without shadow of

reason or excuse, and not by careless or incompetent
persons alone. I believe it may be laid down that whenever
an instrument will succeed syringing would also succeed,
and that when proper syringing will not succeed all
instruments are full of danger. But syringing in the
right way and patiently repeated scarcely ever fails,
and if had recourse to before violence has been used
would probably in all cases remove the offending body
in ample time to prevent mischief. For the presence of
an unirritating foreign body in the meatus is generally
quite innocuous : I have known pieces of tobacco-pipe
to remain in it for about thirty years, according to the
best evidence attainable, with no appreciable damage.
And even when irritation has been produced by interference, and the foreign body has consequently been
irremovable for an indefinite period, I have never
known it to fail to be removed in the end. In these cases
what might be described as an "effort of nature" seems
to take place : I have three times seen a foreign body
extruded by a process of inflammation ; granulations—
a flat sort of polypus—spring up and push the substance
before it until it approaches the orifice and easily comes
away. I do not say it is desirable to let this process
take place : the membrane in each case was perforated,
and though reparation set in, probably the ear would
never entirely recover ; but inflammation had been set
up by instrumental efforts at extraction. Perhaps a
certain proportion of the cases of perforation that occur

arise in this way. In one case Gruber saw an irremovable foreign body become encysted in the tympanum;
and Löwenberg states that he saw one enter the tympanum through an orifice in the membrane which afterwards became too small for it to pass: an incision was
made and after a few weeks it escaped.

The first step to take is, of course, to ascertain that a
foreign body is present : parents not seldom are very
sure of this when either none has entered the meatus or
it has already escaped. A full examination with good
light will settle this point—that is generally; but not
quite always, for it has happened to me to have asserted
that the meatus was empty when a small bead, or
similar object, has been concealed in the hollow formed
by the anterior wall of the meatus just in front of the
membrane. The mode of removing foreign bodies is
syringing, but in the proper way ; that is, with gravity
favouring their escape. The head should be placed
horizontally (a child is easily held so on its mother's lap),
but the face should be turned a little upwards, to allow
for the bend of the anterior wall. A stream of warm
water, or soap and water, should be syringed with fair
force directly upwards, along whichever wall of the meatus
the body seems to be least in contact with. If a few
minutes' work do not bring it away, let oil be poured in
frequently, and renew the syringing daily. The failures
on this plan would be very few, but there are three other
methods which are also free from risk : (1.) To apply a

strong solution of glue, by means of a camel's hair brush,
to the body, letting it remain till it has dried, using
currents of dry air if there is much moisture in the ear.
Considerable force may be exerted in this way, and Dr.
Löwenberg, who suggests it, urges that it should have
the preference whenever a perforation exists, as the
syringe may drive the body into the tympanum. Of
course when perforation is present the obvious resource
of inflation of the ear by Politzer's bag would not be
overlooked. Dr. Clark, of Boston, has succeeded in a
similar way by passing a small plate of adhesive plaster
down to the foreign body and concentrating on it the
rays of the sun. (2.) A sucker, such as boys make by a
disc of india-rubber, may be applied; and (3.) Non-
metallic bodies may be partly destroyed by the galvanic
cautery. I have also diminished the size of beans by
carefully scraping out a portion by a small sharp-pointed
knife. Of all "instruments" the least objectionable is
a thin loop of wire passed around the body, if there is
any part of the meatus with which it is not in contact,
as suggested by Mr. Hutchinson. Dr. Morland removed
a firmly impacted metal button by means of a small steel
drill. Von Tröltsch renews an old suggestion as a last
resort; that of cutting into the tube at its superior part
behind the auricle, or in front of the tragus.

A case that occurred to me suggests that the possible
presence of a foreign substance might be borne in mind
in every case of obstinate suppurative perforation in

children.   A boy, aged twelve, was brought to me suffering with what appeared to [be an ordinary perforation
with a spongy condition of the exposed mucous membrane. The ordinary treatment by lotions, with passage
of air freely through the Eustachian tube, was carried out
at intervals but without effect for four or five weeks; when
there appeared at the orifice of the meatus that which his
friends took to be a small splinter of wood ; and the discharge at once abated. It was then remembered that
some years ago a fruit basket had been thrown at him
and struck him on the ear. I did not, however, see
either the splinter or the boy after its escape.

Foreign bodies sometimes give rise to paroxysms of
coughing, which cease on their removal. Dr. Fox,* of
Scarborough, has drawn attention to this class of cases
under the head of *ear cough;* an affection treated in vain
unless the meatus is examined. He found that in about
20 per cent. out of a hundred and eight persons examined
tickling the meatus produced cough, while in two or three
nausea ensued. The nerve concerned is a branch of the
auriculo temporal of the fifth, and the connection with
the larynx takes place in the floor of the fourth
ventricle. In one case Dr. Denton found that cough and
nausea were produced by irritation of the left meatus,
while vertigo alone followed similar irritation of the right.
It is possible that if more frequent inquiry were made, a
cough of this character would be found common among

* See Report of Dr. Burnett, " Tr. Amer. Ot. Soc." 1873, p. 15.

aural patients; but I have not found it often made a subject of complaint.

There is a certain physiological parallelism, however, between the ear and the lungs, which in this connection we may recall. For the conducting portion of the ear is an offshoot from the respiratory tract, and it consists of (1.) a tube to permit the passage of air; and (2.) an air-containing cavity. Almost, we might say, the tympanum and its appendages represent a modified lung; even as it is a transformation of the branchial arch, the respiratory function giving place to that of hearing. Now, may it be that the cough which is sometimes elicited by irritation of the meatus bears a relation to this deeper connection; which thus gives witness that it has left a memorial of itself in the nervous centres? *

Cases in which foreign bodies have given rise to epilepsy, convulsion, or paralysis, which have ceased on their removal, are referred to by Dr. Von Tröltsch.†

Cotton wool is often found pressed into the meatus. In

---

* I do not know whether it will appear merely fanciful, but I cannot help drawing a parallel between the relation of the tympanum and labyrinth, and that of the lungs and heart. The spiral cochlea divided into two portions with different relations, the one to the air-containing tympanum, the other to the vestibule and canals, seems to me to recall, with more than a fancied resemblance, the not less distinctly spiral and divided heart, with its twofold relation; on one side to the air-containing lungs, on the other to the mass of the body. In a word, may not the conjoined respiratory and vascular system give us a clue to the conjoined tympanum and labyrinth, as if the formative impulses and conditions had been parallel in each case, though so diversely modified?

† "Surgical Diseases of the Ear." (Sydenham Society.)

one case I extracted by the forceps three distinct masses
firmly pressed down upon the membrane. It is of importance that those who have recourse to it should use portions large enough to avoid this danger. Gruber objects
to cotton wool altogether, as liable to produce irritation by its loose filaments, and recommends charpie
instead.

I have not myself seen living insects in the meatus,
though I have many times syringed out dead ones. But
several cases have been reported: they seem to be much
more frequent in warmer countries. A case was mentioned to me as occurring in India, of a girl who suffered
from frequently-recurring earache; on one occasion she
fell violently to the ground and a white ant rolled out of
the ear; the symptoms ceasing from that time. Maggots
also are said to be found in the ear in the disease called
peenash—a collection of maggots in the nostril. The affection seems sometimes to follow sleeping on the ground,
but on other occasions flies have been supposed to be
attracted by discharge from the ear. M. Guerin reported
at the Société de Chirurgie the case of a soldier who had
returned from Mexico, seven months previously, suffering
from facial neuralgia and other affections, and from whose
ear an *Ixodes hominis* escaped, with entire relief. Oil
poured into the meatus is the treatment recommended, and
if there be irritation, lotio nigra. Dr. Morton, of America,
described a case in which maggots had to be removed by
forceps from within the tympanum, and Dr. Blake, of

Boston,[*] has described them as burrowing into the tissues by means of two large and strong hooks attached to a horny framework. Possibly among labourers in English country districts they might be met with. Pouchet[†] has found bacteria and vibrios in a discharge from the meatus, attended with itching; they were also met with in the discharge from the bronchi and nose.

2. Of cerumen, it is enough to note that the deafness it produces is very apt to come on suddenly, and that it may produce by its pressure great giddiness or even staggering, besides distressing tinnitus, for which patients have been treated with leeches and mercury. And on the other hand, when the ear has not been properly examined, syringing has been had recourse to for several days in vain while the presence of cerumen was after all the sole affection. It is needless now to remark how unworthy of a scientific profession was the practice of syringing the meatus unexamined on the chance that wax was present. The practice was as little *safe* as it was rational : serious mischiefs have arisen from it. Often it is advisable to soften the wax before removing it ; warm water, or a warm solution of soda, or if there be no irritation, ether ʒj to glycerine ʒj may be used.

The effect of using water in syringing either very hot or too cold, is to produce giddiness. On one occasion,

---

[*] "Monatsschr." iii. No. 3.
"Compt. Rend.," 1864, p. 148.

in my hands, with no fault of temperature, and without either rupture or inflammation of the membrane, severe vomiting, lasting almost an hour, followed a very slight syringing. The patient, a lady of middle age, exclaimed, as soon as the stream began, "O, that is pleasant;" and almost immediately became violently sick. When the cerumen is removed the treatment is often but commenced. Dr. Pomeroy, of New York, found the ear thoroughly healthy in but twenty-seven cases out of two hundred. But time should be given for gradual recovery, and of course a thickening of the external layer of the membrane may be the mere result of pressure.

I have no experience of any treatment that diminishes the tendency to excess of wax. But repeated suction on the meatus, or the use of a stimulating lotion, when these are otherwise indicated, seem to have a certain power of re-exciting the secretion when it has failed.

Dr. Weir, of America, found in three cases that the hairs of the meatus by growing inwards irritated the membrane and produced a dry rattling noise in eating and yawning, all relieved by their removal. In one case the hairs could be seen to rub against the membrane on moving the jaw.

3. Much more serious in its effects is the accumulation in the meatus of layers of epidermis. Dr. Von Tröltsch has controverted Mr. Toynbee's view that, besides occurring in the form of aggregated laminæ, these epidermic

masses are found in the meatus or tympanum as distinct tumours, growing and infringing upon the neighbouring parts as other tumours do (sebaceous tumours). Which-ever view be true, it is certain that fatal results ensue from the affection ; that the mass, however its increase be effected, exerts pressure, eats away the bone, passes even into the cerebral cavity and may excite fatal disturbance there. My own opinion agrees with Mr. Toynbee's. I have met with distinctly formed, isolated tumours of this kind, closely resembling ant's eggs, within the tympanum.

Wherever occurring, the treatment demanded is to remove by a firmly-holding forceps not only the epi-dermic layers, but the dense membrane which surrounds them. An interesting case in which this was done, with relief to pain and tinnitus, is reported by Mr. Wilders in the British Medical Journal, September 30, 1873. They are frequent enough to constitute a serious danger.

4. But apart from these tumours, layers of epidermis collect in the meatus in dense and sometimes immense masses, press upon and disorganise the membrane, and by forcing it inwards even obliterate the tympanic cavity ; * at least this is the apparent order of events. Even after the removal of comparatively small masses the membrane is often seen flattened and white, and with

* See Atlas, Plate xxiv. Nos. 1, 2, and 3 ; and Plate xxv. Nos. 1, 3, and 5.

G

a red and fleshy swelling protruding from it, generally at the upper part. In these latter cases, is not the fleshy surface rather the source of the secreted flakes, than the result of their pressure ? The treatment is the same as for the roots of polypi, and for chronic catarrh of the tympanic cavity, which is also generally involved. It is an inquiry deserving the utmost attention how far the habit of cleaning out children's ears with the screwed-up corner of a towel produces these accumulations, which I have known lead to inflammation of the mastoid process. Quite frequently thêy give rise to intense distress and even danger ; for if the meatus becomes inflamed during their presence it swells externally to them, and their removal becomes at once imperative and difficult. It may, however, be accomplished by patient softening of the mass with lotions containing borax and liquor opii, &c., and repeated cautious syringing, and use of a looped forceps. These masses generally have smooth casts of the membrana tympani upon their inner surfaces ; in the case of a boy of fifteen I removed two masses ending in such casts, one beneath the other.

Dr. Lucae has recently * reported twelve cases of epidermic accumulation : he also holds that they occur in the two forms of aggregated flakes and distinct tumours. One of such tumours he found within the tympanum without either perforation or any disease of the mucous

* " Archiv für Ohrenheilkunde," 1873, p. 255.

lining. He recommends trephining the mastoid process
for their removal if they produce symptoms of irritation
and cannot be otherwise removed. Whether the membrane is perforated or not, cases of this kind treated with
continued gentle syringing and withdrawal of the successively protruding masses, aided by the use of Politzer's bag,
will recover to all appearance perfectly, though the hearing may remain impaired. Some of the worst and most
obstinate cases of perforation are caused by these masses
ulcerating through the membrane; the destruction then
commences generally at the upper part, and the symptoms,
not so much of acute pain as of continued distress and
brain irritation, are severe. In one well-marked case in
which a healthy condition was regained after the repeated
evacuation of large solid masses, the earlier stages of the
affection seemed to be connected with a diseased tooth of
the same side, from which a sudden pain shot into the
ear, and the extraction of the tooth was followed by great
temporary relief. Incision of the membrane seems indicated, but in the few cases in which I have tried it, the
results have been negative. The diagnosis is difficult
in the early stage, and the mass seems to tend to collect
so much quite at the upper part of the cavity that its
removal through an incision cannot be ensured.

5. Vegetable fungi are found within the meatus. The
most frequent is the aspergillus (flavus, glaucus or nigri-
cans); but besides this, penicillium glaucum, graphium
penicilloides, and tricothecium roseum have been de-

G 2

scribed ; and a peculiar encysted form was met with by
Meyer in 1844.   Schwartze * was the first to make
generally known the presence of aspergillus, and Dr.
Wreden at St. Petersburg seems to have found it very
common.†   It is the same as the mould that occurs on
damp walls.   Dr. Roosa is of opinion, not only that the

FUNGUS FROM THE MEATUS (after Blake).

fungus is always secondary to some disease that loosens
the epidermis, but also that the disease is usually eczema.
I think the occurrence of fungi in the meatus must be
more common both on the Continent and in America than
in England.   Dr. Bezold of Munich ‡ brings ten cases to
prove that the affection is due to the habit of dropping
oil into the ears ; and probably this practice is less common here than in some other countries.   This view of
the cause (which would represent the parasite as not
necessarily depending on prior disease) is supported by
the following case given by Dr. J. Green of St. Louis.   A
gentleman, æt. thirty-eight, remembered that two years ago
an insect entered the right meatus.   It was destroyed by

* " Arch. f. Ohr.," 1867, p. 7.
† Ib., 1868, p. 1.
‡ " Monatsschr. f. Ohr.," July, 1873.

pouring oil into the ear. Eight months ago he was seized with pain in the ear and became deaf. The meatus was plugged with epidermic masses, including a small cockroach. The walls of the meatus were red and covered with flakes of adherent epidermis. Six months after the symptoms returned; the meatus was full of a white substance of exactly the appearance of cotton, mingled with a little pus. Dark specks appeared upon the flakes; and examination showed the mass to be identical with the blue mould formed upon a crust of bread.* Dr. Orne Green † reports his own case. He had several times suffered from furuncles, the last time nearly two years ago. During June and July, 1865, he was treating a case of aspergillus glaucus, and was at the time perfect in health and ears. In August he felt some ill-defined irritation in the ears attended by a slight serous discharge, just enough to be felt by the fingers, but soon ceasing. In November it returned with pricking, itching, and occasional slight pain and feeling of fulness in the ears. The meatus on each side showed patches of deep congestion and small white masses apparently of epidermis. Recovery took place in six weeks. Dr. Green tried solutions of carbolic acid, of soda, and of hypochlorate of lime. The latter he found very soothing. Wreden, from experiments, pronounces it the most powerful parasiticide; he recommends gr. ij to the ℥j,

---

* "Tr. Am. Ot. Soc.," 1870.
† Ibid. 1869, p. 23.

freshly mixed on account of the chlorine and oxygen set free. Regular cleansing by warm water alone however seems to suffice for the cure. Dr. Roosa pencils the meatus with a strong solution of nitrate of silver to remove the inflammation. My friend, Dr. McCall Anderson, of Glasgow, also finds fungus in the meatus very rare ; he recommends as a lotion Hydr. perchlor. gr. j—ʒj. In a case reported by Zaufal,* the fungus was found after the occurrence of a blue discharge, attended with *bacteria.*

6. Thickening of the walls, or their falling together from lack of natural elasticity, occurs in the old. The remedy is a small silver tube, about ¾ inch long, and made to fit the meatus, with a small flat portion externally to lie in the concha. An abnormal formation of the cartilaginous portion of the meatus sometimes occurs also in the young, which is best remedied in this way; the tube appearing as it were slightly too long, and curved downwards. When the thickening due to chronic eczema is not removable, a similar tube is indicated. It is in such cases alone that the small advertised tubes are of use.

7. Polypi occur more frequently with ruptured membrane, and will be spoken of hereafter; but a careful watch should be maintained for granular swellings of the superior or posterior wall of the meatus, which indicate affections of the bone. I have seen a case,† unique

* " Arch. f. Ohr.," B. vi.
† See Atlas, Plate xxv., No. 6.

in my experience, in which a polypoid mass appeared
growing from the upper wall of a much enlarged meatus,
and on its removal, which required, besides the snare,
a continued application of caustics, there appeared a
circular orifice in the bone, a third of an inch in diameter,
the basis of which became, as the granulations disappeared, of a dull greyish hue and of an even surface—
evidently the interior of the horizontal portion of the
mastoid cells ; the probe could be passed in for half an
inch without meeting firm resistance. The edges of the
orifice were smooth, and no dead bone could be anywhere detected. The patient was a healthy girl of 12.
The origin of the disease was ascribed to a blow on the
head by a door during play. The membrane had lost its
transparency and was of a dense bluish yellow colour, irregularly convex, the malleus seemed short and thick as if
imperfectly developed. The other ear was natural. The
hearing remained much impaired, but all active disease
disappeared. The nature of the case appears to me
obscure, but my thoughts tend to connect it with the
idea of a sebaceous tumour, that had probably expanded
the meatus and destroyed part of the wall, and had
come away. At other times large fleshy growths are
connected with caries of the posterior or lower wall of
the meatus, and it becomes urgently necessary to prevent
them from interfering with the free escape of pus.

Inflammatory affections of the meatus seem sometimes to result in complete closure of the canal. Dr.

Engelmann* has seen a case in which granulations growing from opposite walls united in the centre, and suggests this as a mode in which the occlusion occurs. No very good success has generally attended the attempt to restore the tube in such cases owing to the great tendency to contract and reunite. F. Weber Liel,† however, in a case in which complete occlusion occurred after a bullet wound, succeeded in permanently restoring the opening by means of the galvanic cautery, the wire passing upwards and backwards for about an inch, and sanious pus escaping with some improvement of the hearing: laminaria bougies enlarged the opening, and it remained permanent.

8. Exostoses in the meatus are frequent. Often they are congenital. Mr. Toynbee suggested their connection with gout or rheumatism, but I have not been able to trace any relation to special diatheses. They may occur in all parts of the meatus, and even in the tympanum,‡ and may be of any size. So long as even a minute passage remains their effect on the hearing is very slight; but when they are of large size they predispose to attacks of deafness by blocking of the passage. Cerumen or exuviated epidermis is apt to collect behind them, and of course a very small quantity of abnormal secretion will obliterate a passage already reduced perhaps to the

* "Monatsschr.," April, 1871.
† "Archiv," vol. 3, p. ii.
‡ Atlas, Plate xix., figs. 1-6.

dimensions of a pin's head. But in such cases the
hearing can be restored by patient use of an alkaline
lotion, or of one containing pot. iod.; syringing being
repeated at intervals. And I have found the application
of Argent. Nit. ʒj—ʒj, by means of a camel's hair brush,
very useful. I have not myself undertaken the removal of
such a growth when entirely closing the canal, by opera-
tive procedure, but I have had the pleasure of witnessing a case in which this was done with most gratifying
success. The patient, a girl of 15, was under the care of
Dr. T. E. Clark, of Bristol.* The exostosis was at first
concealed by a polypus which disappeared under the
application of tannic acid, it was then found almost
filling the meatus, which it rapidly completely closed.
At this stage I saw it. The hardness of hearing was
extremely great, but the tuning-fork was heard best
on the affected side. Dr. Clark suggested the application of the continuous current, under chloroform. On
August 29th he introduced three needles, two at the
base, close to its attachment to the posterior wall, and
one at its anterior edge. The former were attached to
the negative pole, and the latter to the positive; and the
application was continued for three minutes. This produced a large coagulum at the point of entrance of the
needles, and rendered the whole tumour white. There
was no subsequent irritation or pain produced. The
battery used was Dr. E. Stöhrer's (six pairs of plates).

* It is reported in " Brit. Med. Jour.," Dec. 6, 1873.

"September 12th. Two needles were introduced while she was under chloroform; and in introducing them the resistance was very slight, whereas at the first application one of the needle-points broke on account of the great hardness of the growth. The connections were similar to the last, but were continued for five minutes. No ill effect. Some diminution followed.

" October 4th. She was again placed under chloroform; and upon examining the exostosis, it gave the idea of being loose; and on pressure with a closed scissors against its base, it came away entire. Only a few drops of blood followed. There was no subsequent pain.

" On examination of the growth, the front, or part facing the anterior wall of the meatus, was seen to be convex, with slight depressions above and below, covered with periosteum. The posterior part, or its attached surface, was hollowed out corresponding to where the needles had passed, or absorbed to a mere point; and thus it was that it broke away so readily.

" The tympanum was perfect. Hearing was also perfect."

I have also seen a case in which Dr. Bonnafont, of Paris, restored fair hearing by boring with a drill through an exostosis that completely filled the meatus. The skin covering it was first destroyed with nitrate of silver, and the drill used at intervals till the whole thickness was penetrated : laminaria bougies of increasing thickness were used, and a sufficient passage maintained.

There is therefore more than one resource against this affection even in its completest form. Sometimes polypi form not only in front of these growths but apparently behind them, or by their side, and protrude externally. In one such case the exostosis almost entirely filled the passage and caused great pain.* For such a case electrolytic treatment appears admirably adapted.

But the most remarkable event connected with exostosis of the meatus that has come under my observation is the following :—A gentleman, aged sixty-five, healthy, but of nervous temperament, consulted me for deafness, with slight discharge on the right side. He had been under my care with some benefit two years previously. The meatus was nearly filled by a large and solid exostosis, entirely concealing the membrane, through an orifice in which, however, air could be passed. The throat was much thickened, and in the course of the treatment I applied a solution of nitrate of silver, $\ni j$—$\bar{3}j$, to the mouth of the tube by the Eustachian catheter. More of the solution appeared to enter the tympanum than I desired ; and tho' the solution was not very strong, it excited considerable pain, lasting till evening. Two days later the portio dura on the same side was paralyzed ; and this continued for five or six weeks, recovering finally under the local use of electricity, the hearing, however, remaining impaired. But during the paralysis, and before the use of the electricity, the exostosis that had

* See Atlas, xix., fig. 2.

before nearly filled the meatus became very much diminished in size, indeed, almost disappeared. It did not
come away as a mass, nor was the discharge or the
irritation of the meatus at all considerable; but the
passage almost regained its natural form, so that the
membrane could be clearly seen.

Diffuse inflammation of the external meatus is generally connected with inflammation of the whole tympanic
region, with perforation of the membrane. Even when
this is not the case, unless some merely local cause have
operated, I believe it is almost always symptomatic of
inflammatory, or at least congestive, disorder within the
tympanum. Mr. Toynbee laid stress on this "sympathetic" character of inflammation of the meatus, and my
observation has entirely confirmed his opinion. This is
especially the case with chronic and obstinately recurring
forms of the affection: they are obstinate because their
real source lies deeper. It continually happens that
even when in such a case the membrane shows no signs
of disease, or none beyond slight whiteness, the air on
the patient's own inflation enters with a distinctly moist
sound, showing hyper-secretion within the drum. It
has become an axiom with me, in the treatment of
almost all chronic inflammations of the meatus, to regard
not only the tympanum but the throat.

The amount of watery discharge that may flow from
the meatus, and indeed within a few hours from the
beginning of the attack, is sometimes enormous. It

may be mistaken for the flow that follows fracture of the skull thro' the labyrinth, attended with rupture of the membrane. But the absence of rupture may be easily determined by inflation of the drum. At the Irish College of Physicians (Feb. 17, 1869) Dr. Stokes related a case, in which during recovery from typhoid fever, a most extraordinary serous discharge had taken place from the ear; it reached to several gallons, and was so great that it soaked thro' the bed, mattrass, &c., and dropped into a vessel placed to receive it.

I also think that there is no form in which a gouty affection of the ear is so clearly marked as in a peculiar obstinate irritability of the meatus, attended with slight serous or sticky discharge, with itching and pricking pain, the walls being somewhat swollen, with a tendency to purple in their redness. In these cases the membrane also is congested, but the structures of the tympanum may apparently scarcely be involved.

When the inflammation of the meatus is acute, it commences with itching and fulness, rapidly developing into pain, which may be intensely severe, and is especially aggravated on any movement of the jaw, and the parts around are tender. Fever is present; and indeed it should not be forgotten that an inflammation of this part, by virtue of its close connection with the mastoid cells and lateral sinus, always carries with it a possibility of serious danger. In the inner part of the canal its lining membrane is also the periosteum of the bone. An inflammation beginning in the meatus may spread to the membrane,* and in rare cases perforation appears to arise in this way, the membrane becoming intensely vascular, and ulceration taking place. It can, however, never be determined that perforation has been produced from without unless the membrane has been seen complete, and the process of its ulceration followed. Inflation of the tympanum must be used to decide whether an orifice be present. The direct application of irritants, or mechanical injury, are the chief causes of diffuse inflammation of the meatus, but the condition of the teeth (as indeed in every irritative lesion of the ear) should also be looked to.

The treatment is antiphlogistic : especially leeches applied close to the meatus (protected by cotton wool), or to the tragus ; hot fomentations, and a stream of warm water, or poppy water, suffered frequently to run into the ear. Dr. Clarke's ear-douche is very serviceable for this purpose, as also for syringing the ears of children. It consists of a cup made of soft rubber for convenience, into the lower part of which an india rubber tube is introduced, the tube ending in a small nozzle to be applied to the meatus.† Poultices should be avoided, or used but for a very brief period. They promote perforation, and stimulate remarkably the growth of granulations. Dr. Roosa gives details of the formation of large polypi under their use in a few days. He also

* See Atlas, Plate xxi., fig. 3.

† To be obtained at Fisher and Haselden's, 18, Conduit Street.

states that children who awake with earache may often
be soothed to sleep again by breathing into the ear. He
speaks well also of a small conical flax seed poultice
introduced *into* the meatus.* The best authorities seem
to agree in recommending early free incisions in cases
that are at all severe ; but on this point I must abstain
from giving an opinion. It is doubtless urgently necessary to incise freely if the least risk of bone affection
appears. When the bony wall of the meatus is affected,
besides implicating the mastoid cells, it will sometimes
result in the formation of a sinus, opening immediately
below the attachment of the auricle. Such a sinus may
furnish the first indication of the bone disease.

In the later stages of the affection, or more chronic
forms, I find lead a good application. I use it generally
in the formula :—

℞ Liq. plumbi diacet.	ℳ x—xxx
Acid acét. del.	ℳ iii—x
Liq. Opii	ℳ xx
Aq. dest.	ad ℥j

With it I combine counter-irritation and careful attention to the throat. I find the same lotion useful, at first,
in the excoriated and swollen condition of the meatus
that often co-exists with affections of the tympanum in
children, especially if neglected.

In furuncles as the rule a free incision by a curved
bistoury is always desirable ; there seems to be no rule for

* Loc. Cit., pp. 121, 125, 126.

preventing their recurrence. It is striking how frequently
they form again and again in the meatus when the rest
of the body is entirely free. Local irritations have
much to do with their occurrence, and I think I have
noticed that excitement of the tympanum by stimulating
remedies has a tendency to induce them. Sometimes
they have seemed to me to expedite the subsidence of
deeper seated inflammation. In one case an obstinate
attack followed fatigue, induced by excessive railway
travelling.

For eczema every one has his own treatment. Thorough
cleansing of the canal by the free use of warm water is
imperative. I think I have found the lotion of lead with
dilute acetic acid as useful as any; and for the thickening
of the walls that is so apt to remain, pencilling with nitrate
of silver. Central galvanism is said, by some American
physicians, to be very successful.

Syphilitic ulceration of the orifice of the meatus occurs
sometimes in connection with similar affections of the
throat; and disappears under lotio nigra. But the part
played by acquired syphilis in affections of the ear is, as
yet, very undecided. It can hardly be the cause of any
considerable number of chronic affections of the middle
ear, or these affections would preponderate in the male
sex much more decidedly than they do. It seems to me
that of aural affections, probably traceable to syphilis,
the most frequent are obscure affections of the temporal
bone occurring long after the primary disease, and giving

rise to anomalous symptoms, chiefly of a nervous character.

Bleeding from the ears occurs rarely, as from other parts in some cases of suppressed menstruation. It is preceded by pain and fulness, to which it gives relief.

CHAPTER IV.

THE structure of the Eustachian tube has been best investigated by Rüdinger, of Munich.* By his researches and those of others it seems established that the tube in man consists of two portions, one the chief passage, normally open only on swallowing, and the other a small tube—situated at the upper part, and bounded off by a rim of cartilage—which is practically pervious to air, acting probably as a "weak valve;" a view suggested, tho' with less minuteness, long ago by Dr. Wharton Jones (Fig. 6). This upper portion of the tube appears to permit the entrance and exit of air to and from the tympanum to a small extent during respiration, in some cases in which the nasal mucous membrane is much swollen ; the passage of the air may sometimes be plainly heard, and thinned parts of the membrane, when these exist, may be seen to move in and out. But that in the normal state the interchange of air thus effected must be very slow, is shown by the injurious effects of greatly increased air pressure even in the healthy, unless the precaution of swallowing or inflating the drum is taken. Many instances of rupture of

* See his *Atlas des Menschlichen Gehörorgans.*

the membrane from such increased pressure in those employed in laying the foundations of bridges, piers, &c.,

FIG. 6.

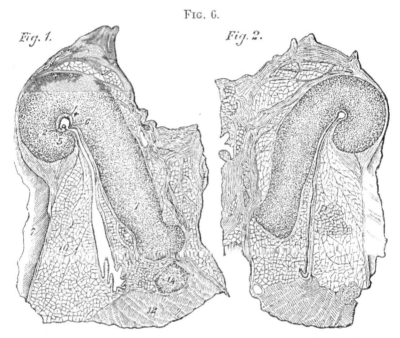

Fig. 1.   *Fig. 2.*

TRANSVERSE SECTION OF THE EUSTACHIAN TUBE:—I. AT LOWER
THIRD; II. AT UPPER THIRD.—1. The median cartilage bounding
the tube, and terminating above in a hook-shaped process;
2 and 6. Folds of mucus membrane running along the tube at
the junction of its inferior and superior portions; 4. The small
canal constituting the upper part of the tube; 5. End of the
hook-shaped portion of the cartilage; 7. The tensor palati, or
dilator of the tube; 10. Mass of fatty tissue between the membranous portion of the tube and the tensor palati; 12. Levator
palati; 14. Gland between this muscle and the basilar fibro-
cartilage (After Rüdinger.)

have been recorded,* but the opinion of those who have
observed these cases seems to be that they do not occur

* See Magnus, "Arch f. Ohr.," B. I. p. 270. Roosa, pp. 225—8.

except where there has been previous disease impeding
the passage of air thro' the tube.   I have met with only
one case in which *permanent* relief to deafness ensued
from exposure to compressed air ; that of a youth, whose
ears " opened " on going down in a diving-bell : apparently a slight case of simple closure of the Eustachian
tube.

On the mode by which the opening of the tube is
effected during swallowing, fresh light has been cast by
the investigations of Mr. C. J. F. Yule,* who can himself
voluntarily open the tube and contract the tensor tympani.   The account given by him is as follows :—

" It is noticed during the contraction for opening the
tube : First, that the velum palati does not change either
its position or shape, in fact, that it remains unmoved ;
and further, that it does not become tense, but hangs as
soft and flaccid to the touch as at ordinary times of rest.
Secondly, that the only parts that do move are the two
posterior pillars of the pharynx ; and their motion is
ample and decided, and altogether unmistakeable.   They
both move inwards simultaneously towards the middle
line, moving from their old position from one-half to three-
fourths of an inch.   This action is not spasmodic, but
perfectly steady, and can be sustained for some considerable time at will, the pillars maintaining their new position all the while.   Now I am quite satisfied and certain
that during this period the Eustachian tube is open.   It

* " Journ. of Anat. and Phys.," Nov. 1873.

will be noted that from the flaccid condition of the velum, and also from the fact of its position and form remaining unaltered, the tensor and levator palati can have no participation in the opening of the tube, and that the muscles most evidently concerned are the palato pharyngei." The

Fig. 7.

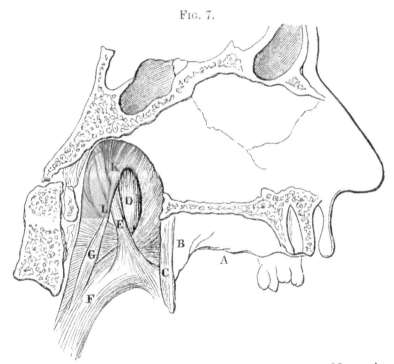

Cavity of the pharynx viewed from the right side in Man.—A. Hard palate. B. Velum Palati. C. Azygos Uvulæ. D. Tensor Palati. E. Levator Palati. F. Palato-pharyngeus. G. Salpyngo-pharyngeus uniting below with the Palato-pharyngeus. K. Lateral cartilaginous lobe of the Salpynx. L. Tendinous insertion of the Salpyngo-pharyngeus.

mode of operation is this : the salpingo pharyngeus is united at its lower attachment with the palato pharyngeus, and, as this muscle during swallowing is drawn inwards, the salpingo pharyngeus is drawn inwards also, and so draws the projecting cartilaginous lobe of the tube, to which it is attached superiorly, away from the opposite wall. The new direction given to the salpingo pharyngeus by the movement inwards of the pillars of the fauces is the cause of the opening of the tube.* (See Fig. 7.)

From the observation of cases I am convinced that there exists a constrictor as well as a dilator of the tube; because mere mechanical irritation of the adjacent part of the fauces, as by the presence of the catheter, will sometimes evidently cause firm closure of the tube when it has before been pervious. Further evidence in the same direction is given by the fact that the vapour of chloroform will often enter an obstructed tube with ease, when air will not; and Dr. Von Tröltsch,† on anatomical grounds, asserts the existence of a constrictor of the tube; assigning this function to the levator palati. Dr. Wolf‡ also reports that in a case of defective palate the Eustachian tube was seen to open during swallowing, and that in the act of retching it could be felt by the finger forcibly to close.

Mr. Yule confirms the statements of Drs. Jago and Rumbold respecting the effect of an abnormally open

* I am indebted to the kindness of Mr. Yule and Dr. Humphry for permission to use the accompanying cut from the "Journal of Anatomy and Physiology."
† "Arch f. Ohr.," I. p. 25.
‡ Loc. cit.

Eustachian tube in intensifying any sounds produced in
the patient's own throat. And I had the opportunity of
demonstrating that the cause is rightly assigned, by introducing into his tube a vulcanite Eustachian catheter, in
the curve of which an orifice was cut, so as to establish
a continuous passage from the throat to within the tube,
when the very same effects that result from his own
muscular action were produced. I could not, however,
during the time the passage was thus open, perceive any
appreciable change in the curvature of the membrane. It
appears that air passes thro' the tube more freely into
than from the tympanum. In the case of a patient with
a large destruction of the membrane but fairly pervious
tube, Mr. Yule demonstrated that the resistance to the
passage of a warm solution of soda thro' the tube from
the meatus to the fauces, raised a column of mercury
four inches.

Voluntary contraction of the tensor tympani causes the
membrane to move inwards, as tested by the manometer.
It does not, however, cause the clicking sound once
ascribed to it,* which is due to the separation of the walls
of the tube ; but it produces a loud muscular sound, which
is of a high pitch, and which renders inaudible all vibrations
below seventy in a second. In Dr. Schapringer's case,
another observer, listening by an otoscope, heard all notes
above E' louder during the contraction of the muscle, but
he himself did not: this is perhaps due to increased vi-

* "Schapringer Sitzb. d. K. Acad. d. Wissensch.," Oct. 1870.

brations of the membrane, which are not perceived by the subject owing to the rigidity of the ossicula and the sound produced by the muscle. The proper tone of the membrane, produced by air blown upon it, evidently lost its deeper constituents; and the resonance of the meatus sank from 5340 vibrations to 3700. But no evidence of its action in *adapting* the membrane could be gained; that is, no effect appreciable on the manometer ensued on listening to sounds of different pitch. Dr. C. Blake[*] found that a concave membrane favours the perception of a higher tone than a less concave one; and also that an electric current, the cathode being applied in front of the ear, increased the perception of high tones, probably indicating, therefore, contraction of the tensor tympani.

Sometimes the tensor tympani contracts during mastication. Dr. Moos[†] reports a case in which this occurred on the left side only; the membrane moved to and fro, and a grating sound was heard. The hearing on that side was diminished, and the sounds C' and C" of the tuning-fork placed on the head were heard better by the patient but worse by another observer; that is, were *less* transmitted through the tympanum. Hearing worse during eating is a symptom very frequently complained of by patients suffering from moderate degrees of deafness. Finding that it did not seem to correspond to any con-

---

* "Rep. Am. Ot. Soc.," 1873, p. 40.
† "Arch. of Oph. and Otol.," II. 1, p. 356.

stant condition, I have been in the habit of referring it
merely to the fact that mastication always diminishes
the sharpness of hearing, and that this occasioned inconvenience to those in whom it was already impaired.
But it is worth more enquiry whether an involun-
tary contraction of the tensor tympani be not often
concerned.

The most frequent morbid condition of the Eustachian
tube is simple closure from thickening of the mucous
membrane, most commonly met with in children, and
often attended with an excess of viscid secretion clogging
its walls. The presence of plugs of mucus in these cases,
is proved by the fact that in later stages, after incision of
the membrane, long and dense strings, precisely of the
shape of the tube, may be not infrequently syringed out
by a stream of liquid passed from the meatus through the
tube. The symptoms in these cases are recurring attacks
of deafness during colds, increasing in degree and duration
as they are repeated; swelling and congestion of the
throat, often also of the tonsils; sniffing of the nose,
with indisposition to blow it; and in bad cases, snoring
from inability to sleep with the mouth closed. The
whole aspect of the patient is apt to be characteristic;
the full throat and heavy expression telling the tale at
once. The degree of deafness is very variable; never, I
think, extreme, unless from other conditions co-existing;
the tuning-fork is heard well. But the diagnosis rests
on the appearance of the membrane, which is pressed

inwards towards the tympanic wall, in a manner perfectly characteristic. The malleus appears foreshortened,
and the membrane has a tense, stretched look, like a
drawn-back curtain, often falling into similar folds.
The colour is various, {generally white and dull,
but sometimes, especially in the earlier stages, the
congested mucous lining of the tympanum shines
through it.*

With this condition there co-exists, more frequently
than not, an excess of mucous secretion within the
tympanum indicated by one or other of the signs before
described, and giving generally a moist sound on inflation
by Politzer's bag.

The right treatment for this condition I must hold to
be yet not fully determined. The inflation of the
drum by Politzer's process gives, in uncomplicated cases,
instant relief, and followed up by measures adapted to
restore the throat to health, may not even need repeating.
In such a case there can be no doubt that the artificial
inflation of the drum is a pure gain, indeed, simply a
cure; and its prompt employment wards off many
ill consequences, such as undue stretching of the membrane, danger of its becoming fixed in an abnormal
position, derangement of the vascular system of the tympanum by diminished air pressure, and, in all probability,
injurious effects on the labyrinth from increased pressure
exerted on it thro' the stapes. The inflation of the

* Atlas, Plate III. figs. 1, 2, and 3.

tympanum on Politzer's method, accordingly, may always
be had recourse to with confidence, in every case of
obstructed Eustachian tube, and its delightful, and even
wonderful, results in at once restoring hearing cannot be
too highly extolled. It is as valuable for warding off
future danger as for relieving immediate inconvenience.
But often the effect is temporary, and needs frequent
repetition [even apart from the presence of mucus, which
seems always to prevent the full effect of the inflation],
and then other considerations come in ; namely, whether
the repeated use of the bag lays a basis for future evils,
for the sake of avoiding which it is better to be content
with less speedy results : whether, in a word, a patient
use of the remedies adapted to restore the faucial and
tympanic mucous membrane to a healthy state, and
waiting for the muscles to open the tube in the natural
way, would not be a better practice in the end ? On this
point I do not offer an opinion, feeling only that the
brilliant results of the artificial inflation, simple and
effective as it is, must be adapted to lead us astray in
this respect ; and that only prolonged and careful com-
parisons, including the history of the patients during
many years, can satisfactorily determine it. Of course,
these remarks are quite irrespective of the abuse to
which patients may carry the use of the bag when placed
in their own hands, a matter which needs very careful
guarding.

Whether the bag be frequently used or not, the utmost

attention must, of course, be given to the general and
local treatment. Besides fresh air, good food, exercise,
warm feet, and steel (which I often combine at first with
acid and sulphate of magnesia), I place my reliance chiefly
on cleansing and astringent solutions syringed through the
nostrils, and on the application, twice a week, by a curved
brush, of a solution of the perchloride of iron (ʒj—ʒj) to
the faucial openings of the tubes. The cleansing solutions I use are of common salt, chlorate of potash, or
alum, about five grains to the ounce; and I generally
direct them to be syringed, tepid, into one nostril, with
the head held slightly forward, so that they escape thro'
the other. The syringe is the ordinary glass syringe
with a shortened nozzle, and with gentleness its use does
not alarm the most timid child. For adults, drawing the
solution thro' the nostrils, letting it escape by the mouth,
is often still more effective, and indeed the use of salt
and water in this way may soon become a luxury.
Among excellent means are, of course, to be included
spray, and especially a spray of nitrate of silver (gr.
v.—ɔj ad. ʒj) applied to the region of the Eustachian
tube, by means of a silver tube perforated at the extremity.
Dr. Rumbold insists also on the necessity of carrying the
spray of astringent solutions into the upper part of the
nasal cavity, and uses, for that purpose, tubes perforated
with holes that project the spray directly upwards.

The figure below represents an Eustachian catheter,
which may be introduced by the mouth. Dr. Pomeroy,

who suggests it, states that by it, spray may be caused
to pass well up the tube. The ordinary nose douche
is open to question, since various observers have re-

FIG. 8.

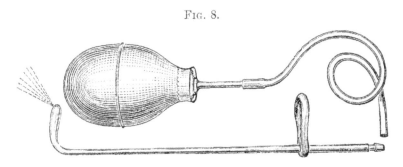

ported cases in which the current has entered the
Eustachian tube with force and injured the tympanum;
Dr. Roosa* especially has collected eighteen cases in which
this misfortune has occurred. I have met with but one
case of this accident, and then the douche had been
advised by a most competent and careful physician; the
patient was a clergyman, aged seventy, and severe inflammation was set up in each ear: the liquid had a fall
of about five feet. Possibly the danger is greater in
advanced age, owing to the wasting of the tissues. When,
however, the Eustachian tube is abnormally closed, the
use of the douche is wholly without risk.

For the most part, when the Eustachian tube is closed
the tympanum also is affected; but this is not always
the case, at least in the early stages; and Dr. Pomeroy's

* Loc. cit., p. 291.

statement that in morbid conditions that travel along
the tube the tympanic affection is apt to increase as
that of the faucial portion of the tube passes away, is
supported by a great deal of evidence. When the
obstruction of the tube is so complete that neither
Politzer's bag, nor the Eustachian catheter, with vapour
of chloroform, avail to open it, the use of bougies, if
fairly continued, will almost without exception restore
the passage; at least, I have not for many years met
with a case in which they failed. I use bougies of
laminaria, which, however, require to be made thinner
than are usually met with. None thicker than about
one-half of a line in diameter should be passed thro' the
narrowest part of the tube, which lies about two-thirds
of the distance up, at the junction of the bony and
cartilaginous part; but others, of larger size, may be
kept for the purpose of expanding the faucial portion of
the tube. When I have succeeded in introducing one
of the bougies (often only a very short distance, at first),
I generally leave it in the tube for fifteen or twenty
minutes, during which time it swells, often to twice its
original bulk, and is firmly retained in the tube after
the catheter is withdrawn. The catheter should always
be removed first; or at least the bougie and catheter
together; the attempt to withdraw the bougie thro' the
catheter of course breaks off the swollen portion within
the tube. Twice it has happened to me to break a
laminaria bougie in the tube; on the first occasion,

to my great alarm, a full inch was left behind. No mischief, however, resulted, nor even any pain; a warm nose douche of soda was used freely night and morning, and in four days it came away, resolved into a mass of

FIG. 9.

LAMINARIA BOUGIE, after remaining fifteen minutes in the Eustachian tube, indicating constricted portions.

pulp. The tube remained open, and the result was very satisfactory. Another time a small portion broke off beyond the isthmus, and some temporary irritation ensued.

Another accident that occurs when the bougie is used without proper precautions is emphysema of the cellular tissue in its neighbourhood. This also has a serious aspect, but * is entirely free from danger. It may also be avoided with absolute certainty by never endeavouring to inflate the tympanum with air on the same day after the bougie has been used. It occurred, without any detriment, in the following case, which I report here, because the chief morbid condition, and the one that presented the main difficulty in the treatment, was the closure of the tube, although other conditions, not yet discussed, were also present. Not only laminaria bougies were used to overcome the constriction, but smaller

* Unless one of the two cases of death after the air-douche under Dr. Turnbull, reported many years ago, was caused by it.

catheters were introduced thro' the usual sized ones, as far as they would reach, and fluids injected thro' them.*

Mucous accumulation in each tympanum; on the right side deafness since childhood; obstruction of the Eustachian tube; treatment by bougies and incision; perfect recovery of hearing.†

August 3rd, 1868.—L. E—, æt. 19. On the right side she had been deaf as long as she could remember, and her mother traced it to some affection of the ear occurring at the age of six weeks. The left ear had been liable to attacks of deafness during colds for some years, and has now been deaf for a fortnight. In each ear she has had occasional attacks of pain. Watch, r., $\frac{0}{40}$ (contact); l., $\frac{3}{40}$. Tuning-fork well heard on the vertex; louder on the deafer side. R. M. T. very concave, dark, and shining, with the glistening appearance of yellowish fluid just visible posteriorly. L. M. T. also very concave, thick, and white. On inflation air entered the left ear only, with a wheezing sound, raising the hearing to $\frac{14}{40}$. The right membrane was incised, and a little viscid mucus oozed out. No air could be passed through the tube; but the hearing improved for the time to $\frac{10}{40}$: this gain, however, was almost wholly lost as soon as the incision healed. Three times the incision was repeated with the same result, all attempts to gain a passage through the incised membrane, without too much pressure, being in vain; and on October 21st, 1868, considering that the evidently morbid condition of the other (the left) ear rendered it the more desirable to restore the right if possible, I addressed myself thoroughly to the attempt to gain a passage through the tube. The means used [besides various applications to the throat] were at first the introduction, every other day, of bougies,

---

* These smaller catheters were first suggested for the more exact medication of the tympanum, by F. Weber-Liel.

† See Atlas of Diseases of Membrana Tympani, Plate XVII. Nos 3 and 4.

either elastic, or of laminaria, or of softened whalebone, followed by the syringing of astringent solutions into the tube.

On November 17th, while inflating by the nostril, after the use of a laminaria bougie, the air escaped into the cellular tissue, causing some swelling of the soft palate and uvula. These were pricked, and in two days all swelling had subsided. Treatment, however, was omitted for three weeks, at the end of which time it was resumed by the intro-duction, at short intervals, of a small elastic tube passed through the catheter as far as possible along the canal, air and a solution of car-bonate of potash being then strongly injected through it. On February the 2nd a small stream of air was in this way distinctly heard to enter the tympanum ; at the same time some mucus, which was plainly visible, was evacuated by incision from the anterior part of the cavity, a solution of soda being syringed through the tympanum and tube in each direction, and the hearing immediately rose to $\frac{35}{40}$. On the next day, however, the tube was closed again, and only a laminaria bougie could be passed along it. For some weeks this continued to be the case, the tube closing immediately after it had been made pervious ; so rapidly indeed, that it happened more than once that I syringed a solution of soda freely and completely *through* the tube in the morning, and in the evening not even air would pass. On the 9th of March the membrane was incised for the last time, and a viscid, very yellow matter was washed out ; but it was not until the 16th of April that the tendency of the tube to close was overcome. On that day I syringed into the tympanum a solution of nitrate of silver (gr. v to the ounce) occasioning temporary pain. In the evening the pain returned severely, lasting for some hours ; the next day the ear was easy ; and on the following one, while blowing her nose, the air suddenly entered the tympanum. From that time she was able to inflate it easily; and the hearing, so far as I could judge, was perfect. The watch was heard at forty inches, the full average distance, and a low whisper at over six yards. The membrane regained, after an interval of seven months, an almost perfectly normal appearance; but for many weeks it was much relaxed ; and on inflation assumed an extremely convex form, while a smaller portion posteriorly bulged out into a globular projection. This relaxation of the membrane was due, in my opinion, to the tension under which it had been placed through the long-continued closure of tube, probably since infancy, increased

I

by the pressure of the dense collected mucus, and possibly by contact with the promontory.

This was the most obstinate case of closure of the tube that I have met with, and its great tendency to return, even after the passage had been made pervious, often made me doubtful of permanent success. Until the bougie can be passed the whole length of the tube it is well to introduce it once a week, using the inflation by Politzer's bag on intervening days. After the tube has been once completely opened, the occasional introduction of a bougie thro' the isthmus of the tube is desirable until it remains pervious, and the spray of sulphate of zinc or nitrate of silver should be applied weekly. I have not found obstructions of the tube once thoro'ly treated in this way apt to recur.—The bougie is oiled, or, if of laminaria, moistened. I generally precede its use by injecting a warm solution of Pot. Iod. into the part of the tube that is open. The length of the catheter is marked on the bougie, and at an inch and a third beyond it is placed a second mark, to guide the surgeon as to the position of the point.

The introduction of the bougie, of course, needs practice, which should be gained upon the dead subject. Sometimes it seems as if the catheter, to permit the passage of the bougie, needed to be turned a little more *upwards* than the position most favourable for the entrance of air or liquids. It is very easy to be deceived as to the entrance of the bougie into the mouth of the tube, since, unless it is very rigid, it may bend at its exit from the catheter; but this is indicated by the catheter tending to change its position. Of course when a bougie lies well in the tube, it supports the catheter·in its place. When we can be sure the catheter is rightly placed, repeated failures to gain entrance, even for a firm bougie, need not discourage us; and when the extremity is once grasped by the orifice, nothing but patience is needed, according to my experience, to ensure a perfect entrance. But cases of bony stricture of the canal and of firm scars at its mouth have been reported as found in dissection, which of course could not have been overcome.

Of course if symptoms of destruction of the nervous power exist, no attempts with the bougie, which must be more or less painful, would be suggested.

On one occasion, in a case of large perforation of the membrane, with obstructed tube, where, owing to limitation of time, I wished to restore its patency as quickly as possible, I passed, without designing it, a small elastic bougie thro' the orifice in the membrane into the meatus. My impression was that the bougie had bent, and was lying in the throat, though something unusual induced me to persevere with its introduction. On turning to examine the membrane, I found the end of the bougie lying at the outer part of the meatus. I gently drew it on, and its whole length passed without pain thro' the tympanum, and out at the external ear. The tube remained open, the hearing improved, and was rendered satisfactory by aid of the artificial membrane.

In respect to the use of bougies, however, it should be mentioned that some excellent practitioners scarcely ever employ them ; and, in particular, Dr. Roosa states that by the use of weak chloroform vapour on Politzer's plan, following the introduction of the catheter, he scarcely ever fails to gain an entrance into the tympanum. I should, however, entertain the suspicion that in the drier climate of America a very confirmed occlusion of the tube may be less frequent than it is in our moister air. An easy method of introducing chloroform or iodine vapour into the tube consists in attaching to a pair of India rubber balls (as used for the spray-producer) a small perforated box, containing a piece of sponge, upon which a few drops of chloroform or a few crystals of iodine may be placed. The box is provided with a nose-piece, perforated by small holes, which is introduced into one nostril, and air injected, as in Politzer's plan.* Whether iodine vapour thus employed has much advantage over air alone, I have not yet been able to decide.

The effects of different climates on the forms assumed by affections of the ear seem to me to be probably very considerable, and to give a key to variations in experience not otherwise to be explained. Among these may, perhaps, be included a greater frequency in America of

* See Fig. 3, p. 45.

the opposite condition to obstruction of the Eustachian tube, namely, an abnormal patency. Of the occasional existence of this condition here, there is no doubt, tho' among the usual class of patients it very seldom presents itself. One painful case I witnessed in a man aged fifty-six dying of phthisis; he complained of a constant rustling in the left ear with the respiration, and of his own voice rushing up into it in a way that distressed him greatly. The membrane appeared normal; nor did I notice any change from the usual concavity, and the hearing was not appreciably affected; but on listening to each ear, by means of an India rubber tube while he spoke, the sound evidently passed with .. great intensity out of the left meatus.

I was not able materially to relieve him; indeed, he was unable to bear treatment. In this case one naturally supposed a thinning or wasting of the walls of the tube, which the smooth and pallid condition of the fauces rendered more probable. And it is possible in like manner that abnormal patency of the tube is more frequent in drier climates than in ours.

Of course spasm of the dilator, or inaction of the constrictor, of the tube [the salpingo-pharyngeus, and the levator palati respectively], might have part in maintaining this condition; but it appears generally to co-exist with more or less catarrh. The injection of a small amount of liquid into the tube gave temporary relief in Dr. Rumbold's hands; and, so far as appears at present, the treatment that is effective for chronic catarrh (with the omission of the inflation of the tympanum), is also best adapted to relieve insufficient closure.

Dr. Jago describes a smacking or cracking sound as accompanying the first opening of the tubes, from the sundering of its walls and sudden yielding of the membrane. He observed patency of the tube after the excision of a portion of the uvula, in the case of a woman in whom it had been so relaxed as to be caught by the muscles in the act of swallowing. Only about an eighth of it was cut off; but a great contraction followed, with a twisting of the stump to the right side, so pulling upon the muscular fibres, extending along the right arches of the palate. The right tube was subject to the abnormal patency.

A few cases are reported of small foreign bodies, such as grains of barley, entering the tubes from the faucial side. My only experience of anything like this was in the case of a youth who suffered from acute catarrh of the tympanum, with perforation, and who shortly after the commencement of the symptoms, in clearing his throat, hawked up a grain of bearded grass which he felt to come from the neighbourhood of the affected ear.

CHAPTER V.

Not only are the inflammatory affections of the membrane, almost if not quite universally, parts of a larger morbid condition affecting also the meatus or tympanum, but by far the larger part of the other morbid conditions that are met with in it are the result of tympanic disease, inflammatory or other, and can rightly be spoken of only after the diseases of the tympanum have been discussed. But there are some abnormal states which seem to involve the membrane alone. One appearance has often attracted my attention, and I hardly know whether to consider it an abnormal one or not — a more than customary thinness and transparence of the membrane,* which permits the incus, stapes, and internal tympanic wall to be very distinctly seen. It is true there is no absolute standard of transparence for the membrane, and that this character is affected by the slightest changes in the epidermis that covers it; but it is none the less true, also, that some membranes give at once to the eye the impression of an unusual thinness, and experience has taught me to connect with this appearance a distinctly

* See Atlas, Plate I., fig. 2 ; also Plate XVII., fig. 4.

unfavourable prognosis; even as we are compelled to do
with "hearing better in a noise," though we cannot give a
satisfactory account of the reason. I have a feeling that
an unusual thinness of the membrane, without other
change, is very apt to exist in persons in whom the
function of the auditory nerve is impaired in unexplained
ways; whether it be a coincidence merely, or have any
relation to the deeper-seated affection, I do not know. I
think it is common in young people born in India, in whom,
about the age of puberty, a failure of the nervous power,
without visible cause, seems apt to occur. In such cases
the tympanum may be demonstrated healthy by the use of
the tuning-fork, closure of the meatus having the normal
effect in increasing the sound. Possibly, if this connection
were confirmed, it might become an aid to the distinction
of a class of cases having other characters in common, and
even a guide to treatment. I have recourse to tonic
measures, and *rest* of the ear, but cannot boast of my
results.

(2). Cretaceous deposits are quite frequent, even in
healthy membranes. They lie in the fibrous layers, and
are oval or crescentic in shape.* They may co-exist with
perfect and even with acute hearing, and appear sometimes to arise quite apart from disease; altho' they are
also one of the most frequent results of its long continuance.

(3). Sometimes, tho' much more rarely, the substance

* See Atlas, Plates I. and II.

of the membrane itself seems somewhat thickened without any appreciable impairment of the hearing;* this is interesting because, on the other hand, slight degrees of abnormal *tension* seem to render the membrane a great hindrance to the perception of sound ; as is shown by the frequency with which a mere linear incision produces, until it closes, great improvement. It would seem that the peculiar structure of the membrane has less to do with its transmission of vibrations than it might be natural to suppose: if only the stapes be well balanced, it seems to matter comparatively little what lies external to it. But in reference to this it has been remarked, by Mr. Moon, that when an organ has once been educated, an impaired structure will suffice to maintain a perfectness of function that it could never have acquired.

(4). Injuries to the membrane arise chiefly in one of three ways: from direct application of violence, from blows to the head, or from explosions. Direct injury arises generally from something introduced by the patient into the ear ; most frequently hair-pins.† The most dangerous results, however, ensue when a needle or other sharp body is introduced by another person into the meatus, and the patient suddenly turns his head. This is sometimes done with pens or pencils by boys at school

* See Atlas, Plate I., fig. 3.
† Plate IX. of the Atlas, fig. 1, shows the prick of a hair-pin in the membrane ; healing without ill-result.

to one another, and the danger should not be forgotten by their instructors. A case of fracture of the malleus, with total loss of hearing, came under my notice in a man who had placed in his ear the rod of the pendulum of a clock he was carrying, and received a blow on his hand from a passer-by.* Death has resulted in the course of a few days from a crochet-needle entering the meatus on a sharp turn of the head; pus being found in the subarachnoid space in the neighbourhood of the ear. The practice of using ear-scoops or hair-pins to the meatus, on any pretence, is therefore doubly to be discouraged; besides its invariable irritating effect upon the passage, it involves a real risk to life. Slight perforations almost always heal very readily; but mild depleting measures may be necessary if any inflammation arises.

Boxes on the ear are the practically most important form in which violence to the head produces injury of the membrane, and every trainer of youth should be impressed with the imperative duty of avoiding that form of punishment. At the same time I may say, that I think in every case of rupture of the membrane from this cause that I have seen there has been reason to believe that its structure was previously weakened. Gruber's experiments upon the resisting power of the normal membrane would favour this view, since he found that it resisted a pressure of more than four atmospheres; indeed, by forcing air into the meatus by a syringe he

* See Atlas, Plate XI., fig. 6.

never succeeded in rupturing it. But probably no more cruel injustice is done than that which is inflicted in boxing children's ears for "inattention." Children are not inattentive, but distinctly curious and alert, and a child who incurs boxes on the ears on such ground is probably doubly injured : in mind as well as body—by the injustice as well as the hurtfulness of the blow. I have known a youth die of brain disease from inflammation of the ear, whose history was that when young his father used often to box his ears for not attending.

Rupture occurs also sometimes in hanging, and in fracture of the base of the skull. In the latter case, the question whether the liquid that escapes from the ear is cerebro-spinal fluid or not may be solved by chemical and microscopical examination. Once, in removing the petrous bone from the skull in a case in which there had been a fall on the head but no fracture had been dis- covered after death, a distinct fracture of the bones of the base took place, extending thro' the petrous bone, before any force adapted to produce it had been em- ployed. Is it not possible, therefore, that there may exist a sort of virtual or latent fracture of the base of the skull, in which the continuity is loosened but not distinctly broken, and that this may, perhaps, per- manently affect the function of the ear ?

Injury to the membrane from explosions of artillery or otherwise are not very frequent. I have seen but one case of rupture from heavy guns; the patient was a naval

officer ; the rupture healed and the hearing was regained.
Dr. Orne Green* reports several cases of injury to the
ear from an explosion of chemical substances. In half of
them there was a previous history of slight disease of
the tympanum; the injury found was of two kinds:
rupture, with or without discharge, soon healing ; and a
forcing inwards of the membrane, causing deafness and
tinnitus, relieved by the introduction of air into the
tympanum, and so restoring the membrane to its normal
position.

In the year 1863 a young woman applied to me, into
whose right ear undiluted nitric acid had been poured by
accident. The face and the outer part of the meatus
were excoriated by the acid ; the hearing seemed almost
totally abolished on that side, but the membrane presented only a dull and rather opaque appearance. In
the "British Medical Journal" for August 2nd, 1873,
Mr. Lee reports the case of a man struck by lightning.
Among other injuries, there was excoriation of the right
auricle and bleeding from the meatus. He was also
deaf in the right ear, and on examination by Dr. Allen,
a laceration of the membrane was found : pain followed
after a fortnight, but was relieved by discharge ; the
hearing had not returned.

(5). Inflammatory perforation of the membrane sometimes occurs as the result of inflammation of the meatus,
tho' much more rarely than from inflammation within

* "Tr. Amer. Ot. Soc.," 1872, p. 88.

the tympanum. One such case I had the opportunity
of observing from an early stage.*

The patient was a healthy girl, aged eight years, who
had suffered for four years with repeated attacks of
discharge from the right ear, often attended with pain,
and brought on first by chewed paper put into the ear by
a companion. On examination, the meatus was found
somewhat red, swollen, and covered with discharge; on
the membrane, which was of a dull grey hue, with a
purplish tint, besides a general congestion of its vessels,
there was, just beneath the end of the malleus, a small
red surface, bounded below and in front by a white
portion of the membrane, apparently a thickened patch of
epidermis. This red surface appeared raw and slightly
depressed, and had the aspect of a superficial ulceration.
The membrane was entire, as proved by the fact that air
passed into the tympanum, through the Eustachian tube,
moved the membrane forward, but did not pass through
it. On the next day, at the anterior extremity of the
red patch, a small darker spot was seen, visibly pulsating,
and through which, on the inflation of the tympanum, air
passed outwards with the usual slight screeching sound.
No fluid, however, escaped with the air.

When next seen, eleven days after, the red surface was
no longer to be distinguished, the perforation had healed,
a slight depressed point alone marking its position;
the general aspect of the membrane was much more

* See Atlas, Plate XIX., fig. 3.

transparent than before, and less vascular, but it looked too concave and somewhat irregular. It moved outward on inflation, by which the hearing distance also was improved. The membrane gradually became free from opacity; and the position which was occupied by the red surface appeared as a slightly depressed, thinner, and more transparent portion, resembling a scar, but perhaps yielding less on inflation.

CHAPTER VI.

Acute and Chronic Catarrh: Suppuration.

OUR knowledge of the diseases of the tympanum has greatly advanced in the last few years, especially in the form of bringing into doubt much that has passed current as ascertained. In regarding the subject the surgeon feels like a person suddenly released from bonds to which he had grown accustomed—conscious of a new liberty, but uncertain in what direction it may lead him.

Acute and chronic catarrh, with free exudation, or with dry thickening [sclerosis] of the mucous membrane, going on to anchylosis, at one time nearly exhausted the pathology of the tympanum; but the ill success which attended the treatment of a large class of cases left the mind dissatisfied. And investigations taking in a wider scope have at least sufficed to show that the range of aural disease is less contracted than had been supposed, and is therefore probably open to a wider application of remedies. In this condition of our knowledge, however, it would be unfit to dogmatize; and I shall endeavour not to mark out the various kinds of disease with definite limits, but rather to suggest the lines in which observation should run.

One disease, however, retains its pre-eminence: the acute catarrhal inflammation of the mucous membrane of the tympanum, with its minor degrees, down to the slight stuffiness which attends a cold, and in which the presence of an increased secretion is shown by the squeaking sound which attends our own inflation of the drum. The symptoms of this disease in its acute form are too striking to be overlooked—*except in young children, in whom they are constantly overlooked.* The intense severity which the pain may reach within a few hours of its commencement as a slight tickling in the bottom of the ear, the fever, not seldom attended even with delirium, the shooting pains over the side of the head, increased by each beat of the pulse, and by swallowing [but less increased by motion of the jaw than when the meatus is chiefly attacked], the tenderness of the scalp, with the hissing and roaring noises in the ear, leave no doubt of the nature of the affection. Except as connected with specific exanthemata, I do not know that it has any other exciting cause than cold, or direct irritation. It may supervene on chronic morbid conditions of the ear; but my experience would induce me to think that, owing perhaps to better precautions, or a more rational treatment, it is less frequent now than it was formerly. On examination, the meatus is generally found somewhat tumid and tender, but not necessarily reddened. The membrane is at first slightly congested, the vessels at the circumference and along the malleus being the first to become enlarged; but in severe cases the whole surface soon becomes intensely red, at first with a distinct vascular network, but after a few days assuming a velvety appearance; and its natural concavity is lost. In the meantime the Eustachian tube is closed by swelling, so that the patient cannot inflate the drum; but if Politzer's bag be used, with just sufficient force, as it is very desirable it should be every day, the air enters with a creaking, gurgling sound, indicating the presence of tenacious secretion shut up, no doubt under strong pressure, by the swollen mucous membrane. The throat almost always participates in the inflammation.

When the inflammation reaches the severity indicated above, I believe the membrane always gives way, or at least that it is very desirable it should give way, and the secretion, almost always purulent, escapes outwardly. If this result takes place, the membrane may undergo extraordinary changes of appearance, bulging into large, irregular, udder-like protuberances, from which yellowish matter may be seen to ooze, and seeming to undergo a degree of distension from which it would be impossible for it to recover.* But there is no real danger in this condition; if only the matter be freely discharged, the membrane and all the other structures soon recover themselves, and the hearing perfectly returns. Perhaps

* For a drawing of this condition, see Atlas, Plate XIX., fig. 5.

K

not even a scar may permanently remain. In fact, formidable as are the symptoms of the acute form of inflammation of the drum, it is, in a healthy subject, and provided the inflammation do not extend to the bone or mastoid cells, and is early treated with moderate care, scarcely dangerous to hearing: when once discharge takes place thro' the membrane, the irritation speedily abates, healing then rapidly sets in, and the hearing, if unimpaired before, is wholly restored in a few weeks or months. Not acute, but insidiously recurring, chronic affections of the mucous membrane of the tympanum destroy the hearing.

The treatment of these cases speaks for itself: free depletion by leeches (below the ear, or around the meatus, which should be closed by a small piece of sponge), or by the artificial leech, is universally recommended; the hottest fomentations, but not poultices—or if at all, for a very few hours—and warm water freely poured into the meatus; purgatives, and sedatives sufficient to give sleep; inflation of the tympanum daily by Politzer's bag, to give exit to the pent-up secretion, if it be possible, thro' the Eustachian tube. To these means I should add a mild nose douche, injecting a warm solution of borax or chlorate of potash, or common salt, thro' one nostril by a small glass syringe, and letting it escape by the other; thus fomenting the internal orifice of the Eustachian tube. Since the real relief of the symptoms depends upon the escape of the matter through the membrane, it would seem an obvious inference that the membrane should be, at the earliest possible period, incised. And this is recommended by almost every writer; but experience of this method has left a doubt upon my mind. In the few cases in which I have had recourse to it during the acute stage of an inflammation, I have not found the results very satisfactory, and in two instances in which the inflammation existed on both sides, and I incised one membrane only, the progress of recovery seemed retarded rather than expedited. I must therefore hold an undetermined· position on this question. The following case is a well-marked one, in which incision was performed on one side and omitted on the other.*

June 20th, 1868.—M. M., æt. 20 ; healthy, but not strong. Eight days previously felt a sudden giddiness on rising, followed by pain first over the eyes, next in the face, then in the teeth, and finally settling in the ears. The giddiness was followed by vomiting and purging. On the third day of the pain he became deaf. The next day a slight discharge of matter tinged with blood occurred from the left ear, with scarcely any relief. There had been no affection of the ears before, except one night's severe pain on one side four years ago. On examination, each membrane was seen intensely red, and of fleshy appearance, bulging a little superiorly, most on the right side ; on the left there was a small dimple like a pin-hole, but no orifice. Air entered each, by Politzer's bag, with a creaky sound. Tuning-fork well heard ; but a loud watch only on contact, best on the left side.

A prick was made in the right membrane with a cataract knife, which

* In Plate XIX. of the Atlas, fig. 4 shows the membrane in a case of acute inflammation of the tympanum opened by incision, and fig. 5, giving way of itself.

K 2

was covered with a whitish fluid on withdrawal, but no fluid escaped, tho' air passed thro'.

On the 24th, the left membrane had become immensely protuberant and had given way, and masses of viscid secretion were removed. In the right membrane the puncture seemed to have closed, and it was intensely red and swollen. A more free incision, three'lines in length, was made on the right side, at the lower and posterior part; thick and viscid secretion escaped, and he blew thro' the orifice.

26th.—There was no pain, and each ear was discharging freely from the tympanum. From this time the left ear progressed favourably, the protuberance of the membrane diminished as the viscid secretion was evacuated, and on the 28th July it was healed. W. $\frac{3}{40}$. The right tympanum did not appear to discharge itself effectively thro' the incision, tho' it continued widely open, about the size of a cress seed; and the membrane bulged and ulcerated in a manner very similar to the left. It was not till August 30th that it had fairly healed. On that day the hearing was r. $\frac{10}{40}$, l. $\frac{24}{40}$. On Nov. 1st, the scar on each side was diminished to a small yellow spot, and the hearing seemed perfect. On the 1st May, 1869, he wrote to me: "I have quite regained the use of both ears, except, perhaps, that the ringing of bells is not quite so audible to me as it used to be, while sharp sounds, such as the engine whistle, &c., sometimes quite hurt the ear. The only other effect of my illness is an occasional sharp pang thro' either ear when I am tired." He has perfectly recovered since.

In this case it is possible that the incisions of the right membrane really did good, altho' the disease on that side ran the more tedious course; but a few other instances also have occurred to me in which the un-incised membrane has recovered the more quickly. Possibly the period at which it is made is an important element. Many good authorities concur in advising the third day. Free scarifications of the substance of the swollen membrane also are advised by Gruber and others.

But whatever may be the best method of treatment in simple acute catarrh of the tympanum, there seems to be no doubt that immense evil might be prevented by free incisions of the membrane in very many of the cases in which it becomes inflamed during the course of the exanthemata. This is a subject that has hitherto received scarcely any attention; but Mr. Harvey has reported cases in which, during the severity of an attack of scarlatina, he has incised the membrane and evacuated thick discharge, with obvious relief to the severity of the symptoms, and with perfect preservation of the hearing. Much less permanent deafness, even less deaf-mutism, will affect the people, when the profession make it part of their duty to study the condition of the tympanum in every case of scarlatina, measles, or hooping-cough. And there can be little doubt, I think, that the mortality at least from scarlatina might be appreciably diminished by treatment directed to the ear.

When the catarrhal affection of the tympanum is less severe, it may terminate in the escape of the secretion by the Eustachian tube, the swelling of the mucous membrane subsiding sufficiently to give it exit; as in the following case, which occurred in a very intelligent student :—

October 7th, 1865.—W. J., æt. 20, was quite well up to midnight, but at 4 A.M. was awakened by great pain about the ear and right side of the head, of a neuralgic character. This pain was not referable to any deep-seated structure, as was the pain which followed it; but affected the teeth of that side. Hot fomentations were applied at once, which afforded partial relief.

The day following, the pain increased in severity, and altered in character, being now localized in the ear, more deeply seated and far more intense. Tincture of opium and olive oil were dropped in warm, and increased the pain, which now became paroxysmal in its attacks, and accompanied with a feeling of bursting and distension, quite distinct from the pain itself, and referable to the membrana tympani ; also now accompanied with feverishness, tinnitus, partial deafness, beating noises, loud and painful, synchronous with pulse, inability to lay head on pillow or lift it off without assistance, sensibility to sound, and sleeplessness. Pain always worse at night. On inspection the membrane was seen bulged out externally, and the parts around much inflamed, especially the floor of the meatus. Blister, and fomentations continued.

On about the fifth day from the commencement of the attack, an oozing into the pharynx commenced, first of blood and mucus, and afterwards of mucus alone, of a bright yellow colour, and very tenacious. This seemed to relieve the feeling of distension before referred to, and continued for a couple of days, when complete freedom from pain was experienced.

At present (October 26th) slight deafness ; sometimes noises as of distant ringing, feeling of uneasiness high up in throat, unpleasant sensation sometimes after swallowing, as if the tympanic cavity were thereby over distended with air. Also sometimes noise as if the membrane were loose and hanging, and then suddenly made tense by the entrance of air from the pharynx.

On the 1st of December I examined him again. The membrane was natural in appearance, and air entered the drum fairly on inflation ; but a slight diminution of hearing remained.

In reference to every similar case, also, the question arises whether the Eustachian tube, narrow as it is, and situated not at the most dependent part of the tympanum, really affords sufficient exit for the viscid secretion that collects, and whether its exit through the membrane is not really a better result, as being less liable to leave portions of unremoved secretion which may become a cause of deafness in the future.

Besides these more acute forms of inflammation there occur, and apparently much more frequently, two forms of chronic inflammation : the catarrhal, with excess of free secretion, and the dry, or " proliferous "—the " thickening of the mucous membrane of the tympanum " of Mr. Toynbee. Of the frequency of the former affection, and of the correctness in the main of the views entertained respecting it, I think there is good evidence ; but the basis on which the views hitherto generally entertained respecting the latter—or " dry catarrh "—rest, appears to demand reconsideration. That a certain proportion of the cases hitherto put down as pertaining to this class belong really to the former, and that the symptoms in them depend not so much upon " sclerosis " of the mucous membrane as on gradually increasing dryness of the viscid secretions that have been poured into the tympanum, and the rigidity that thus results, I think is proved by the results alike of dissection and of treatment. But even when these cases are allowed for, there remains a large class of diseases of the tympanum, the pathology of which has yet to be finally decided.

The chronic *catarrhal* inflammation of the tympanum differs from the acuter forms in its less intensity. It is

the deafness that recurs with colds, and gives rise to
the "earaches" so frequent in the young. In its more
considerable degrees, when seen in the early stage,
the membrane may be seen congested, with distinct red
vessels along the malleus, its surface shining, with a hazy
whiteness showing beneath it, as it were, caused by the
swelling and diminished transparency of its mucous layer.
It is generally drawn in, owing to closure of the tube ;
and on inflation of the drum, which needs Politzer's bag
to effect it, the air enters with the characteristic gurgling
sound. With a little care, or even without it, the affection
subsides ; but its consequences do not cease. In milder
degrees still, nothing is felt but recurring attacks of
"stuffiness" in the ear ; and in some of these cases,
especially after inflation, a whitish viscid fluid may be
seen lying in contact with the inner surface of the
membrane.* Such attacks will frequently follow careless
bathing,† or come as the sequelæ of affections of the
lungs, but more often still with no assignable occasion.
Wet feet, however, are a frequent cause, and even cold-
ness to the feet may bring it on in very susceptible
persons. One man assured me that even putting on cold
boots made his hearing worse. Mr. Toynbee relates the
case of an elderly lady in whom he entirely relieved
recurring attacks of catarrhal deafness by saving the feet

---

* See Atlas, Plate XIII., fig. 7, and Plate XVIII., fig. 5.

† It is said that water-dogs become deaf, but only from being thrown
into the water, not from entering it naturally.

from cold. Some light may be thrown upon these cases by a condition that I observed in a fairly healthy man of thirty. The meatus were narrow, and during wet weather the orifice on the left side would become so tumid as greatly to constrict the passage : perhaps an analogous effect may be produced upon the tympanic mucous membrane.

On the other hand, instances occur in which the hearing is made better for the time by acute affections of the throat, and even by scarlatina.*

The treatment of recurrent catarrh naturally consists in the avoidance of colds and bracing up of the whole faucio-tympanic mucous membrane. Salt and water or alum and water drawn thro' the nostrils, the use of the perchloride of iron by a brush to the orifice of the Eustachian tube, and very small blisters used for a long while, with suitable regimen, suggest themselves.† But if the catarrhal attacks continue, the natural results follow ; one of the chief of which is the gradual collection of mucous secretion, more or less dense, within the tympanum.

* Two such cases are related in the Guy's Hospital Reports for 1865.
† Turpentine in full doses has been much recommended by Weber-Liel for the acuter forms of tympanic inflammation.

CHAPTER VII.

(a) *Accumulation of Mucus in the Tympanum.*

THIS result of the milder and more chronic forms of catarrhal inflammation of the tympanum comes before us in two forms, or rather stages; those, namely, of recent secretion and of old accumulation. Every case of catarrh, in which the secretion does not discharge itself thro' the membrane, or completely escape by the tube, presents the former condition. In how large a proportion of cases the latter condition—that of old accumulation remaining after all inflammatory action has ceased—exists, and constitutes a main cause of impaired function, is a question for the future. My own little experience would tend to assign it a very important part.

For recent collections of mucous secretion in the tympanum three methods of treatment are presented for our choice; two that seek to effect the removal of the fluid, and the ordinary treatment, relying on general means, and seeking to induce its escape or re-absorption. I do not feel that the question between these methods is yet decided. Under the latter, more or less success for the time can almost always be gained; but the point that

needs decision is whether the results are permanent.
When the appearance of the membrane, the sound on
inflation, the history of colds, the condition of the throat,
indicate that swelling and congestion of the mucous membrane of the tympanum with excess of secretion are
present, certain remedies are obvious : occasional inflation with Politzer's bag ; iron, or nitrate of silver, or spray
to the naso-pharyngeal mucous membrane, or syringing
of alum, &c., thro' the nostrils ; counter-irritation, very
slight but long continued ; the use of an ointment containing pot. iod., with tincture of capsicum, behind the
jaw ; and purgatives combined with steel and other tonics.
To these may be added, in the more confirmed cases,
an injection into the tympanum, once or twice a week
for a few times, of a warm solution of sulphate of zinc,
gr. i.—ii., ad ℥ i. Nor will these means often palpably
fail, altho' their use may be very tedious, and relapses
will be very apt to occur. It has appeared to me,
indeed, that the presence of an excess of secretion
in the tympanum has kept up the irritation in the throat
and prevented it from subsiding, as if there were a
nervous sympathy between them. But supposing the
treatment to have been apparently successful, little doubt
can remain that if the secretion have been profuse and
viscid, it will not have been entirely absorbed, nor probably
have completely escaped by the tube, so that there will still
remain a certain residuum of the more solid portions, which
may lay a basis for permanent deafness in the future.

Accordingly two methods have been proposed for the evacuation of the secretion: one, the incision of the membrane, revived recently by Schwartze; the other the introduction of a very thin elastic catheter thro' the Eustachian tube completely into the tympanum, to withdraw the contained secretion by suction; suggested by Weber-Liel. Of these two plans, both having their advocates, I should certainly incline to the incision, as being, if more formidable in sound, certainly less irritating in reality, and likely to be much more effective.

Schwartze has most fully reported on incision of the membrane in this class of cases. Out of 163 of his cases only five remained quite unimproved; and 87 were "completely cured."—The incision was repeated in 47 cases only; in 16 cases the treatment lasted only eight days, and only in 23 did it extend over four weeks; showing a great advantage in point of brevity. The operation was repeated twelve times in one case, with the use of various solvents, with no benefit but *without ill effect*. But Schwartze has found irritation (without permanent mischief) follow in every fifth case; tho' Politzer, in 220 cases has never seen inflammation follow. Also, without any local irritation, he has seen on the third day fever with frequent vomiting, in a child, without any apparent cause. In one case also, in which I incised at the same time both membranes in a young child, in a case of intense deafness, convulsions occurred on the next day, but with no permanent ill result. I do not now incise both membranes at the same time, or very rarely indeed; but Schwartze not only does this in cases of double disease, but even incises sometimes a healthy membrane for the sake of being able better to pass fluid thro' the Eustachian tube of the diseased side : so convinced is he [and, indeed, so far as my observation goes, truly convinced] of the harmlessness of the proceeding.*

In most chronic cases, Schwartze finds the secretion not muco-purulent but purely mucus; and it is not found that serous and mucous accumulations respectively are characteristic of acute and chronic inflammation. It is often very tenacious, drawing out into long threads like isinglass. It contains numerous cells like white blood-corpuscles, mucous corpuscles in all stages of destruction, some squamous epithelium, and often cholesterine. Sometimes it is citron yellow from previous destruction of the corpuscular elements; or grey from black pigment. In 97 chronic cases, the contents were serous in 8; sero-mucous in 14; purely mucous in 67; muco-purulent in 8. Carbonate of soda has no effect on lumps of the mucus, but they dissolve in a few minutes in a 3 or 4 per cent. solution of caustic soda. It has an alkaline reaction.

If after closure of the wound bubbling is still heard on

* A most exaggerated feeling prevails respecting the danger of making incisions in the membrane, which is curious when we consider how freely the cornea is operated upon. Voltolini in doubtful cases makes an incision to examine the condition of the intra-tympanic structures. It is difficult to keep the cut open for so long as four days.

inflation, Schwartze uses alkaline injections to insure absorption of the remaining mucus or its escape thro' the tube; and if the tube is not freely pervious, weak injections of zinci sulph. may be used to render it so.

The following is a case of this kind in which the treatment was thoroughly successful, while no other means seemed to me to afford any real hope.*

Repeated attacks of tympanic catarrh on each side; at length bulging of the right membrane; incision, and escape of much thick matter; return after nine months; re-incision; permanent recovery.

H. C—, healthy and strong, but with a decided hæmorrhagic diathesis, frequently suffering from epistaxis which ceased only on his becoming faint. No deafness in the family; his own attacks most frequently following bleedings of the nose. At the age of four or five he had a slight discharge from one meatus, and had been occasionally hard of hearing at that time and since. At nine he had an attack of deafness attended with pain in the head, especially at the back part, and great tinnitus, with feverishness. Throat relaxed, and tonsils somewhat enlarged. Each membrana tympani appeared dull and rather flattened. Iodine was painted around the ears for a few days. In two months the hearing was nearly perfect; but again fell back after an attack of epistaxis; the ears feeling stuffed and stopped up, and the tinnitus violent; membranes of a pearly opacity. From this attack he soon recovered, and the hearing continued pretty good for about a year, the left, however, being the better; he had occasional tinnitus. During the attacks of catarrh he could not inflate the ears, and on account of the tendency to epistaxis air was not passed in artificially until a later period, and then but seldom and very gently.

June 3rd, 1864 (at age of ten) an attack of fulness and tinnitus in *left* ear. Watch, l. $\frac{3}{40}$ [right, perfect]. Right membrana tympani appeared normal : on the left side the malleus was slightly prominent ; delicate red vessels running beside and in front of it, and radiating to the circumference : at the superior part of the membrane a marking of delicate oval lines, exactly representing bubbles, which doubtless they were, of mixed air and fluid within the tympanum. ·

In a week the left ear had improved, but the right had become affected. Watch, right, $\frac{3}{40}$; left, $\frac{20}{40}$. Right membrana tympani of a dull porcelain-like whiteness, with red vessels radiating over its surface ; malleus white and clear ; behind it at the upper part a small patch of bright redness, and another rather larger in front of it, the surface of the membrane looking red and swollen, but no distinct vessels being traceable there. This appearance ceased after a few days, as also did the appearance of *bubbles* on the left side. By the end of the month the hearing had much improved, and he left town.

In November of the same year (1864), after a nose-bleeding and exposure to draught, he had a slight attack of bronchitis, and the left ear became again affected, but soon recovered. In February, 1865, on the third day of a severe cold in the head, pain and deafness occurred in the right ear, soon followed by a watery discharge. The meatus was somewhat swollen and contained much soft sodden epidermis, hiding the membrane, which was afterwards seen slightly vascular and dull. In a few days there was a little discharge also from the left ear, in each case coming evidently only from the meatus. On March 1st and 2nd, a nose-bleeding, after which he gradually improved. In July he had scarlatina very slightly, the ears not being affected by it.

September 9th, 1866 (æt. 12).—The hearing has been good until about a fortnight ago, when he became very deaf. He had had a severe bleeding a few days before. Hearing now much better ; watch, each ear, about thirty inches. The appearance of the right membrana tympani seemed to indicate a thickened mucous layer ; anteriorly at the upper part was a white circular spot suggestive of a white substance within the tympanum ; and the whole membrane presented a mottled patchy whiteness, evidently seated internally and seen through the external more transparent layers. This was most marked posteriorly and above, where it formed a broadish crescent. Concavity not excessive. Left membrana tympani appeared healthy ; being compared with that of a well-hearing brother.   Liniment of ammonia and iodine.   Alum by spray-producer to the throat and nose.

January 2nd, 1867.—He recovered soon from the last attack, and remained hearing fairly. Two days ago, however, he had a severe nose-bleeding, and last night was kept awake by pain in left ear. Watch, right, $\frac{20}{40}$; left, $\frac{5}{40}$. Right membrana tympani appears less white than on the last report ; left meatus swollen a little, and near the membrane its posterior wall is red. The posterior portion of left membrana tympani is of a dark frosted aspect, the malleus appears only as a broad red streak. A chlorate of potash lotion was used and counter-irritation ; and this attack also subsided.

On November 4th, however, he had epistaxis, and again after a week ; and immediately after the second bleeding he had a slight ear-ache on each side, and became deaf. I saw him on the 18th ; throat a little tumid ; left tonsil somewhat large. Watch, right, two inches ; left, four inches. The right membrana tympani presented a distinct bulging of circular form, occupying all the posterior superior part, and of a silvery white surface (like very fine "ice-glass") : the lower portion of the membrane was flat and of a pale violet hue ; malleus visible only as a red streak ; posterior wall of meatus also red.

An incision was made, about a line in length in the most bulging part, and a little fluid escaped ; but on passing air on Politzer's plan a large quantity of dark-coloured viscid mucus began to run out of the meatus. The inflation was repeated three times and fully a drachm of mucus was removed. The hearing rose to fifteen inches. A small blister. Alum in powder to the throat. Tinct. ferri perchlorid. M x, ter die.

The next day the orifice was closed, at least air could not be passed through it ; and the hearing had again diminished. The malleus and the meatus were less red. In the position of the former bulging was a shallow oval depression, bounded above by a broad white curved ridge. On inflation this was blown out into a bladdery appearance. On the fourth day no scar was visible ; but the bulging had re-formed, projecting below into a small white nipple. He could inflate the ear. Watch, four inches. On the fifth day, the bulging being very decided, I again incised the membrane, and again there escaped—after his own inflation—a large amount of similar viscid mucus, scarcely less than before. Watch, fifteen inches. Fluid continued to escape for some hours, but had ceased on the next day ; he blew through the orifice a small bubble of mucus. Membrana tympani flat and white ; watch, twelve inches. The second incision healed in two days, its position being marked by a thin depressed oval spot, to which a small red vessel ran from the posterior border : superior part of the membrane white and thick ; lower portion healthy. Vascularity of malleus almost disappeared. At first the membrane bulged on inflation into a bladdery projection, but this ceased in a few days, and the hearing, which had again sunk to two inches, gradually rose. A severe nose-bleeding which now occurred did not interfere with the progress of the case, and in the course of a month the hearing had become quite good ; watch six feet.

August 10th.—Nine months after, during a severe cold, deafness returned in the right ear, and on examination the membrane was seen again to be bulging in the same position as before. This was incised again with a similar result, closing in thirty-six hours. The patient went on the third day to Scotland, where a discharge continued for fourteen days. On October 25th the hearing was found perfect. Watch between five and six feet ; membrana tympani healthy, with the exception of a whiteness at the upper part.

During this attack the left ear showed no very distinct signs of fluid ; the membrana tympani was white posteriorly and appeared slightly prominent, but was thin and indrawn anteriorly. Redness along malleus. After a few days he was able to inflate the tympanum, and the hearing gradually returned. Six years after, his hearing continued perfect.

It is interesting to note, as bearing upon the question of the tendency of inflammatory affections of the tympanum to implicate the labyrinth, that during one at least of these catarrhal attacks the hearing of the tuning-fork placed upon the head was to a certain extent diminished, returning again as the other symptoms disappeared. During the last attack, also, closure of each meatus *diminished* instead of increasing the sound of the tuning-fork upon the head.

How far the mucous accumulation in the right ear was merely a recent incident, or a gradual result of the repeated attacks of tympanic catarrh, the evidence does not suffice to show. My own impression would be that it had gradually collected during a considerable period,

L

doubtless with intervals of diminution. The position in which the bulging presented itself was decidedly in the superior part of the membrane.

A still more chronic case of an essentially similar sort came before me in the following instance.*

Deafness, with recurrent attacks of inflammation in each tympanum, since scarlatina six years previously. Evacuation of small dense masses of mucus by incision.

May 14th, 1868.—M. G—, æt. 12, a healthy boy; at age of 6 had scarlatina, followed by discharge from the right ear lasting only about fourteen days. Ever since he had been decidedly deaf in the right ear, and, with the exception of two years, had been more or less so in the left, and subject also to frequent attacks of pain, during which any sound as music, &c., became painful. Yesterday he was so deaf that he did not hear an express train passing. My watch was heard on contact on the right side, and $\frac{1}{15}$ on the left; the tuning-fork was heard well upon the vertex, louder in the better ear. Each membrane appeared very concave, especially the right ; and on this also there existed a small white *dimple* anteriorly, apparently a healed perforation. The throat was turgid and pale. He could not inflate the tympana. Air was blown through the Eustachian tubes while he swallowed, without much difficulty, entering the tympanum with a sharp sudden sound, and improving the hearing on the right side to three inches, and on the left to twenty-four, the membranes appearing afterwards convex posteriorly. Ferri perchlor., Lin. Iodinii. Salt and water to be drawn through the nose.

In a week the improvement only partially continued, and the inflation was repeated, again with advantage, the sound on the entrance of the air being a moist squeak. He went into the country, where deafness returned in three weeks. It was again removed by inflation on four or five occasions in the course of four months ; general treatment and appli-

---

* See Atlas, Plate XIV., figs. 1 and 2.

cations to the throat being carefully carried out. But the effect of introducing air into the tympanum became less with its repetition. The sound was always sharp and moist. In November he had an attack of pain in the right ear; treated by two leeches, fomentations, &c.

Jan. 4th, 1869.—I saw the patient with Dr. Bickersteth, of Liverpool. The right ear had remained very deaf, and had lately been subject to pain again; the left ear for three or four days had been in acute pain, attended with some discharge, but not relieved by it. Watch not heard on right side, and only in contact on the left. The right membrane was of a dull grey, and somewhat prominent posteriorly. The left meatus was red, and covered with loose flakes of epidermis. The membrane was red and swollen, and bulging posteriorly. Inflation again improved the hearing somewhat. A leech was applied below the left ear, a solution of bicarbonate of soda syringed through the nostrils daily, a lotion of borax and opium poured into the left ear, and an ointment of iodide of potassium and aconite applied around it. The ears to be inflated every alternate day.

In a week he was much better, the redness and pain were gone; watch heard at each side at fourteen inches. As, however, I had formed the decided opinion that the continued liability to pain and deafness depended upon the presence of retained secretion in the tympanum, and that its removal afforded the only prospect of permanent benefit, I made the usual incision in the right membrane, viz., between the positions of the malleus and incus, and extending nearly from the upper to the lower border of the membrane. I then, after passing air through the Eustachian tube, syringed through it, by means of the catheter and an elastic bag, a solution of sodæ carb. (gr. xx. to the ounce). The effect produced by this was that there protruded from the incision a white shining mass, which partly receded on ceasing the pressure, and that neither air nor fluid could be passed through it. The orifice was, in short, evidently filled by a firm substance, the appearance being that of fluid enclosed in a membranous bag. For the next four days the injections of air and solution of soda through the Eustachian tube were repeated, and with the effect of washing out, through the perforation, small dense masses of white mucus; on the fifth day the incision was healed. The same treatment was then adopted for the left ear, and with very similar result. At first, on injecting the liquid the incision became plugged, but after repeatedly passing air into the tympanum, a small viscid mass, about the size of a pea, escaped. The incision healed on the third day. The improvement of the hearing on each side was decided, but not complete, and it appeared evident to me that part only of the abnormal contents of the tympanum had been removed; accordingly the incision was repeated, and with precisely similar results—the gradual forcing out of small dense masses of mucus—twice more on each side. No irritation whatever followed, and the hearing of both ears became, so far as I could judge, absolutely perfect, the lowest whisper being heard at a distance of six yards. It was striking to observe, indeed, how perfect the hearing remained, even immediately after the solution of soda had been passed freely through the tympanum. The filling of the ear with the liquid evidently did not even for the moment impair the transmission of sound. The right ear, which had been continuously deaf for six years, appears to have recovered as completely as the left.

In this case the membranæ tympani exhibited a peculiar degree of relaxation, so much so that they *flapped* visibly and audibly, in and out, as the patient forced air into the tympana or withdrew it. In their usual position they lay nearly or quite in contact with the inner wall of the tympanum, and on inflation started out into a kind of bladder, bulging up around the malleus, so far as almost to conceal that bone. The inflation was attended with a slight improvement of hearing for the time. After the evacuation of the mucus the membranes gradually re$_c$overed their tone, and assumed their normal position.

I believe that relaxation of the membrana tympani, more frequently, however, partial than general, and often accompanied with a distinct *thinning* of its substance, is a very frequent effect of the protracted presence of the mucus within the tympanum. I have, at least, frequently observed the coincidence : nor—apart from the presence of *scars*, which are generally thin—have I distinctly traced a relaxed condition of the membrane to any other cause. This relaxation and thinning of the membrane accompanying the presence of retained mucus, together with the frequent closure of the Eustachian tube, is probably the reason of a fact that would not at first have seemed probable, but which I have continually noticed, viz., that when mucus is present in the tympanum the membrane is more often sunk in, at least in parts, than protruding outwards.

Another point which this case illustrates is the existence of abnormal secretion in the tympanum after a perforation has healed. From many observations I am induced to think that when a perforation is small this frequently occurs, the tendency to heal in the membrane being so strong; hence it is by no means uncommon to find, in an acute attack of catarrh of the tympanum, in which the membrane has given way and, after a discharge of matter of more or less duration, has closed, that after a short interval the discharge recurs, and on examination the orifice is found open.

In both these cases it appears to me that deafness would certainly have become permanent if the dense secretion had not been removed. Not only must it, so far as can be imagined, have clogged more and more the motions of the ossicula, or obstructed the fenestra rotunda, or by its pressure injured the membrana tympani, but the very presence of the secretion within the tympanum appeared manifestly to act as an irritant, and induce repetitions of the inflammatory attacks, which after its thoro' removal ceased to recur.

A farther stage of the same affection is presented in such a case as the following.* A healthy youth, aged 14, the son of a medical man, had been subject ever since he was a child to attacks of deafness during colds. On examination of the ears each membrane was seen white, and somewhat drawn in, while at the posterior superior part there was a thinner and more transparent part thro' which the long process of the incus was not only plainly visible, but almost projecting. On inflation of the ear,

* See Atlas, Plate XVIII., fig. 6.

a very slight improvement in hearing took place, the
sound was muffled and obscure as if the air were forcing
its way thro' a thick substance, and the thin portion of
the membrane bulged prominently out before a whitish
mass. After a little general treatment, incision of the
membrane was performed; the incision being carried, as
I always carry it in cases of *old* accumulations, parallel
and posterior to the handle of the malleus between it and
the long process of the incus, and from about the lower
third of the membrane upwards completely to the superior
border. A little thick mucus escaped, and on renewing
the inflation more protruded. I laid hold of it with a
forceps and drew out from the tympanum a string of
viscid mucus, which extended, without giving way, an
inch beyond the orifice of the meatus. Further quantities were removed on the two days following; no irritation occurred; the wound healed on the fourth day,
and the hearing had become almost perfect. The other
ear was then treated in the same way. I saw the patient
occasionally afterwards, for he was still subject to be
slightly deaf during a cold, but these attacks abated.
Five years after the incision the hearing was good, and
the membrane presented no trace of scar.

In this case there was presented the beginning of a
process which seems to me one of constant occurrence;
the gradual drying up of the viscid secretion into a denser
form, and partial atrophy of the membrane from its
pressure. For, on the one hand, a process of drying up

could hardly fail to occur, both because the more fluid
parts of the secretion would be absorbed, and because the
tympanum contains air not too moist, probably, to have
a drying effect; and, on the other hand, the Eustachian
tube being kept closed by the swollen mucous membrane,
the membrana tympani would be drawn inwards, and so
pressed upon the hardening mass. The position of the
thinned part of the membrane at the upper and posterior
part was characteristic.

Bearing in mind these natural results of collection of
mucus within the tympanum, it seems to me that its effects,
as they are presented in practice, may be clearly traced out,
and the very varied appearances which they present understood. I have enumerated some of these in speaking of
the general diagnosis, but no catalogue could detail them.
They are, every form and degree of thinning, thickening,
discoloration, bulging out, sinking in, and distortion of
every kind, which a thin and delicate membrane can
undergo from vascular derangement, local pressure, agglu-
tination with irregular structures behind it, a constant
weight of atmospheric air without, and sudden and
irregular impulses of air from within, and the shining
thro' it of variously coloured fluids. But it should be
remembered that owing to the almost constant closure of
the tube in confirmed cases, sinking in of the membrane,
and especially a strong depression of small portions, is
a much frequent condition in long-standing accumulations
than the opposite condition of bulging. But a distinct

protrusion of a thinned portion of the membrane on inflation, not rapidly receding, and revealing a yellowish colour within, may be taken as a conclusive sign.

Sometimes, however, dense mucus is present, and impairs the hearing when no sign of its presence is visible in the membrane, which may present merely a uniform whiteness and flatness, such as might naturally be ascribed to chronic thickening; and no characteristic sound may be given by inflation. At other times a more local whiteness posteriorly gives a more distinctive indication. In some such cases I have acted upon the history alone; in one case in particular with most marked and immediate success, a large mass of yellowish mucus being at once removed with very great improvement; the history being distinct that the deafness came on gradually during a cold caught by falling into a stream. The incision is so free from danger that any just ground for believing that collected secretion is the cause of the symptoms fully justifies the attempt to give relief by means of it. Indeed the case in which I gained at once the most striking results and most instruction for myself, was one in which (having then had little experience in the plan) I incised the membrane with no distinct reason, but merely in a kind of despair. The case was the following :—

Extreme deafness, greatest on the left side ; disease of the tympana, complicated with nerve affection ; evacuation of semi-solid masses from the left tympanum by incision; partial improvement.

January 18th, 1868.—Miss S. A., æt. 24, healthy, but rather weak; about ten months previously subjected to severe mental shocks, which, however, have left no indications of general nervous derangement. Six years ago had rheumatic fever; for about two years subject to severe vertex headaches. About nine months ago the left ear became deaf, with severe tinnitus. She had a cold, and spoke thickly at the time; shortly before, she had suffered from giddiness. This and the headache became better at a water-cure establishment where she went three months ago. Shortly after, the right ear had also become deaf. The deafness varies much in the right ear; when she is most deaf she sleeps much: hears better in a noise. Catamenia regular; throat tumid, and often relaxed. She required a loud voice on the right side; on the left no word could be understood, nor could she hear a piano. The crack of the nails was heard on the right side at fifteen inches, on the left at two. One of König's large tuning-forks was not heard on the head, and very imperfectly on the teeth; best on the right side; closure of the meatus increased the sound slightly on the right side, not on the left.

Right membrana tympani of dullish-grey hue, except a small spot anteriorly, which appears thin and relaxed. Can inflate the right ear, the membrane yielding slightly, without effect on the hearing.

Left M. T. of an uniform dull white appearance, slightly flat. Tympanum not inflated: air passed on Politzer's plan entered the right ear only.

Tonics were given; iodine and ammonia applied externally; Politzer's inflation used to the right ear, and the left Eustachian tube opened by the catheter and bougies; vapour of iodine, and afterwards a solution of hydrochlorate of ammonia (gr. v.— xx.) were introduced into the tympanum. In three weeks both ears were improved; on the right side a moderate voice was heard with ease, and the watch at four inches; with the left she could hear distinctly-spoken words, and the watch on contact. The hearing, however, was subject to very sudden and rapid variations, apparently of a nervous character. Air blown into the left ear entered with a slightly moist sound, and the membrane would sometimes bulge strongly, with a thick white aspect, around the malleus.

In about six weeks, soon after hearing of a very affecting death, she became a good deal worse again in hearing, and again came to me. Watch just heard on right side ; left ear about as at first. She was seen with me by Dr. Hughlings Jackson, who discovered no indications of general nervous disease. *R* Pot. Bromid. gr. x. ; Liq. ferri perchlor. ℳ. x. ter die. Alum and sugar in powder to the throat daily. A solution of Ammon. hydrochl. injected into left tympanum three times a week.

On the tenth day, as that ear was practically useless, I incised the membrane posteriorly. There was scarcely any pain or bleeding, and the membrane felt tough and resisting. No fluid escaped ; after using Politzer's inflation there seemed to be mucus *at* the wound, but none came through it. Accordingly, a solution of iodide of potassium was syringed through the ear by means of the Eustachian catheter, with the effect of washing out a mass of firm solidified secretion, of a dry white colour, nearly as large as a pea. On the two following days, three more similar masses were in like manner washed out of the tympanum, the whole forming a mass as large as the kernel of a nut. In two days the orifice had closed. The hearing at once improved, becoming about equal to that of the better ear at her first visit. She was able, also, to hear with the left ear the upper notes of the piano correctly; the lower ones were also heard, but without any musical tone. The right ear had also improved again ; watch four inches. She left London, the medicine being continued ; solution of soda syringed through the nose, and afterwards sulphuric acid spray employed. Since this time the hearing has varied, though it has been on the whole much better. Subsequently the symptoms many times returned, incision of the left membrane having been repeated with excellent results, the hearing becoming "very good." The right membrane also was incised, and some mucus, less dense, removed, with improvement. But great variations, apparently connected with nervous conditions, supervened after a few years.*

In this case the mingling of tympanic and nerve symptoms will at once be recognised. The deafness was

---

* The *right* membrane is shown in the Atlas, Plate XIX., fig. 1. The left membrane, behind which the densest masses of mucus lay, was very similar in appearance.

not greater at the catamenial period; there was no mark of hereditary disease. I would suggest whether the pent-up secretion within the left tympanum may not have had much to do with putting the nervous apparatus out of gear; and whether scientific surgery would not have demanded its removal at a much earlier period.

Equally dense masses I have never since removed, but I think this may be partly due to the fact that I have almost always adopted the plan of using injections of iodide of potassium for several days before making the incision. I have a suspicion, indeed, that in at least the greater number of the cases in which alkaline solutions injected into the tympanum improve the hearing (and these are very numerous), the improvement is due to softening of dried up mucus. But this needs further investigation. Another characteristic case´ is the following :—*

Catarrh of each tympanum; mucus remaining in the cavity; incision first of the right and afterwards of the left membrane; complete recovery.

Harriet C—, æt. 48, unmarried and somewhat delicate, living in a damp situation, applied to me on May 16th, 1868. Her hearing had been quite good until December last, when, during a severe cold, she became gradually deaf with some pain, but not severe, in the throat and ears. She had been carefully treated with applications of nitrate of silver and other means, and had tried change of air. The throat had become much better, but the deafness, though better at times, continued

---

* See Atlas, Plate XVI., figs. 1—3.

on the whole unchanged. She required a raised voice ; watch heard only on the left side, $\frac{1}{20}$. The tuning-fork was well heard on the head, loudest on the left side. The membrana tympani on each side was bright and thin, extremely concave, the malleus running almost horizontally backwards ; on the right side it had a translucent pink hue, but the outline of the tympanic wall was distinctly visible. The Eustachian tubes were impervious, but on using Politzer's inflation, air entertained each tympanum with a faint moist sound, causing a slight bulging of the membranes, and the appearance of a yellow fluid within. The hearing was improved : watch, right, one inch ; left, five inches.

A solution of soda to be syringed through the nostrils ; a liniment of iodine, ammonia, and chloroform; potassæ chlorat. gr. x. acid. hydrochl. ɱ. x. ter die.

May 18th.—The improvement continues in part ; the membranes are less drawn in, but the fluid behind them is still more plainly visible. On inflating the ears the hearing rose on the left side to twenty-four inches ; on the right to two inches only. The case appeared to me a very suitable one for testing the treatment by incision, especially as each ear presented a similar condition, but to a greater extent on the right side ; and as the patient came from the country it was desirable not to delay. Accordingly an incision, one line and a half in length, was made in the right membrane at the inferior and posterior part, and on the patient forcing air through the drum, a limpid, brownish fluid escaped, to the amount of fully 3ʃs, and ran out of the meatus. At the same time the dark colour disappeared from the membrane, and the hearing rose to ten inches. Powdered alum was applied to the faucial openings of the Eustachian tubes. Cont.

19th.—Thick white mucus was blown out from the right tympanum (by Politzer's inflation) through the incision. The appearance of fluid behind the left membrane was more marked.

20th.—The incision had closed ; air blown in entered with a sharp dry sound, but there appeared at the upper and anterior part a bladdery swelling of red colour, about two lines in diameter. This swelling was incised, a little thin reddish fluid escaped, and it entirely disappeared. Watch, each side, thirty-six inches.

On the 22nd the patient returned home, hearing moderately well on each side, though by no means cured of the disease. The inflation of the tympanum was not repeated, owing to the effect it had produced on the right ear. She was directed to continue the treatment and to return in three weeks.

On June 13th, accordingly, I saw her again. As was to be expected, the hearing had fallen back, but the right side (the one operated on) was now the better, and was considerably better than at the first visit. This was not the case with the left. Watch, right, one inch ; left, contact.

The right membrane was of a dull patchy white colour, a good deal drawn in anteriorly ; the left was as much drawn in as at first, and presented the dull dark colour of fluid within. Eustachian tubes impervious. On inflating the ears, the hearing rose on the right side to thirty inches, on the left to five inches only, and a distinct bulging presented itself at the posterior part of the left membrane.

The advantage of the previous incision being thus in my judgment sufficiently proved, a similar one was made in the left membrane, and a brown limpid fluid escaped. After repeatedly passing air through the tympanum, the hearing rose to twenty inches.

From this time the *right* ear continued quite well, the Eustachian tube remained pervious, and the hearing good ; fully forty inches for the watch. On the left side a boil formed in the outer part of the meatus, causing a good deal of pain. The incision closed on the fourth day, although air was passed daily through it, but another bulging of the membrane formed on the tenth day and was incised, giving exit to a large quantity of viscid mucus. A solution of carbonate of potash was syringed from the meatus through the Eustachian tube into the throat. On the twelfth and fourteenth days more mucus was evacuated by means of Politzer's inflation, the secretion being so viscid as to clog the orifice in the membrane. At the end of three weeks there was no longer any appearance of fluid ; the membrane had regained its natural curve, though not its perfect transparency ; the Eustachian tube was pervious, and the hearing, although not quite equal to that of the right ear, was entirely satisfactory to the patient ; for the watch $\frac{30}{40}$.

In this case the advantage of the treatment by incision of the membrana tympani seems proved by the comparative progress of the disease on the two sides. In fact, at the time when the ear first treated by incision was fairly well, the other remained practically in its original condition ; and this although the case was comparatively recent, and the coincident affection of the throat, or at least of the pharynx, had been subdued. The patient suffered under a long-standing relaxation of the mucous membrane of the larynx.

It will be observed that the hearing was temporarily much improved, in the ear in which the incision was deferred, by the mere inflation of the tympanum with air, but that this effect was only temporary and could not be reproduced at a subsequent period, and, also, that though the ear last incised (the left) was on the first visit the less affected, yet— possibly from the longer continuance of the viscid mucus within the tympanum—its treatment was the more tedious of the two, repeated incisions being needed. After the evacuation of the mucus the deafness on the right side partly returned (as was indeed to be expected), but it was due merely to a closed condition of the Eustachian tube, and was removed at once, and permanently, by the introduction of air into the tympanic cavity. The patient subsequently died from cancer of the throat.

In this instance good success attended the incision altho' the circumstances were very unfavourable. But it is not only for the sake of the hearing that the evacuation of inspissated secretion from the tympanum may be needed. The most serious symptoms may apparently be relieved by means of it.

Inflammation of the left tympanum, with discharge, five years before; partial recovery; twelve months ago return of discharge from the ear, with pain extending over the head; three " epileptic" fits; polypus in the meatus; membrana tympani incised, and masses of dense mucus removed.

October 9, 1864.—T. N—, æt. 20 ; fair complexion and healthy.

Father lately somewhat deaf ; an elder sister had died from abscess in the brain, caused by disease of the petrous bone, treated as neuralgia. Six months before, he had pain in the left ear, which subsided without discharge. Three months ago there came from it a discharge of matter and blood, which still continues to a slight extent. No pain, but a constant loud noise in the ear, like two men sawing wood. Watch r. $\frac{40}{40}$, 1, $\frac{3}{40}$; right ear healthy : from the left some flaky discharge was syringed, and the membrane presented a peculiar appearance, due partly, as it afterwards appeared, to a collection of epidermoid scales at the upper part, surrounding a depressed spot, possibly a minute perforation, but no air escaped on inflation. The rest of the membrane was rough and somewhat red, and irregularly drawn in. On inflation, air entered with a harsh clap ; the hearing being somewhat improved, and the tinnitus rapidly ceasing. He was treated with lotions, applications to the throat, repeated inflation of the tympanum, and iron and quinine ; the discharge entirely ceased ; the hearing rose to eight inches ; the membrane became of natural appearance, except just above the short process, where there was visible a small, dark, shining spot, surrounded by a dull white surface, like a depression with raised edges. (In all probability the dark spot was the enlarged foramen of Rimini, and the white ring around was constituted by matter collected around the neck and head of the malleus.) The ear felt quite well, the health stronger, and the hearing sufficiently good. On the 12th of February, 1865 (two months later) the condition was the same.

I did not hear of the patient again until the 14th of September, 1869, when he came to me suffering considerable distress, and with the following history : Until about twelve months before he had continued well, then without cause the discharge returned from the left ear, and it became very deaf. There was no pain for two months, then it became severe, but did not seem deep in. Tinnitus was present then but had now ceased. Six months ago he became very ill, having severe shivering and fainting. His medical attendant states that he had at that time two "fits" of decidedly epileptic character, and a few slight ones since. There was no pain in the ear then, but the day before he became ill the discharge ceased, and it returned as he got better. The ear was tender after lying on it. Lately he has had pains drawing across the forehead and concentrating themselves in the ear, lasting a day or so. He was blistered, and brought under the influence of Ung. Hydrarg., and then the head symptoms ceased.

A polypus, about the size of a horse-bean, was found growing from the upper part of the membrana tympani and adjacent roof of the meatus. This was removed, and the upper wall of the meatus being red and swollen and very tender, an incision was made along it through the periosteum. The bone was not rough. The membrane was not perforated. Air entered, when blown in, with a loud moist sound, increasing the hearing to four inches for the watch. The incision of the meatus gave partial relief, but as there was evidently fluid within the tympanum, the membrane was incised on the next day, and a solution of soda syringed through the cavity of the meatus. On two successive days this brought away a large quantity of tenacious mucus of dark colour, with a complete sense of relief to the head, and immediate improvement of the hearing to twenty inches. In five days the membrane was healed, and under the application of chloroacetic acid the polypus had entirely disappeared in a fortnight more.

Four years afterwards this patient called on me for a trifling catarrhal affection. The ear had continued healthy, and he had had no more giddiness or pain.

Quite lately I have carried out the same treatment in the case of a Catholic priest, aged 32, whose case presents a few peculiarities. He first called upon me in the year 1871, having then been becoming deaf about four years, chiefly on the left side. The deafness began with an attack of pain and discharge, apparently brought on by sea-bathing. The membranes were of white and thick appearance, especially on the left side. Watch r. $\frac{6}{40}$; l. $\frac{1}{40}$. Tuning fork fairly heard, alike on each side. A constant humming tinnitus, and on the left side *an occasional sound like a musical note caused by any metallic musical sound or by shaking the head. These ceased later,*

on the incision. Politzer's inflation and injection of sodæ
bicarb. into the left tympanum produced a little improvement, and incision of the left membrane was proposed, but
deferred. Two years afterwards he returned: the deafness had considerably increased: w. r. $\frac{2}{10}$ l. contact.
The left membrane was incised, the hearing immediately
rising several inches; the next four days a considerable
flow of yellow viscid liquid took place, and some was
also removed by syringing thro' the meatus. At his own
request, after the left membrane had healed the right was
also incised: a slight improvement took place, but this
was lost after syringing a warm solution of soda thro'
the ear, altho' a discharge of yellowish fluid took place
also on this side, not less, in his judgment, than on
the other. The syringing thro' the ear was repeated
only once, because a slight irritation of the meatus arose
and delayed the healing; and also the hearing became
very much more impaired. A loud click of the nails
was heard only at a short distance, and the tuning fork
was heard decidedly best on the left side, thus giving an
indication in respect to the right side that usually im
plies an affection of the nerve. This condition continued
for nearly a fortnight, when, the membrane having healed
for some days, I injected again [at the patient's own
suggestion] a warm solution of pot. iod., gr. v.—ʒj; an
immediate improvement followed, and after it had been
repeated every fourth day for eight times, the hearing had
reached $\frac{48}{40}$ for the watch, and a whisper was well heard

at a distance of five yards: about the same amount of
hearing had been gained also on the left side, and the
patient has continued for five months to be perfectly
capable of work in the confessional.* The chief points of
interest in this case are—(1) the continuous increase of
the deafness until the incision was made; (2) the ceasing
of the musical sound after the incision, and which has not
returned; (3) the apparent severe affection of the nerve on
the right side, after the incision and syringing, which yet
yielded entirely to a few injections of the tympanum.

One other case I may briefly report. It is that of a
healthy and well educated girl of 17, who had suffered
for about eight months from a feeling of stoppage in the
left ear, " as if something came in it;" for about three
months pain had come on, not constant, but occurring
nearly every evening, beginning in the ear and passing
over the head, sometimes severe : used to fancy she
heard clocks striking; now tinnitus. A year ago_ a
venetian blind had fallen on her head, but with no ill
result. W. r. $\frac{20}{40}$ l. $\frac{18}{40}$. T. F. well heard, loudest on the
right side; closure of the meatus increases its sound on
each side. Right M. T. healthy, the left only slightly dull,
but on inflation air entered the left ear with a louder
and deader sound than on the right; the left membrane
also yielded more before it, and on examination afterwards, at the upper and posterior part, just behind the
short process, there was seen a small whitish prominence

* Eight months after he writes me that the ears still improve.

which seemed to indicate the presence of a dense substance within.* Tonics and general treatment of the
throat were employed, with no effect. Dr. Wilks was
then consulted and found no cause for the pain complained of; but bromide of potassium was given for a
short time. The symptoms, however, continuing unchanged, I incised the membrane, and by syringing thro'
the ear, removed small masses of semi-solid mucus.
The relief was complete, and the hearing became equal to
that on the right side. Twelve months afterwards, feelings of fulness and discomfort were again complained of,
but abated under general management. Whether this
was a case really of hysteria I will not undertake to
decide ; but Dr. Wilks's opinion was that the symptoms
indicated some local cause. When the pain threatened
to return, both the patient and her friends were almost
urgent for a repetition of the operation.

The knife I use is a small lance-shaped one, about
half an inch long, with a light handle. I do not prefer
the handle bent. As I have said, I make the incision
(unless a visible accumulation presents itself elsewhere)
behind the handle of the malleus, between it and the
long process of the incus, and carry it upwards, from
about the lower third of the membrane fully to its
superior border. The object in this is to wash the
mucus well from the *upper* part of the tympanum. I
almost always prepare by injecting some weak alkaline

---

* See Atlas, Plate XVII., figs. 5 and 6.

solution into the drum two or three times a week for six or
eight times, but I am not sure that this is a good plan,
or whether, in some cases, the dried mucus might
not come away more easily if no attempt were first made
to dissolve it.   After the incision, I pass air freely by
Politzer's plan; and then syringe a warm solution of
soda, gr. v.—ʒj completely thro' the ear and tube, in each
direction, generally first from the meatus, and relying most
on syringing in that direction : the head is held slightly
forward, and the mouth open.   (Schwartze, and others I
believe, adopt exclusively the opposite plan, and force
the fluids they use altogether outwards, thro' the tubes,
preferring, accordingly, always to operate on both ears at
once.)

I find a sudden stoppage in the passage of the liquid
thro' the ear a good sign : it seems to imply that the
tube is occupied by a mass too large to pass.   In such
case I never use force; nor of course, unless the tube
is freely open, do I ever attempt syringing in that way.
Very frequently a repetition of the incision is called for,
and I find it better to repeat it than to try to keep the
previous one open when it tends to heal.   I have known
the sixth incision produce a permanent good effect; and
I have persevered in this way, when I have believed that
I have plainly seen masses of mucus within the tympanum, tho' I have failed to remove them.   But I have
adopted the rule never to repeat the incision within
fourteen days of healing.   In one case in which the

effects of the first incision had been excellent, I was
induced to repeat it after five days, and inflammation set
in, demanding in the end an incision over the mastoid
process; but even this did not prevent a strikingly
good result in the end. This is the only case of serious
inflammation I have known to follow the incision; altho'
sometimes the meatus will inflame in a painful way; but
if caution is used in respect to the pressure of the syringe
upon the meatus in forcing the liquid thro' the drum,
this may almost always be avoided. The nozzle of the
syringe I use is made of wood, large enough nearly to fill
the meatus, and is surrounded by a short piece of india-
rubber tubing doubled on itself.

Of course I have failed many times, and often have
selected my cases injudiciously. I believe also it is quite
possible that I may, in several cases, have diminished,
instead of increasing, the hearing. But of such cases I
know of only two : one being that of a gentleman who had
resided in India, and in whom, on account of his nervous
debility, it was doubtless injudicious to have operated.
From one patient, whose membrane I twice incised, I
received, after about eighteen months, a letter containing
bitter complaints of the injury he had suffered, both to his
hearing and his general health ; his better ear, he said,
had been made deaf, and his nerves so shaken that he had
been forced to resign his occupation. Having by a soft
answer succeeded in turning away his wrath, I had shortly
after the opportunity of seeing the patient, when I found

his condition the following:—(1) He was in fair health. (2) The right ear, the one operated on, which had been the worse, was then the better of the two : it was also better than at the time of his first application to me ; having improved from contact to one and a half inch by the watch. (3) The ear that had been the better, and was not touched by me, had sunk from twenty-four inches to contact. (4) He had not become ill till a fortnight after my treatment had ceased ; and the better ear had not begun to grow more deaf until two months after.

But I have failed even in cases in which I have fully expected to succeed, and I do not know the reason ; sometimes when large masses of dense mucus have come certainly from the tympanum (being withdrawn by the meatus), no improvement has followed. And in some other cases, in which, after removal of mucus, a great improvement has followed and lasted for some days, I have not been able to make it permanent. One source of error needs to be carefully guarded against ; it has deceived me two or three times ; namely, that the power of hearing is capable of being really and truly increased by causes which excite general or local nervous irritation. In some cases, tho' I think they are not many, the hearing becomes really better for a time after incision and syringing, simply thro' the excitement of the nerves that is produced. But I do not think permanent mischief need result from this.

In one case in which I failed, I was misled by an

preted to mean the presence of secretion behind it.

Deafness on the right side, eighteen months, tinnitus : incision without effect.

January 26th, 1869.—Mrs. H. J—, æt. 49 ; healthy, not subject to nervous attacks nor to colds ; found herself deaf in the right ear eighteen months ago after a "bilious attack ;" no pain in the ear, but from about that time has been subject to a frequent roaring like the sea. W., r., one inch ; left, thirty inches. Tuning-fork heard fairly on the vertex alike in each ear ; louder on the vertex than before the right meatus ; closing the meatus increases its sound on the left side ; has no effect on the right. R. m. t. moderate curve, of a streaky whiteness posteriorly ; anteriorly of a shining yellow appearance, generally of a *rigid* look. Inflation of air produced no effect. A solution of hydrochlorate of ammonia (gr. x.) with Hydrarg, Perchlor (gr. ½ to the ounce) was injected into the right tympanum by the catheter weekly for seven weeks. The immediate effect was to dull the hearing, but it always fully recovered, and the patient thought she was less affected than usual by a cold which she caught. On April 19th the appearance of the membrane had altered somewhat, and there appeared at the lower and anterior part a distinct yellowish prominence, brightly shining. An incision was made in this part, immediately after which the tinnitus was less, and the hearing slightly improved. Alkaline solutions were syringed through the tympanum for five days, but without effect. The incision healed without irritation, and the hearing continued uninfluenced.*

Here there was a palpable error in diagnosis, but happily no permanent mischief resulted. It is hard to say on reviewing the symptoms whether they most indicate a tympanic or a nerve affection; the "bilious attack" is very suggestive of the latter; but probably a slight tympanic affection existed before, and the patient's

* See Atlas, Plate XVI., fig. 6.

attention was called to her deafness only when the tinnitus set in.

Examinations of the tympanum after death afford
sufficient evidence of the collection of dense mucus as
a fact.

In October, 1863, a boy, aged 6, died in Guy's Hospital three days
after admission, with acute inflammation of the kidneys and broncho-
pneumonia. He had been exposed to the poison of scarlatina about
two months before. The sister did not notice him to be deaf. Each
tympanum was full of a thick, glairy, tenacious secretion, tending to be
purulent on the left side, which was most inflamed. The mucous membrane of the tympanum and mastoid cells was red and pulpy. The
lining of the Eustachian tube near the tympanum seemed healthy ; but
it afforded no exit to the secretion. On introducing the beak of a
catheter into the tube and blowing air forcibly into the tympanum, no
mucus escaped from the tube on the left side, and only a little of the
more fluid part on the right. The membrana tympani was of a pale grey
opacity round the border. On the third day after death the malleus and
incus were freely moveable, but the stapes did not yield at all to gentle
pressure.

Schwartze also says that he has many times, in examining the petrous bone, had to use a scalpel to dissect
away the thick adherent mucus. And the following
case, reported by Dr. Magnus of Kœnigsberg, illustrates
the same fact, as well as an important cause of occasional
difficulty in the use of the Eustachian catheter :—*

The patient was a man, æt. 73, but strong and healthy, affected with
great deafness on each side. The right membrane was dull, and of
reddish-grey colour. On inflation a slight temporary improvement ensued, with a yellowish bulging posteriorly. An incision was made, with

* " Arch. f. Ohrenh.," 1873, p. 255.

escape of a little yellowish mucus, and the hearing improved slightly. This was afterwards repeated with similar results, but Dr. Magnus found that even while the incision was open he could not pass air into the tympanum through the catheter, although the Eustachian tube was proved to be free by the unimpeded and painless passage of a bougie its whole length. Having found it impossible to clear the cavity of the tympanum from its abnormal contents by these means, treatment was discontinued. Eighteen months afterwards the patient died with symptoms among which aphasia was a prominent one. The petrous bone was healthy, but an abscess was found in the anterior lobe of the right hemisphere of the brain. The membrana tympani showed no sign of the incisions. On opening the tympanum it was found full of a mass of tough, yellow mucus, mixed with pus-corpuscles, but odourless, and readily drawing out into threads. It could not be removed either with a camel's-hair brush or by a gentle stream of water, and extended into all the adjacent cavities. The mucus membrane was much thickened; the natural ligaments were swollen into soft masses, which invested the ossicula , and one (which, as formerly described by Dr. Magnus, extends from the anterior ligament of the malleus to the bony portion of the Eustachian tube, and overarches its tympanic orifice) formed a kind of valve to the tube, and accounted for the occlusion.

The extent to which the accumulation may sometimes go, when once it has begun, would certainly astonish anyone who had not witnessed it before. Schwartze speaks of masses hanging down from the meatus to the shoulder, and I have found teaspoonful after teaspoonful come away. It evidently collects, packed away, as it were, in the cavities adjacent to the tympanum. And I have often thought that when a temporary great improvement is gained by the removal of a mass, and is lost again in a day or two, it is very likely to be due to more old secretion welling out of the mastoid cells. But when we recall the enormous amount of muco-purulent secretion that may be poured out day after day by the mucous membrane of the tympanum when exposed by a perforation, no quantity that the cavities can hold, packed away in the most inspissated state, can really seem too great to expect to be present. In old cases, when the tendency to secretion has thoro'ly passed away (and it is of such that I have been chiefly speaking in this chapter), I do not think the incision and subsequent treatment, unless pushed to a great extreme, tend to excite any obstinate discharge.

In conclusion, I quote the following case from Dr. Moos :—*

Catarrh of the Eustachian tube on both sides—Sensation of the movement of a fluid in the ear accompanied by improvement in hearing.—Sensation of resonance.— Paracentesis performed with negative result.

"M., 60 years old, merchant, has suffered for eight months from pain in the temple and forehead, especially over the left orbit, and accompanied by a feeling of pressure in the left eye ; the latter, however, only exceptionally present. From time to time these pains increased, extending to the right side of the head (there were no spots of tenderness). Latterly a sensation of stopping in the nose and in both ears has been added to the other discomforts. (Bromide of potassium, quinine, iron, and the whey-cure gave no relief.)

" 'If I recline my head,' said the patient, 'I feel a movement in the ears, especially in the left one, and the ears are suddenly freed from the stoppage; the longer my head rests, the more free it is. When I awake in the morning my ears are perfectly free and the hearing good ; but so.

---

* " Arch. of Oph. and Otol.," Vol. I., No. 2, p. 595.

soon as I raise my head erect the left ear fills itself, and shortly afterwards the right also, and I hear much worse. The head is never entirely free from pain, not even after long remaining in a horizontal position.' The patient denied ever having had pain in the ears, discharge, subjective noises, or vertigo.

"The examination showed both external ears normal. Both tympanic membranes were slightly opaque ; they remained unchanged when the patient bent his head forward. Watch r. 1½ inch, l. 1 inch ; heard on the head. The tuning-fork was negative in its results. The ordinary voice was heard at from 8 to 10 paces.

"On the patient being caused to place himself in the position above described, a gradual increase in the hearing power followed. It increased in proportion as the head was inclined forwards ; on the right side it became 4 feet for the watch, and 18 paces for a whisper, whereas on the left side it reached the normal standard, 30 feet for the watch.

"The head being returned to an erect position, in a few minutes the same diminution in the hearing power appeared as before the experiment. The remarks with which the patient accompanied the movement of the head were curious. With the head inclined forwards, 'Now the ear is empty.' When in an upright position, 'Now it is filling again.'

"On using Politzer's air-douche he experienced no sensation, neither could I determine any important increase in hearing power afterwards. I now used the catheter, and ausculted at the same time. There was a marked difference between the two sides : this difference was also noticed by the patient. Scarcely any air entered on the right side, and the resulting râle resembled a faint creaking ; the patient had no sensation from it in the middle ear, and the hearing power was not increased. On the left side, on the contrary, I heard as if it were in my own ear, a loud blowing sound, readily perceived by the patient, and unaccompanied by bubbling râles. There was an immediate increase in the hearing distance of from 3 to 4 inches. After the operation there was injection of the manubrial plexus on both sides, but no other change. The rhinoscope showed nothing more than a catarrh of the pharynx. The pharyngeal openings of both Eustachian tubes were small, but beyond this nothing remarkable was observed. By the time of his departure the hearing was the same as before the examination. There was no change in the condition of the head, nor in the resonance of his voice; this latter symptom I had forgotten to mention. He described it very characteristically in the words, 'It often seems to me, when I speak, as if I had an echo on the left side of the head.' The patient perceived no cracking sounds accompanying the movements of the head, swallowing, etc. There was no question of dissimulation.

"Although I doubted the presence of a moveable exudation in the middle ear, certain symptoms induced me to perform paracentesis on both sides. These were: the sensation as of movement of a fluid in the ears, accompanied by marked improvement in hearing; and the sensation of resonance particularly on the left side.

" I performed paracentesis and injected air, which passed through the openings on both sides with a hissing noise, and without the appearance of a trace of fluid, although the air-douche was used several times, and repeated a few hours later. The hearing power remained the same as before the paracentesis.

"No reaction followed the operation, and the patient's condition remained in every respect the same, so that on his departure, after a further period of four days devoted to the treatment of the pharynx, nasal passages, and Eustachian tube, we were both much dissatisfied."

Dr. Moos remarks, "the peculiarity of this case is to me inexplicable." I venture to suggest to the readers of this chapter whether the employment of a stream of liquid through the tympanum after the incision might not perhaps have solved it. The age would certainly have been no obstacle to success; in the case of a man aged 62, in whom the membrane was greatly disorganized, being thinned and very much fallen in, with bulging of yellow fluid on inflation, and in whom deafness had existed several months, incision gave perfect relief, which has continued for more than five years.*

* See Atlas, Plate X., figs. 1—4.

CHAPTER VIII.

RESULTS OF CATARRH OF THE TYMPANUM.

Perforation of the Membrana Tympani.

By classing perforations of the membrane as a result of tympanic catarrh, it is not meant to imply that this disease is their sole cause ; but the proportion of cases in which it is so appears to be so large as to make this arrangement practically true. Of course, the inflammation of the tympanum which occurs in scarlatina and the other exanthemata—by far the most frequent cause of chronic perforations—is included under the term catarrh. The immediate cause of the ulceration of the membrane, however, is by no means to be assumed to be the mere presence, or pressure, of the fluid contained within the drum. Much more probably, not only in the specific fevers, but also in the simplest inflammatory affections, the membrane yields only thro' its own structure partaking in the morbid process.

Perforations of the membrane, occurring with discharge from the tympanum, may be of any extent, except that they are never absolutely complete. They vary from the size of a minute pinhole, up to the entire absence of all but a narrow fringe around the border ; this latter con-

dition being attended after a time with a partial wasting
away of the denuded malleus. But there seems to be no
destruction of the membrane so extensive as entirely to
put aside the possibility of repair. I have only once,
however, witnessed its commencement in a case of almost
total loss. The case was that of a girl aged 9,* who had
been subject to discharge from the left ear since the age .
of 3, ascribed to cold after chicken-pox, a not very unfrequent cause of perforation if the statements of patients
are to be relied on. Twelve months before I saw her
the discharge had ceased for a time (under treatment.of
Dr. Turnbull in Paris), but had recurred, and was very
profuse and offensive. There was removed from the ear
a quantity of black grumous matter, evidently deposited
in consequence of the use of a lotion of green tea which .
had been carried on for several months. Of the membrane
only a narrow rim was left; the malleus, however, was
entire and in contact with the promontory. The mucous
membrane of the tympanum was of a livid red, thick and
spongy, the niche for the fenestra rotunda not distin-
guishable, the head of the stapes just appearing, the
incus was apparently lost. The local treatment consisted
in the application of finely powdered *talc*, mixed with a
small quantity of morphia, which was gently blown into
the ear, to cover all the exposed portion, every third day
for three weeks, the powder being carefully removed by
inflation and syringing before being re-applied. Iodine

* See Atlas, Plate VII., figs. 1 and 2.

was applied externally, and the ear was occasionally
washed out by a solution of zinci sulph. or nitrate of
silver. The spongy mucous membrane assumed a healthy
appearance, pale and dry, and the discharge quite ceased.
The hearing continued about as at first ($\frac{4}{46}$), but the
" cotton wool" greatly improved it. Three years subsequently I saw the patient again ; the handle of the
malleus had partly disappeared ; but there was a distinct
formation of new membrane posteriorly and below,
equalling fully half of the lost portion. It was thin and of
a bluish hue ; and the mucous membrane still exposed
was pale and healthy. The next year the repair did not
seem to have advanced farther.

But a still more complete healing of a wholly destroyed
membrane may take place. Moos* affirms that he has twice
seen the whole membrane destroyed, except the part immediately attached to the handle of the malleus, and that
from this the whole aperture has been closed with new
tissue. A case that I examined in 1865 appeared to be
one of complete formation of a substitute for the
membrane.

. G. F.—, æt 52, a healthy man of dark complexion. When a child,
deafness and an eruption on the scalp alternated with each other.
Remembers that when the head was better he was more deaf. No
discharge for several years ; not much tinnitus. About fourteen years
ago, after looking over some business papers, he became all at once " as
deaf as a post. This happens often." At first my watch was not heard
on either side, but on his pushing the right tragus in a peculiar manner

---

* "Klinik der Ohrenkrankheiten," p. 133.

somewhat upwards and backwards, it was heard on that side at two inches. He can almost always produce temporary improvement in this way. The right membrane was irregularly thinned in various parts, giving the appearance of numerous small depressions, which bulged out on inflating the tympanum and fell back on swallowing. It was also a good deal fallen inwards, and the short process of the malleus projected much. A hard accumulation of epidermis was removed from the roof of the meatus, and the tympanum freely inflated, by which the hearing was much improved, varying from six to sixteen inches. From the left meatus a great accumulation of soft but adherent epidermis was removed, a pale irregular polypoid growth was then seen anteriorly, touching and partly hiding the membrane, which appeared white, of a soft thick look and irregular surface. The tympanum could not be inflated without the catheter, from which air entered it with a loud harsh blowing sound; afterwards a watch was heard one inch, and he could inflate the ear. The improvement continued the next day. The polypus was then removed by Wilde's snare, when it appeared that in the membranous septum which occupied the position of the membrana tympani there was a small orifice, like a pin-hole, previously closed by the polypus; for now when he inflated the ear the air passed out of this small aperture with a whistling sound, whereas, before, the membrane had bulged before it. The polypus itself appeared to have been developed from, or around, a small projecting spicula of bone, which yielded to a slight pressure and came away. On exploring farther, none of the ossicula could be discerned, but in the position usually occupied by the short process of the malleus the probe came in contact with a flattened bony surface. In contact with this was the thick white membrane (covered in parts with flakes of epidermis) which I had taken for the altered membrana tympani, but which on further examination appeared to have a different character. For around the inferior two-thirds of the meatus, in the usual position of the membrana tympani, and just in front of the white septum referred to, there was perceived a rim of thick tough membrane, resembling soaked chamois leather. This membranous rim was about two lines in width, it was firmly attached externally to the meatus, and its inner margin was free. On applying traction to a part of it by the forceps, the patient complained that I seemed to be "pulling away a part of the real organ," different from the pain given by the removal of the polypus or the adherent epidermis. In short, this membranous rim answered, in all respects, to a remnant of the natural membrane attached to the cartilaginous ring, which was plainly visible. But the septum which closed the meatus appeared to be quite disconnected with this. It was attached, inferiorly, evidently *within* the position occupied by the remnant of the membrane, with which it had no visible connection. It appeared like an entirely new formation of thick, strong, though flabby tissue. The next day the small perforation noticed was no more to be seen, the septum bulged on inflation, which slightly improved the hearing, but pressure on the tragus improved it more, raising the hearing distance for the watch to twelve inches. This action made no visible change in the ear, but the effect seemed to depend, in part, on the closure of the meatus, since the presence of even the smallest speculum entirely prevented it. The vapour of acetic ether was passed warm into the right tympanum with improvement of the hearing, and the patient left me with each ear performing its function moderately well. Tonics, with astringents to the throat, and a lotion of carbolic acid to the left ear were advised, but the hearing again diminished, and in five weeks he returned. Watch, right $\frac{3}{40}$, left $\frac{2}{40}$. The left ear had altered considerably; deep in on the floor of the meatus was seen a small polypus, which fell off without bleeding on being touched by a probe. There was a slight milky discharge, on removing which the portions of membrane before described were seen to have become continuous, forming a white soft septum ; no orifice existed. Inflation of each tympanum again restored the hearing; right to fifteen, and left to twenty inches. This was repeated for three days with the injection of acetic ether vapour by the catheter. At the end of this time all trace of the polypus was gone, and the ears appeared in a healthy condition. The septum above described had evidently grown into one with the circumferential remnants of the membrana tympani, forming a complete membranous layer occupying nearly the ordinary position. The line of junction was visible as a slight ridge. The membrane was of an opaque white, soft-looking, but smooth and bright, and fell slightly into vertical folds, especially at the upper part. It was quite insensitive when touched, and fell inwards towards the promontory, which was easily felt by the probe. There was no trace of malleus or the other ossicula.

N

The patient could generally inflate the tympanum, when it yielded slightly, most at the lower part. The hearing was sometimes a little improved by this ; but it became much better at times without obvious reason. Sometimes a little rub of the meatus would improve it ; at others it was better after the escape of a little fluid from the ear. Believing that these variations depended upon the partial loss of the ossicula, and were determined chiefly by the varying position of the membrane in respect to what remained of them, I introduced the artificial membrana tympani, which had a decidedly good effect, though I did not always succeed in placing it aright. With it the watch was heard often at fifteen or twenty inches, and the voice without difficulty.

I am uncertain what construction to put upon the appearances in this case ; whether an almost entirely new septum was formed after loss of the natural membrane, or whether after a partial loss the relaxed central part had sunk back, and so given the appearance of a mere ring of membrane below, with a new membranous formation behind it. The total disappearance of the malleus, and the entire distinctness of the partial ring of membrane from the septum behind, seem to me to favour the former view.

Since nearly the whole membrane may thus be restored, it is easy to understand that smaller perforations are very apt to heal. And it is probable that if fitting care were taken in cleansing the ear and warding off irritation, the exceptions to this rule would be very few. As it is, however, the number of long standing perforations in which the edges have skinned over, and which no treatment yet tried can close, is very great. In most of them there exist also other conditions of degeneration of the remaining portion, such as especially cretaceous deposits ; * and if the discharge is still con-

* See Atlas, Plates IV., fig. 2.—Plates IV. to IX. represent various forms of perforation.

tinuing, the exposed mucous membrane is thick, spongy, and dark red; often protruding fully to the level of the membrane; which also is very frequently relaxed and fallen back. Sometimes a large portion of the membrane will seem to be wanting when it is not, because it has fallen quite in, and has become red and swollen, so as to be undistinguishable from the exposed tympanic wall.* Often also the membrane has contracted adhesions to the ossicula or wall of the tympanum, though this seems to occur more frequently during healing. The scars of perforations are almost always thinner than the natural membrane, the fibrous layers not being renewed; and they are distinguished by a darker, or more transparent, appearance, by being slightly sunk in, and by bulging slightly on pressure of air from within. But even considerable orifices may in the course of a few months so contract that their scars become inappreciable, at least without a lens. I have known an orifice three lines in diameter heal in a man aged 68. It had probably formed two months previously,

The mere loss of part of the membrane (as is now generally known) by no means always much interferes with hearing; tho', perhaps owing to the exposure of the tympanum, the hearing almost always varies a good deal. Sir W. Wilde noticed what seems to be a fact, that tinnitus, at least in a severe degree, is less frequent

---

* Plate IV., fig. 3, represents a membrane in which this had been the case.

N 2

when perforation exists. It is not very rare to find more than one perforation co-existing; I have several times met with three in the same membrane.

In one unsatisfactory case I saw a second quite distinct perforation form.* The patient was a boy aged 10. When I first saw him he had had a discharge from the left ear for two years, since measles. There was a red and slightly depressed surface occupying the upper two-thirds of the anterior part of the membrane, and at the centre of this space the membrane was wanting to the extent of about two lines in diameter. The membrane was white and flat, with a pinkish hue, from congestion of its mucous layer. He did not improve under treatment, and I lost sight of him. Two years afterwards he came to me, having had hooping-cough eighteen months before; the first perforation had scarcely changed, but posteriorly another had formed of very similar size and appearance. The membrane generally had become more white and thick. Treatment was not carried out, owing to the death of his mother from consumption. This fact, indeed, no doubt gives the key to the tendency of the membrane to ulcerate. Often the edges of a perforation are red and swollen, or covered by granulations, or polypoid formations may grow from them; and sometimes the whole surface of the membrane is spongy and red. In all such cases there is generally an insufficient exit for the discharge, and the mucous membrane of the

* See Atlas, Plate V., figs. 1 and 2. See also figs. 3 and 4.

tympanum is also much inflamed : perhaps by its swelling serving to close up the aperture. In such cases, if the orifice is small, the only really effective treatment often is to enlarge the orifice by a small linear incision, and so permit a more complete escape of the secretion.*

In cases also in which there exists a mere pinhole orifice, and irritation and discharge continue obstinately, it is most advisable not to delay too long a similar procedure. Healing has always ensued, in my experience, very quickly on enlarging these minute orifices ; and in one such case, in the son of a medical man, in whom discharge and deafness, with frequent attacks of pain, had continued for two years, and became no better under any remedies I could devise, enlargement of the orifice downwards rapidly induced perfect recovery, and also was followed by a striking improvement in the opposite ear.† This result I have many times known to follow incision of the membrane when it has been really indicated, and has given relief ; namely, that the opposite ear, if it has been in any way affected, has also greatly improved without treatment. So marked has this coincidence been, in many cases, that it seems to me to prove the existence of a sympathy between the two ears in their morbid conditions ; of which there is

* In Plate IX. of the Atlas, figs. 5 and 6 represent a case in which this treatment was employed and its result. Also in the case shown in Plate IV., fig. 4, the same treatment was employed with perfectly good effect.

† Plate IX., fig. 4.

otherwise little distinct evidence. If polypi are developed on the edge of a perforation they should be treated as when they form elsewhere, by removal and caustic, but the latter should not be stronger than the solid nitrate of silver. Undiluted liquor plumbi also is very useful, applied by means of a camel's-hair brush. It is seldom that in such cases the perforation heals; the best result generally attainable being that the edges of the orifice become pale and dry,* and do not, as they skin over, contract adhesions to the tympanic wall or ossicula. The frequent use of the air douche is a means of guarding against this danger.

The following case illustrates fairly well the process of healing in a perforated membrane, and the conditions on which it depends :—†

The patient was a youth, aged fourteen, delicate, and with the tonsils so much enlarged as nearly to meet. He applied to me in October, 1865, for a painful discharge from the right ear, in which, for two or three years, he had been subject, during frequent colds, to deafness. About six weeks ago, while at the seaside, there had come on in it first a buzzing noise, and then a slight aching, followed by a free discharge with a little bleeding. Three weeks ago he had brought up from his throat a portion of the husk of a grain of oats, which he had swallowed a few days after the discharge commenced. It was now expected that the ear would recover, but it did not. Has lately had a series of boils upon the neck. W. $\frac{9}{40}$. The right membrana tympani was anteriorly thick, and of a dull grey hue, uneven, and the malleus hidden; posteriorly, close to the meatus, was a small mass of fungoid granulations, and just in front of these, and partly hidden by them, an orifice

---

* See Atlas, Plate VII., figs. 5 and 6.
† Plate VII., figs. 1 to 4.

in the membrane the size of which could not be determined on account
of the thickened and granular condition of the surrounding parts. He
could not inflate the tympanum, but air inblown passed readily through
the perforation, bringing with it bubbles and mucus, and improving the
hearing to two inches. The treatment adopted consisted of quinine and
iron internally ; nitrate of silver, and afterwards tannin, to the tonsils,
and finally a solution of alum by means of an atomizer ; moderate
stimulus in the form of light claret ; under which the general condition
and the throat gradually improved. For the ear, various cleansing and
astringent lotions were applied : carbolic acid, nitrate of silver, sulphate
of zinc, borax, and opium; the granulations were touched with caustics,
and air was once or twice a week blown through the tympanum to clear
it, while the meatus was filled with an astringent lotion. Improvement
to a certain extent soon followed, the granulations disappeared and the
orifice contracted, but it did not heal, and showed a continually returning tendency to increase again, and to reassume an irritable character,
the fungoid condition of the meatus recurring more than once after the
caustic applications had removed it.

On the 20th of January, upon examining the ear after it had been
apparently thoroughly cleansed not only by syringing, but by the use
of a lotion of sulphate of zinc and by inflation, I was struck by the
continued presence of viscid mucus within the orifice. To remove it I
placed the patient in a recumbent position, filled the meatus with a
warm solution of sulphate of zinc (gr. iv. ad. ℨj), and, causing him to
swallow some water, passed air into the tympanum (on Politzer's plan)
causing it to bubble up freely through the lotion in the meatus. Then
on syringing the ear, a mass of coagulated mucus the size of a grain of
wheat was removed ; but still, upon examining, more viscid secretion
was perceived within the orifice. The same process was accordingly
repeated, and with the same result, *six times ;* until, at last, on so washing out the tympanum nothing was removed. The effect was decided :
the hearing rose to eight inches, and from that time the perforation
progressed uninterruptedly to a perfect healing, the ear being washed
out daily in a similar manner by the patient. Ten days after, the
fungoid condition had entirely disappeared ; the internal wall of the
tympanum, just discernible, was of a red colour and moist ; there was
no vascularity of the membrana tympani, but its external layers were

opaque and thickened, hiding the handle of the malleus entirely, and presenting an uneven flattened surface instead of the usual delicate concavity. Four days later, the orifice had already greatly contracted, and the membrane had become much clearer, so that the malleus could be traced. Posteriorly the epidermis had become thickened, and over-lapped the posterior border of the orifice (at a later period a thick, hard mass of epidermis was removed from this spot). There was very little discharge. The attempt to blow air through the tympanum was gradually discontinued, and ten days afterwards the orifice was entirely healed, presenting the aspect of a thinned and slightly depressed sur-face. This scar gradually contracted, the edges becoming slightly thickened in the process, giving it a crater-like appearance, and six months later the appearance was that of a minute dark speck sur-rounded by a comparatively broad white rim, and on using the lens the dark central spot was seen to be a very thin concave portion of mem-brane surrounded by a raised and thickened ring. The thinned portion, the new scar tissue, bulged slightly when the tympanum was inflated. The hearing was, for the watch, five inches (after inflation, nine) ; the voice was heard moderately well, though not acutely. The hearing had therefore very considerably improved ; but during the early stages of the healing it had for a time diminished. On the left side the watch was heard at fifty inches, or double what it had been.

Seven years afterwards this patient again suffered from catarrh of each tympanum, the membranes ulcerating and becoming spongy. The affection was very obstinate, and enormous quantities of semi-purulent secretion came away ; the right ear, however, did not suffer more than the left, and eventually both healed, with nearly perfect hearing.

In this case I believe the chief secret of the treatment of perforations of the membrane is indicated; namely, the perfect evacuation of the viscid mucus which collects (as it is evident it must) in the various recesses and around the irregular structures of the tympanum, and clings to them in a manner that defies ordinary methods of cleansing. When the membrane is largely wanting, dense masses of mucus may often be seen descending along the inner wall of the tympanum, even after the ear has been well syringed, and as the process of cleaning is carried out, the head of the stapes may often be seen as it were emerging from the dense masses that had enwrapped it. Accordingly I have of late directed my attention, in all cases of unhealed perforation, chiefly to the thoro' cleansing of the tympanum, and use for the purpose the same method as that which I employ after incision ; namely, syringing a stream of warm solution of soda from the meatus thro' the Eustachian tube so as to escape by the nostril. The following case was in this respect very instructive to me :—

19th May, 1870.—Miss A. E——, æt. 11 ; healthy ; between two and three years ago had scarlatina very severely, which left her very deaf, and with a discharge from both ears. For two years she was under the care of one of the most justly respected aural surgeons of the Continent at various intervals ; he had last seen her during the previous July, when the discharge had entirely ceased, and he had said that there was nothing more at that time to be done for her. The deafness, however, continued very considerable, and lately there had been some slight return of the discharge. The treatment had been by the Eustachian catheter and the use of lotions, among which was one of sulphate of zinc.

On examination I found the nervous power on the left side apparently very much injured ; the membrane was extremely collapsed. On the right side my watch was heard at three inches, and the nervous power seemed unimpaired. The membrane was destroyed for about a third of its extent anteriorly. Air passed through the Eustachian tube. Syringing removed only small flakes of recent secretion, but the appearance of the remaining portion of the membrane suggested to me the presence of retained secretion behind it, and the treatment above described was had recourse to. On the first two or three occasions nothing was removed, but an alkaline lotion was employed, and very shortly the solution, as it escaped from the nostrils, brought with it dense brown masses of secretion that had palpably been lying concealed for months. At the same time, on exploring the meatus, the same kind of matter was found to have exuded into the exposed part of the tympanum, and was removed by the syringe. This was continued day after day with the same result, the quantity of the retained matter being quite inexplicable except on the supposition that it had filled the mastoid cells, and was being gradually washed out from thence. Coincidently, the portion of the membrane remaining assumed a more natural appearance, and resumed more nearly its normal position, and the hearing decidedly though slowly improved.

In the autumn the child returned to me; the hearing had remained better; a slight discharge had continued for the most part. On renewing the treatment still more of the same discoloured discharge was removed, and was proved in the same way as before to come from portions of the tympanum inaccessible to syringing. When the whole was apparently removed, alum was substituted for the alkali, and the discharge disappeared.

Since this case, which had been treated according to the very best recognised practice, I have felt indisposed to the treatment of perforations by astringents, until at least I have thoro'ly assured myself of the complete freedom of the tympanum from old discharge. Accordingly I almost always have recourse first to *solvent* lotions, of a mild kind however. (It might be worth while trying weak solutions of caustic soda or potash, which has a really solvent power on mucus.) And then, when the tympanum is clear, I use chlorate of potash, or alum. Of course, unless the Eustachian tube is free no attempt would be made to pass a liquid thro' it; and sometimes there seems to be a resistance in the direction from without inwards, even when air passes freely from within, as if a valvular arrangement existed. In these cases, either the catheter may be used, or the patient may himself pass liquids thro' the tube and tympanum (in the manner described in Chapter IV.). But I seem to have found syringing from without inwards the most efficient. It often produces a slight temporary giddiness, but unless very injudiciously used seems to me to be wholly free from objection. When the tympanum is free from secretion, astringent lotions may be used : sulphate of zinc (gr. ij—ʒj) holds the pre-eminence; carbolic acid or tincture of opium, or both, may be combined with it; or the perchloride of mercury (gr. ½ to gr. i—ʒj) with opium. A little glycerine added to the lotions seems often to add to their efficiency, probably by keeping them longer in contact with the surface. At the same time, if the exposed mucous membrane continues swollen, I paint it with argenti nitr. (ʒj—ʒj) on a piece of cotton wool; and always use cleansing and bracing applications to the throat. Indeed it seems to me that a tympanic affection can scarcely ever be treated thoro'ly without the throat being also directly treated.

Other methods of treatment of perforations of the membrane are, that described above of filling the meatus with a lotion and forcing air into it thro' the Eustachian tube by the elastic bag, recommended by Politzer; or the plan recommended by Schwartze, of introducing into the meatus a solution of nitrate of silver (gr. v.—xl. ad ʒj), and then *blowing* it, by a tube fitting the meatus, thro' the Eustachian tube into the throat; following it immediately by a solution of common salt to neutralise it. This is a plan I find needlessly severe, and the precipitate of chloride of silver, which is formed in all parts of the cavity, seems to be open to objection. But in some obstinate cases it seems useful to force a weak solution of nitrate of silver completely thro' the tube in that way, tho' if the strength exceeds ten grains to the ounce the (English) patient is sure to make great complaint. Of course, if any tenderness of the meatus, or general irritation of the organ exists, no plan that involves any use of force would be employed. But the *local* application of nitrate of silver (ʒj—ʒj) is in almost every case healthful and soothing.

I have mentioned the application of *talc* in powder to the exposed mucous membrane. I often found it successful, before adopting my present methods, and I still have recourse to it in cases that prove untractable. If the powder is blown in so as fully to cover the secreting surface, and carefully removed and renewed every second or third day, the ear being well cleansed and dried before it is applied, it generally brings the tumid and unhealthy parts very speedily into a healthy state. I should prefer it decidedly to the mere use of astringents, but the plan of thoro' cleansing often leaves no necessity for supplementary treatment.

There is another plan I ought to mention, tho' I have neither adopted it nor seen it applied, and it impresses me as needlessly dangerous; but I have heard more than one patient describe it as having been entirely and rapidly successful. It is that recommended a few years ago by the late Mr. Yearsley, of closely covering the discharging surface with a film of cotton wool gently pressed down upon it "almost thread by thread." On the other hand, Mr. Toynbee stated that he had seen cases of extreme irritation excited by it. Mr. Toynbee adopted once a similar method for polypi; namely, applying pressure to them by a small piece of fine sponge, and sometimes with good success; but the same risk would seem to apply to every such procedure.

When healing takes place it is quite common to find a temporary diminution of the hearing, as if from contraction of the scar. This, I think, usually passes off; and as the rule, a thoro'ly treated case of perforation, even of large size, whether it heals or not, if there is no other disease, regains a degree of hearing sufficient for all purposes. If this is not the case the artificial membrane should be had recourse to.

The question whether the ARTIFICIAL MEMBRANE operates by closing the orifice in the membrana tympani, or supporting the ossicula and especially the stapes, is now decided in favour of the latter view; and accordingly

in introducing it I always endeavour to place it in contact
with the head of that bone ; that is, I introduce it along
the roof of the meatus to the superior posterior portion of
the tympanum.   If this fails, however, I do not desist
until I have tried every part.   The wire attached to Mr.
Toynbee's membrane has been deemed objectionable, but
a piece of thread may easily be substituted for it, and a
small forceps used for its introduction.   Another form is
that of a small bladder of thin India rubber, which will
succeed sometimes when the flat membrane fails.   But in
the majority of cases I give the decided preference to the
cotton wool.   A small portion of cotton wool is moistened
and rolled up between the fingers into the form of a
minute egg, then it is taken up by a thin pair of forceps,
which should be of a very slight *spring*, so as not to give
pain, and introduced as above described.   The patient
will become aware if it reaches the right spot by the
change in his hearing, especially if he stands near a clock,
or the surgeon continues speaking.   I use, to moisten
the cotton-wool, a solution of sulphate of zinc in
glycerine (gr. iv.—ʒj), and it can frequently be worn a
whole week without change.   If water is used it soon
becomes dry, and needs to be renewed.   The improvement effected is often wonderful; from a degree of deafness rendering conversation almost impossible, a patient
may be raised in a moment to a state of hearing that
would betray its imperfection only to an attentive
observer.   No case should be abandoned till every form

of the artificial membrane had been thoro'ly tried. The disc used by Mr. Toynbee sometimes, if worn too long, slips off its wire, and requires removing from the meatus; I know of no other disadvantage attending it. The good effect continues indefinitely, and I think that in every case one might say the use of the artificial membrane tends to improve the hearing, and to render the patient more likely to be able to dispense with it. This might be expected, if its action is to keep the loosened stapes in its place. And that it does operate in this way is confirmed by many evidences. For instance, in one case of a man so deaf from scarlatina in infancy that he habitually pronounced words according to their spelling, and whose tympanum was filled with spongy growths, but on whom, after they were removed, the india-rubber discs had a splendid effect, it frequently happened that while I was cleaning out the tympanum, using a camel's-hair brush or rolled-up cotton-wool to dry it, he would exclaim, " I can hear :" and it was evident that the stapes had been touched. To a similar effect in bracing up the stapes, I ascribe the marked result of the use of lotions of sulphate of zinc upon the hearing ; and sometimes the action of the tensor tympani, or stapedius, appears to operate in the same way. For example, in some cases of perforated membrane I have known the hearing to be decidedly better while a bougie occupied the Eustachian tube, as if thro' stimulating the tensor tympani ; and one patient, a young lady, in whom almost all the membrane

was destroyed, but the malleus was still present, found
that often when listening to music she felt a sudden click
in the ear, and heard better.

Accordingly it is not only in cases in which the membrane is partially destroyed that the artificial membrane
is useful; but perhaps scarcely less frequently, upon the
whole, when there has either been no breach of continuity, or it has been restored. And whensoever, with
the appearance of a scar, or of relaxation of any kind,
or collapse upon the tympanic wall, or any mark of
previous disease that may have been attended with loss,
or dislocation, or any degree of loosening of the connections, of the ossicula, the hearing is defective, and cannot
be otherwise restored, a case exists for a thoro' trial of
each form of the artificial membrane.

The appearances presented by healed perforations are
very various. Generally they are simply thinner and
more concave portions of the membrane, but often they
are very different from this. Sometimes the whole adjacent part of the membrane becomes white, thick, and
dense; * at others it seems to undergo a bony degeneration, as in the following case :—†

J. H—, æt. 32, policeman, was knocked down violently in a struggle
with a burglar in November, 1864. A discharge followed from each ear,
most from the left. He suffered much from severe pains in the head and
dizziness, for which, after fourteen months (in January, 1866), he applied

---

* See Atlas, Plate VIII., fig. 6.
† See Plate XXIV., fig. 5.

to Dr. Wilks. For six weeks three grains of Pot. Iod. were given without much relief, when I was requested to examine the left ear. I found a small polypus on the floor of the meatus, close to the membrane, which was swollen, of a dull grey hue, and traversed by congested vessels. Inferiorly was a roundish perforation, the size of a small pea, through which puriform matter exuded ; Eustachian tube not pervious. The hearing was almost abolished, indicating a lesion deeper than the tympanum. A lotion containing Sulph. Zinc. and Morph. Hydroc. (aa. gr. ii.—ʒj.) was dropped into the ear each night, and the medical treatment continued. On the 8th of March, when he was next seen by me, the perforation had healed ; the upper part of the membrane was opaque, grey, flat, and seeming as if fallen in on the internal tympanic wall. Inferiorly the surface was of a snowy white, and slanted obliquely outwards and downwards. The Eustachian tube still did not yield to the attempt to inflate it. Dried secretion was removed. The pain still continued severe about the occiput. On June 13th air was passed (by Politzer's process) into the tympanum, with but slight relief ; the Eustachian tube continued open ; the pains in the head, though diminished, were still often severe ; the hearing had improved a little, so that words could be distinguished, though with difficulty. The tuning-fork, placed on the head, was also heard very imperfectly. The appearance of the membrane had altered considerably. The upper part was transformed into a dense yellowish mass, feeling to the probe like bone ; the short process of the malleus projected strongly in its place, and the handle could be faintly traced below. Inferiorly was a thin transparent surface of scar-tissue, which projected like a bladder on the inflation of the tympanum.

In this case there has been most probably a slight fracture, involving the left tympanum to some extent, and inducing a slight effusion of blood into the upper part of the cavity. The dense deposit in the upper part of the membrane, the great impairment of hearing, and the serious cerebral symptoms, lead me to this view. In other cases of blows upon the head, and notably in that of a railway guard whose head came in contact with a bridge while travelling, symptoms of a similar kind, attended with analogous lesions of the membrana tympani, have come before me, and have gradually abated, apparently being relieved by means which tended to diminish morbid action within the tympanum.

CHAPTER IX.

POLYPI.

ANY form of irritation in the tympanum or meatus may issue in the growth of polypi: tho', as I have previously stated, their most frequent cause seems to be lack of a free escape for discharge. They grow from every part; he external canal, the outer or inner surface of the membrane, the tympanum, and the walls of the Eustachian tube; nor is it absolutely necessary that the tympanic cavity should be exposed in order for them to form within it. No distinct line can be drawn between mere minute granulations and dense growths that may extend from the walls of the Eustachian tube beyond the orifice of the external meatus, but they nevertheless present quite distinct characters in different forms. The most recent and best account of their structure is given in Mr. Dalby's Lectures on Diseases of the Ear, which the reader may consult with advantage. He has found two prevailing forms: most common, an ordinary fibro-cellular structure, the more fibroid and denser the older it was; and less frequently a myxomatous structure, containing large stellate cells, and covered with pavement epithelium. Both of these forms are moderately easy to eradicate; the latter, how-

ever, which grow only from the mucous surfaces, being
the more apt to recur; but there is also a third form,
fortunately much more rare than the other two, which is
very similar to the "round-celled sarcoma," and seems to
possess a tendency akin to that of true malignant disease
to return. These investigations throw great light upon
the very varying results which the treatment of aural
polypi has hitherto afforded; and if they are confirmed
will enable the surgeon to give, by aid of the microscope,
a much more definite prognosis than heretofore. The
cause of the great tendency of aural polypi to recur, however, is not always the nature of the growth, but seems to
be due sometimes to the fact that several coexist from the
first. I have, after removing a small polypus from the
tympanum, syringed out three minute fleshy masses, each
with a distinct attachment. Now and then, but rarely, a
true malignant growth simulates a polypus, and demands
caution in treatment The general cachexia, the pain,
the livid colour, the great tendency to bleed, and the
swelling which is almost always present around the ear,
serve to distinguish the malignant growth. A soft persistent swelling above the attachment of the auricle,
attended with great pain, I have never known except in
malignant disease.

The *diagnosis* of polypus is easy: it is always to be
suspected if with long discharge there coexists occasional
bleeding from the ear; and after syringiing the meatus it
will be seen as a more or less projecting red mass.

When deeply situated, it can sometimes be distinguished from the swollen mucous membrane of the tympanum only by touching with a probe, which should however be done with a clear view and under a good light. It is well always to test the condition of the membrane by inflation; much the most frequently it will be found perforated. Apparent polypi are sometimes granulations growing

FIG. 10.

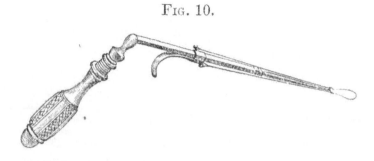

WILDE'S SNARE FOR POLYPI; modified by Dr. Clarke.

from carious bone, and this possibility should always be present to the surgeon's mind.

The treatment of aural polypi is always essentially the same : removal ; thoro' treatment of the Eustachian tube and tympanum ; and applications to the root that shall entirely eradicate the tendency to return. For a growth of any size Wilde's well-known snare, used with jack-line rather than wire, is the most efficient instrument (Fig. 10) ; for small deeply-seated bodies, Mr. Toynbee's ring-forceps, consisting of two fine rings pressed together by a movable tube ; and for growths of larger size situated,

as they often are, in inaccessible corners, various forceps
have been constructed. They should grasp well, and be so
constructed as to open more widely at the end than at any
other part of them that lies within the meatus. The cut
shows one form that I have found useful (Fig. 11). So
much time and pain are saved subsequently by a complete
removal of the growth at first, that I think it is well in a
case of any difficulty to give ether or laughing gas, so as
to be able to take away at once all that can be laid hold

Fig. 11.

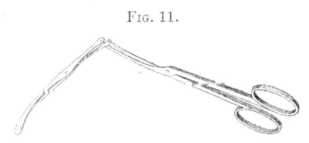

Polypus Forceps; the ends can be made straight, and of
any size.

of. In some cases, where time is no object and the
growth occasions no irritation, something may be done in
the way of deadening and even diminishing the growth by
the application of undiluted liquor plumbi. The removal
is the first (and least) step in the cure. Probably no
pólypus ever existed in the ear without the tympanum
being in an unhealthy state, whether the membrane be
perforated or not. If it be not, most likely on inflation
air will be heard to enter the drum with a moist sound,
the membrane will be injected, or spongy, or thick and

white, and drawn in; the Eustachian tube imperfectly pervious; and the appropriate treatment will be called for. If the membrane be destroyed, in whole or part, the mucous lining of the tympanum will be swollen and congested, and almost certainly masses of accumulated secretion will be present. Indeed very often, and especially when (as frequently happens) intense cerebral distress has been present before the removal of the polypus, thick masses of cheesy substance, of a whitish-yellow hue and offensive odour, will be found pressed up behind it, and will come away for days after on syringing; or instead of a cheesy substance, hard masses of close-packed epidermis, glued together as if by mortar, may be found occupying the whole space of what was once the tympanum, and may require long patience to soften and remove them piecemeal. In all such cases the polypus is threatening the life of the patient. One of the most striking instances I have met with was that of a painter, a man aged 32, who had had a discharge, more or less continuous, from the left ear since scarlatina as a child. He had for years suffered attacks of violent pain in the ear, and had become subject to extreme nervous depression, and inability to attend to his profession. Six months previously a polypus had been removed from the ear with no permanent relief. He could hear on that side only a loud voice close to the ear. A polypus of smooth appearance was seen nearly filling the meatus, and on removing what could be grasped of it by the

snare, a dark hard mass was exposed at the upper part
entirely blocking up the tympanum. Caustics were applied
to the remains of the polypus, and small blisters behind the
ear ; the tympanum was injected about once a week with
a solution of iodide of potassium ; a lotion of the same
was applied to soften the hardened mass, which was
removed flake by flake by the forceps, the process lasting
many weeks ; but even at the last there remained visible
at the bottom of the meatus only a pale red, uneven, solid
surface inferiorly, and superiorly a dark-coloured, dry,
depressed surface, thro' which, however, air could be
blown. Nothing appeared in the slightest degree resembling either the membrane or the wall of the tympanum ;
but, to my great surprise, not only did the discharge
quite cease, and all irritation and nervous distress subside, but the hearing became distinctly very good. A low
whisper was heard at five yards, and the watch $\frac{30}{40}$.

The polypus having been thoro'ly removed and the
tympanum kept clean and free, the application of caustic
will in almost every case restore the diseased surface to a
healthy state. I use the chloro-acetic acid ; and it is
better to apply it for one or two weeks every day, if the
root continues red or swollen. But the length of time
during which caustic needs to be applied varies with every
case ; sometimes a small polypus will come away during
syringing, and not return at all ; at others, six weeks or
more may be needed before a discontinuance of treatment

---

* See Atlas, Plate XXV., fig. 4.

is safe. It is well always to impress on the patient's mind, or his friends', that perseverance till the treatment is completed is absolutely necessary, and that anything less is pain endured for nothing. Merely to remove a polypus and leave it with no further treatment, unless symptoms of irritation render its removal urgent, is to inflict pain uselessly.

The undiluted liquor plumbi may be alternated with the caustic advantageously. Other plans for the removal of polypi have been advocated. One is the galvanic cautery, which, however, seems neither more efficient nor less painful. Another is the injection of liq. ferri per- chloridi into their substance, of which I cannot speak sufficiently. A third is gentle pressure by means of sponge, to which I should never have recourse.

The removal of a completely developed polypus from the tympanum, without any perforation of the membrane, has occurred to me only once. I was quite unprepared for the result, and give an abstract of the case from the " Transactions of the Clinical Society," 1869.

Mrs. H. S——, æt. 44, delicate, but healthy, consulted me on December 12th, 1868.

During a voyage to Australia, sixteen years ago, she caught a violent cold, which caused for the time a loss of hearing, taste, and smell. The taste and smell, and the hearing of the right ear, shortly returned, and it continued fairly good until January, 1869. It was then attacked by severe pain, which, after a few days, was followed by discharge, accompanied at first with a little bleeding. Since this there has been no acute pain, but there have remained more or less constant uneasiness, with deaf- ness, a beating and humming in the ear, and confusion in the head.

The discharge also has continued, and there has been tenderness behind the ear. Lately the glands behind the angle of the jaw have become swollen.

On examination the meatus was seen red and swollen, especially its posterior wall, near the membrana tympani. The membrane was of a dull gray hue, with a patch of vascularity near the centre. It was swollen so that the malleus could not be distinguished, and posteriorly was slightly prominent. At the anterior part was a darker and thinner portion resembling the scar of a former perforation.

A repeater watch was heard only when held close to the ear, but a tuning-fork placed on the head was well heard, and louder on the right (the worse) side, showing that the deafness was due to obstruction within the tympanum. The Eustachian tube was closed, but air was passed through it during the act of swallowing, raising the hearing of the watch to $\frac{4}{40}$.

The upper part of the fauces was washed daily by a solution of soda syringed through the nostrils. A small blister was applied, and a warm lotion of liq. plumbi ℥xx., olei olivæ ℥j., dropped into the ear night and morning.

Some relief was obtained by these means during the next three days; but, judging from the history and the appearance of the membrane that the symptoms were chiefly due to an excess of secretion contained within the tympanum, I made, on the 15th, an incision about two lines in length through the posterior part of the membrana tympani.

Contrary to my expectation, no fluid followed the incision, nor did any escape from the wound when air was passed forcibly through the Eustachian tube; but on examining the membrane after repeating this procedure a few times, a solid mass was seen protruding through the wound. This was afterwards removed by further inflations of the tympanum, followed by syringing, and proved to be a small kidney-shaped mass of bright red colour, about three lines in length by two in breadth. It was of firm consistence, slipping away with a dense elastic feeling when seized by the forceps. Under the microscope it presented only a mass of small cells, with here and there an appearance of slight fibrillation.

From this time all the symptoms rapidly abated. There was no more discharge nor tinnitus. The hearing rose at once to twelve inches, and

in a few days to twenty-four.   In a week the incision was healed, the
redness had almost entirely disappeared, and the membrane had partly
recovered its transparency.

Six months later the patient returned ; the membrane was white and
slightly bulging; it was congested at the superior part ; and a small
mass of granulations had formed close to the membrane below. Another
incision was made, and viscid mucus evacuated ; in a few weeks the
hearing was greatly improved, and all disease had disappeared.*

One of the most difficult forms of polypus to treat is
when it grows from the wall of the tympanum and pro-
trudes thro' a small orifice in the membrane. If removed,
it grows again and again, and the best treatment probably is to enlarge the orifice so as to gain a full command
of the diseased surface.   One such case † was under my
care for many months with no result ; but after seven
years the patient applied to me for another affection, and
I found that the polypus had disappeared, and the hearing
was sufficient.   The orifice, however, still remained, with
slight occasional discharge.

* See Atlas, Plate XXI., figs. 1 and 2.
† See Atlas, Plate XXI., figs. 4, 5, and 6.

CHAPTER X.

AMONG the effects of chronic inflammation of the tympanum, a very frequent one is a thinning and degeneration of the entire membrane, which leads to its falling in upon, and becoming adherent to, the inner wall of the tympanum. In extreme cases of this kind the appearance is almost entirely the same as if the membrane were wanting, but the surface is smooth and shining, and no margin of the membrane is to be seen. Polypi not unfrequently coexist with this condition, and when they have been cured, the surface that remains visible is that of the tympanum covered as with a layer of gold-beater's skin. The malleus may be completely or partly wanting, and generally the head of stapes stands prominently out. Here again the remarkable fact is that the hearing may be very good indeed, even while the collapse is extreme. A girl, aged 16, was brought to me for discharge and deafness lasting since scarlatina at 3. A polypus existed on both sides, which was eradicated on the right only after enlarging the orifice in the membrane and thoro'ly evacuating the tympanum. On the left side, a large polypus occupied almost the whole meatus, and was found, after removal, to have apparently grown from the lower part of the tympanic wall, which was red and fleshy. After a few weeks' treatment, however, it was seen that there was no free margin of membrane, but that the whole internal wall of the tympanum assumed a white and glazy appearance; all its contour could be distinctly traced, but there was no sign of any breach of continuity in the membrane, which could be seen falling inwards from its margin to the promontory. The malleus was much drawn back, and seemed shortened, and the stapes stood out behind it. Air blown thro' the Eustachian tube entered the tympanum, but did not escape, and by repeated inflation, by Politzer's bag and the catheter, the thinned membrane was blown off from the lower and anterior part of the tympanic wall, and she could herself make it bulge into a bladder. The hearing greatly improved, and became quite sufficient for all practical purposes. A whisper was heard at ten feet.* In all such cases, if the hearing does not otherwise return, the artificial membrane should be tried; and if that does not succeed, a small curved knife may be introduced very carefully behind the adherent handle of the malleus, and it may be gently raised from its bound-down position; or the stapes (which is generally plainly to be seen) may have slight incisions carefully made around it, and even very gentle pressure applied to it, to restore its mobility,

* See Atlas, Plate III., fig. 6.

precautions being taken to prevent any risk of sudden movements. I have known measures of this kind render the cotton wool fairly effective in cases in which it was previously of no avail. But all such means would perhaps be avoided or carried out with excessive care if the other ear were lost; or, if the nervous power were destroyed, of course they would be futile.

A slightly different condition is when a part of the membrane has been destroyed and the edges have become adherent to the tympanic wall.* In these cases, if other means are unavailing, cutting round the adherent part with a small sharp knife, and so setting the membrane free, has sometimes had a very good effect. In other instances suction on the meatus—best exerted by the mouth—will, for the time at least, restore the hearing. So that the resources in such cases are: powerful inflation; suction; the artificial membrane; cutting around the scar; and, finally, cautiously endeavouring to liberate the malleus and restore mobility to the stapes. Also the possibility of the presence of old viscid secretion gluing the parts together should not be overlooked, nor an urgent case abandoned (if the nerve-power is good) without a fair attempt being made thoro'ly to clear out the tympanum.

In milder degrees of indrawing of the membrane, when tho' it can be restored to its place by inflation, and temporary improvement follows, it soon falls back again,

* See Atlas, Plate XX., fig. 4.

Politzer introduced, and still speaks highly of, the plan of keeping up an air-tight closure of the meatus. Having well inflated the tympanum, he takes some cotton wool rolled up into a small ball with wax, or ointment, and with it closes the orifice of the meatus; he thus takes off the pressure of the external air, and even turns to account the absorption of air in the meatus, making it tend to draw the membrane outwards, care being always taken to see that the Eustachian tube is free. The ball may be worn for several consecutive nights, and then omitted for a time. When the membrane is atrophied, however, this plan does not succeed. But then excision of the relaxed part, whether it be a scar or a part otherwise thinned, will sometimes be of use. Or if the relaxation has advanced only to a less degree, and the membrane simply lacks the proper tension, simple incisions into the most relaxed part of the membrane help towards a restoration of the normal tension; apparently thro' the contraction that attends their healing. The incisions may be frequently repeated, and at short intervals. But in this climate, and with the kind of patient we usually see, I should prefer always to let fourteen days elapse.

A similar treatment has been found useful also for an opposite condition: namely, for increased tension and rigidity of the membrane, indicated by abnormal prominence of the folds that run anteriorly and posteriorly from the short process to the margin of the membrane. Repeated incision of these folds, especially the posterior one, is said to have often a permanent good effect.*

Also in scars, or slight adhesions, of the membrane it has often been found that a rupture produced by forcible inflation of the drum has permanently improved the hearing.

In some cases of relaxed membrane, with more or less loss of the ossicula, the hearing is improved by the membrane being forced outwards, in others by its being gently pressed inwards. Varying relations between the membrane and the stapes may account for this difference. In one case, in which, on dissection, the incus was wanting, and the thinned membrane lay in contact with the stapes, the hearing had been fairly good.

Very frequently the hearing is at once and greatly improved by mere incision of the membrane, as if it took off a tension or load from the ossicula; but the improvement is lost again as soon as the membrane heals. And this may recur several times. Accordingly every contrivance has been used for keeping incisions in the membrane permanently open, but none of them have succeeded; not even Dr. Wreden's method of cutting away at once the chief part of the membrane and of the handle of the malleus. Politzer, in view of these facts, constructed a small ring of hard rubber, with a slight groove

* In the Atlas, Plate XIX., fig. 2, is shown a case, in which the membrane is seen gaping after incision. The hearing was greatly improved, but for a time only.

around it, to introduce into the incision with the view of its being permanently worn. He has reported good results, but at the best, when the ring is tolerated and keeps its place, it works its way to the edge of the membrane after the lapse of a few weeks. The incision is enlarged by a bougie placed in it for a few hours, and the ring has attached to it a portion of thin thread by which it can be withdrawn.* I have tried it more than once, but have not succeeded. In one case an enormous discharge was excited, but no permanent mischief followed.

Some years ago, when dissections of the ear were just ceasing to be unknown, the extreme frequency with which bands of adhesion are found in the tympanum naturally excited much attention, and seemed to cast a gloom over the prospects of treatment. But farther investigations have thrown a new light upon this condition. The bands so frequently found connecting together, as if by a morbid product, the membrane, ossicles and tympanic wall, are not the result of disease, but represent rather the relics of the mass of cellular tissue by which the tympanum, in fœtal life, is occupied. But tho' not themselves morbid in their origin, they seem to me to have a great influence upon the progress and effects of morbid processes within the tympanum; and that their presence or absence may be one of the determining causes of the very different issue of apparently quite similar

* They may be obtained of Messrs. Meyer and Meltzer, 59, Great Portland Street.

affections of the ear in different persons, and the different
effect of treatment in cases apparently alike, which is one
of the chief sources of difficulty and dissatisfaction in the
treatment of diseases of the ear. For a slight inflammatory affection which would have no permanent effect
upon the structures within the tympanum, or would leave
effects easily removable, if the cavity were freely open and
the parts not joined together by any accidental connections, might produce a very different and much more
serious effect, if bands of thin connective tissue, passed,
as they very frequently do, in all directions between the
ossicles and the tympanic walls. For a very slight inflammatory action might lead to thickening and contraction
of these bands; and secretions that might otherwise
gravitate to the floor of the tympanum, or escape by the
tube, might easily become entangled in their meshes, and
convert them from innocent, because unimpeding, threads
into unyielding or even distorting bands. That such an
effect does take place seems to me proved by facts. In
the following dissection, for example, the bands of
adhesion were as distinct and numerous in the perfect ear
as in the deaf one, but in the latter they had been
evidently changed in their character by an inflammatory
process within the tympanum; and instead of being
loose and thin, had become dense and thick. The effect
of the disease upon the hearing apparently took many
years to develop itself.

Deafness on the left side. Membranous bands in either tympanum; ossicula on the left side drawn together, and less movable than natural.

H. W—,a tall, apparently robust man, died suddenly at the age of 52. The muscular structure of the heart was in a state of degeneration.

History.—He suffered from earache in early life, and was noticed to be slightly deaf at about 26 years of age. For some years past he had been unable to hear without great difficulty with the left ear, and when spoken to would habitually turn the right. He was able, however, to carry on ordinary conversation with perfect facility, the hearing on the right side being very good. He had always been subject to headache, and three years ago had an illness pronounced to be congestion of the brain.

His mother became deaf in both ears at 7 years of age from scarlatina, and her deafness increased as she advanced in life. All his brothers and sisters, of whom there were four, suffered in childhood from pain in the ears. His sister, aged 40, is very deaf, the symptoms indicating an affection of the auditory nerve. His two brothers are deaf in a less degree.

Examination of the petrous bones.—The left ear, in which the hearing was impaired, presented the following appearances : The membrana tympani was slightly opaque, thicker and more concave than natural, and rigid. The mucous membrane of the tympanum was red and thick. The ossicula were *approximated to each other, and firmly bound* by membranous bands, uniting the long crus of the incus to the membrana tympani and to the handle of the malleus, and the stapes to the other ossicles and tympanic walls. The stapes was firmly fixed in the fenestra ovalis, being immovable without considerable pressure. The vestibule and semicircular canals were healthy. The cochlea more vascular than natural. The membrana fenestræ rotundæ was opaque.

Right ear.—The meatus externus contained a small accumulation of soft cerumen. The membrana tympani and mucous membrane of tympanum were healthy. The ossicula were surrounded by membranous bands, connecting the membrana tympani and malleus to the long process of the incus, and the stapes and incus to the posterior wall of the tympanum. The ossicles retained their natural mobility.

The internal ear was healthy, except a slight vascularity of the cochlea and adjacent part of the vestibule.

When adhesions impairing the mobility of the structures can be seen, or their presence otherwise made sure (as, for instance, by suction with Siegle's speculum), their division by means of a small curved knife, with subsequent continued inflation of the drum to prevent re-contraction, has occasionally been found useful. But probably more is to be hoped from the persevering injection of warm solutions of Potass. Iod., or other alkaline salts, than from any other form of treatment; and a certain proportion of the numerous cases in which this treatment does good belongs most probably to this class.

When clinical observation, supplemented by examination after death, shall have thrown more light upon *anchylosis of the stapes*, the diagnosis of ear-disease where it is at present most unsatisfactory will have made a great advance. Mr. Toynbee by his dissections proved that a condition of bony anchylosis of the base of that bone to the vestibular wall was remarkably frequent; he found seventy-two cases of it in the dissection of 1149 diseased ears; but then the greater part of these were met with in aged soldiers and sailors who had been exposed to the sound of artillery. But of " membranous anchylosis " —a fixed condition of the base without formation of new bone—he found 53 ; and of expansion of the bone and

unnatural rigidity 91 more; in all 216, or nearly one in
every five diseased ears. That the prevailing great age of
the subjects of his dissections had much to do with this
result appears certain. In upwards of 500 dissections of
younger subjects that I have made, of which 93 had
histories of deafness, I have never once met with distinct
bony anchylosis, and complete fixity of the base of the
bone was rare, tho' a greater rigidity than natural was
not unfrequent. In one case in which the symptoms
during life had been most obscure, I found not anchylosis,
but apparently congenital malposition of the stapes.

D. R—, æt. 23; very tall, being six feet three inches in height; thin,
of dark complexion, general good health; working hard as a student.
Had scarlatina at seven years of age. This was not noticed to affect
his hearing, but he had always seemed rather dull in that respect.
For a year or two this dulness had increased, without apparent cause,
and was now become practically inconvenient. There was an occasional
humming or buzzing noise in the ears.

November 20th, 1863.—Watch r. $\frac{4}{10}$, l. $\frac{10}{40}$; heard also on any part of
the skull. A plug of hard wax was syringed from the right ear with no
change for the watch but slight improvement for the voice, soon lost
again; inner part of each meatus somewhat congested, membrana
tympani normal; Eustachian tubes free.

April 15th, 1864.—He died quite unexpectedly on the fourth day of
what appeared to be an attack of rheumatic fever, proceeding favourably.
Nothing was found to account for the fatal issue; neither the heart nor
the brain was visibly diseased. The petrous bones were removed about
sixty hours after death. The membrana tympani on each side was
normal. The mucous membrane of the tympanum exhibited numerous
congested vessels, giving it a markedly vascular appearance. This was
probably connected with the fatal illness. It was not thick or soft.
The articulation of the stapes to the vestibule presented certain peculiarities. On each side the anterior crus (opposite to the attachment of

the stapedius muscle) was of an opaque white, quite unlike the rest of the bone, which presented the usual pale-greyish hue, and the base, when viewed on the vestibular aspect, was of a markedly white colour, contrasting much more than is usual with the rest of the vestibular wall. The stapedius muscle on each side was healthy in structure, as shown by the microscope. On the right side the stapes was less freely movable than on the left, and the action of the stapedius seemed to be different from that which is usual. By drawing on the muscle the stapes was, by a very slight amount of motion, pulled down into contact with the promontory, and there fixed; it was scarcely at all withdrawn from the vestibule. On the left side the normal rotatory action was produced.

The membrane of the fenestra rotunda, on the right side, was clear and bright, convex towards the tympanum. On the left side it was covered by a membranoid lamina, which adhered, but was not attached, to the surrounding tympanic wall. This lamina was thick and of dark grey colour, showing under the microscope scarcely any trace of structure; probably it was a mass simply of inspissated mucus.

Under the microscope, the vestibule on the right side appeared normal, the otoconic rather scanty. On the left side, however, it presented in its whole extent numerous large oval or circular outlines, apparently cellular structures, yet greatly exceeding in size the normal vestibular epithelium, being about the $\frac{1}{800}$ of an inch in diameter, and presenting no trace of nucleus or contents. In some parts they were isolated, in others lying in groups, sometimes appearing to run into one another, and exhibiting rather a lobulated outline than distinct forms.

The cochlea appeared healthy. The fibres of the auditory nerve on each side seemed softened and bulging, doubtless from post-mortem change.

Farther examinations must determine how much the abnormal condition of the stapes on the right side had to do with the habitual dulness of hearing. On examination during life there appeared no cause to which the deafness could be assigned. There was some deafness in the family. The appearances found in the vestibule on the left side have been described also by Politzer, Voltolini, and Lucae, and appear not to be necessarily morbid. In one case Lucae succeeded in obtaining from the large globular bodies some small striated particles which gave a blue colour with iodine.

Cases often come before the surgeon, and even in young persons, in respect to which the thoughts irresistibly revert to anchylosis of the stapes; but certainty seems impossible to gain. It is in reference to these, in part, that Voltolini makes the proposal to incise the membrane, with a linear or crucial incision, and explore the tympanic wall. There is every reason to believe that such a procedure would be free from danger, and the question of the mobility or immobility of the stapes might be put to rest. The following is a case in which anchylosis would suggest itself as the diagnosis.

A. M—, æt. 30, a healthy man, has been gradually becoming deaf for ten or twelve years; for about two years the deafness has caused him inconvenience; never any pain in the ears nor tinnitus; does not hear better in a noise; is worse after a hearty meal, or during a cold, if severe. Smokes three or four pipes daily; has travelled much by rail. No relatives deaf; there is much gout in his father's family, but he never had any symptoms of it; sight good; throat slightly relaxed.

Watch, each ear, seven inches, heard also on the forehead; tuning fork well heard, sounding a little louder on the right side, which is a little the worse; *no effect from closing either meatus.*

Right meatus dry; m. t. bright, of natural curve; somewhat milky posteriorly. Left meatus contained several loose flakes of epidermis; m. t. concave, irregular, and its surface rough. Could inflate the right tympanum, not the left. By means of the catheter the left Eustachian tube was opened so that he inflated both tympana, which had at first no effect upon the hearing ; subsequently it appeared somewhat to diminish it. When air was thus forced into the tympanum the malleus was not seen to move, but on each side the membrane yielded very freely at the upper and posterior part.

With this may be contrasted a case of probable nerve-affection.

Miss N—, æt. 52, of languid and worn appearance, had been affected for three or four years with a noise as of rushing water in the right ear, and for about six months with a similar-sound in the left ear, but much more intense. It is constant, and occasions her great distress ; at times, a sudden whistle, like that of a steam-engine, will come in each ear, especially the left, and last a few seconds. During the same period her- hearing has also become impaired. No cause has been observed, except that she has long suffered much from severe pains in the head, which begin generally from the right eye, affecting only half of the head at a time, but involving both sides before they leave her. These return regu- larly every. four or five weeks. The deafness and tinnitus are somewhat worse during the attacks. Two years ago she had small pox, which left her weak, but did not affect the ears. There is much gout on both sides, and she has had slight attacks of it in the knuckles. No relative deaf.

Watch, right, four inches ; left, contact ; t. f. not well heard ; louder on the *right* [the better] side ; *closing either meatus increases the sound ;* membrana tympani bright and natural ; Eustachian tubes pervious ; throat healthy ; inflation of the tympanum produced a slight temporary improvement of hearing for the watch, and exhaustion of air from the meatus gave a little relief for the moment to the tinnitus.

Probably in both cases, in spite of their difference, the gouty diathesis was a chief element. In the one case the tuning-fork was well heard; if anything, louder on the worse side; in the other it was badly heard, louder on the better side; and, again, closure of the meatus had no effect on its sound in the former case,

and increased it in the latter : points which indicate in
the former an obstructed passage of sound thro' the
tympanum ; and in the latter, that the tympanum per-
forms its functions aright. Absence of tinnitus, however,
is by no means a character of anchylosis ; possibly its
presence or absence may depend upon the degree in
which the stapes, together with its abnormal fixity, is
made to project also into the vestibule, a condition which
Mr. Toynbee noted in seven cases. I had the opportunity of examining the ear of a gentleman, who, six years
before, was returning from consulting Mr. Toynbee
for deafness in his right ear. While waiting at the
railway station an engine suddenly came up with a loud
whistle : it seemed to go thro' the patient's ear, and the
hearing returned from that moment. There was nothing
abnormal in the ear when I examined it ; and the idea of
a suddenly loosed anchylosis was the only one that could
be suggested. On the other hand, Moos* reports two
cases that appeared as if sudden loud sounds might be
the *cause of* anchylosis. It is conceivable that thro' an
excessive action of the stapedius both the effects might
be produced ; the more since the function ascribed by
Helmholz to the stapedius is that of protecting the ear
from sound.

For the treatment of bony anchylosis not much can be
suggested, though Mr. Toynbee had some belief in small,
long-continued doses of perchloride of mercury. Injec-

* " Archiv. of Ophth. and Otol." II. vol. I.

tions of iodide of potassium into the tympanum might
benefit the milder forms ; and in some such cases I have
found this injection, used once a week, with the long-
continued administration of Tinct. ferri perchlor. ℥vi—x,
with Hydrarg. perchlor. gr. $\frac{1}{32}$, beneficial. I have used
it in obscure cases with or without history of catarrh,
confining the injections to the worst ear, at first ; the
results of course being much better, as the rule, when
the tuning-fork is well heard, but sometimes being very
satisfactory when the contrary is the case.

Weber-Liel's "koniantron," as he terms a small catheter, adapted to be passed completely into the tympanum
and to direct spray to any portion of it, would probably
find its best use in cases of this kind ; but our diagnosis
must be carried farther before any exactness could be given
to its use : for an anchylosed condition may affect not the
stapes alone, but the other ossicula also ; and especially
the head of the malleus is sometimes firmly bound to the
upper wall of the tympanum : a condition of which the
symptoms would probably be hard to distinguish from
those of a like affection of the other end of the chain.
But a narrow scrutiny of the upper part of the membrane
may in the future contribute farther elements to our
judgment.*

Lucae asks whether, when the hearing is improved by
the inflation of the tympanum, there may not exist a
stiffness of the joint between the malleus and incus, so

---

* Plate XVIII., Fig. 2, in the Atlas, suggests itself as a case of this sort.

that the inflation draws the stapes from the vestibule, which in the normal condition it does not. In one case I found inflating the tympanum produce a marked improvement for the voice, but at the same time a decided diminution of the hearing for the watch. It was a case of chronic catarrh with polypus growing from the meatus. As it recovered, inflation by the bag improved the hearing both for voice and watch.

CHAPTER XI.

In some respects, this is the most important part of the whole subject of diseases of the ear. Not only are aural affections most frequent during early life, but in even the majority, probably, of cases of confirmed deafness at a later period, the foundation is laid then. The affections of the ear in infancy and youth also are often full of peril; and finally remedial measures are more efficient then than at any other period. It is a reasonable belief that if fair care were given to ear disease in childhood, half, at least, of the disease which affects that organ in manhood would never exist. For it continually happens that adults come before us, dating back their deafness a few months or years at most, to whom we say at once, because the condition of the ear betrays it: "You had disease of the ear in childhood;" and find that there existed then a long-continued discharge, for instance, or repeated attack of earache with deafness following.

It is the constant practice of medical men to say to the parents of children who have discharge from the ear, or otherwise suffer in it, that they will grow out of the affection. In the great majority of cases this may be true; in some it certainly is so; but also in others the discharge does not cease, nor the hearing return, but the latter becomes progressively more impaired, and the former continues for thirty or even sixty years. What we want is some basis on which a judgment can be formed, which of the affections of the ear in childhood will advance to a spontaneous recovery, and which will not. It is impossible that such a basis ever should be gained except by a careful examination of the ear in every case—a task which must devolve upon the general medical practitioner. The most probable supposition is that those cases recover well in which there is free escape for all morbid secretion ; and that those in which such escape is impeded continue diseased.

The Exanthemata, as is well known, are the great enemies to the ear in childhood. Their chief result is partial destruction of the membrane, and more or less chronic inflammation of the whole mucous tract behind it. But in their severer forms they do much more than this : scarlatina, especially, often totally abolishing the hearing not only with, but even without, visible injury to the tympanum. Next, or perhaps equal in frequency to scarlatina in this respect, stands mumps, which has an effect on the nervous apparatus of the ear which has yet received no explanation, and affords no clue to the use of remedies ; every part of the ear being normal, so far as examination can extend, but the function almost abolished.

But some cases of damage to the ear from mumps present an intermediate character, showing clear signs of a tympanic disorder mixed with the nervous symptoms. The similarity of the nerve affection that follows mumps to that which ensues upon parturition, is very striking; and the resemblance is increased by the fact that quite frequently the latter affection also is accompanied with symptoms of a catarrhal character.

I have had a few opportunities of studying the mild attacks in children which are called earache, and are followed by a slight discharge; and in the cases I have seen the affection has been a subacute catarrh of the tympanum, with a small perforation of the membrane, soon healing.

May, 1863, I saw a girl, æt. 10, of good constitution, but subject to intermittent albuminuria that had continued since scarlatina two years previously. During a cold she had had an attack of pain, lasting a few hours, in the left ear, which was seen to have at first a flat and slightly dull aspect; afterwards red vessels were visible on its surface, both radiating and around the circumference, and it presented also a peculiar appearance chiefly at its upper part, being marked by faint oval outlines, which appeared to arise from bubbles in contact with its inner surface. The hearing was much dulled. In another week the membrane had become less vascular, but it was decidedly concave, the stapes being plainly visible and apparently in contact with its inner surface. The tympanum was gently inflated twice. The membrane lost its vascularity, and the hearing in a few days became good, but not perfect. (Two feet for a watch heard on the right side at six feet.) Just twelve months after, on May 17th, she woke again in the night with pain in the left ear, followed the next day by a watery discharge. There was a little fever, and the hearing was reduced to ten inches on the right side, and four on the left. The left membrane was white and thick. A saline powder was ordered, and a lotion of three grains of borax. Four days after, the ears being quite easy, there was syringed from the left meatus a small mass of soft flaky discharge, and a circular orifice about the size of a large pin's head was seen at the lower part of the dull white membrane. The next day the orifice was smaller and of an oval form : four days after, it was scarcely to be detected as an orifice, but appeared as a small dark point with somewhat thickened white edges, but air passed through it with a slight dry sound. In three days more no trace of it was visible, and air inblown entered the tympanum with a hollow puff, not escaping. The right ear in this instance was involved as well as the left, being indeed the more deaf of the two, and the membrane becoming for a time uneven, and of a dull, dark grey hue, with a slight tinge of pink.

This is an example of a large number of cases which pass almost or entirely unobserved. There was nothing in the symptoms indicative of anything more than an ordinary slight discharge from the ear. The recovery seemed perfect, though the hearing continued for a long time slightly impaired.

It is interesting to note the presence of an excess of fluid in the tympanum twelve months before the occurrence of the perforation.

Thus, it is probable that perforation of the membrane takes place in slight infantile affections much more often than would be supposed. In one case which followed an attack of bronchitis three months previously, in a boy of four, a bulging of the membrane, of a deep red colour, took place at the upper part. There had been pain, not very severe, for four nights, and the upper and posterior part of the membrane, including the greater portion of its extent, was seen of a bright pink colour, and very prominent. The next day a small perforation had formed a little below the umbó, and thick, white matter was seen escaping. Eight days later, the orifice had healed, but the membrane was white, and much indrawn. On inflation, it resumed its natural position, tho' still white in appearance, and the hearing was found perfect.*

In such cases as these, and in the discharges which occur in the early months of life, and are called "teething discharges," and in which the membrane is also ruptured, the chief demand is to obtain a free evacuation of the secretion from the tympanum. And this is easily done by blowing thro' a flexible tube into one nostril while the child's mouth is closed. The air will whistle thro' the perforation, and after it the syringe will probably remove more discharge (altho' the ear has been well syringed immediately before) and, as I have frequently seen, from that time the affection will begin to subside. I use, generally, a lotion of borax, with a drop or two of tincture of opium to the ounce, for cleanliness, and after two or three inflations such a case, which may have been distressing the child for weeks, will usually get quite well.

But a more serious class of cases is one which is much too frequent: acute inflammation of the tympanum, causing pain and distress of the utmost severity, but altogether overlooked until discharge from the ear suddenly occurs, with relief to all the symptoms. Such cases are generally taken for affections of the brain, and all the

* See Atlas, Plate VI., Figs. 1 to 4.

time during which relief might be given and the ear saved from damage is lost. The following case, for which I am indebted to Dr. Wilks, is a fortunate instance as regards its result; but how great a risk was run, and what, probably needless, pain endured.

"The child of a medical man, æt. 2, was taken ill on March 9th, 1864, with feverish symptoms, &c., and a powder with calomel was given it. On the three following days continued very ill, constantly crying out as if in pain, and with much febrile disturbance.

"On March 15th Dr. Wilks saw him, found him very ill, very rest-less, constantly moving about as if in great pain; skin hot, lips parched, pulse 104. There were no symptoms indicating any cerebral mischief, but the bowels were relaxed, the abdomen full and soft. It was thought, therefore, that his complaint might be dysentery in an early stage, and two grains of Dover's powder were ordered.

"19th.—Appeared better, had slept, and was quieter. After this, however, the former symptoms re-appeared, extreme restlessness, and screaming as if in pain. There was evidently some source for this, but it was difficult to discover. For a week he thus continued, throwing his head about as if in pain, but with no other cerebral symptoms, and the child appeared quite sensible. He then passed a lumbricus, and it was hoped that another purge might relieve him, but it had no such effect.

"22nd.—Appeared worse, never quiet for a moment; lying in his nurse's lap, throwing himself about, his arms, legs and head, as if endeavouring to gain repose from some internal agony. He then began to make curious movements with his mouth, constantly thrusting his tongue out and licking his lips. For nearly another fortnight the child thus continued; with constant restlessness, throwing his head about as if in great pain, and placing his hand over his head and face. The father then lanced the gums, but with no effect. Sometimes for a whole day he never slept, and chloroform was given to soothe him, which generally had the desired effect. About a month after the commence-ment of his illness, and when the child was wasted to a mere shadow, a discharge occurred, first from one ear and then from the other. For a day or two there appeared no relief, but after this the child began to get better, ceased to cry, took its food and grew stout. He is at the present time in good health, and his hearing seems to be good."

A somewhat similar case was brought to me in the year 1867 : a healthy boy, aged 3, had been seized four months before with severe symptoms of fever, restlessness, and pain. Consultations had been held, and various treatment adopted in vain, until, about six weeks from the commencement of the attack, thick matter flowed from each ear with immediate relief. The discharge however continued, and the hearing was much impaired. On examining the ears, each membrane presented a perforation, about two lines in diameter on the left side, and three on the right. The mucous membrane of the tympanum also on the right side was dark-red and greatly swollen. After ten months the left ear had healed, tho' it gave way again afterwards for a time ; but the right membrane was not healed until three years had elapsed, when both membranes were healthy, and the hearing appeared to be perfect, even quick for music.

It seems strange that in the slight affections before referred to the membrane should give way so easily, and in these more severe attacks should resist so long. But it is possible that in the early stages of the severe inflammations a process of thickening takes place in the membrane which renders it more resisting. In the first years of life also the membrane is altogether thicker and firmer than at a later period, and the Eustachian tube is much

Q

wider, being, according to Von Tröltsch, a line and a half at its narrowest part.

Many years ago, while dissecting the ears of the children who died under my observation, I was struck with the extreme frequency with which (whatever the fatal disease) the tympanum showed signs of inflammation, often advancing to an extreme degree.* In the following case the condition of the tympanum seems to have been the source of part of the symptoms.

Samuel H—, æt. 3½, a well-formed child, of dark complexion, was first seen on the evening of 26th May, 1855. He was then in strong convulsions, affecting nearly all the muscles of the body, and resembling an extremely severe form of chorea. He did not appear to be in pain ; there was no heat of skin, or excessive quickness of the pulse ; he took fluids when desired. He continued convulsed during the whole night and died exhausted about two o'clock on the following morning.

His history, so far as it could be ascertained, was as follows : —He was always a very passionate boy, especially during the few last months of his life. He had enjoyed general good health, never complained of headache, *but often seemed more unwilling than other children to have his head touched ;* he always had a habit of putting his fingers in his ears, but never complained of pain in them, nor had there been any discharge from them. *Four or five times he has been noticed to throw himself upon the ground, and roll about, apparently in play, yet so strangely . as to attract particular attention.* Has been deaf when he has had a cold, for some time. About three days before his death he became much more deaf than ever before, and so continued.

He had appeared in his usual health until the 24th, three days before his death, when he seemed to be languid and ill. On the evening of that day he fell, and struck his head against the door, but not violently, and apparently quite recovered from the effects of the blow. The next

* The results of some of these dissections were published in the "Medico-Chirurgical Transactions" for 1856.

day he was feverish, and laid his head upon the pillow. He first became convulsed on the evening of the 26th, and died in fourteen hours afterwards.

Examination twenty-four hours after death.—Appearance of body natural. The sac of the arachnoid contained three or four drachms of clear fluid, and the membranes of the brain generally were much congested. No disease was detected in the substance of the brain, which appeared quite healthy throughout. The spinal cord was not examined. The heart was loosely contracted. A small triangular mass of soft lymph, attached by its base to the apex of the heart, lay in the pericardial sac. There were a few dull white patches on the opposed surfaces of the pericardium, which, however, contained no fluid. Structure of the heart healthy.

The lower lobe of the left lung contained scarcely any air ; it did not collapse when the chest was opened, nor crepitate beneath the finger. It was of a dark reddish hue when cut into, and broke down on firm pressure. Portions of it sank in water.

Examination of temporal bones.—The mucous membrane of the fauces around the orifices of the Eustachian tubes was very greatly swollen, and infiltrated with muco-purulent fluid, which exuded from it in great quantity when it was pressed. The Eustachian tubes were closed, by approximation of the thickened lining membrane, from the faucial extremity to within half an inch of the tympanic opening. The cavity of the tympanum on each side contained a red coloured viscid fluid ; and the mucous membrane was red, thick, and velvety. The membranæ tympani were fallen in towards the promontory ; they were very vascular, and the mucous layer thick.

On the right side, there were many membranous bands uniting the membrana tympani to the wall of the tympanum ; these bands existed also in the mastoid cells, and contained many spots of ecchymosis. The cochlea also (on the right side) was much congested, and contained a red fluid ; and red vessels were seen ramifying on the walls of the vestibule and canals.

Two other children of the family are also deaf with a like condition of the membrane.

Similar conditions were found in young children after

death from bronchitis, from heart disease, from hooping cough, from croup. And in cases of tuberculosis of the brain, I found more than once collections of apparently tubercular matter within the tympanum and mastoid cells.

But the most remarkable fact that has been ascertained respecting inflammatory conditions of the ear in childhood, is one of which every one who has dissected the ears of infants has had proof, but to which Von Tröltsch and Wreden have paid most attention : namely, that in much more than half of all children dying of affections of the lungs or brain, the tympanum, generally on each side, contained pus, and its lining membrane was inflamed and swollen.* Dr. Von Tröltsch found the ear normal but in thirteen cases out of forty-six, and Wreden out of eighty found but fourteen healthy. But the membrane was never perforated in Von Tröltsch's cases, and only once in Wreden's. The oldest of the children was 14 months.

It should be observed that these results were found among the poorest classes of the community, chiefly in the inmates of foundling hospitals. But Von Tröltsch states that whenever the ear was healthy there was no other pathological appearance ; and Wreden's opinion is that in more than half his cases the pus that was present in the tympanum had given rise to consecutive affections which were often the direct cause of death. The signifi-

* "Diseases of the Ear : " by Dr. Anton Von Tröltsch; translated by Dr. St. John Roosa. Pp. 392, 403.

cance of these facts cannot yet be estimated; and especially the relation in which the aural affection stands—
whether as cause or mere concomitant—to the other
morbid conditions and the death of the child, remains for
future determination. I would venture to suggest, merely
as a hypothesis, that the condition is less one of inflammation than of mere breaking down; or, rather, is identical in character with the purulent condition which so
often arises in the tympanum in the last stage of phthisis;
that it is, therefore, probably almost unaccompanied by
pain, and is rather a symptom of dissolution than a
primary constituent of disease. At the same time it
may be true that from it there start, in the weakened condition of the child, the most serious secondary results;
but not local treatment but general support, or rather
such maintenance as should save the patient from ever
sinking into the already almost moribund condition in
which the aural affection has its root, would be the true
remedy. A cause for the tympanum being specially
subject to this degenerative process may perhaps be found
in the active "developmental" changes which take place
in it during the first period of independent life. Von
Tröltsch showed that before birth the tympanum is completely occupied by a cushion of cellular tissue, and
Wreden found that its absorption is normally completed
within twenty-four hours after birth. Possibly this process, when the vital power breaks down, may be prone to
lapse into a purulent degeneration. One slight circum-

stance may tend to confirm this supposition, namely, that
the internal surface of the membrana tympani, which has
less part in forming the pre-natal "cushion," participates
very little in the morbid change.

That a frequent cause of deaf-mutism is to be found
in the occurrence of these conditions of the tympanum,
hardly admits of doubt. And there is another class of
cases that strongly claims the attention of all under whose
care infantile diseases come, those, namely, in which a
child becomes deaf after "convulsions." Frequently, in
such cases, when the hearing is totally destroyed, marks
of inflammation within the tympanum are betrayed by
the appearance of the membrane ; nor can any form of
eccentric irritation be well imagined more likely to express
itself in convulsive seizures.

There is yet another peculiar affection of the ear occurring in children, the true significance of which is yet
undetermined. Voltolini first drew especial attention to
it, and described it as being an inflammation confined to
the labyrinth, but involving both sides. The symptoms
are those of acute fever with implication of the brain—of
meningitis in a word—but after a few days they all disappear, and no result whatever remains except total
abolition of the hearing. The tympanum shows no sign
of disease. The question is whether the affection is one
involving the brain or membranes—whether, for example,
it is to be regarded as a sporadic cerebro-spinal meningitis—or whether the labyrinth alone is its seat. The

chief argument in favour of the latter view is, that an affection of the central organs severe enough to produce the acute initial symptoms, and to entirely abolish the power of hearing, could not pass away so rapidly and leave no other effects. On the other hand, an extreme degree of deafness, for which no reasonable treatment suggests itself, remains sometimes after an attack of cerebro-spinal meningitis: some such cases I saw after the late epidemic in Ireland; and Dr. Down* has lately reported a case in which during an attack of this disease a paralysed condition of several of the motor and sensitive nerves was present, and among the other symptoms was deafness on the right side. On recovery the deafness alone persisted. Unfortunately, the state of the tympanum appears not to have been examined; but supposing it healthy, as is most probable, to what cause should the non-recovery of the hearing alone be ascribed?

* "Brit. Med. Journ.," Feb. 7, 1874.

CHAPTER XII.

THE frequency with which fatal effects follow inflammatory affections of the ear has long attracted attention, Mr.
Toynbee having especially thrown light upon their nature
and pathology; so that it is no longer necessary to dwell
upon the importance of the subject. The fatal result is
the consequence either of caries, affecting the brain or
vessels by continuity, or of poisoning thro' the veins of
the diploe; or abscess may form in the brain in the
neighbourhood of an inflamed tympanum without caries
or any apparent means of propagation of the morbid
action. In addition to these results, fatal hæmorrhage
has taken place from ulceration alike of the carotid artery
and of the lateral sinus. When caries of the roof of the
tympanum exists, it is often covered with a thick layer of
lymph, the value of which as a preservative against the
spread of the disease has been pointed out by Mr. Prescott
Hewitt; and I have observed, in dissecting petrous bones
in which the tympanum had been long diseased, that a
new deposit of bone had been formed beneath the dura

mater, evidently serving to guard against the spread of
the disease. The thin, and often partly deficient, walls of
the tympanum are in contact not only with the dura mater,
but with the lateral and superior petrosal sinuses and
the carotid canal; and from its lining membrane there
extend more than one direct communication with the
vessels of the dura mater. But besides this, the external
meatus borders also on the brain and sinus; and the large
cavity of the mastoid cells, from which, when purulent
action is once set up, a free escape of its products is
extremely difficult, is separated from them but by a
thin layer of bone. Affections of the meatus, therefore,
when they tend to implicate the bone, are not less
dangerous than those of the deeper parts. Indeed, Dr.
J. Gruber gives it as the result of his experience that
fatal affections originate most frequently in diseases of
the external portion of the ear.

Whenever, during the existence of a discharge from the
ear, serious symptoms of brain disturbance set in, or rigors
occur, every surgeon would now give to the local affection
his utmost attention. The only error at all likely to occur
is that, the ear affection being disregarded by the patient,
and not mentioned by him, the surgeon might take the
one affection for fever or treat the other with quinine.
And there is the more danger of such error, because sometimes fatal symptoms will supervene and run a very rapid
course without any warning. Twice in my experience it
has occurred that patients under my care for chronic

inflammation of the tympanum, connected with perforation of the membrane, in whose symptoms neither I nor
any of their friends detected marks of danger, have
succumbed within a few days to brain disease. Both of
the patients were young ; one was a woman of 24, of good
health, who had been subject to discharge since scarlatina
in childhood : the meatus was very narrow and the
mucous membrane was spongy, but it had become almost
healthy under the treatment before described as used by
me in perforations, and the hearing had greatly improved.
Nothing suggested danger to me. The other case was
that of a gentleman aged 26, on whom, two years before,
I had performed incision of the left membrane for old
catarrh of the tympanum attended with discharge from
the meatus, with very satisfactory results, the hearing
being much improved, and all morbid appearances ceasing. The right ear also improved in hearing. The patient
went to Canada, and continued with good hearing and free
from annoyance for more than eighteen months, when a
slight discharge came on. On his calling on me, about
two years from the date of the incision, there was a small
perforation of the membrane, not in the position of the
incision but anteriorly, and the edges were spongy and
granular. I used Politzer's inflation, and applied a
solution (ʒj—ʒj) of nitrate of silver to the granular
surface, and the case appeared to progress perfectly well
till within little more than a week of his death. I do not
know how such cases should be distinguished in the

future. Mr. Toynbee has reported instances in which, after death, abscesses were found in the brain substance, which, from their characters, must have existed for many months ; but it is doubtful if these cases are of the same kind. I had not the opportunity of witnessing the last attack in either case.

When threatening symptoms declare themselves, such as rigors with or without ceasing of the discharge, pain in the ear or side of head, giddiness, fever, or loss of power of any of the muscles, the aim of the treatment is simple ; namely, to subdue any newly arisen inflammation, and above all to secure a perfectly free exit for pus wherever it may be. In the vast majority of cases impeded discharge is or has been the prime cause of the evil. With this view all polypoid growths, or even granulations springing from diseased bone, if they are large, should be removed ; the Eustachian tube should be opened, if it is obstructed, by Politzer's bag, or, with caution, by the catheter, and air passed daily thro' the tube and tympanum. If there be not a free exit for matter contained within the tympanum, the membrane should be incised or the existing orifice enlarged. And the most scrupulous care should be given to detect any symptoms of the presence of matter pent up beneath the periosteum. This is found generally in one of two places ; either over the mastoid process externally, or within the meatus, at the posterior or upper wall. Any redness or swelling, with tenderness of these parts, should prompt to imme-

diate action.* Free incision, carried completely thro'
the periosteum to the bone,† should be made in the.
swollen part. The value of incision over the mastoid
process is now well understood; but this part should not
be regarded to the exclusion of the posterior and upper
wall of the meatus, where an efficient incision will often
give even greater relief. In one case of sudden exacerba-
tion of long-standing discharge, in which the symptoms
were of the gravest character, I incised a red swelling in
this part; no considerable relief followed for three days,
and I was again sent for, but before I arrived a large discharge of pus had escaped from that part, having worked
its way thro' the bone, a small orifice in which could be
felt by the probe. Immediate recovery followed; a very
free discharge of pus continuing for several days. On
one occasion I opened a large abscess over each mastoid
process in a boy of twelve, with entire relief. But if the
division of the periosteum over the mastoid process leaves
the symptoms unchecked, the perforation of the mastoid
cells should not be delayed more than a day or two. It
is easily carried out. Often when pus is contained within
the cells the bone is softened and the knife will penetrate
it, or a strong probe will break it down. When this is
not the case, a gouge or drill may be used; I employ a
drill furnished with a moveable guard, so that the bone
can be penetrated to any desired extent. The best point

---

* I think it may be said that swelling, even tho' painful, in *front* of
the ear, is scarcely ever of serious import.

† Students are very apt to fail in this.

to select is a spot on a level with the upper border of the
meatus and about half an inch behind it; the perforator,
directed slightly forward, may be allowed to penetrate
three-quarters of an inch. Even if no pus immediately
escapes, relief is very often given, and a discharge sets in
afterwards.

In the "Medico Chirurgical Transactions" for 1868,
p. 231, I have reported a case in which relief was given
to most threatening symptoms by perforation of the
mastoid process, in the case of a clergyman, aged 58,
who had suffered for about two months from inflammation of the meatus and tympanum, with perforation of
the membrane, attended all the while with very free discharge. After apparently perfect relief had thus been
given, however, a large abscess formed beneath the
sterno-mastoid muscle, apparently in connection with the
mastoid process, and was freely laid open in its whole
extent. The patient rapidly regained perfect health; the
orifice in the membrane, which had been a line and a half
in diameter, healed, leaving a scarcely detectible scar;
and the hearing became again almost perfect for the
voice, and for the watch $\frac{15}{40}$.*

In this case the soft parts over the bone were swollen
to more than an inch in depth; but redness and swelling
must not be regarded as essential indications for the
operation. Pus and sequestra of dead bone may be con-

* Plate VIII., Figure 3, of the Atlas, shows the healed membrane
about three months after the final operation.

tained within the cells, and give rise to urgent symptoms without any change in the external tissues. It is of the utmost importance not to delay too long; and since the ether spray will generally suffice to deaden the pain, incision over the mastoid process should be had recourse to promptly in every, even doubtful, case. I may repeat that I have never regretted making the incision, and scarcely ever decided against making it without regretting that I did not.

When threatening symptoms first arise, of course vigorous preventive treatment would be adopted: perfect rest, fomentations, mild aperients, sedatives at night, and the free application of leeches. By means of this kind, especially long-continued rest, cases of the gravest aspect have perfectly recovered. Mr. Prescott Hewitt reports the case of a young woman, in whom, after protracted symptoms of pyæmia thro' the lateral sinus, entire restoration was secured by good support.* And the numerous cases in which large masses of dead bone, often including almost the entire labyrinth, have come away, with no permanent·damage to the health, prove how strong are the recuperative powers, provided only free exit for discharge is secured and the strength sustained. Dr. Ogle † mentions the case of a soldier, who suffered from aberration and noises in the ears. After two years a fetid discharge came on, and he became deaf. The discharge

---

* "Pathol. Soc.," May 17, 1864.
† "Med. T. and Gaz.," 1864, p. 566.

and deafness both ceased after a time, but he shortly died of phthisis and softening of the brain, and each tympanum was found diseased, the membranes being destroyed. It is probable that the starting-point of the disease here was in the ear. The patient had been often punished for malingering.

CHAPTER XIII.

THE class of affections which have recently been included under the name of proliferous inflammation of the mucous membrane of the tympanum (Toynbee's thickening and rigidity), constitutes a subject that needs a careful reconsideration. The symptoms which have been supposed to characterize it are similar, only less in degree, to those which indicate anchylosis of the stapes; and are mainly negative. The hearing becomes gradually impaired, tinnitus generally marking the onset and continuing, but as the rule pain has not been present. In uncomplicated cases, or cases which have not advanced to secondary impairment of the nervous function, the tuning-fork is well heard on the teeth, and loudest on the worst side; closure of the meatus does not affect its sound. The Eustachian tube is open, and air enters on inflation with a dry harsh sound, seldom improving the hearing even for a time. Suction of air from the meatus may or may not diminish, momentarily, the tinnitus. The hearing is generally better in a noise.

The membrane is whitish and shining, sometimes of normal curvature, sometimes seeming flat; it moves but
slightly on inflation (unless thro' abuse of that practice
it has been relaxed and bulges in excess). There is
no history of colds, and the throat is not inflamed, but
not unfrequently temporary relief has been given by the
removal of cerumen.

Dr. J. Gruber has given the most detailed account of
this form of disease as it has been supposed to exist, and
the following description is quoted from him.*

"Occasioned by some injurious influence, there arises in some portion
or the whole of the mucous membrane of the middle ear a great
hyperæmia, with swelling, and, in fact, also a new formation of vessels,
and increase of the intercellular fluid. The corpuscles of the connective
tissue multiply by division, and perhaps through other processes also.
These results now increase in the substance of the mucous membrane,
the epithelium of which is swollen. It is generally less moist than in
the other form, and the free exudation, which is formed in part from
the protoplasma of the epithelium, is much less profuse ; in many cases
it is not discoverable. Sometimes the inflammation leads to increased
formation of epithelium, which then undergoes farther metamorphoses,
and may lay a basis for choleastomatous formations.

"As the process advances, the newly-formed elements (which are
either uniformly distributed or found in groups) receive partly or
altogether a higher organization. By outgrowth and division of their
processes, meeting with those of others, there is formed a complex,
intimately-interlaced, soft connective substance, either distributed uniformly, or constituting single or manifold granular excrescences, or even
running on to polypi. It should be expressly mentioned, that in the
continued development of connective tissue and corpuscles, it often
happens that they are not confined to their place of origin, but that they

---

* " Ohrenheilkunde," Wien, 1872, p. 514.

R

extend to quite other surfaces, either by means of the epithelium of the part, or by their freer growth if that be already exfoliated. This occurs in the formation of polypi, but is shown still more strikingly in this affection by the connective threads and membranes which extend in every direction from one part of the tympanum or mastoid cells to another.

"Thus far we have described the development of the newly-produced elements; but it must be observed also that many of these elements undergo a retrograde metamorphosis. They are molecularly disintegrated, become fatty, and are absorbed, or, as sometimes happens in very chronic cases, become chalky.

"Even the newly formed, as well as the simply distended, blood-vessels ulcerate in the course of the process, whereby they are either reduced to simple fibres, or grow fatty or chalky, together with their contents, and gradually become absorbed." (Pp. 514–516.)

Fig. 11.

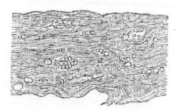

Section of the Mucous Membrane of the Tympanum from a Case of Hypertrophic Inflammation : it was thickened more than fivefold. There are visible scattered chalky masses which undergo characteristic changes on addition of acetic acid. (After Gruber.)

Dr. Gruber's treatment is as follows :—

"We must endeavour to prevent the farther development of the new formed elements, or even to destroy them. For this purpose we possess various methods, according to the portion of the tympanum affected by the inflammation, and the condition of the ear in other

respects. If the tube is chiefly involved, we should seek to maintain its
patency by the air-douche, or by the introduction of laminaria or other
bougies ; at the same time the pressure of the bougie may promote
absorption. If the affection is slight in its degree, and has extended over
the tympanic mucous membrane, benefit may be gained from injections
of caustic potash (gr. ½—1 to ʒj) daily, or at longer intervals; especially by these the epithelium is softened and brought to a speedier
exuviation, the air-douche being then brought into operation to aid the
removal of the free product.

" In this form of inflammation also, dilute acetic acid, used in a
similar way, is sometimes useful in particular cases. Also acetic ether,
iodic ether, and vapour of hydrochlorate of ammonia, give satisfactory
results, and in syphilis the vapour of weak solutions of perchloride of
mercury (gr. ½—1 to ʒj). If the disease is more intense, or if from the
very commencement it is attended with very considerable increase of
substance of the membrane, a more or less concentrated solution of nitrate
of silver (gr. 1—5 to ʒj) is indicated. These solutions are to be syringed
through the Eustachian tube by the catheter, or applied as spray locally
by the very small catheter, which Dr. Weber-Liel recommends to be
introduced completely into the tympanum."

I have tried various injections, especially those of
hydrochlorate of ammonia (gr. ii.— × to the ounce), combined with perchloride of mercury (gr. ⅛—ʒ j) ; but the
treatment that I find on the whole most useful is the
injection by the catheter of a warm solution of iodide
of potash once or twice a week, continued for three or
four weeks, and then intermitted for a time. With this
I have again begun to combine the internal administration of a medicine that was formerly much relied upon
in diseases of the ear, but latterly, in my hands at least,
had fallen out of use : the perchloride of mercury. I give
it with the perchloride of iron, the $\frac{1}{36}$ or $\frac{1}{48}$ of a grain two

or three times a day, and I believe the combination of
these means is often useful. But always, when the introduction of solvent liquids into the tympanum has a good
effect, the question arises whether the condition has been
one of rigidity of the membrane itself, or collection of
hardened secretion on its surface. Dr. Roosa states that
he has found the simple introduction of steam into the
tympanum by the catheter very useful. The steam may,
if preferred, easily be medicated by introducing whatever drug is desired into the hot water and using two
glass tubes, one for the entrance of the air, which may
be pumped in by an elastic bag, and the other for the
exit of the vapour, which may be conveyed to the catheter
by an elastic tube. But my experience has seemed to
be, that in almost every case in which vapour does good,
liquids do more, and are effective also, sometimes,
when no vapour is of any avail. Mr. Dalby* has
remarked the great uncertainty which attends the treatment of cases of this class even when the symptoms
show no difference. This uncertainty depends in part, I
think, upon original differences in the structure of the
tympanum; which, as before remarked, may favour more
or less the occurrence of mechanical adhesions and
other causes of insuperable rigidity.

But probably part of the doubt that envelopes the
subject of proliferous inflammation, is due to the fact
that most cases not only of this affection of the ear,

* " Lectures on Diseases of the Ear."

but of almost all, are not simple specimens of one
morbid condition, but combine the results of several.
Thus the proliferous and the properly catarrhal inflammations may coexist and mask each other's symptoms,
and sympathetic or secondary impairment of the nerve-
function is an event perpetually supervening; while
two other factors in inducing morbid conditions of the
tympanum claim more regard than they have yet received. The first of these is the part played by the
sympathetic or trophic nerves which supply the tympanic
cavity, in producing an irritable or even slight inflammatory condition of its mucous membrane; this abnormal
influence being called into play by cerebral exhaustion.
Many times it has appeared to me that an apparently
catarrhal condition of the tympanum, attended with congestion of the mucous membrane and hypersecretion,
with consequent tinnitus, has had for its cause nothing
whatever but cerebral exhaustion, arising from overwork;
and relief has distinctly followed rest. In other words
there is a form of " nervous-deafness," wholly cerebral in
its origin, which expresses itself not in abnormal function
of the auditory nerve, but in vascular derangement within
the tympanum. The general condition and history of
the patient, and the mingled slightness and obstinacy of
the apparently catarrhal symptoms, will mark out the
cases if the attention is alive to them.

The second element of tympanic disturbance above
referred to is an abnormal condition of the muscles of

the ossicula and Eustachian tube; and in connection
with these, of the muscles of the soft palate and
pharynx. In the year 1866 a case came before me
which first drew my attention to this subject. It was
that of a young lady, aged twenty, who some weeks
before had suffered from a fall on the back of the
head and spine, for which she had been under the care
of Mr. Brodhurst, who had applied heat to the spine
with much benefit. A deafness in the left ear had
rapidly followed. There had been relaxation of the
throat since scarlatina at seven. When she came to me,
a distinct voice was heard on the left side only at two
yards : w. r. $\frac{3}{40}$, l. $\frac{2}{40}$. Tuning fork well heard, loudest
on the left side.

The meatus were very narrow; the left membrane
was somewhat dull and sunk in. The Eustachian tube
was closed, nor could I get air to enter the tympanum,
either by Politzer's bag, or by the catheter. On the use
of Politzer's bag indeed the muscles of the palate seemed
to yield, and it always produced choking. On examining
farther it was found that she had a difficulty in swallowing, and the pharyngeal muscles not only acted imperfectly, but had lost part of their natural sensibility on
the left side; as also had the conjunctiva of the left eye,
which was dry, owing to a great deficiency in the secretion
of tears. Subsequently air was introduced into the
left tympanum by the Eustachian catheter, but with
difficulty and with a creaking sound, as thro' a tube

the walls of which were in contact. The hearing was
improved by it for a time to $\frac{6}{40}$ for the watch. The
diagnosis formed was impaired action of the muscles
connected with the Eustachian tube : local electrization
was proposed, but was not carried out.

This case, in the clearly marked character of its
symptoms, has stood alone in my experience, but if the
diagnosis formed was correct, it indicates that impaired
hearing, accompanied by symptoms similar to those of
catarrh, may have its origin in an impaired innervation
of the muscles of the pharynx and tympanum. In other
cases in which there was an evident preponderance of
nerve disorder, abnormal action of the tympanic muscles,
and slight but obstinate symptoms of catarrh of the
tympanum persisting apart from any faucial affection,
have appeared to me to coexist in a marked manner, and
to be alike amenable only to remedies which restored the
nervous tone.

But recently Dr. F. Weber-Liel has suggested * a new
interpretation even of the largest number of cases of
gradually progressive deafness. His views may be sum-
marised thus :—

Perfect hearing demands a normal balance of tension
between the pharyngeal, tubal, and tympanic muscles :
derangement of this tension in any one of these muscles
brings about secondary vaso-motor changes in all the
parts within the tympanum. Such disturbance begins

* " Progressive Schwerhörigkeit." Berlin, 1873.

most frequently in the form of a loss of power in the
tensor palati; and it induces a gradually increasing
deafness and tinnitus, which may assume the form alike
of sclerosis or of catarrh of the mucous membrane of the
tympanum; and that accordingly the chief aim of treatment in the majority of such cases should be the
restoration of the normal muscular power, the disturbance of which is the source of the vascular and other
changes. The treatment best adapted to do this is
local electrization of the pharyngeal and tubal muscles,
the continuous current being the most generally efficient;
but this must always be combined with careful attention
to the general strength, and when the paralysed condition has gone on to fatty degeneration it is unavailing.
Sea-bathing, which is generally counted dangerous,
Weber-Liel thinks beneficial, with prudence, except in
rheumatic patients, in whose case mineral baths may be
substituted. When there is hereditary tendency to the
affection there is not much hope. He finds that diminution of the tinnitus as the first result of treatment is
the most favourable sign, and that improvement of
hearing while the tinnitus is unrelieved is seldom permanent. The application of very mild astringent spray
by the small catheter introduced *into* the tympanum may
be added to the other means. Guided by Dr. Jago's
report of an unnaturally open condition of the Eustachian
tube on one side having been produced by excision of
the uvula, he suggests that in cases in which the tube

cannot otherwise be kept from closure (owing to paralysis of the muscles) a small portion should be excised from the soft palate, so that in the contraction of its healing the patency of the tube may be mechanically restored. Finally, when the retraction of the tendon of the tensor tympani is very excessive, and the pressure so produced upon the labyrinth is the cause of intense deafness and intolerable tinnitus, he advises the division of its tendon; an operation the value of which in mitigating distressing tinnitus, in some cases, is confirmed by some other surgeons. One symptom of the retraction of the muscle is that the malleus is not only drawn in, but slightly twisted on its axis, so that its anterior surface is directed a little forwards

It is, perhaps, worth while to give one of Weber-Liel's cases.

"Nov. 1869—A. P—, aged 45, weakly: constant tinnitus on both sides; giddiness, and rapidly increasing deafness; commencing the previous year, during convalescence from illness of a febrile character, and after much trouble. She could not follow rapid conversation at all, but could hear slow and distinct whispering near the ear. The membrane showed only a little abnormal concavity. On suction it moved outward less than natural. No catarrh. The velum hung loose, and in speaking and swallowing showed very slight marks of muscular tension. Her voice failed after long talking; she could not swallow twice together, and the act had little audible effect on the tube. Only when she supported the upper part of the throat with her hand did swallowing force air into the tympanum (?). Its effect was : increase of the tinnitus, and a momentary attack of giddiness. A bougie passed readily along the tube, and no secretion was withdrawn from the tympanum by suction thro' a small catheter introduced into it. Electricity was applied to the tube; one pole being introduced into it half a centimetre, and moved to and fro with the current applied to its anterior wall; the other pole to the neck. Clicking sounds were produced in each ear. The patient felt much fatigued, but greatly relieved in the head : the tinnitus was removed for the time ; for the watch the distance was trebled on the right side, and increased a third on the left. (Tonics, rest, and to avoid conversation.) In a fortnight, stronger, but hearing and tinnitus the same. A stream of six elements was applied, with increased and more lasting effect ; and this was continued every two or three days, to one ear at a time, for six weeks : the constant stream was found the best, one pole in the tube, the other moved upwards on the mastoid process. The cure seemed perfect; during the last two weeks the stream was applied only every fourth day. The electricity must not be omitted too soon ; especially not until the tinnitus is entirely removed."

There are evident imperfections in the report of this case, as, for instance, in respect to tests applied to the auditory nerve, and I abstain from any opinion on the views I have quoted farther than to say that they seem at least exaggerated. I believe no other surgeon has yet found electricity of similar avail in disease of the ear. My own trials of it have been wholly negative in their results; and at the last Conference of Aural Surgeons at Dresden * the opinion of its very rare and limited value was unanimously expressed. Information respecting it may be sought in the works of Dr. Brenner, of St. Petersburg, and Dr. Benedikt, of Vienna. The former asserts that by the constant current a certain definite reaction of the auditory nerve can be obtained, on opening and closing the current, which he terms the normal formula, and that in morbid states deviations

* "Arch. fur Ohrenheilkunde," Jan. 1874, p. 237.

from this formula occur, which may be corrected by the use of the current, and that improvement in the symptoms accompanies such correction. The " normal formula," as asserted by him, is that the healthy acoustic nerve, even with the highest degree of current applicable to the head, receives a sensation of sound only on *closure* and during the *passage* of the current with the cathode applied to the meatus, and on the *opening* of the current with the anode applied to the meatus; while it remains unexcited on the opening of the current with the cathode applied to the meatus, and on closure and during the passage of the current, with the anode there.

The truth of these views is much discussed by the German aural surgeons with a decided preponderance of opinion against them. One of the questions most debated is whether the sounds heard by the patients are due to an effect on the auditory nerve, or to contractions caused in the muscles of the tympanum; and Dr. Löwenberg has proposed, as a test, to apply the current while a manometer, suitably modified, is introduced into the meatus, to indicate whether any change takes place in the position of the membrana tympani. The settlement of these questions, and the recognition of the true place which electricity holds in aural therapeutics, will be a great gain to the art. And if a high value can be shown to belong to it, our power will have received a great extension. Duchenne has found it of avail for " hysteric deafness." And Moos* reports a very severe case, apparently of the same character, which might probably have baffled all other means, in which its efficacy was marked. Mr. R. J. Pye-Smith has reported some cases of galvanization of the *eye* in cases of anæmia of the optic disc, in which, as at least a definite diagnosis could be made, the results obtained possess a certain value, by analogy, for the treatment of the ear. Though no visible change was effected in the condition of the retina, it is satisfactory to learn that some good result was obtained in four cases out of six.†

In conditions of catarrh co-existing with signs of nervous disturbance, indications often exist of an abnormal state of the tympanic muscles; the patient will find, for example, that the ear accustoms itself by degrees to voices; and then if anything is said that it vexes him not to have heard, he becomes agitated, and is worse. In some cases of paralysis of the portio dura there may, perhaps, be detected hereafter symptoms indicative of a paralysis of the stapedius muscle.

* "Arch. of Oph. and Otology," vol. 1, No. 2, p. 464.
† "Brit. Med. and Surg. Jl.," 1872, p. 521.

CHAPTER XIV.

NERVE-DEAFNESS—HEREDITARY SYPHILIS—AFFECTIONS OF
THE EAR IN INDIA.

In this section we approach the darkest part of our
subject, and one which owing to the structure of the
organ must, so far as we can anticipate, always remain a
region for inference rather than for demonstration. It
presents to us a demand for extreme patience ; and even
for suspicion of apparently the best founded means of
investigation. For instance, we have seen that the apparently certain test of the tuning fork—its being heard
louder in the worse ear in tympanic affections, and louder
in the better ear in nerve-affections—has many exceptions.
And with regard to the morbid conditions of the nervous
apparatus, though dissection has made known to us the
occasional presence of many, hardly one of them has yet
been connected with characteristic symptoms, and their
most formidable signs are sometimes simulated by mere
external conditions that give rise to pressure on the
membrane.

But, notwithstanding these disadvantages, we may
fairly claim a certain amount of knowledge, and it is
steadily increasing. In the first place, the morbid con-

ditions which have been found on dissection of the labyrinth are the following :—

Mr. Toynbee found the auditory nerve diseased twelve times—eight times atrophied, twice with blood effused around it, once suppurating, and once having a tumour attached to it. Disease of the labyrinth he observed one hundred and five times ; most frequently atrophy, thickening, deficient endolymph, excess or deficiency of otoconie, deposits of pigment or calcareous matter, exostoses, the endolymph opaque or red, or the blood-vessels enlarged.* He has also seen hæmorrhage into the labyrinth after the poisons of gout, and various fevers.

Politzer also has found ecchymoses accompanying ecchymoses of the tympanum.

Voltolini found most frequently thickening of the membranous structures, cretaceous deposits, deficiency and excess of otoconie, deposit of pigment, amyloid degeneration of the auditory nerve, once a fibroid tumour in the cupola of the cochlea, and once a sarcoma of the nerve. † He found increase of the otoconie one of the first and most common morbid conditions. Förster has also reported sarcoma of the auditory nerve, and Dr. Böttcher has observed deposits of phosphate of lime infringing on the internal auditory canal.

In my own dissections I have found more or less decided morbid conditions of the nervous structures by no

---

* "Medico-Chirurgical Transactions," vol. xxxviii.
† Von Troeltsch, "Ohrenheilkunde," 3rd edition, p. 384.

means very uncommon. Most frequent has been an enlargement and congestion of the vessels of the labyrinth, often of a very extreme degree. This I have observed forty-one times, and chiefly in connection with inflammatory affections of the tympanum. Excluding cases of deaf-dumbness, I have found the membranous labyrinth obviously atrophied sixteen times, soft and swollen ten times, and seeming fatty twice the endolymph opaque or red seventeen times, seeming too abundant three times, and too scanty twice; the otoconie in apparent excess five times, and in apparent deficiency eight times; twice the labyrinth has contained pus, and once cholesterine; once the sacculus had undergone bony degeneration; once the lamina spiralis was thick; once the cochlea contained a fibroid mass, three times an excess of pigment, and twice extravasated blood.

Gruber * has found anæmia and hyperæmia of the labyrinth; inflammation of it, and especially, as he considers, a primary inflammatory affection of it in syphilis, attended with giddiness, &c.; extravasated blood; new formations epithelial and cellular; fibrous adhesions in the vestibule; choleasteatoma; cancerous growth; chalky deposit in the meatus internus; absence, atrophy and degeneration of the auditory nerve.

Gruber also lays stress upon the frequency with which labyrinth affections are secondary to tympanic ones, and

---

* "Lehrbuch der Ohrenheilkunde," Wien, 1870, p. 611.

observes that the secondary nerve-affection may remain permanent tho' the tympanic affection disappears.

In time these conditions may become recognizable during life; the sooner, doubtless, the more carefully unproved assumptions are abstained from.

Perhaps the best ascertained connection of organic lesion of the tympanum with definite symptoms is in the form of disease known as Ménière's disease, or labyrinthine vertigo. This affection has received its name from having been first observed by Ménière, in the case of a girl who caught cold while menstruating, became suddenly deaf, suffered from giddiness and vomiting, and died on the fifth day. No disease was found except a bloody exudation in the canals and vestibules. The symptoms, of course, appear the more easily intelligible thro' the experiments of Flourens, so often repeated, which show marked disorder of motion to result from section of the semicircular canals.

These cases seem to occur very frequently, and have been studied in their general relations, among others, by Dr. Hughlings Jackson. The following is a characteristic case :—

Great deafness on the left side, beginning after attacks of vertigo and faintness three years ago; tinnitus twelve months; tympanum healthy.

D. W—, æt. 50, a perfectly healthy man and of healthy family, with no tendency to deafness. About three years ago he had fits—five or six, at short intervals—of giddiness and vomiting, which he had never suffered from before. He staggered, and thought he was bilious. On such occasions he recovered in a few hours. His medical attendant stated that the fits were like fainting; and he ascribed them to over-work. They reminded him of sea-sickness. They mostly came on in the evening, and in the morning the patient was well. There was nothing to draw attention to the ears, but during their occurrence the medical man noticed him to be deaf on the left side. The patient did not discover this till afterwards. After two years, about twelve months ago, a singing noise in the ear came on suddenly, and has continued ever since; there were no fits or giddiness at that time, but he had been worried. The membrane is perfectly healthy, and to all appearance the cavity of the tympanum. Throat healthy. With the right ear closed, only words spoken in a loud voice near the left ear are heard. Watch (about four feet hearing distance) not heard. The tuning-fork on the teeth heard well, but only on the right side. Music sounds natural. On exhausting the air in the external meatus, so as to draw the membrane outwards, the tinnitus was decidedly diminished for a few minutes.

In this case no cause was apparent beyond the over-work. In the one that follows, a diseased condition of the osseous wall of the canals suggests itself:—

Frequent giddiness and vomiting, with staggering and tendency to turn to the left in walking; deafness of each ear; restricted perception of musical sounds; no apparent disease of tympanum; old disease of sternum.

N. W—, æt. 51, first seen in July, 1871; of moderately healthy family, free from tendency to deafness, but of strumous constitution; a widower seven years; never syphilis, until a mild form three years ago, which appeared to have no influence on his other symptoms. Since he was a child (he believes ever since measles) he has had ulcerated swellings over the sternum and two or three of the ribs of the right side, frequently discharging; no bone has, to his knowledge, come away. For many years,

S

certainly more than twelve, has had frequent fits of giddiness, often with vomiting, and sometimes falling; seven years ago fell and broke his right arm. For about twelve years the left ear had been deaf; the right ear had become so a few months since; this he first discovered by finding that music sounded out of tune, which he had not noticed in regard to the left ear. The tympana were healthy. Watch, right, contact; left not heard; a loud click of the nail heard at 20 inches. Tuning-fork heard badly, most in the right ear. Iodide and bromide of potassium were prescribed by Dr. Wilks.

On November 29th of this year he consulted me again. The hearing had changed slightly, the left ear having become the better, the watch being heard at one inch on the left side and not at all on the right; the tuning-fork was heard most on the left side (that is, still on the better one). He habitually wakes at three in the morning, with feelings of intense depression, and retches. Has fallen several times from giddiness, but not during the last two or three months till five days ago. He does not walk straight, and tends to turn *to the left side*, and to fall forwards.

Is not more deaf after the attacks, nor is there more tinnitus. This, however, is constant, like a shell. Suction produces no effect on it. A few months ago he had a distinct musical note in both ears. The discordant sound of music has diminished, but the hearing in this respect presents marked peculiarities. He can accurately repeat the note of a tuning-fork held to the left ear, but on the right side he says that it sounds much lower : g of the third octave is heard distinctly as c of the octave below, or twelve notes lower; with other notes there is a similar result, but less distinct. On testing the right ear by the piano, he said he heard g'''' more clearly than any other note, and with his back turned at a short distance picked out that note as the only one he heard. This would be explained, probably, by the fact before observed, that the resonance of the meatus is called into play by notes of this octave, especially by c'''' and g''''.

But the distinct hearing of one musical note as another, a difference of which he was quite conscious, is, perhaps, not yet explicable. I do not know that so great a sinking of the note, as from g''' to c'', has been observed before.

With regard to the nature of the affection of the labyrinth, some ground for conjecture is given by the long-standing periosteal affection of the sternum and ribs. Chronic affections of the lining membrane of the labyrinth, resulting in thickening and increased development of bone, have been met with on dissection, and in two cases of deaf and dumb children I found small bony tumours of the scalæ of the cochlea, in one case obliterating the fenestra rotunda. Upon the supposition that some such tendency existed in this case Dr. H. Weber advised iodide and bromide of potassium, and the use of the Kreuznach water. The tendency to turn to the left in walking, that is, towards* the worse side, was distinctly marked.

For the most part attacks of this kind occur suddenly, and without any previous affection of the ear having been noticed; but in the following case the symptoms supervened upon a tympanic disease; and it suggests the question whether, on accurate examination, it might not be found that some degree of tympanic disorder very fre quently preceded the more properly nervous symptoms.

Chronic catarrh ; tinnitus and slight deafness, with hyper-secretion in the tympanum ; sudden attacks of giddiness and sickness.

Nov. 7, 1871.—B. A—, æt. 42, of fair constitution ; no hereditary deafness. Was "bilious" as a boy, and has suffered from dyspepsia. Two years ago was under Dr. Mackenzie for "chronic sore throat." For about three months has suffered from singing and fulness in the left ear. Watch, right, $\frac{3}{40}$, left, $\frac{1}{40}$. Tuning-fork on vertex not perfectly heard, *loudest in the left (the worse)* ear. The membranes were slightly white and opaque, especially on the left side ; no increased vascularity visible ; Eustachian tubes pervious. Small touches of blistering fluid were advised, and a warm solution of carbonate of soda or chlorate of

---

* The observations on this point are as yet not consistent ; see Knapp, "Archiv. of Oph: and Otol.," Vol. ii., No. 1, p. 278.

potash to be syringed through the nostrils, and to the right ear a solution of perchloride of mercury, gr. j, with Ether Sulph., ʒj, in glycerine, ʒj.

On December 28th he reported himself as somewhat better.

On the 3rd of June, 1872, the symptoms were not improved, and on testing by the tuning-fork on the head it was found that it was no more heard best on the left (or worse), but on the better side; the reverse of that which had been the case (and which the patient distinctly remembered) on the first visit.

No mention was made of giddiness, or any similar symptom, but on his subsequently consulting Dr. Hughlings Jackson, the following history was elicited.

In November, 1871, he was walking home before dinner in good health, when he suddenly felt ill, and said to a friend, "By Jove, I am very giddy:" he could not walk straight; the feeling seemed to affect his legs "as if the ground were moving; when he turned his head to look behind he was worse; did not feel sick till he reached home; was better after lying down for half an hour, but when he got up he felt sick and giddy; no vomiting in this attack; the next morning he was well. In May and June he had two attacks in the night; he woke up feeling very giddy, and vomited. The attacks lasted about an hour, after which he slept, and in the morning was well.

In this case, coincidently with the attacks of vertigo, there was a marked change from a condition indicative of a sound to one indicative of a diseased labyrinth, as tested by the tuning-fork placed on the head. But there was no connection in the patient's mind between the condition of the ear and the attacks, nor would he probably, on consultation with a physician, refer to the tympanic disease.

As a rule these affections, when we are consulted for them, offer no prospect of cure. But I have witnessed a few cases which induce me to think that an essentially similar condition exists in a milder form and recovers

perfectly, so that the irremediable cases that we see are
not the sole exemplars of the disease, but the more severe
residuum of a possibly much larger number; and that
there may perhaps be a stage, even in the severer cases, in
which remedial measures might not be thrown away.
The severer cases, utterly incurable as they have proved
themselves, naturally suggest to the observer irremediable
causes; but a wider induction may possibly lead to a juster
diagnosis, one in which a greater place will be ascribed
to causes of disturbance less necessarily permanent.
Some three years ago a surgeon, himself well acquainted
with diseases of the ear, came to inform me that he had
been suddenly attacked with tinnitus and loss of hearing
in the left ear. He was a strong man, aged 30, hearing
fairly well until the day before, though he remembered as
a boy having some affection of one ear. He had been
very much overworked, and on waking one morning
found himself extremely deaf in the left ear, and with a
loud buzzing tinnitus. The tympanum appeared perfectly
healthy; the tuning-fork placed on the head was heard
only on the non-affected side. Our common opinion was
that the hearing was hopelessly lost, and a slight hæmorrhage in the labyrinth suggested itself as the most
plausible hypothesis. In the course of four or five days,
however, the symptoms gradually disappeared, and have
not returned in the course of four years; the hearing
being fairly good.

Another case, attended with a larger number of symptoms, and occurring in a lawyer subject to great over-fatigue, ran a more protracted but not less satisfactory course.

Attacks of giddiness and vomiting ; affection of hearing on both sides ; lack of control over the muscles of the eyes ; recovery.

May 7th, 1863.—S. W——, æt. 38 ; a strongly-made, healthy man ; was delicate and "nervous" as a child ; used to walk in his sleep, and had intense headaches. About Christmas last, having previously had no symptoms connected with the ears, he had taken a warm bath, and had experimented as to how long he could keep his head under water ; the next morning he woke with loud tinnitus in the right ear ; two days after, a plug of wax was syringed out by an aural surgeon, who pronounced the ear healthy, and the noise ceased ; but the next morning it was as bad as before. The sounds were like those of muffled machinery, and interfered with sleep. On Christmas day, while the tinnitus was better, he felt ill and giddy, and vomited.

Since then he has had six or eight of these attacks, some very severe, always on rising, and lasting the whole morning, The hearing was always worse at these times. The last occurred two years ago.

After the first attack he took quinine and rested, but without benefit for a time, the left ear becoming also affected in a less degree. Gradually, however, the noises abated, though any exercise of the ear or overwork would bring them on. As it became less the sound seemed to connect itself with the rhythm of the circulation ; when lying on the side it would cease. He could also obtain a momentary cessation by pressing the tragus into the meatus, or by rapidly withdrawing the finger from the meatus. When at its height every sound was painful, seeming to be heard with morbid intensity. Watch each side $\frac{10}{40}$, the voice not badly. He does not think that he is deaf. Membranes, throat, and tubes healthy. Tuning-fork not heard perfectly ; closing the meatus increases the sound.

His sight is good ; but for many years, when from any cause he has not been perfectly well, his eyes are apt to diverge, so that he sees double any object on which they may be resting without his consciously "looking" at it ; that is, the unconscious convergence of the eyes is liable not to be performed. This divergence of the eyes is visible to others, and has been remarked to him ; the first time several years ago.

During the years 1865-7 he was subject to varying and sometimes considerable deafness on the left side, and an excess of wax would form occasionally in the right, and require removal. There was never any sign of disease of the throat or mucous membrane of the tympanum ; but while the left ear was the worse there was a slight desquamation of the left meatus, and the membrane appeared somewhat the more concave of the two. The hearing is now fairly good; best on the right side ; he suffers very little from the tinnitus ; but any over-exertion of mind will bring it on ; the sound is often like bells.

In this case several of the most marked symptoms of Ménière's disease were present—vertigo, sickness, tinnitus, and deafness—yet the recovery has been almost complete. Nerve-fatigue appears as a direct cause ; and so far as the tinnitus is concerned, the precedent and concurrent affection of the muscles of the eyes, especially of the left, suggests the question : Was it not due to muscular spasm ?

Although there at no time existed the characteristic *clicking sounds* which sometimes accompany spasmodic contractions of the tensor palati, and have been shown by Politzer to depend on the drawing apart of the lips of the Eustachian tube, nor similar sounds, accompanied by visible motion of the membrane, which are due to contractions of the tensor tympani, the symptoms, nevertheless, appear to me to point to disordered muscular action as their chief cause. And this was also the patient's

very decided feeling. It is true no other disorder of any
branch of the facial could be traced, yet with the tendency
to disordered muscular action that existed, it is not hard
to suppose that some slight irritation of the tympanic
mucous membrane induced an irritable or (more likely)
paralytic condition of the stapedius muscle. Among the
reasons for this view are—the suddenness with which
the symptoms would occur, ceasing as suddenly ; a peculiar feeling of tension, as if in the membrana tympani
(sounds would feel painful sometimes, as if striking upon
a non-elastic membrane) ; any *use* of the ear would at
once increase the tinnitus ; and suction on the meatus
would always give momentary relief. In the first case
reported in this chapter suction also relieved the tinnitus.
It seems an interesting question whether to any extent,
and to what, the symptoms in well-marked cases of
Ménière's disease may depend, in fact, on muscular conditions. In the greater number of cases suction on the
meatus, to draw the membrane outwards, has no effect.

Other cases of tinnitus, co-existing with transient
affections of the motor muscles of the eye, have come
under my observation, all of them connected with nerve-
exhaustion ; and in the " American Journal of Medical
Sciences," April, 1863, is reported the case of a married
lady, in good health, but delicate and subject to cold
hands and feet, who, eighteen months before, after studying, had been attacked with double vision, the eyes being
drawn to the left, downwards. Twelve months afterwards

tinnitus came on in both ears. After nine months of hygienic treatment the tinnitus was diminished, the eyes remained the same. The left eye, on examination with the ophthalmoscope, was found normal.

In the two cases I have given of recovery from symptoms like those of Ménière's disease, severe and prolonged mental effort had preceded the attacks. Whether some tympanic disorder had not also been present could not be determined, but there was a history of some affection in childhood in the one case, and in the other the tympanic mucous membrane was evidently prone to congestion, and hardened wax had been removed from the meatus, a condition which we have seen to be generally connected with tympanic disorder. Now cases come before us every now and then, in which persistent deafness of a high degree follows, not long-continued exhaustion, but any mental disturbance, sometimes even of a very slight kind. Thus, besides serious distresses, such as hearing of the death of a friend, or the proposal of an operation upon a husband, I have known it suddenly follow a slight quarrel, or an alarm of thieves, or a slight blow received from a brother.* In another case a strong purge, merely, has seemed to be its cause. But it is difficult to understand that these ordinary events should permanently abolish a

* Perhaps some light is thrown upon cases of this kind by the following instance :—A lady of a gouty family, on hearing of the sudden death of her husband, became immediately extremely deaf ; in the course of two or three days symptoms of gout manifested themselves, and the hearing returned.

sense without some special reason. Nor is it to me at all satisfactory to ascribe loss of hearing, however purely " nervous " the affection may seem, to weakness. I have known one person at least suffering from deafness decidedly of the kind called nervous, who was distinctly apt to hear better when he was particularly weak ; we have seen, too, that hearing may become more acute on the death-bed, or after an attack of paralysis, nor is any effect of extreme exhaustion and debility more charac- teristic than a painful sensitiveness to sound.* A person too weak to hear, and yet capable of performing any of the other functions of life, is not imaginable by me. The question arises, therefore, whether any light can be thrown on the occurrence of deafness in certain cases from apparently quite inadequate causes. It seems to me it is possible that they may be found in the existence of a previously weakened condition of the ear.

The first case which suggested this thought to me was the following :—

B. H.—, æt. 44, consulted me in the year 1863; thinks his hearing was never sharp, though it was good enough for all purposes, and he never had any disease of the ears. At the age of twenty-two, being then in perfect health and possession of all his faculties, he was about to call on the parents of the lady who afterwards became his wife; but on the morning of the proposed visit he woke up almost entirely deaf; "they could not make him hear anything," he said. He had neither pain nor noise in his ears, but there was a stuffed feeling in them, for which they

---

* Jefferson Davis, towards the close of his imprisonment, is reported to have suffered most of all from this symptom.

were shortly afterwards syringed, with no effect. He had gone to bed hearing well. In about a week he began to improve, and was much better in a month; but about two years after he was troubled again by defective hearing, chiefly on the right side, which, within the last two or three years, has become worse. There has been all the while an occasional singing in the ears, most in the right.

He was a perfectly healthy man, of fair complexion; his hair had turned grey within the last two years. His health had always been good; four or five years ago he had been depressed about business and suffered much from his throat, but was not then more deaf; now finds himself made much worse by any excitement, especially of an annoying kind; no members of his family are deaf; there is some tendency to gout, but he never had an attack of it. He is moderate in his habits and a great walker, though lately he has got rather stout. Is more deaf after dinner, or after wine. Does not hear better in a noise. Is a great sportsman.

Watch r. contact, 1 $\frac{3}{10}$. The tuning-fork placed on the head was heard very imperfectly, and less on the right side than the left. The right membrana tympani appeared perfectly healthy; the left, the better ear, was slightly white. He inflated each tympanum with ease, diminishing for the time the hearing of the watch.

Thus far the symptoms appeared to be entirely unaccountable. Unquestionably we all of us in our turn have felt, or may hope to feel, happily nervous under like circumstances to my patient's. But growing stone deaf under them—unless it be to an unfavourable reply—is a phenomenon which pathology refuses to accept. But on carrying my inquiries farther I ascertained, that at the age of eighteen (four years, therefore, before the access of the sudden deafness) he had fallen the distance of twenty feet down the stairs of his college, and cut the vertex severely. He was ill for some time after, and the right pupil was dilated at the time, but neither his eyesight nor his hearing was affected. The right pupil is still somewhat larger than the left, but reacts well to light.

It appeared to me that this circumstance probably contained the key of the case, and that the deafness was due primarily and in chief degree to the apparently innocuous concussion, and only in a minor way to the nervous excitement which seemed to be its cause. My supposition is, that the fall—a cause which so frequently jars the auditory nervous

apparatus into an almost complete paralysis—had in this case jarred it
into a state of extreme liability to this condition. Other cases that I have
met with seem to justify this inference. A butcher's boy applied to me
in May, 1864, suffering from a high degree of deafness, of a month's
duration, with no apparent disease of the organ. He had been thrown
out of a cart a week before the hearing became impaired.

Another case may be worth reporting more in detail :—

Mary B—, a healthy woman, æt. 36, single, applied at Guy's Hospital in April, 1864, on account of deafness which was almost complete.
Four years ago she had fallen downstairs and struck the back of her
head. She was insensible for several days, and on recovering consciousness found herself quite deaf on the left side, and very considerably so
on the right. After three or four months the hearing began to return
in the right ear, and soon became moderately good. Loud sounds, however, were painful to her, and she would become more deaf during a
cold, or if excited. The fall also destroyed the sense of smell.

This condition continued upwards of three years, until eight weeks
ago, when, after returning from a walk during hot weather, but unat-
tended with fatigue, she became again suddenly deaf in the right ear.
Nothing had occurred to agitate her beyond a pleasing invitation. She
had worked and stooped more than usual a fortnight before, and the
day before after riding in a cab had felt somewhat sick. At the time of
becoming deaf she had a pain in the head. Leeches and blisters had
been applied, and medicine given which produced "twitchings ; " she
had been galvanized also, without result. She complained of tinnitus,
like bells, or a piano, in both ears. This had previously existed on the
left side only. She was unable to repeat words shouted into her ear.
The tympana, so far as could be ascertained, were perfectly healthy.
Eighteen months afterwards she had become entirely deaf. Tinnitus
less ; health good. Each membrane was natural in appearance except
a little whiteness at the upper and posterior parts. Other cases also
I have met with in which deafness caused by a blow on the head has
ceased for a time and suddenly returned.

It is only as a suggestion that the idea can be proposed—but is it not possible that in all cases of apparent

loss of hearing from slight causes, it may be found hereafter that some previous source of injury to the ear has existed?

This view has been confirmed in my mind by another series of observations, which have seemed to indicate that one cause of nerve-deafness in after life is the existence of, possibly slight and unregarded, ear-affections during childhood, or perhaps in youth. As bearing on this point I may report two dissections.

E. G—, æt. 10, died in Guy's Hospital on September 28, 1864, of disease of the vertebræ. His hearing had not been much impaired. *Right ear:* Membrana tympani very concave, slightly red at the circumference and along the malleus ; mucous membrane of the tympanum of pinkish colour ; the vestibular surface of the stapes was marked by its red colour ; stapes not fixed, but a soft, thick band extended along its posterior border and filled up the space between the crura ; the blood-vessels of the vestibule, and especially of the ampulla of the external canal, were unusually numerous and large. *Left ear:* The central half of the membrane destroyed ; tympanic cavity nearly obliterated by the thickened mucous membrane, but containing a little purulent matter ; the blood-vessels in the vestibule generally were much enlarged.

Jane E—, æt. 18, died in Guy's Hospital on the 9th November, 1864, apparently from chorea, which became extremely violent two days before death. The cord as well as the brain was examined, but no disease was found, except some very slight vegetations on the mitral valve ; she had become rather deaf a few months back, and on the left side she had had some earache and a little tinnitus. *Right ear:* The tympanic mucous membrane was red, as also was the base of the stapes on its vestibular aspect ; cochlea and vestibule normal ; some few red vessels visible in the latter. *Left ear:* Membrana tympani bright and thin, tympanum containing a little thin mucus, its lining membrane pink ; the cochlea presented numerous full vessels, certainly more than usual ; but the membranous vestibule appeared red even to the eye, and on examining the posterior canal by the microscope it was found congested to an extreme degree, some of the vessels appearing (under ⅕ objective) nearly half an inch in diameter and crowded with blood-globules, many of which had escaped, so that the whole field appeared more or less full of them ; in other respects the vestibule seemed normal.

It is surely a reasonable inference that in the last described condition, had the patient regained her health, a foundation might have been laid for an obscure "nervous deafness." The membrana tympani, not having been involved in the general congestion of the mucous membrane of the tympanum, might have retained its natural appearance, and little would have remained on which to base an opinion of the cause of the disease.

By the side of this case I wish to put the following :

George T—, a bootmaker, of apparently nervous constitution, æt. 32, applied at Guy's Hospital, May 4th, 1864. He had gradually lost his hearing at 14, and for ten years had been able only to distinguish shouted words ; he habitually used a tube ; much tinnitus, like the roar of the sea, and at times like birds or bells ; no pain, except that he had *earache as a child ;* hears grave sounds much better than acute ones, such as bells or music ; men's voices better than women's. His mother's mother was deaf, and a brother when young, but he was cured.

The membranes were rather opaque, but bright and of natural curve ; he inflated each Eustachian tube with a creaking sound. Watch not heard. Tuning-fork heard very badly when made to vibrate on the table, and scarcely at all when placed on the head, unless the meatus was closed, when it was heard decidedly better on each side ; left ear the worst. No reason to suspect syphilis.

Potassii Iodidi gr. v ; Hydrarg. perchlorid. gr. $\frac{1}{16}$ ter die, Pil. Col. co. gr. v. p. r. n.

In a month he reported himself as decidedly better, and could understand a moderately raised voice near him. He could, however, hear a hand bell only when quite near the ear, and then more the "strok of it than the "ring." Could get on without his tube, and the "bird singing" was less. Continued medicine.

August 30*th.*—The Eustachian catheter was introduced on the right side, and air entered the tympanum with a loud harsh rustle, perhaps slightly improving the hearing.

On September 12th his medicine was changed to Quinine gr. ss. ter die, and on the 27th a lotion was ordered, consisting of Tr. Iodin. 3j. Glycerine vij.

On October 13th, after some variations, he was again much better. The left ear, which, before, he did not use at all, was then the better. Watch heard on contact by each ear.

This case is not reported with a view of recommending this particular treatment, which was used experimentally, and undoubtedly cannot be relied upon in all cases that appear similar. But it is a good example of a large class of cases in this, that there was nothing to throw light upon the cause of the disease except the existence of earache as a child.

On such a point as this it is impossible for one individual to adduce more than slightly probable evidence. Only the long continued and combined observation of many could either establish or disprove the connection between early inflammatory affections of the ear, and subsequent deafness of a nervous character: that is, whether certain kinds of inflammatory affection of the tympanum in childhood so far involve the adjacent structures of the labyrinth as to predispose them to a loss of function from causes that would not otherwise lead to that result. The grounds for this view are : First, the results of dissection, which exhibit so frequently vascular engorgement of the labyrinth as a concomitant of tympanic congestion, which is certainly very frequently, if not usually, present in infantile earache; and, secondly, the observation of cases; which, while they present on the one hand continual instances of destruction or collapse of the membrane, polypi, and every variety of inflammatory havoc of the conducting parts of the organ, as the result of such infantile earache or discharge, present scarcely fewer instances of nervous lesion, for which no other cause can be found if this be excluded. It seems to me also that the nervous element is less apt to be present when the early disease has resulted in more or less destruction of the membrane than when the membrane has remained entire.*

The following case shows a loss of nervous power dating from repeated earaches as a child.

B. F—, æt. 41, a healthy man, applied to me in July, 1865. For ten or twelve years had been almost entirely deaf in the left ear, which did

---

* In reference to the connection between congestion of the tympanum and that of the labyrinth, I may observe that anatomists are at issue on the question whether the vessels of the tympanum and labyrinth anastomose. Politzer affirms that they do, by means of twigs which pass through the fenestra ovalis ["Arch. der Ohrenheilk," vol. ii., p. 91]; Von Tröltsch, supported by Hyrtl, says that they do not ["Lehrbuch der Ohrenheilk," 3rd Aufl., p. 399]. My own attention has been particularly attracted to the reddened and vascular appearance of the vestibular aspect of the base of the stapes in cases of tympanic congestion. The tympanum and labyrinth are ossified independently, and supplied with blood from different sources; but the fact of the frequent coexistence of vascular derangement of the two structures, is unquestionable. It rests upon the dissections of Toynbee, confirmed by those of Von Tröltsch, Politzer, Voltolini, and others, as well as by my own.

not vary at all. On the right side he is liable to become very deaf also whenever he catches a cold, and has then a singing tinnitus in the head. He becomes rapidly deaf, but gradually recovers under use of camphor linament and port wine, and after a few days is about as before the cold. He now requires a loud voice to the right ear, having recently caught cold ; with the left scarcely hears words.

Right ear : m. t., a little dull and slightly more concave than natural. Inflation of the tympanum on Politzer's plan made a little improve ment in the hearing.

Left ear : m. t., of white irregular aspect, and somewhat more con- cave than natural. Air entered the tympanum with a harsh sound through the Eustachian catheter, and a little iodine vapour was passed in, without improvement.

He could not hear a tuning fork on the head, nor on the left meatus. It was heard on the right. Closing the meatus, while he maintained a humming sound with closed lips, *increased the sound on both sides ;* it was heard loudest on the right.

A nerve as well as a tympanic affection on the left side is indicated here as well by the degree of the deafness, as by the facts that the tuning fork and his own voice were better heard on the less deaf side, and that closing the meatus had the normal effect. The history was that as a child he suffered repeatedly from earache and deafness. That the left ear bore the main brunt of these attacks is indicated by the greater amount of old disease exhibited by the left membrana tympani. No other cause of deaf- ness appeared.

Miss F. S—, æt. 26, healthy, and of healthy family, except a slight tendency to gout. Is extremely deaf in right ear ; the left ear is good, except occasionally during colds. No tinnitus. Each meatus con- tained a little cerumen pushed down by the attempt to clean it out. Each membrana tympani was of a similar dull white aspect. Inflation of the tympanum a little dulled the hearing on the left side; no effect upon the right. Watch, left, $\frac{40}{18}$; on right side a loud click of the nails was heard only close to the ear; the voice scarcely understood. T. f. on head well heard, but only on the left side; closing the meatus increased the sound on the left, had no effect on the right side. At about five years old she had had a severe attack of earache in the right ear, from which the deafness probably dates. No other cause for it could be discovered.

Here the nerve was unquestionably involved, and it is difficult to suppose a history more decisive. In the next case the inflammatory affection in childhood played a less important part, but probably contributed its share to the result. The case is an instance of the complicated character which ear affections very frequently present.

L. G—, æt. 24, of florid complexion, but languid aspect, 6 feet 3 in. in height. First noticed a hardness of hearing four or five years ago, slowly increasing, especially the last year. No tinnitus; does not hear better in a noise. Had severe earache when a child; none since. Is subject to colds, and is more deaf during them. About the time when his deafness began a gun exploded close to him, and deafened him for a day or so, but he seemed quite to recover. Shoots a good deal, not feeling his hearing worse for it; has a slight liability to rheumatism, and has had an attack of lumbago. His grandparents had gout, and his mother's father died of phthisis; his mother died of kidney disease. No albuminuria.

Watch, r. $\frac{1}{10}$; l. $\frac{2}{10}$; not on the head. T. f. not well heard, but equally in both ears; sound increased on closing either meatus. Membranes thin and bright; long process of incus and promontory very visible; some white opacity about the upper border; throat a little relaxed, not red; inflates each tympanum with scarcely any effect on the hearing. The symptoms indicated a slight chronic catarrhal affection, with a decided, and, probably, a predominating element of nervous failure. The fundus of the eye was examined by Dr. Hughlings Jackson, and found much pigmented, but not abnormal. Steel had been already prescribed. Some treatment was advised for the throat, and on two occasions vapour of acetic ether was introduced through the Eustachian catheter into the left tympanum, producing a certain improvement of the hearing, but also a little tinnitus, both temporary. Much white glairy mucus was removed from the faucial orifice of the tube.

Similar cases are constantly recurring ; and there is an uninterrupted gradation in them up to severe attacks, which tell their story but too plainly, such as the following :—

Laura E—, æt. 30, healthy, but very nervous. Lost her hearing entirely when about a year old, at which time severe cerebral symptoms set in ; the eyes being turned up, and the body stiff for several days ; no distinct convulsions ; both jugulars are said to have been opened, and mercury was rubbed in. Diarrhœa followed, which seems to have relieved the head, but the hearing was gone. An eminent physician said that if it were recovered it would be at the time of cutting the second molars, and at that time (about the age of seven) there came on a slight perception of sound. She was then again treated with mercury, which is supposed to have induced a nervous weakness, without result on the hearing. She appears now totally deaf in the right ear ; the left very gradually advanced till about the age of twenty, and with it and the aid of the eyes she can understand short sentences, but cannot repeat numbers shouted into her ear ; distinguishes sound by the quality of the vibration ; *e. g.* she perceives thunder in the head, guns in the feet. She felt the explosion at Hounslow some years back, at a distance of fifteen miles, when no one else in the neighbourhood was aware of it. Some tinnitus ; does not hear better in a noise. It is said that she heard (comparatively) well on the mountains in Switzerland. Throat healthy.

Meatus narrow ; each membrana tympani bright, inflates left with a slight moist sound ; not the right. The right Eustachian tube being closed, it was in two or three sittings gently made pervious. No change ensued.

If in connection with this case we recall those, referred

to before, of severe fever and almost convulsive restlessness at once relieved by discharge from the ear, must
not the real source of the disease be referred almost
beyond doubt to the tympanum? Suppose the membrane in the former cases had not given way, and so
no relief had been gained, what could have been more
probable than a propagation inwards of the irritation?
Or how should a severe affection of the brain and its
membranes pass away so entirely, leaving no effect but
an abolition of the function of each auditory nerve? If,
as is not uncommon, we find inflammatory affections of
the tympanic mucous membrane inducing abscess of the
cerebral substance without visible disease of the intervening parts, is it not probable that a parallel extension
of morbid action might take place in respect to the more
closely related labyrinth? *

It is not only in this extreme form, however, that
deafness results from apparent "cerebral" affections in
childhood. Among the multitude of children who apply
for assistance, in consequence of disease of the tympanum
or Eustachian tube, there occurs every now and then a
case which, on a hasty examination, would pass as an
ordinary one, but would be sure in time to arrest the
surgeon's attention by its refusal to take the ordinary

---

* Very many cases of deaf mutism—even some supposed congenital
—most probably arise in a similar way. In several instances I have found
on dissection traces of former inflammatory affection of the labyrinth,
especially a roughness and contraction of the first turn of the cochlea at
its junction with the vestibule.

course. Remedies do not tell. Perhaps the Eustachian tubes are obstructed, but opening them has little effect; if the membranes are perforated the condition of the exposed mucous lining of the tympanum may be improved, but the hearing does not advance. Then, perhaps, it begins to be noticed that the child has a peculiar inexpressive look, unlike both the keen inquisitiveness of the congenital deaf mute and the self-absorbed restlessness of the imbecile; and on testing more minutely it is found that the tuning fork is very badly heard, and that, so far as can be elicited from children, the other symptoms of a nerve affection are present. In these cases I have often found on inquiry that there have been, probably some years before, more or less defined convulsive or "cerebral" attacks. For the most part these attacks seem to occur during the first two or three years of life. Sometimes, however, they are deferred to a somewhat later period, as in the following case, in which one ear only was affected :—

CASE 22.—February, 1866. Mary J—, æt. 15, was first noticed to be deaf in the left ear when about 11, having been before supposed inattentive. On examination the hearing on the right side was perfect; on the left the watch was scarcely heard, and a very distinct voice was required close to the ear. Each m. t. bright, but with a crescentic patch of white deposit inferiorly; the left slightly more concave than natural. Passing air into the left tympanum seemed to produce a slight but temporary improvement. The tuning-fork was well heard, but much better on the right side than on the left. Closing the right meatus increased the sound; closing the left seemed to have a varying effect. There appeared evidently to be a nervous lesion on the left side. Her history was that at the age of six or seven she had a severe illness, called at the time congestion of the brain, and after excitement during recovery, had a sort of prolonged fainting fit. She had been a very delicate child, but lately had been healthy : complexion anæmic and dull, lips thick ; subject to headache. A left molar tooth in the upper jaw painful and tender, but never pain in the ear or discharge. Catamenia regular : during one of the periods I saw her, and found that the hearing of the left ear was decidedly worse than either before or after ; the right (good) ear was unaffected.

An observation of Gruber's may throw light on some of these cases; namely, that in some cases of strumous enlargement of the glands he has found marked congestion of the labyrinth.

The following case also indicates the effect which disorder of the tympanum, even after it has ceased, may have in depressing the nervous function :—

D. W—, æt. 50, was sent to me in November, 1865, by Mr. Paget, under whose care he had long been "with various symptoms of *disorder* of his nervous system, and with chronic catarrh of the bladder." He had always been delicate, but had never had syphilis, nor gone to any excess. First noticed himself a little deaf about fifteen years ago, shortly after a box on the ear from one of his children. A singing tinnitus, now constant, has existed about the same time. Left ear always the worst. Some treatment was early tried in vain, and the deafness continued about the same until three weeks ago, when, without any cause, he became very much more deaf in the course of two or three days. He had been troubled with giddiness for a few weeks previously, which has lately been worse. His manner was that of extreme nervousness, and his study of his own symptoms amounted almost to hypochondria. Family healthy ; has had no gout ; but Mr. Paget having thought he observed indications of a gouty tendency, he has found, on inquiry, that his mother's father suffered from it. Four or five years ago, while hunting, he had an attack of double vision, being otherwise well. Mr. Bowman pronounced the eyes right, but that the nerves did not act in unison. This passed off in two or three weeks, but returned about a year ago, and has continued since at intervals, when the eyes are directed to the sides ; has muscæ occasionally ; sees well by each eye with a glass. The right pupil is somewhat larger than the left. No albuminuria.

He required a raised voice on the right side ; on the left could just repeat a monosyllable shouted into the ear. A loud watch was not heard, nor an ordinary tuning-fork placed on the head, except when the right meatus was closed. Right membrana tympani thick, and somewhat concave ; redness along malleus ; left, thick, rigid appearance, decidedly too concave, and drawn inwards. The right Eustachian tube was pervious, and inflating the tympanum somewhat dulled the hearing. The left tube was closed.

Although, from the history of the case, the nervous constitution of the patient, and that the fact that the tuning-fork placed on the vertex was heard on the right side only, it was considered very doubtful whether any improvement to hearing would result from restoring the perviousness of the left Eustachian tube, it was held right to attempt it, not only on account of the deafness, but also with a view of removing a possible cause of general nervous irritation, in the pressure on the labyrinth which exclusion of air from the tympanum seems to involve. The obstruction proved to be considerable, but by the aid of bougies the tube was rendered pervious in the course of a month, so that he could freely inflate the tympanum, the membrana tympani yielding with a jerk before the air, and resuming a natural appearance. A good deal of mucus was withdrawn from the region of the tube, and warm iodine vapour injected a few times. The hearing seemed at times improved, but ultimately remained as at first, and the proceeding was considered a failure. In about a week, however, the hearing began to improve, and in the course of two months it became, without further treatment, in both ears as good as it had been before the last access of deafness.

In the later stages of phthisis, Dr. Moxon states that the auditory nerve sometimes loses its function while the tympanum is found on examination quite healthy. After diphtheria also an almost total deafness may occur with or without other pareses, but with no tympanic affection. In one such case, a girl of 8, the sight had been lost for a time but had suddenly returned. In some rare cases also a child's hearing will return even after it has seemed totally lost. The following case has come before me lately :—

Mary D—, æt. 9, had never had an illness, and came of a healthy family, in which there was no tendency to deafness. Fourteen days before I saw her, while supposed to be hearing well, she had been seized with earache on the left side, apparently not very severe ; she had had a cold a few days before. The next morning her throat was sore, and in two days there was a slight discharge ; this ceased and returned again n three or four days for a short time : the pain seemed not entirely gone. From the beginning of the attack the hearing rapidly failed, and when I saw her she seemed totally deaf. She had had a good ear for music, and had never seemed pained by sound ; was of active brain, small for her age. On examining the ear the meatus was slightly red, but the membrane was quite healthy ; it bulged naturally on inflation by Politzer's bag with no effect on the hearing ; no cause for the deafness was discoverable. A mild tonic treatment was suggested, and a small touch of blistering fluid was applied behind each ear. In two days from the time of her visit her hearing began to return, and in a week was stated by her medical attendant to be as acute as ever ; at the end of a month she seemed to be in perfect health, except a slight enlargement of the tonsils. Two months subsequently she had an attack of eczema of the skin of the same ear, extending into the meatus, but not interfering with the hearing. In a few weeks it disappeared.

In the journal of the Medical Society for 1844, p. 473, is reported a case in which a deaf and dumb child recovered hearing after the discharge from the bowels of eighty-seven lumbrici and innumerable oxyurides.

Whether there is any distinct relation between epilepsy

and affections of the ear seems not yet determined. Dr.
Hughlings Jackson has observed that an "aura" may
start from the ear, as from other parts. And I have mentioned a case in which an attack resembling epilepsy was
caused in a healthy man by the introduction of the
catheter. Dr. Druitt also informed me of an old man in
whom, after a first "fit," deafness of one side ensued;
after a second deafness of the other; and after a third
partial paralysis. A few cases of co-existence of epilepsy
and impaired hearing I have seen, but only one in which
there seemed a close connection between the two affections, and this was in a gentleman aged 35, sent to me
by Dr. Hughlings Jackson, in whom loss of hearing on
the left side and attacks of epilepsy had come on about
three years before. Dr. Budd, of Bristol, had ascribed
the epilepsy to the ear affection; slight deafness had
preceded the fits. There had been no aura from the ear,
and no tinnitus. There was an old perforation of the
membrane, and thick discharge was collected within the
tympanum. But the case in which the effect of epilepsy
seemed most marked was the following :—

9th Oct., 1867. T. C—, æt. 32, healthy, a little gout in the family, but
he was never affected by it. Two months before, had taken pot. iod. and
quinine for an eruption, supposed syphilitic, but said he had never had
syphilis, only twice gonorrhœa ; subsequently Dr. Gull pronounced
that he found no signs of syphilitic disease having existed. For about
six weeks there had been a slight discharge and tenderness of the right
ear, but no deafness had been noticed till three weeks ago, when, without
cause or warning, there came a buzzing in the ears or head, with headache, especially above the eyes, and dizziness. There was no sickness.

He was at the Isle of Wight, where he had been bathing, but not much. The dizziness lasted five or six days and went away before the deafness became considerable. For the last four days has required a loud voice near to the ear. The throat was healthy. Urine pale ; no albumen. The tuning-fork was heard very badly, and closing the meatus on each side made it sound louder. He heard a loud crack of the nails only at about twelve inches on each side. There was a little swelling and redness of the right meatus, and the outer layer of the membrane was white and thick. On the left side the meatus contained a mass of cerumen and epidermis ; the membrane was healthy. The hearing was not altered by syringing.

Nine days after he came again, and said that the day after his former visit, while travelling by train, he had suddenly lost consciousness, probably for half an hour ; a gentleman in the train told him he had a fit. He had bitten his tongue ; did not feel ill either before or after, but for three or four hours heard much better, but became as deaf as ever again before evening. Since then, however, has gradually improved, and now hears a moderate voice two or three yards. Never had a fit before. The tinnitus continues.

The watch was heard on each side $\frac{4}{40}$; the tuning-fork a little better. Dr. Gull ordered pot. bromid. gr. xv. ter die, and claret a pint daily. The tinnitus had continued to diminish and the hearing to improve on his last visit a week later.

Had the "fit," which Dr. Gull considered to have been of an epileptic character, anything to do with the return of the hearing ? Were the symptoms due to syphilis ? I do not clearly remember any other case parallel to this ; but in Sept. 1873, while examining a woman, aged 20, by the tuning-fork placed on the teeth, she fell, lost consciousness, and was very slightly convulsed. On recovering she said the noise she had complained of was gone, and that she could hear quite well. She had been deaf in the left ear with a singing noise about a year. The membranes.

were of healthy appearance, the tuning-fork best heard on
the deaf side. Before the fit, the hearing for the watch on
the left side was half that on the right; after it they were
equal. I saw the patient again about a year after; the
hearing had not continued better.

In this connection the following case also is interesting.
In Oct. 1867, I was consulted by a healthy-looking youth
of 18, who said that two years before, while sitting over
his studies in Germany, and in perfect health, a sudden
rushing noise had come in his right ear, had increased
for three weeks, and had never ceased since ; the hearing
on that side was from the same moment greatly impaired.
He was not at all sick or giddy or in any way ill. The
noise becomes worse after beer or wine, or smoking, or
exertion. He used to stammer, but about two years ago
got over it. The throat was much swollen and red, and
the tonsils, especially on the left (the unaffected side),
were large. The membranes were of healthy appearance,
and perhaps a little more concave on the right side. The
tuning-fork was heard loudest on the left side, but the
watch was heard quite well by each ear; a little better by
the affected one than by the other. This fact was confirmed on previous visits, though he required a loud
voice near him on the right side. An external noise, by
deadening the tinnitus, made him hear better. Inflating
the ears made the better ear deaf for a time, but it was
relieved by swallowing or yawning. Air entered each ear
obscurely, the membranes moving naturally before it. No

treatment was of avail. His family attendant afterwards informed me, that when young he suffered much from swollen tonsils, but was not deaf. His father was healthy, but suffered from swelling of the nasal mucous membrane. His mother, however, was liable to severe congestive headaches with "liver," and was then depressed and restless, with intolerance of light, and a peculiar cast of one eye, and occasionally a hyperæsthesia for sound; a perfect dread of an organ, for example. The other brother had often had congestive headaches, with some temporary derangement of vision. His sister, at five or six, had a passive effusion into the pleura; tubercle was feared, but it passed off. A few years later she suffered from epilepsy, which had ceased. Two years after my patient said he was the same, but the affected ear had scarcely any wax. In this case, possibly, the family history, through the mother, contains the key to the attack. The watch being better heard on the affected side, while the voice was heard much worse, is a condition that I have met with a few times only. In the case of a surgeon, with slight congestion of the tympanum and tinnitus, due to overwork and recovering rapidly on rest, this symptom was very marked, as if there were a hyperæsthesia for mere sound, while the power of following articulate speech was impaired.—Dr. Parkes states that among diseases of the nervous system in soldiers, epilepsy stands first and otitis second.

Dr. Bader has been good enough to examine by the

ophthalmoscope, for several months together, every
patient who came to me with symptoms which I considered of a "nervous" character. With few exceptions
he found hypermetropia present; and he considered it to
be due, not to flatness of the eye-ball, but to " a certain
paralysis of the third nerve." No other affection of the
eye was found to prevail; that is, the muscular rather
than the nervous structure appeared prone to fail. One
case of great deafness and tinnitus, co-existing with
marked congestion of the optic discs, presented itself to
me in the person of a medical man, resident for fifteen
years in India, and hard worked. The tympana were
healthy and conducted sound freely, as proved by the
increased sound of the tuning fork upon the teeth when
the meatus were closed. A single leech repeated, with
other treatment in various hands, was followed by decided
improvement. He thought a lotion of pot. iod. gr. x.,
ether ʒj to the ounce of water did him good.—In another
case, a youth of 22, in whom apoplexy of the retina
existed on each side, with lack of power of directing the
right eye (without evidence of syphilis), there had been
recently a failure of hearing and tinnitus. Watch each
ear $\frac{6}{40}$; the tuning-fork heard imperfectly. The membranes were dull, and appeared rather flat. Both sight
and hearing improved under iodide of potash. Almost
the only case in which I have known tinnitus pronounced
agreeable by the patient was that of a woman of 58, who
had suffered from glaucoma of each eye, one cured by

operation eight years before, the other affected for three years. She had first become slightly deaf after typhus at the age of 22, but was worse after a confinement nineteen years ago. At first there was constant tinnitus; but for some years past it had subsided into a pleasant singing, like serious music, recurring at intervals. As a rule I have come to regard tinnitus of a distinctly musical character as a sign of nerve affection.—A man, aged 40, who was subject to sudden attacks of loss of hearing, with singing noise, and in whom the tympana were healthy, complained also of dimness of vision, and was found to have dark specks upon the yellow spot.*

A common cause of nerve affection is concussion from falls or exposure to loud sounds. In respect to the latter, suddenness adds greatly to the danger. I have known deafness ascribed to the firing of a cannon on a Rhine steamboat to show an echo, the sound being unexpected; and even to the shout of some Indians at an entertainment. The shock of guns often produces it, and in all obscure cases, in men, inquiry should be made whether they ever feel stunned after a day's shooting. Boilermakers continually suffer, and so also do artillery officers. The effect of the near discharge of a large gun is sometimes to rupture the membrane; and when this is the case, I believe the nerve is much less apt to suffer. I have known a large perforation arise from the shock of a gun,

* I owe the opportunity of examining these patients to the kindness of Mr. Hutchinson.

the nerve being unaffected ; and the artificial membrane
almost completely restored the hearing. I was told by an
artillery officer, seventy-nine years old, that when he was
studying at Woolwich, the general in command had made
him (among others), as a punishment, stand near the
mouth of a low-angle mortar when it was fired. A bar-
barous practice like this is of course now impossible. My
patient's hearing had never recovered from the effect. It
would be interesting to determine whether opening the
mouth during the firing of cannon is of any use in
preserving the ear from shock. I have heard the most
opposite statements, all apparently on good authority.

The effect of quinine in disturbing the function of the
ear is very striking Whether permanent deafness can
result from it is very hard to determine, because in almost
all the cases in which it appears to have had this effect
the disease for which it has been given might rather bear
the blame. Dr. Roosa* is of opinion, from observation,
that quinine may not only affect the nervous power but
may excite an inflammatory condition of the meatus and
tympanum. In the New York " Medical and Surgical
Reporter," Nov. 22, 1873, Dr. S. Reynolds points out that
the effect which quinine produces upon the *sight* are of
two kinds : (1) a visible hyperæmia of the retina, which
however subsides, still leaving a dulness of vision without
any ophthalmoscopic appearances; and (2) diplopia arising
from disorder of the muscles.

* Loc. cit.

The following case exhibits "labyrinthine vertigo" complicated with temporary effects from quinine :—

L. C—, æt. 54, a man of fair constitution, with no deafness in the family ; seen first on May 5, 1867. For fifteen years more or less deaf in the right ear, before any symptoms of illness ; but for the last three months had been dyspeptic, with frequent attacks of nervous exhaustion, vertigo, and sickness. For four or five days had felt better, but had noticed for the first time a rumbling noise in the left ear ; yesterday he found that his hearing on that side also was impaired. In the right ear there is a throbbing with the pulse, which has existed long, but not from the beginning of the deafness. The right ear feels dull and dead all round. He does not hear better in a noise. W. r. contact ; l. ${}^{12}_{40}$. Tuning-fork was not well heard ; louder in the better ear (the left), in which also it becomes louder on closure of the meatus. Both membranes healthy and tubes free. Change of scene was advised, and after three months his health improved, and the hearing of the left ear seemed perfectly restored. He then had ague, and took quinine, but in twenty-four hours the deafness returned, but abated again in two days after discontinuing the quinine. He had a few slight attacks of vertigo. About the beginning of October he had influenza, which affected his hearing transiently. On the 16th w. r. $\frac{1}{40}$; l, $\frac{15}{40}$ (a slight improvement) ; but he noticed that he could not sing in tune. Music sounded natural.

The patient was not seen again until November, 1873. He stated that his health got worse for a time. Iron and Pot. Bromid. were tried with little effect ; slight attacks of vertigo were present ; on one occasion he was very giddy and sick, and could not walk alone ; hearing bad. He then wore a Pulvermacher's chain around the waist ; pustules were formed, and about that time he became better, and was not ill again till a month ago. At that time he felt suddenly a sinking in the right leg ; it was but momentary, but it left much depression for some hours. Quinine was given for ten days, and deafness again returned in the left ear, and an attack of swimming in the head followed, with sickness, lasting about an hour. For the last week has had swimming in the head, but no tendency to turn to one side rather than the other. In both ears he has "the sea roaring and the fulness thereof." The throat is somewhat congested, as is usual ; the sight good. The condition of the ears as before. Is often more deaf on waking. The sounds of various tuning-forks are heard alike on both sides, and he can sing short strains correctly, but cannot repeat the notes of a piano. Suction on the meatus had no effect on the tinnitus.

But most of the cases of deafness ascribed to quinine, that I have seen, have occurred in former residents in India, in whom loss of hearing without visible affection of the tympanum is very frequent. The following is a characteristic case :—

A. S—, aged 48, a colonel in the Indian army. " The first trouble I ever had with my ears was the occurrence of abscesses in them at Calcutta, about June, 1872; no deafness remained, as I think, and the abscesses were supposed due to colds resulting from sleeping under punkahs and in thorough draughts.

" In August, 1872, I had ' dengue fever ' which was accompanied by some deafness and various rheumatic affections ; both of these were disappearing gradually, but not quite gone, when I got low fever in September, 1873, when the deafness became more marked again, sup-. posed to be due to quinine ; since then it decreased rapidly at first, but what little there is left, seems stationary.

" The only noticeable deafness in my family is that of my brother, who returned from the Cape of Good Hope somewhat deaf, at the age of 27 ; it has increased with him, and it is necessary to speak very loud to make him hear. We have generally fancied it to be connected with an impediment in his speech, born with him.

"My mother's deafness came on gradually with age, beginning at about 65 years. We have no record of gout in the family."

The membranes were bright and healthy, yielding freely before his inflation of the drum, which slightly diminished for the moment the hearing of the watch. W. r. $\frac{2}{40}$; l. $\frac{3}{40}$. T. f. imperfectly heard, alike on each side, and closing each meatus made it louder. No *local* treatment was advised, except a lotion of pot. iod. with nux vomica.

But there is another side to the effect of the Indian

U

climate. I have been informed of an officer who on
coming to England from India suffered from severe
tinnitus (without deafness) and this continued until his
return to India, when it ceased. The skin did not act in
England.

In many cases of former residents in India, however,
the tympanum is affected with the results of previous
catarrh. In one instance I incised the membrane of a person
who had been six years deaf in China, with good results,
removing a large quantity of thick secretion.* But there
is one result which I think I have noticed from the
climate of India of which I have no explanation. It is,
that children who have been born there, and lived there
during their first years, seem subject to become deaf with
no visible cause as they approach the age of puberty.
The fact of birth in India weighs with me unfavourably
in the prognosis.

For the treatment of nerve-deafness following Indian
fevers no special remedies seem to be of avail. In some
cases strychnia seems to do a little good, or the lotion I
have mentioned before, of Pot. Iod. (gr. x.) with Tr. Nucis
Vom. ʒj to the ounce of rose water. Dr. Hyde Salter † has
found chloroform, abused for asthma, produce deafness,
among other symptoms such as insomnia and general
apathy.

The deafness that arises from hereditary syphilis would

---

* See Atlas, Plate XVI., No. 5.
† "Lancet," Nov. 5, 1864, p. 116.

hardly be mistaken by anyone familiar with the other symptoms of that affection. In doubtful cases, however, the ophthalmoscope may afford aid. It generally comes on about or before the age of puberty, and mostly after the eyes have begun to recover. The deafness rapidly becomes very intense, and is evidently seated in the nerve apparatus, the tuning-fork not being heard; and indeed the degree of the deafness being for the most part greater than any merely tympanic affection causes. The membrane has generally a dull flattened look, but does not exhibit marks of any considerable local disease. Among the poor who are exposed to hardships and overwork, I have found the affection practically unrelievable; but when it occurs among the wealthier classes, not only do its symptoms often appear less severe, but I have frequently found decided amendment ensue. I have no settled plan of treatment, but have found injecting warm iodine vapour into the tympanum, among other things, seem to answer well. The treatment should be continued for a long time, with intermissions.

A pure neuralgia of the tympanum seems to occur, though rarely. The best marked instance of it I have seen occurred in a surgeon, aged 36, healthy, and with no diseased teeth. He had been much overworked for three weeks, when he began to suffer from severe pain in the right ear; it came on at night and would last till about three a.m. It affected first the right ear, then the left, and then the right again. It was centred quite in

u 2

the ear, radiating thence. Hearing not impaired, and
no tinnitus; but his own voice, or cough, &c. rang loud
and unpleasantly in his ears, although no external
sound did so; also he felt the air in his ears whenever he
swallowed. During the whole time, whether the pain
was present or not, inflating the tympanum would cause
pain or even bring on an attack; so that he was afraid
to blow his nose. I did not have the opportunity of
examining the ears at the time, but some months subsequently, after he had suffered from boils in the meatus,
induced apparently by fatigue from railway travelling, I
found them quite healthy. He tried quinine and iron
without benefit, but lost the pain entirely soon after
taking scruple doses of hydrochlorate of ammonia about
an hour before its time of access. Three years previously
he had had a similar attack, pronounced neuralgic by
Mr. Toynbee, and ceasing after forty-eight hours at
the seaside.

This case suggested to me the use of hydrochlorate
of ammonia in scruple doses, in cases of tinnitus that
afforded no rational indications for treatment; treating it
as a neuralgia, in fact. And though the cases of success
are exceptional, I think I can say that I have had more
success with it than with any other merely empirical
remedy, especially more than with the bromide of potassium, of the efficacy of which I have seen very little,
if any, evidence.

With regard to tinnitus, when existing as an isolated

symptom, apart from conditions of vascular congestion or
of pressure exerted on the labyrinth, little that is definite
can be said. Patients suffering from it are often quite
needlessly alarmed lest it should imply cerebral disease;
and in some cases it is attended with the most terrible
depression; it has more than once been assigned as the
reason for suicide. When it exists without impairment
of the hearing nothing can be relied on to relieve it. It
may depend in rare cases on aneurism of some small
vessel, or thrombosis, or contraction of the bony canal
of the carotid artery. But more often it seems to be
independent of any such cause; and the most various
influences give temporary relief. Thus in one case (that
of a surgeon) who was suddenly attacked at 15 with a
whistling and hissing in each ear, most intense in the
best, which continued without cessation into middle life,
extreme physical fatigue would take it almost entirely
away. In another case, that of a hard-working physician,
aged 28, a tap with his finger on the table would stop
it; in another it was stopped by light pressure on any
part near the ear. When suction on the meatus greatly
diminishes it for the moment, I have recommended its
use by the patient himself several times a day, now and
then with success; otherwise rest and tonics are the
remedies that suggest themselves. Among the causes,
sexual excesses seem sometimes to have a place. I have
known it brought permanently back in a case of perforation by the patient simply blowing thro' the ear.

In other cases inflation of the drum takes it away. In a patient of Mr. Toynbee's in whom tinnitus succeeded facial neuralgia, ascribed to gout, the singing ceased after colchicum, but the neuralgia returned.

In November last I saw a man, aged 28, in whom severe tinnitus and deafness had come on coincidently with albuminuria two months previously; he became very deaf in two days without feeling either sick or giddy. The membranes were white, and there was recent hyper-secretion in the tympanum, air entering it with a distinct moist sound, but there was no appearance of hæmorr-hage. The nerve had evidently suffered, the tuning-fork being scarcely heard upon the teeth. In this case Dr. Hughlings Jackson ascribed the loss of hearing to the albuminuria. Dr. Handfield Jones has found tinnitus follow sunstroke and malaria, associated with intermittent blindness and muscæ;* and in another case of fatal general paresis, after sitting on wet grass, it came on after double vision had lasted for a time.†

Often the hearing of certain special notes is disturbed; and this sometimes in comparatively slight affections. Gruber ‡ says that he has known this symptom removed by the mere employment of the air douche.

Often the hearing of certain notes is specially affected, as in the following case. The patient was a musician, and moreover recovery ensued:—

* " Med. J. and Gaz.," Aug. 1865.
† *Ib.* Nov. 1865, p. 490.
‡ Loc. cit., p. 624.

Sudden partial deafness, with anomalous hearing of musical notes; previous neuralgia, ceasing on extraction of teeth; improvement.

Nov. 25th, 1867. H. D—, æt. 30, teacher of music; pale, but healthy; no hereditary deafness. For ten years has suffered much from neuralgia of the face, alternately on each side, but never in the ear. Was getting worse until July last, when he had ten teeth extracted, and since then has been free. The ears were well until a fortnight ago. On Sunday he conducted two services as organist, but was as usual. On going to his first lesson on Monday morning, he found that his hearing was dull, and he thought that the upper notes of the piano were out of tune. Now "he hears the harmonics with the high notes, making the sound not true." The lower notes give him a drumming through his head; and with the lowest is a vibrating sound, as of a loose string in the ear. Constant tinnitus like a shell; feels as if there was a hand over the right ear; does not hear better in a noise. Is very short-sighted. A small piece of wax has been syringed from the right ear. W. r. $\frac{14}{40}$; l. $\frac{40}{40}$. Tuning-fork not perfectly; best on left side; closing the meatus makes it louder. Membranes bright, natural curve, very transparent, the right a little the more so; they yield slightly on in-flation, with slight increase of hearing for the moment; a feeling as of a bladder in the right; no feeling in the left. Throat slightly relaxed. On trying the harmonium there was a drumming with the bass notes; the middle ones had a "mist" over them; the upper ones were the clearest; but from c'' upwards he heard distinctly two sounds—an added harmonic; b' flat sent a shock or beat very strongly into the ear—"made something vibrate in it;" a' and a' flat have a similar effect. (Various tuning-forks seemed to produce the same results; but a piano did not.) Both ears appeared to be affected alike. Rest was advised; a gargle of iodine; a liniment; and ferro-citrate of quinine, with cod-liver oil.

On Jan. 22nd, 1868, two months after, he reported that he could not obtain rest at first, yet in about fourteen days all the sensations ceased. A dulness of hearing has continued in the right ear, but less than it was, and varying; worse in very cold weather. W. r. improved to $\frac{30}{40}$; left as before. His own voice sometimes sounds very loud in the right ear, and less often other persons' voices also. This is never so with music.

Three years after the patient continued free from serious trouble. He said—"After I last saw you, in the course of a few weeks my hearing gradually became better. If I am excessively tired I now sometimes feel something like a bladder forming in my right ear. I notice also at times that a very loud sound in a confined space will produce a similar effect, passing away with the cause, but often leaving a headache. Any discordant sounds or loud shouting will produce the same effect."

In the description of this case the advantage of a musician's analysis of his own sensations of sound is obvious; but to speculate on them would be premature. The hearing of naturally inaudible harmonics would seem to indicate an increased sensibility to certain very acute sounds, as if, perhaps, the conditions which deadened the response to certain sounds were more favourable to the reception of others. The peculiar sensibility to one note of the scale did not, in this case, cor· respond with the resonance of the meatus. The absence of giddiness or vomiting was marked. The recovery, except so far as the dulness of hearing was concerned, took place without rest, and the facial neuralgia, which seems sometimes most seriously to affect the auditory nerve, had ceased for ten months before the aural affection began.

Symptoms of this kind would naturally be ascribed to local disorder of special fibres in the cochlea, and have been so ascribed. But it is necessary to be more patient. Views which will not conform to the evidence existing at a given time, if they are freely surrendered, are often found on fuller knowledge to be the true ones, and it may be so here. In the meantime, thro' the kindness of Dr. Cassels, of Glasgow, I am able to report a case that may be of the greatest importance in the determination of the true function of the labyrinth.

"Janet N—, Oct. 25, 1872, gave the following history. In good health till six months ago. At that time left ear became very painful and discharged matter, and has continued to do so till now. About one month ago, the right became affected similarly to the left, and also continues to discharge very offensive matter. Her hereditary history is good, and she has not undergone any treatment for her ear disease.

" Her *present condition* (2, 4, '73) is as follows :—Watch not heard on either ear on contact, and requires a very loud tone of voice for conversation, even quite near to her.

"The tones of the diapason (Politzer's tuning-fork with movable clamps) transmitted through solid structures of the head are imperfectly heard, and the watch when applied to the cranial bones is not heard at all. She complains of very loud subjective tinnitus, and has done so for several months past. Ordinary noises, whether of human voices or vehicles on the street, sound peculiarly in her ears.

" Both *meatus* contain muco-purulent fluid, on removal of which the soft tissues of the canals are found sodden, thickened, and, at their inner third, somewhat congested.

" The right *membrana tympani* is imperfectly seen, owing to the presence of a vascular polypus springing from the neighbourhood of Schrapnell's space at junction of upper wall of meatus ; what of it is visible presents the appearances usually found in such cases.

"The left *membrana tympani*, in its anterior superior quadrant, is destroyed by ulcerative absorption ; the perforation extends into the inferior quadrant, and is irregular in form. The remaining portions of the membrane are thickened, and have a highly congested viscous surface. The lining membrane of the tympanum seen through the perforation is deeply injected and secreting purulent fluid.

" The *naso-pharynx* is congested, granular and hypertrophied. Both *Eustachian tubes* are open, but relaxed and swollen ; râles rather dry.

" After the Politzerising and catheterisation necessary to diagnose the condition of the tubes and tympana, the hearing when again tested was found to be improved ; the watch being distinctly heard on both ears on contact.

" It was deemed advisable to remove the high degree of inflammatory action in this case by local depletion and the internal administration of mercurials and full doses of opium. In three days, so great an improvement in this respect had taken place that this active treatment was discontinued, and, after the removal of the polypus from the right ear, the case was treated in the usual manner.

"May 2, 1873, she was very much improved ; from this time till Oct. 19, 1873, she did not present herself.   On the latter date, however, she returned and reported that up till three days previously, she had gone on improving, but was then seized with violent pain in her left ear, she now came for advice and treatment.   The right ear still seemed to be doing well, and on examining the left, Dr. Cassels perceived a peculiar mass projecting through the perforation in this membrane.

"Recognising at once its nature he took especial care to remove it entire. On careful examination it proved to be the cochlea in a semi-necrosed state and almost dry; the lamina spiralis ossea being distinctly seen throughout its whole extent.   Previously to its removal, the hearing for conversation was very bad, and the watch not heard on contact; after it, however, the hearing for conversation was improved, and the watch distinctly heard off the ear (about half an inch) and very loudly when held in contact with the auricle.   The patient was ordered to return in a few days for inspection, but she failed to do so ; and as the interest of the case demanded a further and more complete examination of it, search was made for her, and after much trouble the patient was found.   [26th Oct. 1873.]

" An examination of the tissues showed that their condition had improved very considerably since the date of her first attendance in April. The right membrane was ash grey in colour, very concave, opaque, and without lustre.   The perforation in the left membrane appeared to be cicatrised, no air passing through it either on Politzerising or catheterisation.   The copious discharge appeared to be caused by a slight regrowth of the polypus in the right, and a similar new growth in the left meatus.

"Tested on this date, and again on the 1, 12, '73, by the diapason and watch, as well as by the piano, it was not possible to discover, that the patient had suffered any impairment of the perception of the various tones. She distinguished, without any difficulty, all the notes of the scale of the piano, either when sounded singly or when rapidly played, as in the execution of a set piece of music. $C_1 = 512$ and C natural (of the Philharmonic pitch) were both equally well heard either through the cranial bones or held at a few inches from the left auricle.   Care was taken to seal up the right ear quite effectually during one stage of the testing and other sources of error were guarded against.   Tested with the right ear open to the passage of sonorous waves, no difference in the results was perceptible. The high tones were perceived equally well with the lowest of the scale. When she came back she reported that from the former visit (19, 8, '73) till then, she had removed several small portions of bone-like substance at different times from her left ear, but had not preserved any of them. She had during this period much and severe giddiness, frequent fainting and great difficulty of walking, especially at night. The staggering in her gait was very bad while it lasted, and she required the help of another person to enable her to move from place to place; without this help she could not get about. When she attempted to do so she fell to the ground, always to the left side, to which side she declared that she inclined to stagger. She vomited her food very frequently. Her appearance at this time certainly bore out her state-ment that 'she never had felt so ill before.' On this date (26, 10, '73) her hearing for conversation on both ears was very good, and the watch was heard on both sides at the distance of one inch removed from the auricles.

"She was sent to the country to regain her strength, and when she returned (12, 11, '73) she was much improved in general health. The tinnitus which from the outset had been very distressing (like sounding of bells) was nearly removed, and the giddiness and staggering, which had troubled her so much previously, was at times quite gone. Her hearing distance was, for each ear tested separately, 16′ for mono-syllables in a very moderate tone of voice, and the watch nearly one inch. The purulent discharge from both ears had increased during her residence in the country."

Fig. 10.

The Necrosed Portion of the Cochlea; of the natural size, and magnified.

In the year 1864, a professor from the North was sent to me by Mr. Toynbee for examination: the question was, the right cochlea having come away two years ago, is there any hearing power remaining on the right side? The left ear was perfect.

He had first had inflammation of the right ear twenty years ago, after bathing ; deafness and occasional earache since. The attack which ended in the exfoliation of the cochlea came on two years and a half ago after botanising in rough weather. All the symptoms had subsided, and there remained only a slight numbness of the right side of the face, and especially of the right side of the tongue. Only a dark surface, seeming to be dried secretion, was seen at the bottom of the meatus. Air did not enter by the tube. He said he was conscious of hearing a sort of *echo* of sounds in the right ear ; especially any sudden sound that took him unawares. He heard it distinctly in the left ear first, and then distinctly again, but less, in the right ear. He supposed this to be a reflex action in the centre. Could not satisfy himself whether he heard at all on that side or not. I endeavoured in every way I could to test this point. One or two tests seemed to me to give results that could be relied on. For instance : when the meatus of the left or uninjured ear was open, a tuning-fork, held close to the right meatus, or close to the right cheek, was heard alike, being in fact heard by the left ear; but when the left ear was closed, it was heard louder before the right meatus than beside the cheek. Again, closing the left meatus I took a piece of India-rubber tube, held it near the left ear, and made a loud crack of the nails at the farther end. The sound was not heard. I then transferred the tube to the right side (still closing the left ear) and found that the same sound was heard better when the tube was applied to the right meatus than when it was applied to any other part of the skull. I inferred, therefore, either that there remained some power of hearing on the right side, or that the meatus of one ear facilitates the passage of sound to the nerve of the other.

But whatever may be the structural condition on which they depend, the anomalies of hearing in respect to pitch are innumerable : for instance, it is reported of Patti that she naturally sang three notes false, c''' d''' and e''' ; her ear being a quarter of a tone flat for them, and that she corrected them, singing them flat to her own sensation.

In sudden nerve-affections of the ear the possibility of the condition discovered by Mr. Hilton, of closure of the cerebro-spinal foramen would not be overlooked.

It should never be forgotten that by diligent exercise an ear, of which the function is extremely impaired, may be greatly improved. Mr. Toynbee reported to the Medico-Chirurgical Society,* a case in which a person was rescued from being practically a deaf mute by assiduous exercise carried out in this way by her friends. And the benefit is no less decided in cases less extreme; it is especially desirable to bring into use a long disused ear, when the other ear is suffering, as it does frequently, from the fatigue of exclu-

* "Proceedings," 1858.

sive exercise. The following note, made by a girl aged 20, of the effects of her own efforts at listening, seems to me interesting: the left ear is totally lost, the right is gradually advancing from an extreme degree of deafness, chiefly thro' the opening of the Eustachian tube. She says:—" When I try to hear a sermon, after a little while I begin to feel a heavy numbed feeling, till it becomes actual pain about the ears, more especially in my right ear. Last time I heard every word, and could afterwards remember the tone and expression of the clergyman's face, but I can never recall the words, or even sense of what he has said. The feeling is very like waking up after a long dream. I often am so exhausted and tired afterwards that it is a great trouble to move, and my eyes ache very much if I listen for long. Sometimes after reading I feel it, but not often."

In respect to the forms of Hearing-trumpets, the recent paper of Dr. C. J. B. Williams at the Medico-Chirurgical Society, conveys the best information. He points out that the chief objects are to collect the largest amount of vibrations, and to avoid transverse vibrations produced in the trumpet itself: accordingly, the form most to be recommended is a simple cone, truncated obliquely to two-thirds of its extent, resembling the ears of animals.

APPENDIX.

THE STROBOSCOPIC METHOD.*

By means of this method all kinds of motion which exactly repeat themselves can, whatever their rapidity of occurrence, be rendered visible, as if taking place slowly.

Suppose any object to be illumined by flashes of light: owing to the power which the retina possesses of retaining sensation, if these flashes recur within a certain fraction of a second of each other, the body appears continuously visible; this will be the case even if it moves in the interval, and, if its movement has been a complete vibration, it will appear stationary; if, however, it happens not to have returned quite to its original position, or to have returned and commenced another excursion, by the time the next flash of light occurs, it will appear to have moved from its first position to another, and so on; indeed the body may make any number of vibrations between the successive flashes of light, and yet only appear to have moved that small distance which consists of the difference of its positions under the consecutive flashes.

Since the same holds good at any part of the course of the body, it is evident that it will be seen to go through its whole vibration, but less quickly than it actually does, and, moreover, that by a suitable adjustment of the times of the flashes, any

* " Die Spectrale und Strobscopische Untersuchung Tonenden Korper. E. Mach. Prag.," 1873. Abstract by Lucae, in "Archiv für Ohrenheil-kunde," 1873.

degree of apparent slowness may be attained—limited only by
the inability of the retina to retain sensations of light for more
than ·5 of a second; for if the next flash does not occur before
the effect of the first becomes faint, the object will seem to be
flickering, or to start up in different positions.

Let us take the case in which there are ten flashes of light
to eleven vibrations of the body: at each successive flash the
body is seen one-tenth of its whole vibration further on. In
this way at the first flash the body is one-tenth of its way on
its vibration, at the second, two-tenths, and so by the tenth a
whole vibration has been displayed.

INDEX.

THE END.

BRADBURY, AGNEW, & CO., PRINTERS, WHITEFRIARS.

A SELECTION FROM

Messrs. Henry S. King & Co.'s
LIST OF SCIENTIFIC WORKS.

THE QUESTIONS OF AURAL SURGERY. By **James Hinton**, Aural Surgeon to Guy's Hospital. Post 8vo. Price 12s. 6d.

AN ATLAS OF DISEASES OF THE MEMBRANA TYMPANI. With Descriptive Text. By **James Hinton**, Aural Surgeon to Guy's Hospital. Post 8vo. Price £6 6s.

PHYSIOLOGY FOR PRACTICAL USE. By various Writers. Edited by **James Hinton**. 2 vols. Crown 8vo. With 50 Illustrations. 12s. 6d.

THE PRINCIPLES OF MENTAL PHYSIOLOGY. With their Applications to the Training and Discipline of the Mind, and the Study of its Morbid Conditions. By **W. B. Carpenter, LL.D., M.D., F.R.S.**, &c. 8vo. Illustrated. Price 12s.

THE EXPANSE OF HEAVEN. A Series of Essays on the Wonders of the Firmament. By **R. A. Proctor, B.A.** Second Edition. Small crown 8vo. Price 6s.

"A very charming work; cannot fail to lift the reader's mind up 'through nature's work to nature's God.'"—*Standard.* | "Full of thought, readable, and popular."—*Brighton Gazette.*

STUDIES OF BLAST FURNACE PHENOMENA. By **M. L. Gruner.** Translated by **L. D. B. Gordon, F.R.S.E., F.G.S.**, &c. Demy 8vo. Price 7s. 6d.

"The whole subject is dealt with very copiously and clearly in all its parts, and can scarcely fail of appreciation at the | hands of practical men, for whose use it is designed."—*Post.*

A LEGAL HANDBOOK FOR ARCHITECTS. By **Edward Jenkins** and **John Raymond, Esqrs.**, Barristers-at-Law. In 1 vol. Price 6s.

"Architects, builders, and especially the building public will find the volume very useful."—*Freeman.* | "We can confidently recommend this book to all engaged in the building trades."—*Edinburgh Daily Review.*

CONTEMPORARY ENGLISH PSYCHOLOGY. From the French of **Professor Th. Ribot.** Large post 8vo. Price 9s. An Analysis of the Views and Opinions of the following Metaphysicians, as expressed in their writings:—

JAMES MILL, A. BAIN, JOHN STUART MILL, GEORGE H. LEWES, HERBERT SPENCER, SAMUEL BAYLEY.

THE HISTORY OF CREATION, a Popular Account of the Development of the Earth and its Inhabitants, according to the theories of Kant, Laplace, Lamarck, and Darwin. By **Professor Ernst Hæckel**, of the University of Jena. With Coloured Plates and Genealogical Trees of the various groups of both plants and animals. 2 vols. Post 8vo. [*Preparing.*

A New Edition.

CHANGE OF AIR AND SCENE. A Physician's Hints about Doctors, Patients, Hygiène, and Society ; with Notes of Excursions for health in the Pyrenees, and amongst the Watering-places of France (Inland and Seaward), Switzerland, Corsica, and the Mediterranean. By **Dr. Alphonse Donné.** Large post 8vo. Price 9s.

"A very readable and serviceable book. . . . The real value of it is to be found in the accurate and minute information given with regard to a large number of places which have gained a reputation on the | continent for their mineral waters."—*Pall Mall Gazette.*
"A singularly pleasant and chatty as well as instructive book about health."—*Guardian.*

MISS YOUMAN'S FIRST BOOK OF BOTANY. Designed to cultivate the observing powers of Children. From the Author's latest Stereotyped Edition. New and Enlarged Edition, with 300 Engravings. Crown 8vo. Price 5s.

"It is but rarely that a school-book appears which is at once so novel in plan, so successful in execution, and so suited to the general want, as to command universal and unqualified approbation, but such has | been the case with Miss Youman's First Book of Botany. . . . It has been everywhere welcomed as a timely and invaluable contribution to the improvement of primary education."—*Pall Mall Gazette.*

AN ARABIC AND ENGLISH DICTIONARY OF THE KORAN. By **Major J. Penrice, B.A.** 4to. Price 21s.

MODERN GOTHIC ARCHITECTURE. By **T. G. Jackson.** Crown 8vo. Price 5s.

"This thoughtful little Book is worthy of the perusal of all interested in art or architecture."—*Standard.*
"The reader will find some of the most | important doctrines of eminent art teachers practically applied in this little book, which is well written and popular in style."—*Manchester Examiner.*

A TREATISE ON RELAPSING FEVER. By **R. T. Lyons,** Assistant-Surgeon, Bengal Army. Small post 8vo. 7s. 6d.

"A practical work, thoroughly supported in its views by a series of remarkable cases."—*Standard.*

FOUR WORKS BY DR. EDWARD SMITH.

I. HEALTH AND DISEASE, as influenced by the Daily, Seasonal, and other Cyclical Changes in the Human System. A New Edition. 7s. 6d.

II. FOODS. Second Edition. Profusely Illustrated. Price 5s.

III. PRACTICAL DIETARY FOR FAMILIES, SCHOOLS, AND THE LABOURING CLASSES. A New Edition. Price 3s. 6d.

IV. CONSUMPTION IN ITS EARLY AND REMEDIABLE STAGES. A New Edition. 7s. 6d.

CHOLERA: HOW TO AVOID AND TREAT IT. Popular and Practical Notes by **Henry Blanc, M.D.** Crown 8vo. 4s. 6d.

"A very practical manual, based on experience and careful observation, full of | excellent hints on a most dangerous disease."—*Standard.*

THE INTERNATIONAL SCIENTIFIC SERIES.

Fourth Edition.

I. THE FORMS OF WATER IN RAIN AND RIVERS, ICE AND GLACIERS. By **J. Tyndall, LL.D., F.R.S.** With 26 Illustrations. Crown 8vo. Price 5*s.*

Second Edition.

II. PHYSICS AND POLITICS; OR, THOUGHTS ON THE APPLICATION OF THE PRINCIPLES OF "NATURAL SELECTION" AND "INHERITANCE" TO POLITICAL SOCIETY. By **Walter Bagehot.** Crown 8vo. Price 4*s.*

Third Edition.

III. FOODS. By **Dr. Edward Smith.** Profusely Illustrated. Price 5*s.*

Third Edition.

IV. MIND AND BODY: THE THEORIES OF THEIR RELATIONS. By **Alexander Bain, LL.D.,** Professor of Logic at the University of Aberdeen. Four Illustrations. Price 4*s.*

Third Edition.

V. THE STUDY OF SOCIOLOGY. By **Herbert Spencer.** Crown 8vo. Price 5*s.*

Second Edition.

VI. ON THE CONSERVATION OF ENERGY. By **Professor Balfour Stewart.** Fourteen Engravings. Price 5*s.*

Second Edition.

VII. ANIMAL LOCOMOTION ; or, Walking, Swimming, and Flying. By **Dr. J. B. Pettigrew, M.D., F.R.S.** 119 Illustrations. Price 5*s.*

Second Edition.

VIII. RESPONSIBILTY IN MENTAL DISEASE. By **Dr. Henry Maudsley.** Price 5*s.*

Second Edition.

IX. THE NEW CHEMISTRY. By **Professor Josiah P. Cooke,** of the Harvard University. Illustrated. Price 5*s.*

X. THE SCIENCE OF LAW. By **Professor Sheldon Amos.**

FORTHCOMING VOLUMES.

Prof. E. J. MAREY.
The Animal Frame.

{ Rev. M. J. BERKELEY, M.A., F.L.S.,
and M. COOKE, M. A., LL.D.
Fungi ; their Nature, Influences, and Uses.

Prof. OSCAR SCHMIDT (Strasburg Univ.)
The Theory of Descent and Darwinism.

Prof. VOGEL (Polytechnic Acad. of Berlin).
The Chemical Effects of Light.

Prof. LONMEL (University of Erlangen).
Optics.

Prof. W. KINGDOM CLIFFORD, M.A.
The First Principles of the Exact Sciences
explained to the non-mathematical.

Prof. T. H. HUXLEY, LL.D., F.R.S.
Bodily Motion and Consciousness.

Dr. W. B. CARPENTER, LL.D., F.R.S.
The Physical Geography of the Sea.

Prof. WILLIAM ODLING, F.R.S.,
The Old Chemistry viewed from the New
Standpoint.

W. LAUDER LINDSAY, M.D., F.R.S.E.
Mind in the Lower Animals.

Sir JOHN LUBBOCK, Bart., F.R.S.
The Antiquity of Man.

Prof. W. T. THISELTON DYER, B.A.,
B.SC.
Form and Habit in Flowering Plants.

Mr. J. N. LOCKYER, F.R.S.
Spectrum Analysis.

Prof. MICHAEL FOSTER, M.D.
Protoplasm and the Cell Theory.

Prof. W. STANLEY JEVONS.
Money : and the Mechanism of Exchange.

Dr. H. CHARLTON BASTIAN, M.D.
F.R.S.
The Brain as an Organ of Mind.

Prof. A. C. RAMSAY, L.L.D., F.R.S.
Earth Sculpture : Hills, Valleys, Mountains, Plains, Rivers, Lakes ; how they
were Produced, and how they have been
Destroyed.

Prof. RUDOLPH VIRCHOW (BerlinUniv.)
Morbid Physiological Action.

Prof. CLAUDE BERNARD.
Physical and Metaphysical Phenomena of
Life.

Prof. H. SAINTE-CLAIRE DEVILLE.
An Introduction to General Chemistry.

Prof. WURTZ.
Atoms and the Atomic Theory.

Prof. DE QUATREFAGES.
The Negro Races.

Prof. LACAZE-DUTHIERS.
Zoology since Cuvier.

Prof. BERTHELOT.
Chemical Synthesis.

Prof. J. ROSENTHAL.
General Physiology of Muscles and Nerves.

Prof. JAMES D. DANA, M.A., LL.D.
On Cephalization; or, Head-Characters in
the Gradation and Progress of Life.

Prof. S. W. JOHNSON, M.A.
On the Nutrition of Plants.

Prof. AUSTIN FLINT, Jr. M.D.
The Nervous System and its relations to
the Bodily Functions.

Prof. W. D. WHITNEY.
Modern Linguistic Science.

Prof. BERNSTEIN (University of Halle).
Physiology of the Senses.

Prof. FERDINAND COHN (Preslau Univ.)
Thallophytes (Algæ, Lichens, Fungi.)

Prof. HERMANN (University of Zurich).
Respiration.

Prof. LEUCKART (University of Leipsic).
Outlines of Animal Organization.

Prof. LIEBREICH (University of Berlin).
Outlines of Toxicology.

Prof. KUNDT (University of Strasburg).
On Sound.

Prof. REES (University of Erlangen).
On Parasitic Plants.

Prof. STEINTHAL (University of Berlin).
Outlines of the Science of Language.

A CLASSIFIED CATALOGUE OF
HENRY S. KING & CO.'S PUBLICATIONS.

CONTENTS.

HISTORY AND BIOGRAPHY.

AUTOBIOGRAPHY AND OTHER MEMORIALS OF MRS. GILBERT, FORMERLY ANN TAYLOR. By Josiah Gilbert, Author of "The Titian and Cadore Country," &c. In 2 vols. Post 8vo. With Steel Portraits, and several Wood Engravings. [*Preparing.*

AUTOBIOGRAPHY OF DR. A. B. GRANVILLE, M.D., F.R.S., &c. Edited, with a brief account of his concluding years, by his youngest Daughter. 2 vols. Demy 8vo. With a Portrait. [*Preparing.*

SAMUEL LOVER, THE LIFE AND UNPUBLISHED WORKS OF. By Bayle Bernard. In 2 vols. Post 8vo. With a Steel Portrait. [*Preparing.*

A MEMOIR OF THE REV. DR. ROWLAND WILLIAMS, with selections from his Note-books and Correspondence. Edited by Mrs. Rowland Williams. With a Photographic Portrait. In 2 vols. Large post 8vo. [*Shortly.*

POLITICAL WOMEN. By Sutherland Menzies. 2 vols. Post 8vo. Price 24s.

"Has all the information of history, with all the interest that attaches to biography." —*Scotsman.*

"A graceful contribution to the lighter record of history."—*English Churchman.*

65, Cornhill; & 12, Paternoster Row, London.

HISTORY AND BIOGRAPHY—*continued.*

SARA COLERIDGE, MEMOIR AND LETTERS OF. Edited by her **Daughter.** 2 vols. Crown 8vo. With 2 Portraits. Price 24s. Third Edition, Revised and Corrected. With Index.

"Sara Coleridge, as she is revealed, or rather reveals herself, in the correspondence, makes a brilliant addition to a brilliant family reputation."— *Saturday Review.*

"These charming volumes are attractive as a memorial of a most amiable woman of high intellectual mark."—*Athenæum.* "We have read these two volumes with genuine gratification."—*Hour.*

THE LATE REV. F. W. ROBERTSON, M.A., LIFE AND LETTERS OF. Edited by **Stopford Brooke, M.A.,** Chaplain in Ordinary to the Queen.

I. In 2 vols., uniform with the Sermons. Price 7s. 6d.

II. Library Edition, in demy 8vo, with Two Steel Portraits. Price 12s.

III. A Popular Edition, in 1 vol. Price 6s.

NATHANIEL HAWTHORNE, A MEMOIR OF, with Stories now first published in this country. By **H. A. Page.** Large post 8vo. 7s. 6d.

"Seldom has it been our lot to meet with a more appreciative delineation of character than this Memoir of Hawthorne."—*Morning Post.*

"Exhibits a discriminating enthusiasm for one of the most fascinating of novelists."—*Saturday Review.*

LEONORA CHRISTINA, MEMOIRS OF, Daughter of Christian IV. of Denmark : Written during her Imprisonment in the Blue Tower of the Royal Palace at Copenhagen, 1663—1685. Translated by **F. E. Bunnett.** With an Autotype Portrait of the Princess. Medium 8vo. 12s. 6d.

"A valuable addition to history."— *Daily News.*

"A valuable addition to the tragic romance of history."—*Spectator.*

LIVES OF ENGLISH POPULAR LEADERS. No. 1.—STEPHEN LANGTON. By **C. Edmund Maurice.** Crown 8vo. 7s. 6d.

CABINET PORTRAITS. BIOGRAPHICAL SKETCHES OF STATESMEN OF THE DAY. By **T. Wemyss Reid.** 1 vol. Crown 8vo. 7s. 6d.

"We have never met with a work which we can more unreservedly praise. The sketches are absolutely impartial."— *Athenæum.*

"We can heartily commend this work." —*Standard.* "Drawn with a master hand."—*Yorkshire Post.*

THE CHURCH AND THE EMPIRES: Historical Periods. By the late **Henry W. Wilberforce.** Preceded by a Memoir of the Author by the **Rev. John Henry Newman, D.D.** 1 vol. Post 8vo. With a Portrait. Price 10s. 6d.

HISTORY OF THE ENGLISH REVOLUTION OF 1688. By **C. D. Yonge,** Regius Professor, Queen's Coll., Belfast. 1 vol. Crown 8vo. Price 6s.

ALEXIS DE TOCQUEVILLE. Correspondence and Conversations with NASSAU W. SENIOR, from 1833 to 1859. Edited by **Mrs. M. C. M. Simpson.** In 2 vols. Large post 8vo. 21s.

"A book replete with knowledge and thought."—*Quarterly Review.*

"An extremely interesting book."— *Saturday Review.*

JOURNALS KEPT IN FRANCE AND ITALY. From 1848 to 1852. With a Sketch of the Revolution of 1848. By the late **Nassau William Senior.** Edited by his Daughter, **M. C. M. Simpson.** In 2 vols. Post 8vo. 24*s*.

"The book has a genuine historical value."—*Saturday Review.*
" No better, more honest, and more read-

able view of the state of political society during the existence of the second Republic could well be looked for."—*Examiner.*

PERSIA; ANCIENT AND MODERN. By **John Piggot, F.S.A.** Post 8vo. Price 10*s*. 6*d*.

THE HISTORY OF JAPAN. From the Earliest Period to the Present Time. By **Francis Ottiwell Adams,** H.B.M.'s Secretary of Embassy at Berlin, formerly H.B.M.'s Chargé d'Affaires, and Secretary of Legation at Yedo. Demy 8vo. With Map and Plans. Price 21*s*.

THE NORMAN PEOPLE, AND THEIR EXISTING DESCENDANTS IN THE BRITISH DOMINIONS AND THE UNITED STATES OF AMERICA. One handsome vol. 8vo. Price 21*s*.

THE RUSSIANS IN CENTRAL ASIA. A Critical Examination, down to the present time, of the Geography and History of Central Asia. By **Baron F. von Hellwald.** Translated by **Lieut.-Col. Theodore Wirgman, LL.B.** In 1 vol. Large post 8vo, with Map. Price 12*s*.

BOKHARA : ITS HISTORY AND CONQUEST. By **Professor Arminius Vàmbéry,** of the University of Pesth, Author of " Travels in Central Asia," &c. Demy 8vo. Price 18*s*.

" We conclude with a cordial recommen-
dation of this valuable book."—*Saturday Review.*

" Almost every page abounds with composition of peculiar merit." — *Morning
Post.*

THE RELIGIOUS HISTORY OF IRELAND: PRIMITIVE, PAPAL, AND PROTESTANT; including the Evangelical Missions, Catholic Agitations, and Church Progress of the last half Century. By **James Godkin,** Author of "Ireland : her Churches," &c. 1 vol. 8vo. Price 12*s*.

" These latter chapters on the statis-
tics of the various religious denominations
will be welcomed."—*Evening Standard.*
" Mr. Godkin writes with evident honesty,

and the topic on which he writes is one
about which an honest book is greatly
wanted."—*Examiner.*

THE GOVERNMENT OF THE NATIONAL DEFENCE. From the 30th June to the 31st October, 1870. The Plain Statement of a Member. By **Mons. Jules Favre.** 1 vol. Demy 8vo. 10*s*. 6*d*.

" Of all the contributions to the history
of the late war, we have found none more
fascinating and, perhaps, none more
valuable than the 'apology,' by M.

Jules Favre, for the unsuccessful Government of the National Defence."—*Times.*
" A work of the highest interest. The
book is most valuable."—*Athenæum.*

ECHOES OF A FAMOUS YEAR. By **Harriet Parr,** Author of " The Life of Jeanne d'Arc," " In the Silver Age," &c. Crown 8vo. 8*s*. 6*d*.

" Miss Parr has the great gift of charming simplicity of style ; and if children are
not interested in her book, many of their

seniors will be."—*British Quarterly Review.*

4 Works Published by Henry S. King & Co.,

VOYAGES AND TRAVEL.

SOME TIME IN IRELAND; A Recollection. 1 vol. Crown 8vo.
[*Preparing.*

WAYSIDE NOTES IN SCANDINAVIA. Being Notes of Travel in the North of Europe. By **Mark Antony Lower, M.A.** 1 vol. Crown 8vo.
[*Preparing.*

ON THE ROAD TO KHIVA. By **David Ker,** late Khivan Correspondent of the *Daily Telegraph.* Illustrated with Photographs of the Country and its Inhabitants, and a copy of the Official Map in use during the Campaign, from the Survey of CAPTAIN LEUSILIN. 1 vol. Post 8vo. 12s.

VIZCAYA; or, Life in the land of the Carlists at the outbreak of the Insurrection, with some account of the Iron Mines and other characteristics of the country. With a Map and 8 Illustrations. Crown 8vo. [*Just ready.*

ROUGH NOTES OF A VISIT TO BELGIUM, SEDAN, AND PARIS, in September, 1870-71. By **John Ashton.** Crown 8vo, bevelled boards. Price 3s. 6d.

"The author does not attempt to deal with military subjects, but writes sensibly of what he saw in 1870-71."—*John Bull.* "Possesses a certain freshness from the | straightforward simplicity with which it is written."—*Graphic.* "An interesting work by a highly intelligent observer."—*Standard.*

THE ALPS OF ARABIA; or, Travels through Egypt, Sinai, Arabia, and the Holy Land. By **William Charles Maughan.** 1 vol. Demy 8vo, with Map. Price 12s.

"Deeply interesting and valuable."—*Edinburgh Review.* "He writes freshly and with competent knowledge."—*Standard.* "Very readable and instructive. . . . A work far above the average of such publications."—*John Bull.*

THE MISHMEE HILLS: an Account of a Journey made in an Attempt to Penetrate Thibet from Assam, to open New Routes for Commerce. By **T. T. Cooper,** Author of "The Travels of a Pioneer of Commerce." Demy 8vo. With Four Illustrations and Map. Price 10s. 6d.

"The volume, which will be of great use in India and among Indian merchants here, contains a good deal of matter that | will interest ordinary readers. It is especially rich in sporting incidents."—*Standard.*

GOODMAN'S CUBA, THE PEARL OF THE ANTILLES. By **Walter Goodman.** Crown 8vo. Price 7s. 6d.

"A series of vivid and miscellaneous sketches. We can recommend this whole volume as very amusing reading."—*Pall Mall Gazette.* "The whole book deserves the heartiest commendation. . . Sparkling and amusing from beginning to end."—*Spectator.*

FIELD AND FOREST RAMBLES OF A NATURALIST IN NEW BRUNSWICK. With Notes and Observations on the Natural History of Eastern Canada. By **A. Leith Adams, M.A.** In 8vo, cloth. Illustrated. Price 14s.

"Both sportsmen and naturalists will find this work replete with anecdote and carefully-recorded observation, which will entertain them."—*Nature.* "Will be found interesting by those who | take a pleasure either in sport or natural history."—*Athenæum.* "To the naturalist the book will be most valuable. . . To the general reader most interesting."—*Evening Standard.*

ROUND THE WORLD IN 1870. A Volume of Travels, with Maps. By **A. D. Carlisle, B.A.,** Trin. Coll., Camb. Demy 8vo. Price 16s.
"We can only commend, which we do very heartily, an eminently sensible and readable book."—*British Quarterly Review.*

65, *Cornhill;* & 12, *Paternoster Row, London.*

TENT LIFE WITH ENGLISH GIPSIES IN NORWAY. By Hubert Smith.

In 8vo, cloth. Five full-page Engravings, and 31 smaller Illustrations, with Map of the Country showing Routes. Second Edition. Revised and Corrected. Price 21*s.*

"Written in a very lively style, and has throughout a smack of dry humour and satiric reflection which shows the writer to be a keen observer of men and things. We hope that many will read it and find in it the same amusement as ourselves."—*Times.*

FAYOUM; OR, ARTISTS IN EGYPT.

A Tour with M. Gérôme and others. By J. Lenoir. Crown 8vo, cloth. Illustrated. Price 7*s.* 6*d.*

"A pleasantly written and very readable book."—*Examiner.* "The book is very amusing. . . . Who-ever may take it up will find he has with him a bright and pleasant companion."—*Spectator.*

SPITZBERGEN THE GATEWAY TO THE POLYNIA; OR, A VOYAGE TO SPITZBERGEN.

By Captain John C. Wells, R.N. In 8vo, cloth. Profusely Illustrated. Price 21*s.*

"A charming book, remarkably well written and well illustrated."—*Standard.* "Straightforward and clear in style, securing our confidence by its unaffected simplicity and good sense."—*Saturday Review.*

AN AUTUMN TOUR IN THE UNITED STATES AND CANADA.

By Lieut.-Col. J. G. Medley. Crown 8vo. Price 5*s.*

"Colonel Medley's little volume is a pleasantly written account of a two-months' visit to America."—*Hour.* "May be recommended as manly, sensible, and pleasantly written."—*Globe*

THE NILE WITHOUT A DRAGOMAN. By Frederic Eden.

Second Edition. In 1 vol. Crown 8vo, cloth. Price 7*s.* 6*d.*

"Should any of our readers care to imitate Mr. Eden's example, and wish to see things with their own eyes, and shift for themselves, next winter in Upper Egypt, they will find this book a very agreeable guide."—*Times.* "It is a book to read during an autumn holiday."—*Spectator.*

IRELAND IN 1872.

A Tour of Observation, with Remarks on Irish Public Questions. By Dr. James Macaulay. Crown 8vo. Price 7*s.* 6*d.*

"A careful and instructive book. Full of facts, full of information, and full of interest."—*Literary Churchman.* "We have rarely met a book on Ireland which for impartiality of criticism and general accuracy of information could be so well recommended to the fair-minded Irish reader."—*Evening Standard.*

OVER THE DOVREFJELDS. By J. S. Shepard,

Author of "A Ramble through Norway," &c. Crown 8vo. Illustrated. Price 4*s.* 6*d.*

"We have read many books of Norwegian travel, but . . . we have seen none so pleasantly narrative in its style, and so varied in its subject."—*Spectator.* "As interesting a little volume as could be written on the subject. So interesting and shortly written that it will commend itself to all intending tourists."—*Examiner.*

A WINTER IN MOROCCO. By Amelia Perrier.

Large crown 8vo. Illustrated. Price 10*s.* 6*d.*

"Well worth reading, and contains several excellent illustrations."—*Hour.* "Miss Perrier is a very amusing writer. She has a good deal of humour, sees the oddity and quaintness of Oriental life with a quick observant eye, and evidently turned her opportunities of sarcastic examination to account."—*Daily News.*

SCIENCE.

THE QUESTIONS OF AURAL SURGERY. By James Hinton, Aural Surgeon to Guy's Hospital. Post 8vo. Price 12s. 6d.

AN ATLAS OF DISEASES OF THE MEMBRANA TYMPANI. With Descriptive Text. By James Hinton, Aural Surgeon to Guy's Hospital. Post 8vo. Price £6 6s.

PHYSIOLOGY FOR PRACTICAL USE. By various Writers. Edited by James Hinton. 2 vols. Crown 8vo. With 50 Illustrations. 12s. 6d.

THE PRINCIPLES OF MENTAL PHYSIOLOGY. With their Applications to the Training and Discipline of the Mind, and the Study of its Morbid Conditions. By W. B. Carpenter, LL.D., M.D., F.R.S., &c. 8vo. Illustrated. Price 12s.

SENSATION AND INTUITION. By James Sully. 1 vol. Post 8vo. [*Nearly ready.*

THE EXPANSE OF HEAVEN. A Series of Essays on the Wonders of the Firmament. By R. A. Proctor, B.A. Second Edition. With a Frontispiece. Small crown 8vo. Price 6s.

"A very charming work ; cannot fail to lift the reader's mind up ' through nature's work to nature's God.' "—*Standard*. | " Full of thought, readable, and popular." —*Brighton Gazette*.

STUDIES OF BLAST FURNACE PHENOMENA. By M. L. Gruner. Translated by L. D. B. Gordon, F.R.S.E., F.G.S., &c. Demy 8vo. Price 7s. 6d.

"The whole subject is dealt with very copiously and clearly in all its parts, and can scarcely fail of appreciation at the | hands of practical men, for whose use it is designed."—*Post*.

A LEGAL HANDBOOK FOR ARCHITECTS. By Edward Jenkins and John Raymond, Esqrs., Barristers-at-Law. In 1 vol. Price 6s.

"Architects, builders, and especially the building public will find the volume very useful."—*Freeman*. | " We can confidently recommend this book to all engaged in the building trades."—*Edinburgh Daily Review*.

CONTEMPORARY ENGLISH PSYCHOLOGY. From the French of Professor Th. Ribot. Large post 8vo. Price 9s. An Analysis of the Views and Opinions of the following Metaphysicians, as expressed in their writings :—

James Mill, A. Bain, John Stuart Mill, George H. Lewes, Herbert Spencer, Samuel Bailey.

THE HISTORY OF CREATION, a Popular Account of the Development of the Earth and its Inhabitants, according to the theories of Kant, Laplace, Lamarck, and Darwin. By Professor Ernst Hæckel, of the University of Jena. With Coloured Plates and Genealogical Trees of the various groups of both plants and animals. 2 vols. Post 8vo. [*Preparing.*

SCIENCE—*continued.*

A New Edition.

CHANGE OF AIR AND SCENE. A Physician's Hints about Doctors, Patients, Hygiène, and Society; with Notes of Excursions for health in the Pyrenees, and amongst the Watering-places of France (Inland and Seaward), Switzerland, Corsica, and the Mediterranean. By **Dr. Alphonse Donné.** Large post 8vo. Price 9s.

"A very readable and serviceable book. . . . The real value of it is to be found in the accurate and minute information given with regard to a large number of places which have gained a reputation on the continent for their mineral waters."—*Pall Mall Gazette.* "A singularly pleasant and chatty as well as instructive book about health."—*Guardian.*

MISS YOUMANS' FIRST BOOK OF BOTANY. Designed to cultivate the observing powers of Children. From the Author's latest Stereotyped Edition. New and Enlarged Edition, with 300 Engravings. Crown 8vo. Price 5s.

"It is but rarely that a school-book appears which is at once so novel in plan, so successful in execution, and so suited to the general want, as to command universal and unqualified approbation, but such has been the case with Miss Youmans' First Book of Botany. . . . It has been everywhere welcomed as a timely and invaluable contribution to the improvement of primary education."—*Pall Mall Gazette.*

AN ARABIC AND ENGLISH DICTIONARY OF THE KORAN. By **Major J. Penrice, B.A.** 4to. Price 21s.

MODERN GOTHIC ARCHITECTURE. By **T. G. Jackson.** Crown 8vo. Price 5s.

"This thoughtful little book is worthy of the perusal of all interested in art or architecture."—*Standard.* "The reader will find some of the most important doctrines of eminent art teachers practically applied in this little book, which is well written and popular in style."—*Manchester Examiner.*

A TREATISE ON RELAPSING FEVER. By **R. T. Lyons,** Assistant-Surgeon, Bengal Army. Small post 8vo. Price 7s. 6d.

"A practical work, thoroughly supported in its views by a series of remarkable cases."—*Standard.*

FOUR WORKS BY DR. EDWARD SMITH.

I. HEALTH AND DISEASE, as influenced by the Daily, Seasonal, and other Cyclical Changes in the Human System. A New Edition. Price 7s. 6d.

II. FOODS. Second Edition. Profusely Illustrated. Price 5s.

III. PRACTICAL DIETARY FOR FAMILIES, SCHOOLS, AND THE LABOURING CLASSES. A New Edition. Price 3s. 6d.

IV. CONSUMPTION IN ITS EARLY AND REMEDIABLE STAGES. A New Edition. Price 7s. 6d.

CHOLERA: HOW TO AVOID AND TREAT IT. Popular and Practical Notes by **Henry Blanc, M.D.** Crown 8vo. Price 4s. 6d.

"A very practical manual, based on experience and careful observation, full of excellent hints on a most dangerous disease."—*Standard.*

THE INTERNATIONAL SCIENTIFIC SERIES.

Fourth Edition.

I. THE FORMS OF WATER IN RAIN AND RIVERS, ICE AND GLACIERS. By **J. Tyndall, LL.D., F.R.S.** With 26 Illustrations. Crown 8vo. Price 5*s.*

Second Edition.

II. PHYSICS AND POLITICS; OR, THOUGHTS ON THE APPLICATION OF THE PRINCIPLES OF "NATURAL SELECTION" AND "INHERITANCE" TO POLITICAL SOCIETY. By **Walter Bagehot.** Crown 8vo. Price 4*s.*

Third Edition.

III. FOODS. By **Dr. Edward Smith.** Profusely Illustrated. Price 5*s.*

Third Edition.

IV. MIND AND BODY: THE THEORIES OF THEIR RELATIONS. By **Alexander Bain, LL.D.,** Professor of Logic at the University of Aberdeen. Four Illustrations. Price 4*s.*

Third Edition.

V. THE STUDY OF SOCIOLOGY. By **Herbert Spencer.** Crown 8vo. Price 5*s.*

Second Edition.

VI. ON THE CONSERVATION OF ENERGY. By **Professor Balfour Stewart.** Fourteen Engravings. Price 5*s.*

Second Edition.

VII. ANIMAL LOCOMOTION; or, Walking, Swimming, and Flying. By **Dr. J. B. Pettigrew, M.D., F.R.S.** 119 Illustrations. Price 5*s.*

Second Edition.

VIII. RESPONSIBILITY IN MENTAL DISEASE. By **Dr. Henry Maudsley.** Price 5*s.*

Second Edition.

IX. THE NEW CHEMISTRY. By **Professor Josiah P. Cooke,** of the Harvard University. Illustrated. Price 5*s.*

X. THE SCIENCE OF LAW. By **Professor Sheldon Amos.**
[*Just ready.*

THE INTERNATIONAL SCIENTIFIC SERIES—*continued.*

FORTHCOMING VOLUMES.

Prof. E. J. MAREY.
The Animal Frame. [*In the Press.*

Prof. OSCAR SCHMIDT (Strasburg Univ.).
The Theory of Descent and Darwinism.
[*In the Press.*

Prof. VOGEL (Polytechnic Acad. of Berlin).
The Chemical Effects of Light.
[*In the Press.*

Prof. LONMEL (University of Erlangen).
Optics. [*In the Press.*

{ Rev. M. J. BERKELEY, M.A., F.L.S.,
{ and M. COOKE, M.A., LL.D.
Fungi ; their Nature, Influences, and Uses.

Prof. W. KINGDOM CLIFFORD, M.A.
The First Principles of the Exact Sciences
explained to the non-mathematical.

Prof. T. H. HUXLEY, LL.D., F.R.S.
Bodily Motion and Consciousness.

Dr. W. B. CARPENTER, LL.D., F.R.S.
The Physical Geography of the Sea.

Prof. WILLIAM ODLING, F.R.S.
The Old Chemistry viewed from the new
Standpoint.

W. LAUDER LINDSAY, M.D., F.R.S.E.
Mind in the Lower Animals.

Sir JOHN LUBBOCK, Bart., F.R.S.
The Antiquity of Man.

Prof. W. T. THISELTON DYER, B.A.,
B.SC.
Form and Habit in Flowering Plants.

Mr. J. N. LOCKYER, F.R.S.
Spectrum Analysis.

Prof. MICHAEL FOSTER, M.D.
Protoplasm and the Cell Theory.

Prof. W. STANLEY JEVONS.
Money : and the Mechanism of Exchange.

Dr. H. CHARLTON BASTIAN, M.D.,
F.R.S.
The Brain as an Organ of Mind.

Prof. A. C. RAMSAY, LL.D., F.R.S.
Earth Sculpture : Hills, Valleys, Mountains, Plains, Rivers, Lakes ; how they
were Produced, and how they have been
Destroyed.

Prof. RUDOLPH VIRCHOW (Berlin Univ.)
Morbid Physiological Action.

Prof. CLAUDE BERNARD.
Physical and Metaphysical Phenomena of
Life.

Prof. H. SAINTE-CLAIRE DEVILLE.
An Introduction to General Chemistry.

Prof. WURTZ.
Atoms and the Atomic Theory.

Prof. DE QUATREFAGES.
The Negro Races.

Prof. LACAZE-DUTHIERS.
Zoology since Cuvier.

Prof. BERTHELOT.
Chemical Synthesis.

Prof. J. ROSENTHAL.
General Physiology of Muscles and Nerves.

Prof. JAMES D. DANA, M.A., LL.D.
On Cephalization ; or, Head-Characters in
the Conduction and Progress of Life.

Prof. S. W. JOHNSON, M.A.
On the Nutrition of Plants.

Prof. AUSTIN FLINT, Jr. M.D.
The Nervous System and its Relation to
the Bodily Functions.

Prof. W. D. WHITNEY.
Modern Linguistic Science.

Prof. BERNSTEIN (University of Halle).
Physiology of the Senses.

Prof. FERDINAND COHN (Breslau Univ.).
Thallophytes (Algæ, Lichens, Fungi).

Prof. HERMANN (University of Zurich).
Respiration.

Prof. LEUCKART (University of Leipsic).
Outlines of Animal Organization.

Prof. LIEBREICH (University of Berlin).
Outlines of Toxicology.

Prof. KUNDT (University of Strasburg).
On Sound.

Prof. REES (University of Erlangen).
On Parasitic Plants.

Prof. STEINTHAL (University of Berlin).
Outlines of the Science of Language.

ESSAYS, LECTURES, AND COLLECTED PAPERS.

IN STRANGE COMPANY; or, The Note Book of a Roving Correspondent. By **James Greenwood**, "The Amateur Casual." Second Edition. Crown 8vo. 6s.

"A bright, lively book."—*Standard.* "Has all the interest of romance."— *Queen.*

"Some of the papers remind us of Charles Lamb on beggars and chimney sweeps."—*Echo.*

MASTER-SPIRITS. By **Robert Buchanan**. Post 8vo. 10s. 6d.

"Good Books are the precious life-blood of Master-Spirits."—*Milton.*

"Full of fresh and vigorous writing, such as can only be produced by a man of keen and independent intellect."—*Saturday Review.* "A very pleasant and readable book."— *Examiner.*

"Written with a beauty of language and a spirit of vigorous enthusiasm rare even in our best living word-painters."—*Standard.* "Mr. Buchanan is a writer whose books the critics may always open with satisfaction . . . both manly and artistic."—*Hour.*

THEOLOGY IN THE ENGLISH POETS; COWPER, COLERIDGE, WORDSWORTH, and BURNS. Being Lectures delivered by the **Rev. Stopford A. Brooke**, Chaplain in Ordinary to Her Majesty the Queen. Crown 8vo. 9s.

SHORT LECTURES ON THE LAND LAWS. Delivered before the Working Men's College. By **T. Lean Wilkinson**. Crown 8vo, limp cloth. 2s.

"A very handy and intelligible epitome of the general principles of existing land laws."—*Standard.*

AN ESSAY ON THE CULTURE OF THE OBSERVING POWERS OF CHILDREN, especially in connection with the Study of Botany. By **Eliza A. Youmans**. Edited, with Notes and a Supplement, by **Joseph Payne**, F.C.P., Author of "Lectures on the Science and Art of Education," &c. Crown 8vo. 2s. 6d.

"This study, according to her just notions on the subject, is to be fundamentally based on the exercise of the pupil's own powers of observation. He is to see and

examine the properties of plants and flowers at first hand, not merely to be informed of what others have seen and examined."—*Pall Mall Gazette.*

THE GENIUS OF CHRISTIANITY UNVEILED. Being Essays by **William Godwin**, Author of "Political Justice," &c. Never before published. 1 vol. Crown 8vo. 7s. 6d.

"Few have thought more clearly and directly than William Godwin, or expressed their reflections with more simplicity and unreserve."—*Examiner.*

"The deliberate thoughts of Godwin deserve to be put before the world for reading and consideration."—*Athenæum.*

MILITARY WORKS.

—◆—

RUSSIA'S ADVANCE EASTWARD; Translated from the German of LIEUT. STUMM. By **Lt. C. E. H. Vincent.** 1 vol. Crown 8vo. With a Map.

THE VOLUNTEER, THE MILITIAMAN, AND THE REGULAR SOLDIER; a Conservative View of the Armies of England, Past, Present, and Future, as Seen in January, 1874. By **A Public School Boy.** 1 vol. Crown 8vo.

THE OPERATIONS OF THE FIRST ARMY, UNDER STEINMETZ. By **Major von Schell.** Translated by **Captain E. O. Hollist.** Demy 8vo. Uniform with the other volumes in the Series. Price 10s. 6d.

THE OPERATIONS OF THE FIRST ARMY UNDER GEN. VON GOEBEN. By **Major von Schell.** Translated by **Col. C. H. von Wright.** Four Maps. Demy 8vo. Price 9s.

THE OPERATIONS OF THE FIRST ARMY IN NORTHERN FRANCE AGAINST FAIDHERBE. By **Colonel Count Hermann von Wartensleben,** Chief of the Staff of the First Army. Translated by **Colonel C. H. von Wright.** In demy 8vo. Uniform with the above. Price 9s.

"Very clear, simple, yet eminently instructive, is this history. It is not overladen with useless details, is written in good taste, and possesses the inestimable | value of being in great measure the record of operations actually witnessed by the author, supplemented by official documents."—*Athenæum.*

THE GERMAN ARTILLERY IN THE BATTLES NEAR METZ. Based on the official reports of the German Artillery. By **Captain Hoffbauer,** Instructor in the German Artillery and Engineer School. Translated by **Capt. E. O. Hollist.** [*Preparing.*

THE OPERATIONS OF THE BAVARIAN ARMY CORPS. By **Captain Hugo Helvig.** Translated by **Captain G. S. Schwabe.** With 5 large Maps. Demy 8vo. In 2 vols. Price 24s. Uniform with the other Books in the Series.

AUSTRIAN CAVALRY EXERCISE. From an Abridged Edition compiled by CAPTAIN ILLIA WOINOVITS, of the General Staff, on the Tactical Regulations of the Austrian Army, and prefaced by a General Sketch of the Organisation, &c., of the Country. Translated by **Captain W. S. Cooke.** Crown 8vo, cloth. Price 7s.

History of the Organisation, Equipment, and War Services of

THE REGIMENT OF BENGAL ARTILLERY. Compiled from Published Official and other Records, and various private sources, by **Major Francis W. Stubbs,** Royal (late Bengal) Artillery. Vol. I. will contain WAR SERVICES. The Second Volume will be published separately, and will contain the HISTORY OF THE ORGANISATION AND EQUIPMENT OF THE REGIMENT. In 2 vols. 8vo. With Maps and Plans. [*Preparing.*

MILITARY WORKS—*continued.*

VICTORIES AND DEFEATS. An Attempt to explain the Causes which have led to them. An Officer's Manual. By **Col. R. P. Anderson.** Demy 8vo. Price 14*s.*

"The present book proves that he is a diligent student of military history, his illustrations ranging over a wide field, and including ancient and modern Indian and European warfare."—*Standard.*
"The young officer should have it al-

ways at hand to open anywhere and read a bit, and we warrant him that let that bit be ever so small it will give him material for an hour's thinking."—*United Service Gazette.*

THE FRONTAL ATTACK OF INFANTRY. By **Capt. Laymann,** Instructor of Tactics at the Military College, Neisse. Translated by **Colonel Edward Newdigate.** Crown 8vo, limp cloth. Price 2*s. 6d.*

"An exceedingly useful kind of book. A valuable acquisition to the military student's library. It recounts, in the first place, the opinions and tactical formations which regulated the German army during the early battles of the late war; explains

how these were modified in the course of the campaign by the terrible and unanticipated effect of the fire: and how, accordingly, troops should be trained to attack in future wars." — *Naval and Military Gazette.*

ELEMENTARY MILITARY GEOGRAPHY, RECONNOITRING, AND SKETCHING. Compiled for Non-Commissioned Officers and Soldiers of all Arms. By **Lieut. C. E. H. Vincent,** Royal Welsh Fusiliers. Small crown 8vo. Price 2*s. 6d.*

"This manual takes into view the necessity of every soldier knowing how to read a military map, in order to know to what points in an enemy's country to direct his attention; and provides for this necessity

by giving, in terse and sensible language, definitions of varieties of ground and the advantages they present in warfare, together with a number of useful hints in military sketching."—*Naval and Military Gazette.*

THREE WORKS BY LIEUT.-COL. THE HON. A. ANSON, V.C., M.P.

THE ABOLITION OF PURCHASE AND THE ARMY REGULATION BILL OF 1871. Crown 8vo. Price One Shilling.

ARMY RESERVES AND MILITIA REFORMS. Crown 8vo. Sewed. Price One Shilling.
THE STORY OF THE SUPERSESSIONS. Crown 8vo. Price Sixpence.

STUDIES IN THE NEW INFANTRY TACTICS. Parts I. & II. By **Major W. von Schereff.** Translated from the German by **Col. Lumley Graham.** Price 7*s. 6d.*

"The subject of the respective advantages of attack and defence, and of the methods in which each form of battle should be carried out under the fire of modern arms, is exhaustively and admir-

ably treated; indeed, we cannot but consider it to be decidedly superior to any work which has hitherto appeared in English upon this all-important subject."—*Standard.*

Second Edition. Revised and Corrected.
TACTICAL DEDUCTIONS FROM THE WAR OF 1870—71. By **Captain A. von Boguslawski.** Translated by **Colonel Lumley Graham,** late 18th (Royal Irish) Regiment. Demy 8vo. Uniform with the above. Price 7*s.*

"We must, without delay, impress brain and forethought into the British Service; and we cannot commence the good work too soon, or better, than by placing the two books ('The Operations of

the German Armies' and 'Tactical Deductions') we have here criticised, in every military library, and introducing them as class-books in every tactical school."—*United Service Gazette.*

THE OPERATIONS OF THE SOUTH ARMY IN JANUARY AND FEBRUARY, 1871. Compiled from the Official War Documents of the Head-quarters of the Southern Army. By **Count Hermann von Wartensleben,** Colonel in the Prussian General Staff. Translated by **Colonel C. H. von Wright.** Demy 8vo, with Maps. Uniform with the above. Price 6*s.*

THE ARMY OF THE NORTH-GERMAN CONFEDERATION.

A Brief Description of its Organisation, of the different Branches of the Service and their "Rôle" in War, of its Mode of Fighting, &c. By a **Prussian General.** Translated from the German by **Col. Edward Newdigate.** Demy 8vo. Price 5s.

"The work is quite essential to the full use of the other volumes of the 'German Military Series,' which Messrs. King are now producing in handsome uniform style."—*United Service Magazine.*

"Every page of the book deserves attentive study.... The information given on mobilisation, garrison troops, keeping up establishment during war, and on the employment of the different branches of the service, is of great value."—*Standard.*

THE OPERATIONS OF THE GERMAN ARMIES IN FRANCE, FROM SEDAN TO THE END OF THE WAR OF 1870-71.

With Large Official Map. From the Journals of the Head-quarters Staff, by **Major Wm. Blume.** Translated by **E. M. Jones,** Major 20th Foot, late Professor of Military History, Sandhurst. Demy 8vo. Price 9s.

"The book is of absolute necessity to the military student. . . . The work is one of high merit."—*United Service Gazette.*

"The work of Major von Blume in its English dress forms the most valuable addition to our stock of works upon the war that our press has put forth. Our space forbids our doing more than commending it earnestly as the most authentic and instructive narrative of the second section of the war that has yet appeared."—*Saturday Review.*

HASTY INTRENCHMENTS.

By **Colonel A. Brialmont.** Translated by **Lieutenant Charles A. Empson, R.A.** Demy 8vo. Nine Plates. Price 6s.

"A valuable contribution to military literature."—*Athenæum.*

"In seven short chapters it gives plain directions for forming shelter-trenches, with the best method of carrying the necessary tools, and it offers practical illustrations of the use of hasty intrenchments on the field of battle."—*United Service Magazine.*

"It supplies that which our own text-books give but imperfectly, viz., hints as to how a position can best be strengthened by means . . . of such extemporised intrenchments and batteries as can be thrown up by infantry in the space of four or five hours . . . deserves to become a standard military work."—*Standard.*

STUDIES IN LEADING TROOPS.

By **Colonel von Verdy Du Vernois.** An authorised and accurate Translation by **Lieutenant H. J. T. Hildyard,** 71st Foot. Parts I. and II. Demy 8vo. Price 7s.

*** General BEAUCHAMP WALKER says of this work:—"I recommend the first two numbers of Colonel von Verdy's 'Studies' to the attentive perusal of my brother officers. They supply a want which I have often felt during my service in this country, namely, a minuter tactical detail of the minor operations of war than any but the most observant and fortunately-placed staff-officer is in a position to give. I have read and re-read them very carefully, I hope with profit, certainly with great interest, and believe that practice, in the sense of these 'Studies,' would be a valuable preparation for manœuvres on a more extended scale."—Berlin, June, 1872.

CAVALRY FIELD DUTY.

By **Major-General von Mirus.** Translated by **Captain Frank S. Russell,** 14th (King's) Hussars. Crown 8vo, limp cloth. Price 7s. 6d.

DISCIPLINE AND DRILL.

Four Lectures delivered to the London Scottish Rifle Volunteers. By **Captain S. Flood Page.** A New and Cheaper Edition. Price 1s.

"An admirable collection of lectures."—*Times.*

"The very useful and interesting work."—*Volunteer Service Gazette.*

INDIA AND THE EAST.

THE THREATENED FAMINE IN BENGAL; How it may be Met, and the Recurrence of Famines in India prevented. Being No. 1 of "Occasional Notes on Indian Affairs." By **Sir H. Bartle E. Frere, G.C.B., G.C.S.I.,** &c. &c. Crown 8vo. With 3 Maps. Price 5s.

THE ORIENTAL SPORTING MAGAZINE. A Reprint of the first 5 Volumes, in 2 Volumes, demy 8vo. Price 28s.

"Lovers of sport will find ample amusement in the varied contents of these two volumes."—*Allen's Indian Mail.*
"Full of interest for the sportsman and naturalist. Full of thrilling adventures of sportsmen who have attacked the fiercest and most gigantic specimens of the animal world in their native jungle. It is seldom we get so many exciting incidents in a similar amount of space ... Well suited to the libraries of country gentlemen and all those who are interested in sporting matters."—*Civil Service Gazette.*

THE EUROPEAN IN INDIA. A Hand-book of Practical Information for those proceeding to, or residing in, the East Indies, relating to Outfits, Routes, Time for Departure, Indian Climate, &c. By **Edmund C. P. Hull.** With a MEDICAL GUIDE FOR ANGLO-INDIANS. Being a Compendium of Advice to Europeans in India, relating to the Preservation and Regulation of Health. By **R. S. Mair, M.D., F.R.C.S.E.,** late Deputy Coroner of Madras. In 1 vol. Post 8vo. Price 6s.

"Full of all sorts of useful information to the English settler or traveller in India." —*Standard.*
"One of the most valuable books ever published in India—valuable for its sound information, its careful array of pertinent facts, and its sterling common sense. It supplies a want which few persons may have discovered, but which everybody will at once recognise when once the contents of the book have been mastered. The medical part of the work is invaluable."—*Calcutta Guardian.*

THE MEDICAL GUIDE FOR ANGLO-INDIANS. Being a Compendium of advice to Europeans in India, relating to the Preservation and Regulation of Health. By **R. S. Mair, F.R.C.S.E.,** late Deputy Coroner of Madras. Reprinted, with numerous additions and corrections, from "The European in India."

EASTERN EXPERIENCES. By **L. Bowring, C.S.I.,** Lord Canning's Private Secretary, and for many years the Chief Commissioner of Mysore and Coorg. In 1 vol. Demy 8vo. Price 16s. Illustrated with Maps and Diagrams.

"An admirable and exhaustive geographical, political, and industrial survey."—*Athenæum.*
"This compact and methodical summary of the most authentic information relating to countries whose welfare is intimately connected with our own."—*Daily News.*
"Interesting even to the general reader, but more especially so to those who may have a special concern in that portion of our Indian Empire."—*Post.*

INDIA AND THE EAST—*continued.*

TAS-HĪL UL KALĀM; OR, HINDUSTANI MADE EASY. By **Captain W. R. M. Holroyd**, Bengal Staff Corps, Director of Public Instruction, Punjab. Crown 8vo. Price 5*s*.

"As clear and as instructive as possible." —*Standard.*

"Contains a great deal of most necessary information, that is not to be found in any other work on the subject that has crossed our path."—*Homeward Mail.*

Second Edition.

WESTERN INDIA BEFORE AND DURING THE MUTINIES.
Pictures drawn from Life. By **Major-Gen. Sir George Le Grand Jacob, K.C.S.I., C.B.** In 1 vol. Crown 8vo. Price 7*s*. 6*d*.

"The most important contribution to the history of Western India during the Mutinies which has yet, in a popular form, been made public."—*Athenæum.*

" Few men more competent than himself to speak authoritatively concerning Indian affairs."—*Standard.*

EDUCATIONAL COURSE OF SECULAR SCHOOL BOOKS FOR INDIA. Edited by **J. S. Laurie**, of the Inner Temple, Barrister-at-Law; formerly H.M. Inspector of Schools, England; Assistant Royal Commissioner, Ireland; Special Commissioner, African Settlements; Director of Public Instruction, Ceylon.

"These valuable little works will prove of real service to many of our readers, especially to those who intend entering the Civil Service of India." — *Civil Service Gazette.*

The following Works are now ready:—

	s.	d.		s.	d.
THE FIRST HINDUSTANI READER, stiff linen wrapper .	. 0	6	GEOGRAPHY OF INDIA, with Maps and Historical Appendix, tracing the growth of the British Empire in Hindustan. 128 pp.		
Ditto ditto strongly bound in cloth .	0	9			
THE SECOND HINDUSTANI READER, stiff linen wrapper .	. 0	6	Cloth	. 1	6
Ditto ditto strongly bound in cloth .	0	9			

In the Press.

ELEMENTARY GEOGRAPHY OF INDIA.

FACTS AND FEATURES OF INDIAN HISTORY, in a series of alternating Reading Lessons and Memory Exercises.

EXCHANGE TABLES OF STERLING AND INDIAN RUPEE CURRENCY, UPON A NEW AND EXTENDED SYSTEM, embracing Values from One Farthing to One Hundred Thousand Pounds, and at rates progressing, in Sixteenths of a Penny, from 1*s*. 9*d*. to 2*s*. 3*d*. per Rupee. By **Donald Fraser**, Accountant to the British Indian Steam Navigation Co. Limited. Royal 8vo. Price 10*s*. 6*d*.

"The calculations must have entailed great labour on the author, but the work is one which we fancy must become a standard one in all business houses which have dealings with any country where the rupee and the English pound are standard coins of currency."—*Inverness Courier.*

BOOKS FOR THE YOUNG AND FOR LENDING LIBRARIES.

---+---

AUNT MARY'S BRAN PIE. By the Author of "St. Olave's," "When I was a Little Girl," &c. [*In the Press.*

BY STILL WATERS. A Story in One Volume. By **Edward Garrett.** [*Preparing.*

WAKING AND WORKING; OR, FROM GIRLHOOD TO WOMANHOOD. By **Mrs. G. S. Reaney.** 1 vol. Crown 8vo. Illustrated. [*Preparing.*

PRETTY LESSONS IN VERSE FOR GOOD CHILDREN, with some Lessons in Latin, in Easy Rhyme. By **Sara Coleridge.** A New Edition. [*Preparing.*

NEW WORKS BY HESBA STRETTON.

CASSY. A New Story, by **Hesba Stretton.** Square crown 8vo, Illustrated, uniform with "Lost Gip." Price 1s. 6d.

THE KING'S SERVANTS. By **Hesba Stretton,** Author of "Lost Gip." Square crown 8vo, uniform with "Lost Gip." 8 Illustrations. Price 1s. 6d.

Part I.—Faithful in Little. Part II.—Unfaithful. Part III.—Faithful in Much.

LOST GIP. By **Hesba Stretton,** Author of "Little Meg," "Alone in London." Square crown 8vo. Six Illustrations. Price 1s. 6d.

** *A HANDSOMELY BOUND EDITION, WITH TWELVE ILLUSTRA-TIONS, PRICE HALF-A-CROWN.*

DADDY'S PET. By **Mrs. Ellen Ross (Nelsie Brook).** Square crown 8vo, uniform with "Lost Gip." 6 Illustrations. Price 1s.

"We have been more than pleased with this simple bit of writing."—*Christian World.* | "Full of deep feeling and true and noble sentiment."—*Brighton Gazette.*

SEEKING HIS FORTUNE, AND OTHER STORIES. Crown 8vo. Four Illustrations. Price 3s. 6d.

CONTENTS.—Seeking his Fortune.—Oluf and Stephanoff.—What's in a Name?—Contrast.—Onesta.

Three Works by MARTHA FARQUHARSON.

I. **ELSIE DINSMORE.** Crown 8vo. 3s. 6d.

II. **ELSIE'S GIRLHOOD.** Crown 8vo. 3s. 6d.

III. **ELSIE'S HOLIDAYS AT ROSELANDS.** Crown 8vo. 3s. 6d.

Each Story is independent and complete in itself. They are published in uniform size and price, and are elegantly bound and illustrated.

THE AFRICAN CRUISER. A Midshipman's Adventures on the West Coast. A Book for Boys. By C. Whitchurch Sadler, R.N., Author of "Marshall Vavasour." Illustrations. Crown 8vo. 3s. 6d.

"A capital story of youthful adventure. . . . Sea-loving boys will find few pleasanter gift books this season than 'The African Cruiser.'"—*Hour.* | "Sea yarns have always been in favour with boys, but this, written in a brisk style by a thorough sailor, is crammed full of adventures."—*Times.*

BOOKS FOR THE YOUNG, ETC.—*continued*.

THE LITTLE WONDER-HORN. By **Jean Ingelow.** A Second Series of "*Stories told to a Child.*" Fifteen Illustrations. Cloth, gilt. 3*s.* 6*d.*

"We like all the contents of the 'Little Wonder-Horn' very much."—*Athenæum.* "We recommend it with confidence."—*Pall Mall Gazette.*

"Full of fresh and vigorous fancy : it is worthy of the author of some of the best of our modern verse."—*Standard.*

BRAVE MEN'S FOOTSTEPS. A Book of Example and Anecdote for Young People. Second Edition. By the Editor of "**Men who have Risen.**" With Four Illustrations, by **C. Doyle.** 3*s.* 6*d.*

"A readable and instructive volume."—*Examiner.* "The little volume is precisely of the stamp to win the favour of those who, in

choosing a gift for a boy, would consult his moral development as well as his temporary pleasure."—*Daily Telegraph.*

PLUCKY FELLOWS. A Book for Boys. By **Stephen J. Mac Kenna.** With Six Illustrations. Second Edition. Crown 8vo. 3*s.* 6*d.*

"This is one of the very best 'Books for Boys' which have been issued this year."—*Morning Advertiser.* "A thorough book for boys . . . written

throughout in a manly straightforward manner that is sure to win the hearts of the children."—*London Society.*

GUTTA-PERCHA WILLIE, THE WORKING GENIUS. By **George Macdonald.** With Illustrations by **Arthur Hughes.** Crown 8vo. Second Edition. 3*s.* 6*d.*

"The cleverest child we know assures us she has read this story through five times. Mr. Macdonald will, we are convinced,

accept that verdict upon his little work as final."—*Spectator.*

THE TRAVELLING MENAGERIE. By **Charles Camden,** Author of "Hoity Toity." Illustrated by **J. Mahoney.** Crown 8vo. 3*s.* 6*d.*

"A capital little book . . . . deserves a wide circulation among our boys and girls."—*Hour.*

"A very attractive story." — *Public Opinion.*

THE DESERT PASTOR, JEAN JAROUSSEAU. Translated from the French of **Eugene Pelletan.** By Colonel **E. P. De L'Hoste.** In fcap. 8vo, with an Engraved Frontispiece. New Edition. 3*s.* 6*d.*

"A touching record of the struggles in the cause of religious liberty of a real man."—*Graphic.* "There is a poetical simplicity and picturesqueness ; the noblest heroism ; unpre-

tentious religion ; pure love, and the spectacle of a household brought up in the fear of the Lord. . . . ."—*Illustrated London News.*

THE DESERTED SHIP. A Real Story of the Atlantic. By **Cupples Howe,** Master Mariner. Illustrated by **Townley Green.** Crown 8vo. 3*s.* 6*d.*

"Curious adventures with bears, seals, and other Arctic animals, and with scarcely more human Esquimaux, form the mass of

material with which the story deals, and will much interest boys who have a spice of romance in their composition."—*Courant.*

HOITY TOITY, THE GOOD LITTLE FELLOW. By **Charles Camden.** Illustrated. Crown 8vo. 3*s.* 6*d.*

"Relates very pleasantly the history of a charming little fellow who meddles always with a kindly disposition with other people's

affairs and helps them to do right. There are many shrewd lessons to be picked up in this clever little story."—*Public Opinion.*

18   *Works Published by Henry S. King & Co.,*

BOOKS FOR THE YOUNG, ETC.—*continued.*

SLAVONIC FAIRY TALES. From Russian, Servian, Polish, and Bohemian Sources. Translated by **John T. Naaké.** Crown 8vo. Illustrated. Price 5s.

AT SCHOOL WITH AN OLD DRAGOON. By **Stephen J. Mac Kenna.** Crown 8vo. Six Illustrations. Price 5s.

"Consisting almost entirely of startling stories of military adventure . . . Boys will find them sufficiently exciting reading."— *Times.*

"These yarns give some very spirited and interesting descriptions of soldiering in various parts of the world."—*Spectator.*

"Mr. Mac Kenna's former work, 'Plucky Fellows,' is already a general favourite, and those who read the stories of the Old Dragoon will find that he has still plenty of materials at hand for pleasant tales, and has lost none of his power in telling them well."—*Standard.*

FANTASTIC STORIES. Translated from the German of **Richard Leander,** by **Paulina B. Granville.** Crown 8vo. Eight full-page Illustrations, by **M. E. Fraser-Tytler.** Price 5s.

"Short, quaint, and, as they are fitly called, fantastic, they deal with all manner of subjects."—*Guardian.*

"'Fantastic' is certainly the right epithet to apply to some of these strange tales."— *Examiner*

Third Edition.

STORIES IN PRECIOUS STONES. By **Helen Zimmern.** With Six Illustrations. Crown 8vo. Price 5s.

"A pretty little book which fanciful young persons will appreciate, and which will remind its readers of many a legend, and many an imaginary virtue attached to the gems they are so fond of wearing."—*Post.*

"A series of pretty tales which are half fantastic, half natural, and pleasantly quaint, as befits stories intended for the young."—*Daily Telegraph.*

THE GREAT DUTCH ADMIRALS. By **Jacob de Liefde.** Crown 8vo. Illustrated. Price 5s.

"May be recommended as a wholesome present for boys. They will find in it numerous tales of adventure."—*Athenæum.*

"A really good book."—*Standard.*
"A really excellent book."—*Spectator.*

PHANTASMION. A Fairy Romance. A new Edition. By **Sara Coleridge.** With an Introductory Preface by the **Right Hon. Lord Coleridge of Ottery S. Mary.** In 1 vol. Crown 8vo. Price 7s. 6d.

LAYS OF A KNIGHT ERRANT IN MANY LANDS. By **Major-General Sir Vincent Eyre, C.B., G.C.S.I., &c.** Square crown 8vo. Six Illustrations. Price 7s. 6d.

Pharaoh Land.
Home Land.
Wonder Land.
Rhine Land.

BEATRICE AYLMER AND OTHER TALES. By the Author of "Brompton Rectory." 1 vol. Crown 8vo. [*Preparing.*

THE TASMANIAN LILY. By **James Bonwick.** Crown 8vo. Illustrated. Price 5s.

"An interesting and useful work."— *Hour.*
"The characters of the story are capitally

conceived, and are full of those touches which give them a natural appearance."— *Public Opinion.*

MIKE HOWE, THE BUSHRANGER OF VAN DIEMEN'S LAND. By **James Bonwick,** Author of "The Tasmanian Lily," &c. Crown 8vo. With a Frontispiece.

"He illustrates the career of the bushranger half a century ago; and this he does in a highly creditable manner; his delineations of life in the bush are, to say

the least, exquisite, and his representations of character are very marked."—*Edinburgh Courant.*

65, *Cornhill;* & 12, *Paternoster Row, London.*

WORKS BY ALFRED TENNYSON, D.C.L.,

POET LAUREATE.

THE CABINET EDITION.

Messrs. HENRY S. KING & Co. have the pleasure to announce that they will immediately issue an Edition of the Laureate's works, in *Ten Monthly Volumes*, foolscap 8vo, to be entitled "The Cabinet Edition," at *Half-a-Crown each*, which will contain the whole of Mr. Tennyson's works. The first volume will be illustrated by a beautiful Photographic Portrait, and subsequent Volumes will each contain a Frontispiece. They will be tastefully bound in Crimson Cloth, and will be issued in the following order :—

Vol.		Vol.	
1.	EARLY POEMS.	6.	IDYLLS OF THE KING.
2.	ENGLISH IDYLLS & OTHER POEMS.	7.	IDYLL OF THE KING.
3.	LOCKSLEY HALL & OTHER POEMS.	8.	THE PRINCESS.
4.	AYLMER'S FIELD & OTHER POEMS.	9.	MAUD AND ENOCH ARDEN.
5.	IDYLLS OF THE KING.	10.	IN MEMORIAM.

Subscribers' names received by all Booksellers.

	PRICE.
	s. d.
POEMS. Small 8vo.	9 0
MAUD AND OTHER POEMS. Small 8vo.	5 0
THE PRINCESS. Small 8vo.	5 0
IDYLLS OF THE KING. Small 8vo.	7 0
,, ,, Collected. Small 8vo.	12 0
ENOCH ARDEN, &c. Small 8vo.	6 0
THE HOLY GRAIL, AND OTHER POEMS. Small 8vo.	7 0
GARETH AND LYNETTE. Small 8vo.	5 0
SELECTIONS FROM THE ABOVE WORKS. Square 8vo, cloth extra . .	5 0
SONGS FROM THE ABOVE WORKS. Square 8vo, cloth extra . . .	5 0
IN MEMORIAM. Small 8vo.	6 0
LIBRARY EDITION OF MR. TENNYSON'S WORKS. 6 vols. Post 8vo, each	10 6
POCKET VOLUME EDITION OF MR. TENNYSON'S WORKS. 10 vols., in	
neat case	45 0
,, gilt edges . . . . , . .	50 0
THE WINDOW; OR, THE SONGS OF THE WRENS. A Series of Songs.	
By ALFRED TENNYSON. With Music by ARTHUR SULLIVAN. 4to, cloth, gilt extra	21 0

POETRY.

LYRICS OF LOVE, Selected and arranged from Shakspeare to Tennyson, by **W. Davenport Adams**. Fcap. 8vo. Price 3s. 6d.

"We cannot too highly commend this work, delightful in its contents and so pretty in its outward adornings."—*Standard.*

"Carefully selected and elegantly got up . . It is particularly rich in poems from living writers."—*John Bull.*

WILLIAM CULLEN BRYANT'S POEMS. Red-line Edition. Handsomely bound. With Illustrations and Portrait of the Author. Price 7s. 6d. A Cheaper Edition is also published. Price 3s. 6d.

These are the only complete English Editions sanctioned by the Author.

ENGLISH SONNETS. Collected and Arranged by **John Dennis**. Small crown 8vo. Elegantly bound. Price 3s. 6d.

"An exquisite selection, a selection which every lover of poetry will consult again and again with delight. The notes are very useful. . . . The volume is one for which

English literature owes Mr. Dennis the heartiest thanks."—*Spectator.*
"Mr. Dennis has shown great judgment in this selection."—*Saturday Review.*

Second Edition.
HOME-SONGS FOR QUIET HOURS. By the **Rev. Canon R. H. Baynes**, Editor of "English Lyrics" and "Lyra Anglicana." Handsomely printed and bound. Price 3s. 6d.

POEMS. By **Annette F. C. Knight.** Fcap. 8vo.   [*Preparing.*

POEMS. By the **Rev. J. W. A. Taylor.** Fcap. 8vo.   [*In the Press.*

ALEXANDER THE GREAT. A Dramatic Poem. By **Aubrey de Vere**, Author of "The Legends of St. Patrick," &c. Crown 8vo.
[*Nearly ready.*

THE DISCIPLES. A New Poem. By **Harriet Eleanor Hamilton King.** Crown 8vo. Price 7s. 6d.

ASPROMONTE, AND OTHER POEMS. Second Edition. Cloth, 4s. 6d.

"The volume is anonymous, but there is no reason for the author to be ashamed of it. The 'Poems of Italy' are evidently inspired by genuine enthusiasm in the cause espoused ; and one of them, 'The

Execution of Felice Orsini,' has much poetic merit, the event celebrated being told with dramatic force."—*Athenæum.*
"The verse is fluent and free."—*Spectator.*

SONGS FOR MUSIC. By **Four Friends.** Square crown 8vo. Price 5s.

CONTAINING SONGS BY

Reginald A. Gatty.   Stephen H. Gatty.
Greville J. Chester.   Juliana H. Ewing.

"A charming gift-book, which will be very popular with lovers of poetry."—*John Bull.*

ROBERT BUCHANAN, THE POETICAL AND PROSE WORKS OF. Collected Edition, in 5 Vols. Vol. I. contains,—"Ballads and Romances ;" "Ballads and Poems of Life," and a Portrait of the Author.

Vol. II.—"Ballads and Poems of Life ;" "Allegories and Sonnets."

Vol. III.—"Cruiskeen Sonnets ;" "Book of Orm ;" "Political Mystics."

The Contents of the remaining Volumes will be duly announced.

THOUGHTS IN VERSE. Small crown 8vo. Price 1s. 6d.

This is a Collection of Verses expressive of religious feeling, written from a Theistic stand-point.

POETRY—*continued.*

COSMOS. A Poem. Small crown 8vo. Price 3s. 6d.

SUBJECT.—Nature in the Past and in the Present.—Man in the Past and in the Present.—The Future.

NARCISSUS AND OTHER POEMS. By E. Carpenter. Small crown 8vo. Price 5s.

"Displays considerable poetic force."—*Queen.*

A TALE OF THE SEA, SONNETS, AND OTHER POEMS. By James Howell. Crown 8vo. Cloth, 5s.

"Mr. Howell has a keen perception of the beauties of nature, and a just appreciation of the charities of life. . . . Mr. Howell's book deserves, and will probably receive, a warm reception."—*Pall Mall Gazette.*

IMITATIONS FROM THE GERMAN OF SPITTA AND TERSTEGEN. By Lady Durand. Crown 8vo. 4s.

"A charming little volume. . . . Will be a very valuable assistance to peaceful, meditative souls."—*Church Herald.*

Second Edition.

VIGNETTES IN RHYME. Collected Verses. By Austin Dobson. Crown 8vo. Price 5s.

"Clever, clear-cut, and careful."—*———*

"As a writer of Vers de Société, Mr. Dobson is almost, if not quite, unrivalled."—*Examiner.*

"Lively, innocent, elegant in expression, and graceful in fancy."—*Morning Post.*

ON VIOL AND FLUTE. A New Volume of Poems, by Edmund W. Gosse. With a Frontispiece by W. B. Scott. Crown 8vo. 5s.

"A careful perusal of his verses will show that he is a poet. . . . His song has the grateful, murmuring sound which reminds one of the softness and deliciousness of summer time. . . . There is much that is good in the volume."—*Spectator.*

METRICAL TRANSLATIONS FROM THE GREEK AND LATIN POETS, AND OTHER POEMS. By R. B. Boswell, M.A. Oxon. Crown 8vo. 5s.

EASTERN LEGENDS AND STORIES IN ENGLISH VERSE. By Lieutenant Norton Powlett, Royal Artillery. Crown 8vo. 5s.

"There is a rollicking sense of fun about the stories, joined to marvellous power of rhyming, and plenty of swing, which irresistibly reminds us of our old favourite."—*Graphic.*

EDITH; OR, LOVE AND LIFE IN CHESHIRE. By T. Ashe, Author of the "Sorrows of Hypsipyle," etc. Sewed. Price 6d.

"A really fine poem, full of tender, subtle touches of feeling."—*Manchester News.*

"Pregnant from beginning to end with the results of careful observation and imaginative power."—*Chester Chronicle.*

THE GALLERY OF PIGEONS, AND OTHER POEMS. By Theo. Marzials. Crown 8vo. 4s. 6d.

"A conceit abounding in prettiness."—*Examiner.*

"The rush of fresh, sparkling fancies is too rapid, too sustained, too abundant, not to be spontaneous."—*Academy.*

THE INN OF STRANGE MEETINGS, AND OTHER POEMS. By Mortimer Collins. Crown 8vo. 5s.

"Abounding in quiet humour, in bright fancy, in sweetness and melody of expression, and, at times, in the tenderest touches of pathos."—*Graphic.*

"Mr. Collins has an undercurrent of chivalry and romance beneath the trifling vein of good-humoured banter which is the special characteristic of his verse."—*Athenæum.*

EROS AGONISTES. By E. B. D. Crown 8vo. 3s. 6d.

"It is not the least merit of these pages that they are everywhere illumined with moral and religious sentiment suggested, not paraded, of the brightest, purest character."—*Standard.*

CALDERON'S DRAMAS. Translated from the Spanish. By Denis Florence MacCarthy. 10s.

"The lambent verse flows with an ease, spirit, and music perfectly natural, liberal, and harmonious."—*Spectator.*

"It is impossible to speak too highly of this beautiful work."—*Month.*

SONGS FOR SAILORS. By Dr. W. C. Bennett. Dedicated by Special Request to H. R. H. the Duke of Edinburgh. Crown 8vo. 3s. 6d. With Steel Portrait and Illustrations.

An Edition in Illustrated paper Covers. Price 1s.

WALLED IN, AND OTHER POEMS. By the Rev. Henry J. Bulkeley. Crown 8vo. 5s.

"A remarkable book of genuine poetry."—*Evening Standard.*

"Genuine power displayed."—*Examiner.*

"Poetical feeling is manifest here, and the diction of the poem is unimpeachable."—*Pall Mall Gazette.*

POETRY—*continued.*

SONGS OF LIFE AND DEATH. By John Payne, Author of "Intaglios," "Sonnets," "The Masque of Shadows," etc. Crown 8vo. 5*s.*

"The art of ballad-writing has long been lost in England, and Mr. Payne may claim to be its restorer. It is a perfect delight to meet with such a ballad as 'May Margaret' in the present volume." — *Westminster Review.*

A NEW VOLUME OF SONNETS. By the Rev. C. Tennyson Turner. Crown 8vo. 4*s.* 6*d.*

"Mr. Turner is a genuine poet; his song is sweet and pure, beautiful in expression, and often subtle in thought."—*Pall Mall Gazette.*

"The light of a devout, gentle, and kindly spirit, a delicate and graceful fancy, a keen intelligence irradiates these thoughts."— *Contemporary Review.*

THE DREAM AND THE DEED, AND OTHER POEMS. By Patrick Scott, Author of "Footpaths between Two Worlds," etc. Fcap. 8vo. Cloth, 5*s.*

"A bitter and able satire on the vice and follies of the day, literary, social, and political."—*Standard.*

"Shows real poetic power coupled with evidences of satirical energy."—*Edinburgh Daily Review.*

GOETHE'S FAUST. A New Translation in Rime. By the Rev. C. Kegan Paul. Crown 8vo. 6*s.*

"His translation is the most minutely accurate that has yet been produced. . . " —*Examiner.*

"Mr. Paul is a zealous and a faithful interpreter."—*Saturday Review.*

SONGS OF TWO WORLDS. First Series. By a New Writer. Fcap. 8vo, cloth, 5*s.* Second Edition.

"These poems will assuredly take high rank among the class to which they belong." —*British Quarterly Review, April 1st.*

"No extracts could do justice to the exquisite tones, the felicitous phrasing and delicately wrought harmonies of some of these poems." — *Nonconformist.*

"A purity and delicacy of feeling like morning air."—*Graphic.*

SONGS OF TWO WORLDS. Second Series. By the Author of "Songs of Two Worlds." Crown 8vo.   [*In the Press.*

THE LEGENDS OF ST. PATRICK AND OTHER POEMS. By Aubrey de Vere. Crown 8vo. 5*s.*

"Mr. De Vere's versification in his earlier poems is characterised by great sweetness and simplicity. He is master of his instrument, and rarely offends the ear with false notes."—*Pall Mall Gazette.*

"We have but space to commend the varied structure of his verse, the carefulness of his grammar, and his excellent English."—*Saturday Review.*

FICTION.

AILEEN FERRERS. By Susan Morley. In 2 vols. Crown 8vo, cloth.
     [*Immediately.*

IDOLATRY. A Romance. By Julian Hawthorne. Author of "Bressant." 2 vols. Crown 8vo, cloth.

VANESSA. By the Author of "Thomasina," "Dorothy," etc. 2 vols. Crown 8vo.

CIVIL SERVICE. By J. P. Listado. Author of "Maurice Rhynhart." 2 vols. Crown 8vo.

JUDITH GWYNNE. By Lisle Carr. In 3 vols. Crown 8vo, cloth.

TOO LATE. By Mrs. Newman. 2 vols. Crown 8vo.

LADY MORETOUN'S DAUGHTER. By Mrs. Eiloart. In 3 vols. Crown 8vo, cloth.

MARGARET AND ELIZABETH. A Story of the Sea. By Katherine Saunders, Author of "Gideon's Rock," etc. In 1 vol. Cloth, crown 8vo.

"Simply yet powerfully told. . . . This opening picture is so exquisitely drawn as to be a fit introduction to a story of such simple pathos and power. . . . A very beautiful story closes as it began, in a tender and touching picture of homely happiness." —*Pall Mall Gazette.*

FICTION—*continued*.

MR. CARINGTON. A Tale of Love and Conspiracy. By Robert Turner Cotton. In 3 vols. Cloth, crown 8vo.

"A novel in so many ways good, as in a fresh and elastic diction, stout unconventionality, and happy boldness of conception and execution. His novels, though free spoken, will be some of the healthiest of our day."—*Examiner*.

TWO GIRLS. By Frederick Wedmore, Author of "A Snapt Gold Ring." In 2 vols. Cloth, crown 8vo. [*Just out*.

"A carefully-written novel of character, contrasting the two heroines of one love tale, an English lady and a French actress. Cicely is charming ; the introductory description of her is a good specimen of the well-balanced sketches in which the author shines."—*Athenæum*.

HEATHERGATE. In 2 vols. Crown 8vo, cloth. A Story of Scottish Life and Character. By a new Author.

"Its merit lies in the marked antithesis of strongly developed characters, in different ranks of life, and resembling each other in nothing but their marked nationality."—*Athenæum*.

THE QUEEN'S SHILLING. By Captain Arthur Griffiths, Author of " Peccavi," 2 vols.

"Every scene, character, and incident of the book are so life-like that they seem drawn from life direct."—*Pall Mall Gazette*.

MIRANDA. A Midsummer Madness. By Mortimer Collins. 3 vols.

"Not a dull page in the whole three volumes."—*Standard*.

"The work of a man who is at once a thinker and a poet."—*Hour*.

SQUIRE SILCHESTER'S WHIM. By Mortimer Collins, Author of " Marquis and Merchant," " The Princess Clarice," etc. 3 vols. Crown 8vo.

"We think it the best (story) Mr. Collins has yet written. Full of incident and adventure."—*Pall Mall Gazette*.

"So clever, so irritating, and so charming a story."—*Standard*.

THE PRINCESS CLARICE. A Story of 1871. By Mortimer Collins. 2 vols. Crown 8vo.

"Mr. Collins has produced a readable book, amusingly characteristic."—*Athenæum*.

"A bright, fresh, and original book."—*Standard*.

REGINALD BRAMBLE. A Cynic of the 19th Century. An Autobiography. 1 vol.

"There is plenty of vivacity in Mr. Bramble's narrative."—*Athenæum*.

"Written in a lively and readable style."—*Hour*.

EFFIE'S GAME; How she Lost and how she Won. By Cecil Clayton. 2 vols.

"Well written. The characters move, and act, and, above all, talk like human beings, and we have liked reading about them."—*Spectator*.

CHESTERLEIGH. By Ansley Conyers. 3 vols. Crown 8vo.

"We have gained much enjoyment from the book."—*Spectator*.

BRESSANT. A Romance. By Julian Hawthorne. 2 vols. Crown 8vo.

"One of the most powerful with which we are acquainted."—*Times*.

"We shall once more have reason to rejoice whenever we hear that a new work is coming out written by one who bears the honoured name of Hawthorne."—*Saturday Review*.

HONOR BLAKE: The Story of a Plain Woman. By Mrs. Maitland, Author of English Homes in India," etc. 2 vols. Crown 8vo.

"One of the best novels we have met with for some time."—*Morning Post*.

"A story which must do good to all, young and old, who read it."—*Daily News*.

OFF THE SKELLIGS. By Jean Ingelow. (Her First Romance.) In 4 vols. Crown 8vo.

"Clever and sparkling."—*Standard*.

"We read each succeeding volume with increasing interest, going almost to the point of wishing there was a fifth."—*Athenæum*.

SEETA. By Colonel Meadows Taylor, Author of " Tara," " Ralph Darnell," etc. 3 vols. Crown 8vo.

"Well told, native life is admirably described, and the petty intrigues of native rulers, and their hatred of the English mingled with fear lest the latter should eventually prove the victors, are cleverly depicted."—*Athenæum*.

"Thoroughly interesting and enjoyable reading."—*Examiner*.

WHAT 'TIS TO LOVE. By the Author of " Flora Adair," " The Value of Fosterstown." 3 vols.

FICTION—*continued.*

HESTER MORLEY'S PROMISE. By Hesba Stretton. 3 vols.

"Much better than the average novels of the day; has much more claim to critical consideration as a piece of literary work,—very clever."—*Spectator.*

"All the characters stand out clearly and are well sustained, and the interest of the story never flags."—*Observer.*

THE DOCTOR'S DILEMMA. By Hesba Stretton, Author of "Little Meg," &c. &c. 3 vols. Crown 8vo.

"A fascinating story which scarcely flags in interest from the first page to the last."—*British Quarterly Review.*

THE ROMANTIC ANNALS OF A NAVAL FAMILY. By Mrs. Arthur Traherne. Crown 8vo. 10s. 6d.

"Some interesting letters are introduced; amongst others, several from the late King William IV."—*Spectator.*

"Well and pleasantly told."—*Evening Standard.*

THOMASINA. By the Author of "Dorothy," "De Cressy," &c. 2 vols. Crown 8vo.

"A finished and delicate cabinet picture; no line is without its purpose."—*Athenæum.*

JOHANNES OLAF. By E. de Wille. Translated by F. E. Bunnett. 3 vols. Crown 8vo.

"The art of description is fully exhibited; perception of character and capacity for delineating it are obvious; while there is great breadth and comprehensiveness in the plan of the story."—*Morning Post.*

THE STORY OF SIR EDWARD'S WIFE. By Hamilton Marshall, Author of "For Very Life." 1 vol. Crown 8vo.

"A quiet, graceful little story."—*Spectator.*

"Mr. Hamilton Marshall can tell a story closely and pleasantly."—*Pall Mall Gaz.*

HERMANN AGHA. An Eastern Narrative. By W. Gifford Palgrave. 2 vols. Crown 8vo, cloth, extra gilt. 18s.

"There is a positive fragrance as of newly-mown hay about it, as compared with the artificially perfumed passions which are detailed to us with such gusto by our ordinary novel-writers in their endless volumes."—*Observer.*

A GOOD MATCH. By Amelia Perrier, Author of "Mea Culpa." 2 vols.

"Racy and lively."—*Athenæum.*

"This clever and amusing novel."—*Pall Mall Gazette.*

LINKED AT LAST. By F. E. Bunnett. 1 vol. Crown 8vo.

"The reader who once takes it up will not be inclined to relinquish it without concluding the volume."—*Morning Post.*

"A very charming story."—*John Bull.*

THE SPINSTERS OF BLATCHINGTON. By Mar. Travers. 2 vols. Crown 8vo.

"A pretty story. Deserving of a favourable reception."—*Graphic.*

"A book of more than average merits."—*Examiner.*

PERPLEXITY. By Sydney Mostyn. 3 vols. Crown 8vo.

"Written with very considerable power, great cleverness, and sustained interest."—*Standard.*

"The literary workmanship is good, and the story forcibly and graphically told."—*Daily News.*

MEMOIRS OF MRS. LÆTITIA BOOTHBY. By William Clark Russell, Author of "The Book of Authors." Crown 8vo. 7s. 6d.

"Clever and ingenious."—*Saturday Review.*

"Very clever book."—*Guardian.*

CRUEL AS THE GRAVE. By the Countess Von Bothmer. 3 vols. Crown 8vo.

"*Jealousy is cruel as the Grave.*"

"Interesting, though somewhat tragic."—*Athenæum.*

"Agreeable, unaffected, and eminently readable."—*Daily News.*

HER TITLE OF HONOUR. By Holme Lee. Second Edition. 1 vol. Crown 8vo.

"With the interest of a pathetic story is united the value of a definite and high purpose."—*Spectator.*

"A most exquisitely written story."—*Literary Churchman.*

SEPTIMIUS. A Romance. By Nathaniel Hawthorne. Second Edition. 1 vol. Crown 8vo, cloth, extra gilt. 9s.

The *Athenæum* says that "the book is full of Hawthorne's most characteristic writing."

COL. MEADOWS TAYLOR'S INDIAN TALES.

THE CONFESSIONS OF A THUG

Is now ready, and is the Volume of A New and Cheaper Edition, in 1 vol. each, Illustrated, price 6s. It will be followed by "TARA" (now in the press) "RALPH DARNELL," and "TIPPOO SULTAN."

THE CORNHILL LIBRARY OF FICTION.

3s. 6d. per Volume.

IT is intended in this Series to produce books of such merit that readers will care to preserve them on their shelves. They are well printed on good paper, handsomely bound, with a Frontispiece, and are sold at the moderate price of **3s. 6d.** each.

THE HOUSE OF RABY. By Mrs. G. Hooper.

A FIGHT FOR LIFE. By Moy Thomas.

ROBIN GRAY. By Charles Gibbon.

"Pure in sentiment, well written, and cleverly constructed."—*British Quarterly Review.*
"A pretty tale, prettily told."—*Athenæum.*

"A novel of tender and pathetic interest."—*Globe.*
"An unassuming, characteristic, and entertaining novel."—*John Bull.*

KITTY. By Miss M. Betham-Edwards.

"Lively and clever . . . There is a certain dash in every description ; the dialogue is bright and sparkling."—*Athenæum.*

"Very pleasant and amusing."—*Globe.*
"A charming novel."—*John Bull.*

HIRELL. By John Saunders.

"A powerful novel . . . a tale written by a poet."—*Spectator.*
"A novel of extraordinary merit."—*Morning Post.*

"We have nothing but words of praise to offer for its style and composition."—*Examiner.*

ONE OF TWO; or, The left-handed Bride. By J. H. Friswell.

"Told with spirit . . . the plot is skilfully made."—*Spectator.*

"Admirably narrated, and intensely interesting."—*Public Opinion.*

READY-MONEY MORTIBOY. A Matter-of-Fact Story.

"There is not a dull page in the whole story."—*Standard.*
"A very interesting and uncommon story."—*Vanity Fair.*

"One of the most remarkable novels which has appeared of late."—*Pall Mall Gazette.*

GOD'S PROVIDENCE HOUSE. By Mrs. G. L. Banks.

"Far above the run of common three-volume novels, evincing much literary power in not a few graphic descriptions of manners and local customs. . . . A genuine sketch."—*Spectator.*

"Possesses the merit of care, industry, and local knowledge."—*Athenæum.*
"Wonderfully readable. The style is very simple and natural."—*Morning Post.*

FOR LACK OF GOLD. By Charles Gibbon.

"A powerfully written nervous story."—*Athenæum.*
"A piece of very genuine workmanship."—*British Quarterly Review.*
"There are few recent novels more powerful and engrossing."—*Examiner.*

ABEL DRAKE'S WIFE. By John Saunders.

"A striking book, clever, interesting, and original. We have seldom met with a book so thoroughly true to life, so deeply

interesting in its detail, and so touching in its simple pathos."—*Athenæum.*

OTHER STANDARD NOVELS TO FOLLOW.

THEOLOGICAL.

WORDS OF TRUTH AND CHEER. A Mission of Instruction and Suggestion. By the **Rev. Archer P. Gurney.** 1 vol. Crown 8vo. Price 6s.   [*In the Press.*

THE GOSPEL ITS OWN WITNESS. Being the Hulsean Lectures for 1873. By the **Rev. Stanley Leathes.** 1 vol. Crown 8vo.

THE CHURCH AND THE EMPIRES: Historical Periods. By **Henry W. Wilberforce.** Preceded by a Memoir of the Author, by J. H. Newman, D.D. 1 vol. Post 8vo. Price 10s. 6d.

THE HIGHER LIFE. A New Volume by the **Rev. J. Baldwin Brown,** Author of "The Soul's Exodus," etc. 1 vol. Crown 8vo. Price 7s. 6d.

HARTHAM CONFERENCES; OR, DISCUSSIONS UPON SOME OF THE RELIGIOUS TOPICS OF THE DAY. By the **Rev. F. W. Kingsford, M.A.,** Vicar of S. Thomas's, Stamford Hill; late Chaplain H. E. I. C. (Bengal Presidency). "Audi alteram partem." Crown 8vo. Price 3s. 6d.

STUDIES IN MODERN PROBLEMS. A Series of Essays by various Writers. Edited by the **Rev. Orby Shipley, M.A.** Vol. I. Cr. 8vo. Price 5s.

CONTENTS.

Sacramental Confession. A. H. WARD, B.A.	Retreats for Persons Living in the World.
Abolition of the 39 Articles.	T. T. CARTER, M.A.
NICHOLAS POCOCK, M.A.	Catholic and Protestant.
The Sanctity of Marriage.	EDWARD L. BLENKINSOPP, M.A.
JOHN WALTER LEA, B.A.	The Bishops on Confession. THE EDITOR.
Creation and Modern Science.	
GEORGE GREENWOOD, M.A.	

A Second Series is being published, price 6d. each part.

UNTIL THE DAY DAWN. Four Advent Lectures delivered in the Episcopal Chapel, Milverton, Warwickshire, on the Sunday Evenings during Advent, 1870. By the **Rev. Marmaduke E. Browne.** Crown 8vo. Price 2s. 6d.

"Four really original and stirring sermons."—*John Bull.*

A SCOTCH COMMUNION SUNDAY. To which are added Discourses from a Certain University City. Second Edition. By **A. K. H. B.,** Author of "The Recreations of a Country Parson." Crown 8vo. Second Edition. Price 5s.

"Some discourses are added, which are couched in language of rare power."—*John Bull.*
"Exceedingly fresh and readable."—*Glasgow News.*

"We commend this volume as full of interest to all our readers. It is written with much ability and good feeling, with excellent taste and marvellous tact."—*Church Herald.*

EVERY DAY A PORTION: Adapted from the Bible and the Prayer Book, for the Private Devotions of those living in Widowhood. Collected and Edited by the **Lady Mary Vyner.** Square crown 8vo, printed on good paper, elegantly bound. Price 5s.

"Now she that is a widow indeed, and desolate, trusteth in God."

CHURCH THOUGHT AND CHURCH WORK. Edited by the Rev. Chas. Anderson, M.A., Editor of "Words and Works in a London Parish." Demy 8vo. Pp. 250. 7s. 6d. Containing Articles by the Rev. J. LL. DAVIES, J. M. CAPES, HARRY JONES, BROOKE LAMBERT, A. J. ROSS, Professor CHEETHAM, the EDITOR, and others.

Second Edition.

WORDS AND WORKS IN A LONDON PARISH. Edited by the Rev. Charles Anderson, M.A. Demy 8vo. 6s.

"It has an interest of its own for not a few minds, to whom the question 'Is the National Church worth preserving as such, and if so, how best increase its vital power?' is of deep and grave importance." —*Spectator.*

ESSAYS ON RELIGION AND LITERATURE. By Various Writers. Edited by the Most Reverend Archbishop Manning. Demy 8vo. 10s. 6d.

CONTENTS :—The Philosophy of Christianity.—Mystical Elements of Religion.—Controversy with the Agnostics.—A Reasoning Thought.—Darwinism brought to Book.—Mr. Mill on Liberty of the Press.— Christianity in relation to Society.—The Religious Condition of Germany.—The Philosophy of Bacon.—Catholic Laymen and Scholastic Philosophy.

WHY AM I A CHRISTIAN? By Viscount Stratford de Redcliffe, P.C., K.G., G.C.B. Crown 8vo. 3s. Third Edition.

"Has a peculiar interest, as exhibiting the convictions of an earnest, intelligent, and practical man."—*Contemporary Review,*

THEOLOGY AND MORALITY. Being Essays by the Rev. J. Llewellyn Davies. 1 vol. 8vo. Price 7s. 6d.

"The position taken up by Mr. Llewellyn Davies is well worth a careful survey on the part of philosophical students, for it represents the closest approximation of any theological system yet formulated to the religion of philosophy. . . We have not space to do more with regard to the social essays of the work before us, than to testify to the kindliness of spirit, sobriety, and earnest thought by which they are uniformly characterised."—*Examiner.*

THE RECONCILIATION OF RELIGION AND SCIENCE. Being Essays by the Rev. T. W. Fowle, M.A. 1 vol. 8vo. 10s. 6d.

"A book which requires and deserves the respectful attention of all reflecting Churchmen. It is earnest, reverent, thoughtful, and courageous. . . . There is scarcely a page in the book which is not equally worthy of a thoughtful pause."—*Literary Churchman.*

HYMNS AND SACRED LYRICS. By the Rev. Godfrey Thring, B.A. 1 vol. Crown 8vo.

HYMNS AND VERSES, Original and Translated. By the Rev. Henry Downton. Small crown 8vo. 3s. 6d.

"Considerable force and beauty characterise some of these verses."—*Watchman.* "Mr. Downton's 'Hymns and Verses' are worthy of all praise." — *English Churchman.* "Will, we do not doubt, be welcome as a permanent possession to those for whom they have been composed or to whom they have been originally addressed."—*Church Herald.*

THEOLOGICAL—*continued.*

MISSIONARY ENTERPRISE IN THE EAST. By the Rev. Richard Collins. Illustrated. Crown 8vo. 6s.

"A very graphic story told in lucid, simple, and modest style." — *English Churchman.*
"A readable and very interesting volume."—*Church Review.*

"We may judge from our own experience, no one who takes up this charming little volume will lay it down again till he has got to the last word."—*John Bull.*

MISSIONARY LIFE IN THE SOUTH SEAS. By James Hutton. 1 vol. Crown 8vo. [*In the Press.*

THE ETERNAL LIFE. Being Fourteen Sermons. By the Rev. Jas. Noble Bennie, M.A. Crown 8vo. 6s.

"The whole volume is replete with matter for thought and study."—*John Bull.*
"Mr. Bennie preaches earnestly and well."—*Literary Churchman.*

"We recommend these sermons as wholesome Sunday reading."—*English Churchman.*

THE REALM OF TRUTH. By Miss E. T. Carne. Crown 8vo. 5s. 6d.

"A singularly calm, thoughtful, and philosophical inquiry into what Truth is, and what its authority."—*Leeds Mercury.*
"It tells the world what it does not like to hear, but what it cannot be told too often,

that Truth is something stronger and more enduring than our little doings, and speakings, and actings." — *Literary Churchman.*

LIFE : Conferences delivered at Toulouse. By the Rev. Père Lacordaire. Crown 8vo. 6s.

"Let the serious reader cast his eye upon any single page in this volume, and he will find there words which will arrest his attention and give him a desire to know

more of the teachings of this worthy follower of the saintly St. Dominick."—*Morning Post.*

Second Edition.

CATHOLICISM AND THE VATICAN. With a Narrative of the Old Catholic Congress at Munich. By J. Lowry Whittle, A.M., Trin. Coll., Dublin. Crown 8vo. 4s. 6d.

"We may cordially recommend his book to all who wish to follow the course of the

Old Catholic movement." — *Saturday Review.*

SIX PRIVY COUNCIL JUDGMENTS — 1850-1872. Annotated by W. G. Brooke, M.A., Barrister-at-Law. Crown 8vo. 9s.

"The volume is a valuable record of cases forming precedents for the future."—*Athenæum.*
"A very timely and important publication. It brings into one view the great

judgments of the last twenty years, which will constitute the unwritten law of the English Establishment." — *British Quarterly Review.*

THE MOST COMPLETE HYMN BOOK PUBLISHED.

HYMNS FOR THE CHURCH AND HOME. Selected and Edited by the Rev. W. Fleming Stevenson, Author of "Praying and Working."

The Hymn-book consists of Three Parts :—I. For Public Worship.—II. For Family and Private Worship.—III. For Children : and contains Biographical Notices of nearly 300 Hymn-writers, with Notes upon their Hymns.

*** *Published in various forms and prices, the latter ranging from 8d. to 6s. Lists and full particulars will be furnished on application to the Publisher.*

THEOLOGICAL—*continued.*

WORKS BY THE REV. H. R. HAWEIS, M.A.

Sixth Edition.

THOUGHTS FOR THE TIMES. By the **Rev. H. R. Haweis, M.A.**, "Author of Music and Morals," etc. Crown 8vo. Price 7s. 6d.

"Bears marks of much originality of thought and individuality of expression."— *Pall Mall Gazette.*

"Mr. Haweis writes not only fearlessly,

but with remarkable freshness and vigour. In all that he says we perceive a transparent honesty and singleness of purpose." —*Saturday Review.*

SPEECH IN SEASON. A New Volume of Sermons. By the **Rev. H. R. Haweis.** Crown 8vo. Price 9s.

UNSECTARIAN FAMILY PRAYERS, for Morning and Evening for a Week, with short selected passages from the Bible. By the **Rev. H. R. Haweis, M.A.** Square crown 8vo. Price 3s. 6d.

WORKS BY THE REV. C. J. VAUGHAN, D.D.

THE SOLIDITY OF TRUE RELIGION. [*In the Press.*]

FORGET THINE OWN PEOPLE. An Appeal for Missions. Small Crown 8vo. Price 3s. 6d.

WORDS OF HOPE FROM THE PULPIT OF THE TEMPLE CHURCH. Crown 8vo. Price 5s.

Fourth Edition.

THE YOUNG LIFE EQUIPPING IT-SELF FOR GOD'S SERVICE. Being Four Sermons Preached before the University of Cambridge, in November, 1872. Crown 8vo. Price 3s. 6d.

"Has all the writer's characteristics of devotedness, purity, and high moral tone."—*London Quarterly Review.*

"As earnest, eloquent, and as liberal as everything else that he writes."—*Examiner.*

WORKS BY THE REV. G. S. DREW, M.A.,
VICAR OF TRINITY, LAMBETH.

Second Edition.

SCRIPTURE LANDS IN CONNECTION WITH THEIR HISTORY. Bevelled Boards, 8vo. Price 10s. 6d.

"Mr. Drew has invented a new method of illustrating Scripture history — from observation of the countries. Instead of narrating his travels, and referring from time to time to the facts of sacred history belonging to the different countries, he writes an outline history of the Hebrew nation from Abraham downwards, with special reference to the various points in which the geography illustrates the history. . . He is very successful in picturing to his readers the scenes before his own mind."—*Saturday Review.*

Second Edition.

NAZARETH: ITS LIFE AND LESSONS. Second Edition. In small 8vo, cloth. Price 5s.

"We have read the volume with great interest. It is at once succinct and suggestive, reverent and ingenious, observant of small details, and yet not forgetful of great principles."—*British Quarterly Review.*

"A very reverent attempt to elicit and develop Scripture intimations respecting our Lord's thirty years' sojourn at Nazareth. The author has wrought well at the unworked mine, and has produced a very valuable series of Scripture lessons, which will be found both profitable and singularly interesting."—*Guardian.*

THE DIVINE KINGDOM ON EARTH AS IT IS IN HEAVEN. In demy 8vo, bound in cloth. Price 10s. 6d.

"Entirely valuable and satisfactory. . . . . . . There is no living divine to whom the authorship would not be a credit."—*Literary Churchman.*

"Thoughtful and eloquent. . . . Full of original thinking admirably expressed."—*British Quarterly Review.*

THEOLOGICAL—*continued.*

WORKS OF THE LATE REV. F. W. ROBERTSON.

NEW AND CHEAPER EDITIONS.

SERMONS.

Vol. I. Small crown 8vo. Price 3s. 6d.
Vol. II. Small crown 8vo. Price 3s. 6d.
Vol. III. Small crown 8vo. Price 3s. 6d.
Vol. IV. Small crown 8vo. Price 3s. 6d.

EXPOSITORY LECTURES ON ST. PAUL'S EPISTLE TO THE CORINTHIANS. Small crown 8vo. 5s.

AN ANALYSIS OF MR. TENNYSON'S "IN MEMORIAM." (Dedicated by permission to the Poet-Laureate.) Fcap. 8vo. 2s.

THE EDUCATION OF THE HUMAN RACE. Translated from the German of Gotthold Ephraim Lessing. Fcap. 8vo. 2s. 6d.

LECTURES AND ADDRESSES, WITH OTHER LITERARY REMAINS. A New Edition. With Introduction by the Rev. Stopford A. Brooke, M.A. In One Vol. Uniform with the Sermons. 5s. [Preparing.

A LECTURE ON FRED. W. ROBERTSON, M.A. By the Rev. F. A. Noble. Delivered before the Young Men's Christian Association of Pittsburgh, U.S. 1s. 6d.

WORKS BY THE REV. STOPFORD A. BROOKE, M.A.

Chaplain in Ordinary to Her Majesty the Queen.

THE LATE REV. F. W. ROBERTSON, M.A., LIFE AND LETTERS OF. Edited by Stopford Brooke, M.A.

I. In 2 vols., uniform with the Sermons. 7s. 6d.

II. Library Edition, in demy 8vo, with Two Steel Portraits. 12s.

III. A Popular Edition, in 1 vol. 6s.

THEOLOGY IN THE ENGLISH POETS. Being Lectures delivered by the Rev. Stopford A. Brooke. 9s.

Seventh Edition.

CHRIST IN MODERN LIFE. Sermons Preached in St. James's Chapel, York Street, London. Crown 8vo. 7s. 6d.

"Nobly fearless, and singularly strong. . . . carries our admiration throughout." —*British Quarterly Review.*

Second Edition.

FREEDOM IN THE CHURCH OF ENGLAND. Six Sermons suggested by the Voysey Judgment. In 1 vol. Crown 8vo, cloth. 3s. 6d.

"A very fair statement of the views in respect to freedom of thought held by the liberal party in the Church of England."— *Blackwood's Magazine.*

"Interesting and readable, and characterised by great clearness of thought, frankness of statement, and moderation of tone."—*Church Opinion.*

Seventh Edition.

SERMONS Preached in St. James's Chapel, York Street, London. Crown 8vo. 6s.

"No one who reads these sermons will wonder that Mr. Brooke is a great power in London, that his chapel is thronged, and his followers large and enthusiastic. They are fiery, energetic, impetuous sermons, rich with the treasures of a cultivated imagination."—*Guardian.*

THE LIFE AND WORK OF FREDERICK DENISON MAURICE: A Memorial Sermon. Crown 8vo, sewed. 1s.

A NEW VOLUME OF SERMONS IS IN THE PRESS.

MISCELLANEOUS.

VILLAGE HEALTH. By **Horace Swete, M.D.** [*In the Press.*

THE POPULAR EDITION OF THE DAILY NEWS' NARRA-TIVE OF THE ASHANTEE WAR. 1 vol. Crown 8vo. [*In the Press.*

HAKAYET ABDULLA. A Tale of the early British Settlement in the Malaccas. By a **Native**. Translated by **John T. Thompson.** 1 vol. Post 8vo.

THE SHAKESPEARE ARGOSY: containing much of the wealth of Shakespeare's Wisdom and Wit, alphabetically arranged by **Captain A. Harcourt.** Crown 8vo. [*In the Press.*

SOCIALISM: its Nature, its Dangers, and its Remedies considered by the **Rev. M. Kaufman, B.A.** 1 vol. Crown 8vo. [*In the Press.*

CHARACTERISTICS FROM THE WRITINGS OF Dr. J. H. NEWMAN: being Selections' Personal, Historical, Philosophical, and Religious ; from his various Works. Arranged with the Author's personal approval. 1 vol. With a Portrait.

Second Edition.
CREMATION; THE TREATMENT OF THE BODY AFTER DEATH: with a Description of the Process and necessary Apparatus. Crown 8vo, sewed. 1*s.*

'ILAM EN NAS. Historical Tales and Anecdotes of the Times of the Early Khalifahs. Translated from the Arabic Originals. By **Mrs. Godfrey Clerk**, Author of "The Antipodes and Round the World." Crown 8vo. Price 7*s.*

"As full of valuable information as it is of amusing incident."—*EveningStandard.* "Those who like stories full of the | genuine colour and fragrance of the East should by all means read Mrs. Godfrey Clerk's volume."—*Spectator.*

THE PLACE OF THE PHYSICIAN. Being the Introductory Lecture at Guy's Hospital, 1873-74 ; to which is added ESSAYS ON THE LAW OF HUMAN LIFE AND ON THE RELATION BETWEEN ORGANIC AND INORGANIC WORLDS. By **James Hinton**, Author of "Man and His Dwelling-Place." Crown 8vo, cloth. Price 3*s.* 6*d.*

Third Edition.
LITTLE DINNERS; HOW TO SERVE THEM WITH ELE-GANCE AND ECONOMY. By **Mary Hooper**, Author of "The Handbook of the Breakfast Table." 1 vol. Crown 8vo. Price 5*s.*

THE PORT OF REFUGE; OR, COUNSEL AND AID TO SHIPMASTERS IN DIFFICULTY, DOUBT, OR DISTRESS. By **Manley Hopkins,** Author of "A Handbook of Average," "A Manual of Insurance," &c. Cr. 8vo. Price 6*s.*

SUBJECTS :—The Shipmaster's Position and Duties.—Agents and Agency.—Average.—Bottomry, and other Means of Raising Money.—The Charter-Party, and Bill-of-Lading. Stoppage in Transitu ; and the Shipowner's Lien.—Collision.

32 *Works Published by Henry S. King & Co.,*

MISCELLANEOUS—*continued.*

LOMBARD STREET. A Description of the Money Market. By **Walter Bagehot.** Large crown 8vo. Fourth Edition. 7s. 6d.

"Mr. Bagehot touches incidentally a hundred points connected with his subject, and pours serene white light upon them all."—*Spectator.*
"Anybody who wishes to have a clear idea of the workings of what is called the Money Market should procure a little

volume which Mr. Bagehot has just published, and he will there find the whole thing in a nut-shell." — *Saturday Review.*
"Full of the most interesting economic history."—*Athenæum.*

THE ENGLISH CONSTITUTION. By **Walter Bagehot.** A New Edition, revised and corrected, with an Introductory Dissertation on recent Changes and Events. Crown 8vo. 7s. 6d.

"A pleasing and clever study on the department of higher politics."—*Guardian.*
"No writer before him had set out so

clearly what the efficient part of the English Constitution really is."—*Pall Mall Gazette.*

NEWMARKET AND ARABIA; AN EXAMINATION OF THE DESCENT OF RACERS AND COURSERS. By **Roger D. Upton,** Captain late 9th Royal Lancers. Post 8vo. With Pedigrees and Coloured Frontispiece. 9s.

"It contains a good deal of truth, and it abounds with valuable suggestions." — *Saturday Review.*
"A remarkable volume. The breeder can well ponder over its pages."—*Bell's Life.*

"A thoughtful and intelligent book. . . A contribution to the history of the horse of remarkable interest and importance."— *Baily's Magazine.*

MOUNTAIN, MEADOW, AND MERE: a Series of Outdoor Sketches of Sport, Scenery, Adventures, and Natural History. By **G. Christopher Davies.** With 16 Illustrations by W. HARCOURT. Crown 8vo. Price 6s.

"Mr. Davies writes pleasantly, graphically, with the pen of a lover of nature, a naturalist, and a sportsman."—*Field.*
"Pervaded throughout by the graceful

melody of a natural idyl, and the details of sport are subordinated to a dominating sense of the beautiful and picturesque." —*Saturday Review.*

HOW TO AMUSE AND EMPLOY OUR INVALIDS. By **Harriet Power.** Fcap. 8vo. 2s. 6d.

"A very useful little brochure . . . Will become a universal favourite with the class for whom it is intended, while it will afford

many a useful hint to those who live with them."—*John Bull.*

REPUBLICAN SUPERSTITIONS. Illustrated by the Political History of the United States. Including a Correspondence with M. Louis Blanc. By **Moncure D. Conway.** Crown 8vo. 5s.

"A very able exposure of the most plausible fallacies of Republicanism, by a writer of remarkable vigour and purity of style."—*Standard.*

"Mr. Conway writes with ardent sincerity. He gives us some good anecdotes, and he is occasionally almost eloquent."— *Guardian.*

STREAMS FROM HIDDEN SOURCES. By **B. Montgomerie Ranking.** Crown 8vo. 6s.

"We doubt not that Mr. Ranking's enthusiasm will communicate itself to many of his readers, and induce them in like manner to follow back these streamlets to their parent river."—*Graphic.*

"The effect of reading the seven tales he presents to us is to make us wish for some seven more of the same kind."—*Pall Mall Gazette.*

GLANCES AT INNER ENGLAND. A Lecture delivered in the United States and Canada. By **Edward Jenkins, M.P.,** Author of "Ginx's Baby," &c. Crown 8vo. 5s.

MISCELLANEOUS--*continued.*

Thirty-Second Edition.
GINX'S BABY: HIS BIRTH AND OTHER MISFORTUNES.
By **Edward Jenkins.** Crown 8vo. Price 2s.

Fourteenth Thousand.
LITTLE HODGE. A Christmas Country Carol. By **Edward Jenkins,** Author of " Ginx's Baby," &c. Illustrated. Crown 8vo. 5s.
A Cheap Edition in paper covers, price 1s.

Sixth Edition.
LORD BANTAM. By **Edward Jenkins,** Author of " Ginx's Baby." Crown 8vo. Price 2s. 6d.

LUCHMEE AND DILLOO. A Story of West Indian Life. By **Edward Jenkins,** Author of " Ginx's Baby," "Little Hodge," &c. 2 vols. Demy 8vo. Illustrated. [*Preparing.*

TALES OF THE ZENANA, OR A NUWAB'S LEISURE HOURS. In 2 Vols. Crown 8vo. [*Preparing.*

PANDURANG HARI; or, MEMOIRS OF A HINDOO. A Tale of Mahratta Life sixty years ago. With a Preface by **Sir H. Bartle E. Frere, G.C.S.I.,** &c. 2 vols. Crown 8vo. Price 21s.

"There is a quaintness and simplicity in the roguery of the hero that makes his life as attractive as that of Guzman d'Alfarache or Gil Blas, and so we advise our readers	not to be dismayed at the length of Pandurang Hari, but to read it resolutely through. If they do this they cannot, we think, fail to be both amused and interested."—*Times.*

GIDEON'S ROCK, and other Stories. By **Katherine Saunders.** In 1 vol. Crown 8vo. Price 6s. [*Just out.*
CONTENTS.—Gideon's Rock.—Old Matthew's Puzzle.—Gentle Jack.—Uncle Ned.— The Retired Apothecary.

JOAN MERRYWEATHER, and other Stories. By **Katherine Saunders.** In 1 vol. Crown 8vo.
CONTENTS.—The Haunted Crust.—The Flower-Girl.—Joan Merryweather.—The Watchman's Story.—An Old Letter.

MODERN PARISH CHURCHES; THEIR PLAN, DESIGN, AND FURNITURE. By **J. T. Micklethwaite.** Crown 8vo. Price 7s. 6d.

LONGEVITY; THE MEANS OF PROLONGING LIFE AFTER MIDDLE AGE. By **Dr. John Gardner,** Author of " A Handbook of Domestic Medicine," &c. Small Crown 8vo.

STUDIES AND ROMANCES. By **H. Schutz Wilson.** 1 vol. Crown 8vo. Price 7s. 6d.

" Open the book, however, at what page the reader may, he will find something to amuse and instruct, and he must be very hard to please if he finds nothing to suit	him, either grave or gay, stirring or romantic, in the capital stories collected in this well-got-up volume."—*John Bull.*

THE PELICAN PAPERS. Reminiscences and Remains of a Dweller in the Wilderness. By **James Ashcroft Noble.** Crown 8vo. 6s.

" Written somewhat after the fashion of Mr. Helps's ' Friends in Council.' "—*Examiner.*	" Will well repay perusal by all thoughtful and intelligent readers."—*Liverpool Leader.*

MISCELLANEOUS—*continued.*

BRIEFS AND PAPERS. Being Sketches of the Bar and the Press. By **Two Idle Apprentices.** Crown 8vo. 7s. 6d.

"Written with spirit and knowledge, and give some curious glimpses into what the majority will regard as strange and unknown territories."—*Daily News.*

"This is one of the best books to while away an hour and cause a generous laugh that we have come across for a long time."—*John Bull.*

THE SECRET OF LONG LIFE. Dedicated by Special Permission to Lord St. Leonards. Third Edition. Large crown 8vo. 5s.

"A charming little volume."—*Times.*
"A very pleasant little book, cheerful, genial, scholarly."—*Spectator.*

"Entitled to the warmest admiration."—*Pall Mall Gazette.*

SOLDIERING AND SCRIBBLING. By **Archibald Forbes,** of the *Daily News,* Author of "My Experience of the War between France and Germany." Crown 8vo. 7s. 6d.

"All who open it will be inclined to read through for the varied entertainment which it affords."—*Daily News.*

"There is a good deal of instruction to outsiders touching military life, in this volume."—*Evening Standard.*

BRADBURY, AGNEW, & CO., PRINTERS, WHITEFRIARS.

9 783368 847166